Three Little Words

Jessica Thompson

KT-233-579 KA1

W F HOWES LTD

This large print edition published in 2014 by
W F Howes Ltd
Unit 4, Rearsby Business Park, Gaddesby Lane,
Rearsby, Leicester LE7 4YH

1 3 5 7 9 10 8 6 4 2

First published in the United Kingdom in 2013
by Coronet

Copyright © Jessica Thompson, 2013

The right of Jessica Thompson to be identified as
the author of this work has been asserted by her
in accordance with the Copyright, Designs and
Patents Act, 1988.

All rights reserved

A CIP catalogue record for this book is available
from the British Library

ISBN 978 1 47127 646 0

Typeset by Palimpsest Book Production Limited,
Falkirk, Stirlingshire
Printed and bound by
www.printondemand-worldwide.com
of Peterborough, England

Mixed Sources
Product group from well-managed
forests, and other controlled sources
FSC www.fsc.org Cert no. TT-COC-002641
© 1996 Forest Stewardship Council

PEFC Certified
This product is
from sustainably
managed forests
and controlled
sources
PEFC www.pefc.org
PEFC/16-33-415

This book is made entirely of chain-of-custody materials

For the girls

Forgive *vb to give up, cease to harbour (resentment, wrath)*

Oxford English Dictionary

'To err is human, to forgive Divine.'
Alexander Pope

CHAPTER 1

HE WISHED HE'D SHAVED.

Wednesday 1 April 2009
Angel, north London
1 p.m.

*G*od, *she's beautiful*, Adam thought, as he peered at the girl through the rickety shelves loaded with chocolate powder and packets of sugar.

She'd been coming in to his workplace a lot over the past fortnight, sitting at a round, wooden table right by the window, looking out at the Angel street scene. He didn't know her name or anything like that. There was something about her that gave him the impression his usual banter with customers wouldn't be welcome.

He liked that about her. She was a mystery. Adam noticed her beautiful skin dotted with tiny freckles. As the sun had been out for the past few days, those freckles had been joined by new, smaller ones, nestling between them like stars. Her eyes were a piercing green and she had defined cheekbones that gave her the clean, natural look of a supermodel. But she wasn't *too* perfect, Adam

1

thought: the delicate smile-creases around her eyes and a tiny silver scar just below her bottom lip reminded him that there was something very real and altogether tangible about her. It only made her more beautiful to him.

Her dark auburn hair was normally swept back into a neat ponytail, but today it was in a messy bun and she wore huge sunglasses as if London was in the middle of a scorching summer. *Fuck me, she's amazing*, Adam whispered to himself.

'Adam, get on with your work, will you?' Tara shouted, and it made Adam jump so much he bashed his head against the shelves, causing everything to rattle like it was laughing at him.

'Sorry, bwaaass,' he responded, in a cartoon American accent laden with sarcasm, while stepping away from the shelf and all that mocked. He started pretending to wash up, jabbing a chocolate-coated glass into the warm, foamy water, and wondering if there was any way a guy like him could go over to a girl like her and string together a legitimate sentence.

He'd already imagined how it might go: 'Hi . . . name? . . . mine . . . Adam . . . ergghhh!'

'Table ten, please, Ad. And get on it,' Tara barked once more, placing a stern hand on Adam's back. He wished he could tell her to stuff her job sometimes, but then he thought about the rising pile of credit card bills in the hallway, and was suddenly able to keep his mouth shut.

'Of course, sorry,' Adam spluttered, fully aware

that table ten had *the* girl on it. He was hoping not to serve her this time; she was starting to make him nervous. It was a proper crush now.

He shuffled through the café, aware that his bright blue boxers were probably hanging out of his uniform. *Fuck it*, he thought. *We're in London. We're young and we're trendy. We can get away with this sort of thing. Can't we?*

'Hey, what can I get you?' he asked the girl, sweeping a hand casually through his recently cut dark brown hair and suddenly noticing his fringe was missing, giving him the 'phantom limb' feeling.

At the same time, he thought that she wouldn't look at all out of place as the beautiful heroine in a black and white film.

He wished he'd shaved.

The thing is, Adam knew the question he'd just asked was pointless, because he already knew the answer. She always had the same thing, and she always asked for it in the same way. The girl started by turning to him with a shy half-smile, revealing a row of straight, white teeth. But she didn't seem to mean it, really – it was more as if she'd stepped on an upturned plug, or walked into a glass door, and it was so painful, but people were watching so she had to just smile through it. Then she said, 'Er, hi, thanks. Yes, you can get me . . .'

She always began that way before straightening her back slightly in the wooden seat, which in turn extended her neck gracefully, revealing the most perfect collarbone Adam had ever seen. She tapped

3

her fingers on the table as if she was thinking about what she wanted. He stood; pencil poised, his little green notebook almost stuck to his sweaty palm.

'Can I have a decaf latte with one sugar, please?' she then asked, in a voice soaked in sadness. Like all the decaf lattes in the universe would never make it better. Whatever 'it' was.

'Cream?' he always asked this, even though the cream was normally for hot chocolates and not lattes.

'No, thanks,' she said. She always said no. But he still asked. Adam thought she deserved the cream. And the sprinkles, too.

She then turned her head and looked out of the window. Always the same. Every time.

All the other staff had started asking him who 'that girl' was: finally noticing something other than the limescale build-up in the coffee machine or the mousetrap that never seemed to bear any fruit. They asked who she was, the one who sat on table ten, every few days for hours at a time, watching the world go by, with the sadness they couldn't fathom.

CHAPTER 2

IT'S GETTING ON A BIT NOW, ISN'T IT?

Thursday 12 March 2009
Finsbury Park, north London
11.30 p.m.

Keon Hendry was crouched behind a bush near Finsbury Park underground station, both hands shaking a little.

His heart was racing in his chest and he was so nervous he felt like he might lose control at any second. He was also acutely aware that he felt completely and totally alive.

'So you know what you have to do, right?' whispered Steve Jeffery, wiping a layer of sweat from his pale forehead with the sleeve of his fake navy Barbour jacket. His eyes were glazed from an afternoon of weed puffing at the recreation ground nearby. It had been a wet spring day, and the clouds of sweet-smelling smoke had floated away like unwanted balloons, absorbed by the rain.

Keon screwed his nose up slightly and took a good sniff of the damp air around him, not knowing what to say. His black tracksuit bottoms were far too big for him, and he yanked them up at the back.

He was unsure of how it had ever got to this stage. Recently, things had got a little out of hand among his schoolmates. Some of them had always carried knives – just small ones. The kind you might take camping and only ever end up using to cut the string between the sausages. He himself was quite at home with the switchblade he normally had in his pocket. He forgot it was there, usually. But then the knives had got bigger – mothers all over north London must have been wondering where their kitchen utensils were disappearing to. Even so, no one intended to actually *use* them . . . or, at least, that was what Keon thought. But he was starting to wonder if maybe he was a little naïve. It was just that the more boys were carrying knives on the streets, the more you needed one; and if they got one that was bigger, then you had to upsize, too. It was just the way modern-day life was. It wasn't his fault. At least, that's what he'd told himself, to try and make it OK in his head.

Keon shifted uncomfortably on the cold concrete, bringing his left knee down beside his other so that he was kneeling now. He considered for a moment how uncomfortable this all was, and how he wished he was at home instead watching a film and eating chips with his sister, Reb. He considered for a few moments how disgusted she would be if she knew he was crouching in a bush near

Finsbury Park tube, preparing to scare the living daylights out of someone.

'Keon? Are you there? Earth to Keon!' Steve almost barked now, frustration in his voice. His forehead crunched up in anger; soft, white skin over his sharp bone structure.

'Yes, yes, all right! When he comes out of the station we'll give him a fright. I get it,' Keon responded in a low voice, almost growling, wondering if it would be too late to walk away from all of this.

'And don't take it too far, OK? We don't want to get in trouble for this. Just do whatever you have to do to stop the little shit giving us grief, all right?' continued Steve, putting a cigarette between his thin lips and lighting it with a Zippo. His eyes were like satellite dishes, huge and watery. Thread-like blood vessels had risen to the surface of his eyeballs, making the whites of his eyes a soft pink.

''Course I'm not actually going to hurt him. Who do you think I am?' said Keon, unconsciously running his index finger over the cold, smooth metal that was pushed against the soft skin of his stomach by the band of his boxer shorts. He felt his heart rate pick up again. He might not be planning to hurt Ricky Watson, but he knew that this was definitely wrong. This was the kind of very bad behaviour that would make his mother go to church more often, and cry a lot.

He couldn't believe how much he got away with

behind her back. It brought shivers of guilt over him every time he thought about it. How often he would roll home with the munchies, stoned out of his brains, and how his mother would nod and smile with pride, commenting on how he was a 'growing lad' while he ate so much pasta he nearly burst.

Keon, however, had always managed to sidestep serious trouble somehow, while still hanging out with the bad boys. He was always on the periphery, laughing at the right jokes, wearing the right clothes, but somehow never getting his hands dirty. He was always secretly glad he had managed to get in with the most respected crowd at school and felt sorry for the kids who hid their faces behind thick fringes, carrying their insecurities around with them in their grubby, heavy backpacks.

Lately, though, everyone in Keon's gang had been urging him to do something big. And he felt like if he didn't, he was going to be rumbled – turfed out and rejected by his brothers. He knew he needed all the respect he could get from his boys, and this would get it. After this, he could step back out of things again. Move away from the crazy power-struggle that had whipped up among most of the lads in the Fairgrove Estate and at Elm High School. He would be known as the one who made Ricky Watson wind his neck in for ever. The one who had made the fighting stop, by simply scaring him into submission.

Even though this evening was just about giving Ricky a fright, it was still the most aggressive thing he'd ever been involved with. But Keon hated Ricky with a passion. He'd beaten up too many of Keon's friends, and then he had nicked money from Steve's little sister. That was too much. He had this coming to him. So tonight, Keon Hendry would make his mark, and no one would step to him ever again. He just wanted to set the score straight, make sure no one messed with his gang again and then, maybe, he could put all this behind him. Go to college and concentrate on getting his A-levels. Maybe even go to university, like his mum had wanted for so long.

'When's he coming, anyway? It's getting on a bit now, isn't it?' asked Keon, looking down at his big watch face, packed with fake diamonds, and quietly hoping that he could still get out of this. Raindrops started falling from the sky.

11.35 p.m.

'Yeah, yeah, it's cool,' replied Steve, stubbing out his cigarette with his foot, the crunching sound of gravel underfoot loud as he shuffled around. 'He goes boxing on a Thursday night every week and gets the tube back. If he's not here within the next ten minutes, we'll have to try again next week.' He looked at Keon from the corner of his eye. 'You've got the balls, yeah, Keon? You're the main man. Come on, like I said, no one gets hurt, all right?'

Keon shifted uncomfortably again. A giant wall

9

to their left was covered in brightly coloured graffiti that the council hadn't painted over because it was deemed to be artwork. Looking at it now to distract himself, Keon thought for a moment about the fine line between crime and art. *What I'm doing isn't a crime, surely?* he thought. He wasn't going to use what he was carrying as such; he was just going to scare someone. Make an impact. Change something.

A drunk man in his fifties walked towards the bush and stood there for a moment. The boys could just about make him out through the leaves and branches sheltering them; a streak of grey hair and a furrowed brow visible from beneath the undergrowth. Wobbling backwards and forwards, he was trying to whistle the *Coronation Street* theme but it wasn't going well.

'Fuck's sake . . .' whispered Keon.

The lads stayed dead still, their eyes shining in the streetlight. The man stood there for a moment before unzipping the flies of his brown trousers and urinating on the bush, just a few centimetres away from Steve. Steve flinched and gritted his teeth, clenching a fist. The strong stench of the man's piss filled the air around them.

Keon stifled his laughter and looked down at his Air Force 1 trainers, trying to divert his attention from the humour of the moment by rubbing a scuffmark from the top of his left shoe. Eventually the man left, taking his balding head and tweed jacket with him.

'That was close, man,' Steve said, sounding more than a little irritated.

'That guy pissed like a camel,' Keon replied, his face scrunched up in laughter lines. But soon the silence descended on the pair again, the atmosphere thick. The rain was coming down harder now.

11.41 p.m.

Suddenly steps could be heard coming through the passageway from the underground and up to street level, starting off quietly and echoing, but getting louder and crisper. *They could be anyone's,* Keon told himself.

The usual crowd of commuters and late-night drunks waiting for the W3 bus had dispersed, and the station and its surroundings were empty. The boys got up on their haunches, one hand on the ground, like Olympic athletes ready to sprint. Attack.

Keon felt sick.

'There he is,' Steve suddenly cried, pushing Keon into the outside world before he could have the chance to wimp out. The bush spat him out into the street, his feet thumping against the ground.

Rick, a tall, white guy was in a black jacket, walking with his hood up, his face angled towards the ground to protect himself from the rain.

Keon rushed towards him. His heart was beating so hard now he could barely control his fingers. Adrenaline was rendering him useless, his legs felt like rubber bands. He reached Rick in three long

11

paces. 'Come 'ere, you fucking prick!' Keon shouted, as he pulled him round by his shoulder, and shoved a gun into his chest.

But there was a sound.

A shot. A bang so loud that Keon almost believed it had come from elsewhere. The hairs on his arms stood on end. *No. Surely not?* His index finger twitched once more, the gun hanging limply from his right hand by his leg. But the trigger was as far towards the metal body of the gun as it could go. It *must* have been him.

Maybe this was a dream, a nightmare, in fact? The kind that had him sitting up in his bed and choking for his own breath, legs tangled in a mass of sweaty sheets.

The guy's face turned towards his and crumpled in raw, naked agony. Every frame in slow motion.

'Oh, fuck,' the man gasped, a look of utter horror flickering in his eyes. He clutched his torso with his right hand, a satchel dropping to the ground.

But those features painted in the last moments of life didn't belong to Rick . . . Those lips, which were pursed together in fear, were not Rick's. Those cheeks from which the colour had drained were not . . .

Keon looked around him for back-up. Steve had fled, and he could only hear the fading sound of his shoes thudding down the street. Gone. Nowhere to be seen.

The man. This guy, whoever he was, landed on the floor like a sack of potatoes and curled himself up. 'Fuck, shit. You shot me . . . Why did you shoot me?' he cried, his breath starting to rasp.

Keon stood and stared down at the man as blood started to trickle from his body and form a small pool on the ground. Chunks of vomit filled Keon's throat.

He imagined for a fleeting moment that this was just a Saturday morning football session, and he was looking at an injured footballer, one of his team-mates maybe, and that in just a minute he would get up, sweat on his brow, and laugh about it before wiping down his shorts and spitting onto the grass. But, no . . . this guy's breathing was thick and irregular, like it was being obstructed by something, and instead of the green grass at the recreation ground, this man was lying on the cold, wet streets of London.

Just a small whimper came from the guy's mouth, which was now spilling blood onto the dirty concrete.

Keon dropped the gun with a loud clatter and stood there for a few seconds. His vision had started twitching and jerking like he was on a fairground waltzer, and nausea had set in. Pure panic. His lungs started aggressively squeezing the air from his body in loud gasps.

A woman with wiry hair appeared as if from nowhere, and stood a few metres back, her hands over her mouth. From a distance she was hardly noticeable, bar her cream coat, which was illuminated a sharp white under the streetlight. She had stepped out of the darkness and onto some kind of stage where a real-life tragedy was being played out. And now she was a part of it, with no script, and no idea how this scene would end.

Keon turned and stared at her, breathing hard and fast before looking back at the man he might have killed. Their eyes met and there were a few long seconds of confusion. He could try and save this guy; he looked like he was a nice man. He didn't know for sure, but he was probably somebody's son, somebody's husband, somebody's dad, even . . . The man was clutching onto his brown leather satchel. It looked expensive. Maybe he was a banker? An accountant? A lawyer? he wondered.

But there was nothing he could do now so he ran, fighting to hold back the sick and acid building up in his throat. He had to get away. Away from all this. Away from the man who lay dying in the street.

'Hey, you! Come back!' the woman shouted. Her voice was gruff, tainted by the smoke of a thousand cigarettes.

His legs, which were now twitching hard with fear, carried him into the night with a speed he thought was impossible. Each strike of his trainers on the ground echoed in the streets, bouncing back to his ears to taunt him. A sound that would rattle in his brain for the rest of his life, reminding him of the night he ruined more than just one human life.

The woman ran towards the man, tears filling

her eyes. She fell to her knees in the pouring rain, and pushed her fingers into his chest, feeling the warm damp of his blood soaking into his clothes. She lifted her fingers to the glow from a nearby streetlight, and felt her stomach fold as her eyes met the bright red stains at her touch.

He reached into his pocket, panting as he did so. The woman looked down at him, confused, as he pulled something out of his pocket and pushed it into her hand. She didn't look at what she was given, she just put it in her own coat pocket, too busy focusing on him.

'Give this to . . . please give this to . . .' he spluttered.

The man was no longer able to talk, and there was a deadness creeping into his eyes. All she could hear was his laboured breathing, broken by desperate, tearful whimpers.

'Come back, please,' she whispered, pushing her face against his. She pulled at the skin on his cheeks as if she might somehow stop him falling asleep for ever, leaving a sad finger-painting of his own blood on his cheeks.

With shaking hands she called for an ambulance. 'Hi, yeah. My name's Lisa. We need an ambulance quickly. Please hurry; I've got a guy here. He's been shot.'

As soon as the phone call ended she held his hand. He was squeezing back at first, and then eventually he let go.

CHAPTER 3

IT WAS THE PERFECT CLAUSTROPHOBIA.

Thursday 12 March 2009
Finsbury Park, north London
10.30 p.m.

Bryony Weaver shuffled her body down into the bed, feeling the covers crinkle and curl around her bare, freshly shaved legs. *That's a great feeling*, she thought.

Just half an hour before, she had been running a razor over the contours of her shins and knees, accidentally cutting herself. Twice. Just like she always did. 'Shit, shit, shit . . .' she had said quietly under her breath, as she'd felt the blade grip onto a piece of skin and slice it away. *Not again* . . . One nick under her knee, and one just above her left ankle.

The little cuts had stopped bleeding after what seemed like an age – and a whole roll of toilet paper. She had then slipped on a black vest top and some green checked shorts – ones that always reminded her of the wallpaper in American teen movie bedrooms – and she had swept up her long,

16

thick hair into a sleek ponytail. She could feel the breeze from her open window touch the back of her neck.

She swooshed her limbs around a little more, feeling the cool material of the duvet. The bed seemed like a never-ending landscape without Max. When he was home, she was continually woken by a misplaced arm or a gentle head-bump as he thrashed around a little, dreaming of his last assignment at work. His job was so varied and, at times, so scary, that he never seemed able to properly switch off, and he had vivid dreams. It had been that way since he had started his job as a television cameraman. One minute he would be in Fiji, filming celebrities eating live insects, and the next he would be chasing around a disused industrial warehouse in Africa, capturing vital footage for his latest documentary. Whenever he came home, for some time after he would have things dancing through his mind when he went to sleep at night, like the flickering pictures on a zoetrope. He lived and breathed his job – it was the only thing in the world he loved nearly as much as Bryony Weaver.

When Max was around, Bryony reflected now, filling the room with the smell of the same after-shave he had worn since he was nineteen, it seemed like they were suffocating in each other's company. She loved it, though. It was the perfect claustrophobia.

It seemed a little strange to be alone – she

should be used to it by now, what with him travelling around the world so much in the past. But, recently, he had been filming day shifts in London studios.

She picked up her phone and scrolled down to the last message he had sent her that morning: 'Filming in west London tonight, bloody last-minute shift. Sorry, beautiful. Will be back tomorrow morning. Look in the fridge, bottom shelf. Love you. Maximus x'

She reached over to the small bedside table next to her, which she had decorated with some edgy wallpaper that Max hated, and picked up a blue side plate. On it was the treat Max had bought for her and hidden in the fridge as a surprise. Lemon drizzle cake. Her favourite.

She sank her teeth into it, feeling the icing break gently before hitting the soft sponge inside. The bitter lemon taste was sharp. It was 10.35 p.m. on a Thursday night and this was *her* time. Although she missed Max, she knew she would crave her time alone as soon as he was back and up to his usual tricks, like trying to iron his clothes on the bed because he couldn't be bothered to set up the ironing board.

When she finished the cake, she slid the plate back onto the bedside table and felt around for her book. She plumped up some of the striped cushions behind her and slid her fingers between the pages of George Orwell's *1984*. It was a really old copy; just how she liked it, doused in tea stains and smelling of cigarettes – an odour not found in modern bookshops. Bryony brought the book up to her face and buried her nose between the pages, taking a deep breath in, imagining the memories it held that were not hers. The smell of the book alone could tell more stories than the words it held.

She closed her eyes and sniffed again, this time letting the smell of smoke take her back to a time in her past. Bryony was transported to May 2002, to the beer garden of a little pub in Shoreditch. She'd been gripping on to a cigarette between her thumb and index finger, holding it like it was a joint and squinting at a man sitting opposite her whom she had never seen before.

'Smoking's fucking bad for you,' he had said, taking a huge lug from his own cigarette and gripping on to a cold beer with his free hand. Condensation had dripped down the outside of the bottle, gathering at his fingers.

Bryony had been pretty pissed for the hour, and had been wondering whether, if she put one hand over her left eye and just looked at him with the right . . . would he notice? Just for clarity, of course . . . 'I'm sorry, who are you?' she had asked, horribly aware she might be slurring her words.

The man in front of her was so handsome it scared her, but all the wine she had consumed that afternoon stopped her from doing the usual, which was making an excuse and darting away before she had the chance to make a fool of herself. The young Bryony Weaver had had little confidence.

He had been wearing a navy blue and white striped T-shirt with effortless cool, while his dark brown hair had been cut really short on both sides and left to grow a little wild on top. His fringe was so long it sloped down into a point, almost covering his eyes. There was a certain mystery about him. He looked kind of dirty, like he needed a good scrub. But she hadn't liked the idea of him lathering it away as it would have spoiled him somewhat.

Bryony smiled widely into her book as she remembered that day.

He had had a certain roguish charm about him, a look of adventure, as if he could persuade her to just pack in her life and jump into a car for a road trip into the unknown. It was an unusual man that made a girl feel like that.

Bryony, at twenty-one, liked the boys in Shoreditch and their grubby hands after a long day of painting some sad, naked figure in a dusty art studio. They looked intelligent, perceptive and creative. There was just a little something special about them. She had despised the City slickers in their smooth suits and how they hung around in Bank nightclubs looking for something to take home to ease the bitter loneliness of working life. They represented everything she hated.

Looking back, she found this funny.

But, as much as she liked the arty lads, she had

found them intimidating with their fashion choices, and their talk of politics they never seemed to actually understand. University had failed to knock out of her a crushing shyness, which saw a dark crimson rush to her cheeks whenever there was a good-looking man around. She had hated this about herself.

'I'm Max Tooley,' he had said. His dark brown eyes had met hers and made what she thought was a disturbingly strong connection. It had felt a little like an electric current being passed through her body.

He had a great nose . . . She hadn't been sure what it was about the nose that was so good, but it *was* good – a sign of character, perhaps? But it had been a little too early to tell at that stage. But it was straight. Not too big, not too small. Just perfect.

Max had pursed his lips as if in thought, before looking up and flashing her a cheeky smile. He'd extended a hand over the faded wooden bench and it hovered there for a moment.

She'd noticed his fingers were free of paint, chalk or cuts from metal work and instantly wondered what exactly it was that he did.

'You going to shake my hand or what?' he had said, laughing a little, his cigarette quivering between his beautiful lips. He had looked so mischievous.

She'd paused for a few moments. Totally in control for once, thanks to the anaesthetising effect of the wine on her habitual shyness, and raising her right eyebrow as she scoped him out. 'Hi, Max, it's nice to meet you.' She had put her hand out into the void between them, an eccentric ring on her index finger glinting in the early-evening sun. It was noticeably heavier after her flatmate had glued a jet-black stone on to it.

But as soon as she did so, Max pulled his hand away, like a child. 'Ha, ha! Too late!' he yelled, laughing mischievously and slamming the withdrawn hand onto the bench, making the empty glasses there chime loudly as they clattered against each other.

She had withdrawn her hand quickly too, embarrassed and instantly irritated by him. 'That's mature,' she had said flatly, staring at him with dead eyes.

She realised she was probably coming across as pretty rude, and so had smiled. It was an attempt to retract the attitude she had, caused entirely by shyness; it only ever seemed to repel nice men.

'That's a lovely set of gnashers you've got there, er . . . what's your name, sorry?' Max had asked, stubbing the remains of his roll-up into a glass ashtray with one hand and gesturing extravagantly with the other.

'Bryony,' she said, flicking her cigarette butt into a bush behind her, in tipsy rebellion against the system.

He frowned at her, for littering.

'Gnashers?' she asked, the word unfamiliar to her.

'Teeth. You've got pretty teeth,' he said, before jumping up from the bench and darting back into the pub like he'd sat on an ant's nest.

She'd spent the whole of that evening decoding the encounter with her flatmate, Eliza, a budding jewellery designer, who kept over-enthusiastically attaching jewels onto Bryony's rings and necklaces at every opportunity with a glue gun that dripped like the mouth of a ferocious dog.

'What does it mean if a man says you have nice teeth, Eliza? Does he like you?' Bryony asked, hanging upside down from her bed, her long hair spreading out over the carpet. She had not been able to shift the image of Max Tooley from her head.

Eliza had been curling a small metal wire with an impossibly small pair of pliers, her toes twisting in concentration.

'Er, teeth? Teeth . . . errrm. I don't know, Bryony. I mean, it wasn't like he said you had a nice bum or legs or whatever, was it?' she said, looking up with a painful honesty in her eyes.

Bryony had sighed deeply.

'And what sort of boy talks about teeth? He sounds like a weirdo to me,' Eliza added, trailing off slightly, before loosening the miniature vice holding the ring she was trying to make. She had raised her creation up to the light and inspected her handiwork, her mouth twisted into a dissatis-fied pout.

'This is shit, Bryony! Utter shit,' she had cried with frustration, before throwing it in the metal bin. It made a loud pinging noise as it rattled to the bottom. The sound of failure, which echoed far too often in their £700 per month bedsit.

'Don't do that, Eliza. I love the things you make,' Bryony said, rolling her eyes towards the shag pile. 'So should I just forget about Max, then?' she had asked one more time, hoping her faithful friend would give her the confidence she needed to go back down to the pub and ask for his number. He might still be there . . . Maybe, if she got Eliza's seal of approval, she could dig out her most flattering bra and tight black vest top, run a brush through her wild mane, slick on some lipstick in pillar-box red and just turn up there again, while still looking casual . . . Somehow . . .

'Yeah, I think so, sweetheart,' Eliza had said, before abandoning her miniature workshop and shuffling out to the kitchen, which had no door because her ex-boyfriend had punched a hole right through it four months before. They had decided to take the door off the frame altogether because people kept asking what happened to it, and then not quite believing the cover-up story that a drunken Bryony had fallen against the door while singing Pulp's 'Common People' into a mop. For a long time afterwards, the mere mention of her ex made Eliza disappear to the bathroom, emerging ten minutes later with blotched eyes, and stinking of weed and tequila. 'I don't know why you bother with the lads around here,' she said, calling out from the fridge as she rooted around for something to spread on toast.

Bryony had slid off the bed and was quietly searching in the bin for the reject ring, which she found hiding under a screwed-up bank statement. She had picked it out and put it on her finger. It fitted perfectly. *It's awesome*, she thought. She would add it to the box she had hidden in her top drawer, full of Eliza's 'shit' jewellery, which she adored and wore in secret.

'I mean, they're so scruffy. And they all have these big dreams to be the next big artist, never growing up. Never really facing reality and all its bills and social responsibility. Do you understand what I mean?' Eliza said, pulling her face out of the fridge. A slice of processed burger cheese fell out and landed on the floor with a slap.

'I do understand,' said Bryony, hiding her hand under the duvet before Eliza noticed she had adopted the ring as her own. 'But some people *have* to have a big dream, don't they? And if no one took risks and worked hard, then we would never have great artists, or athletes, or musicians. Would we?' she continued, as she watched the slim-framed Eliza liberally piling peanut butter onto her slice of toast. 'I mean, what about you with your jewellery dream? You want to be the next big thing, right?'

There was a brief silence. This was a sore point.

'That's true,' said Eliza, grudgingly, after a moment. 'You've a good point. But as for your bloke, Bryony, I don't really know what to say except that if he was that bothered, he probably wouldn't have leapt up and disappeared like that, would he?' She stood in the open doorway, holding her small plate in one hand and wrinkling her nose slightly, her spiralling mane of thick, blonde hair forming its own little dreadlocks. Her nose piercing glinted in the low light.

She was *horribly* honest sometimes.

Bryony had almost given up at that very moment.

She could remember feeling disappointed and getting into bed with a book rather than the man she had fallen for during a drunken two-minute conversation. She had wondered if it would ever just be simple.

But it was now.

She was all grown up. Twenty-eight. Had a steady, well-paid job in PR, had a clean driving licence and was capable of rustling up more than just cheese on toast and a beer bong. Plus she had a gorgeous boyfriend.

Max Tooley.

He had gone from being her impossible crush to her day-to-day reality after he had accidentally spilled a whole pint of Foster's down her white dress on a summer afternoon, just a few weeks after they had first met.

She had thought she would never see him again, and was surprised to find his shocked face before her as he had stood, holding an empty pint glass at an angle, the almost ice-cold liquid seeping through the soft material of her dress and onto her skin. He had laughed at her polka dot bra and she had slapped his cheek.

He spent the whole summer hand-delivering roses to the vintage clothes shop she worked in and hated, making the summer of 2002 one of the best of her life. Better than the summer of 1999 spent backpacking in Australia. Better than the summer of 2000 when she first discovered the joys of partying until 7 a.m. And even better than the summer of 1996 when she learned to cartwheel after umpteen attempts and a broken arm.

Bryony had been reluctant to let him in at first. She enjoyed the flowers first of all, and the attention, of course. She had liked how the girls she worked with swooned behind the counter and played with their fringes every time he came in. She adored the cute desperation of love etched in his features . . .

Bryony smiled and opened her book, switching off her bedside lamp so there was nothing but the light of five candles shining around her. Just enough light to read. But she was distracted a little. She felt unsettled, excited and strangely alive.

She turned her head to the right and looked out of the open window into the Finsbury Park street she lived on. Underneath the window was a huge leather weekend bag, waiting to be packed for the trip she and Max were taking to Amsterdam that weekend.

She couldn't wait but, at the same time, she was slightly suspicious of Max's behaviour of late. The weekend away . . . the cake . . . the increased appetite for sex . . . It was like he was falling in love with her all over again, and she couldn't help but wonder why.

Their apartment was on the second floor, so she could see rows and rows of windows in from hers. There were a lot more cosy lights flickering behind curtains, and Bryony wondered what was going on in each room. She hoped the people behind them were as happy as she was.

Some of the curtains were modern and brightly coloured, pinks, greens and reds.

Some were ragged, old-fashioned lace disasters that reminded her of the white knitted skirts on loo-roll topper dolls.

She turned her attention back to her book but, just as she started to read, she heard a bang. It was so loud, the sound ricocheted in the street, bouncing from house to flat to shop and then back again. But she could still tell the source of it was several hundred yards away.

It made her jump a little in bed and she pushed her book down into the duvet, her heart racing a little.

The city was full of unexplained sounds; the residents of Finsbury Park rarely batted an eyelid at most of them. There was the usual clatter of bins, the wailing of cats that sometimes sounded like a girl in distress, the rattle of a fox discarding an empty tin of beans, backfiring car engines and the hysterical scream of ambulances. But there was something about this sound that made Bryony sit up for a moment and raise her hand to her chest, unconsciously pushing her index finger into the soft hollow of her throat. She swallowed hard.

Silence.

And then, a little later, sirens.

CHAPTER 4

'I SUPPOSE WE CAN DO SOME WINDOW SHOPPING.'

Thursday 12 March 2009
Crouch End, north London
4.55 p.m.

'**G**et off work. I need wine and cigarettes. It's urgent. Tanya x'
The message was short and to the point. But Sara knew the only way she could get out of work in time was by changing her shift.

She slipped her white iPhone back into her pocket and took a deep breath as she surveyed the scene around her. She was looking at the beautiful, clean, classy and – dare she say it – trendy, White Rope restaurant, in Crouch End, London.

Her restaurant.

Well, not *her* restaurant . . . she had been given the lofty position of 'manager'. But it was, for her, a dream come true. Finally, at the age of twenty-eight, Sara was where she wanted to be.

Dreams. Do. Come. True she had typed in four text messages to her husband the moment she had got the news from Mauro Dellati.

Mauro, an ageing Italian man and the owner of White Rope, carried the heavy burden of unrealised, life-long dreams on his shoulders. As a child, he had imagined taking over the world with his deliciously decadent food empire, making elaborate 'things on ciabatta' in his mother's cluttered kitchen, standing on a pile of phonebooks to get to the worktop.

Mauro, aged eight, covered in flour.

Mauro, aged nine, successfully creating his first paella.

By ten, Mauro knew how to make fresh pasta, his bemused mother looking on as she painted shocking red lipstick on her mouth, her hair twisted and locked tight in giant rollers.

But things hadn't worked out as he'd hoped, and the years had slipped by until his dreams were all too far from reach. It haunted him. The onset of crippling arthritis and an ever-growing drink problem had eventually put a stop to his working days, so now he just took part of the profit from the restaurant and shared out the responsibilities. He would only visit on Sunday evenings, clutching a walking stick and sipping cold white wine in the corner of the restaurant, while looking out wistfully at the business he had used to run.

'You, Sara, my darling, will make this place your own,' he had said with teary brown eyes, the October before. Both his hands had been on her slim shoulders, which had been barely covered by a delicate vest top, as if he were about to hand down a knighthood. She had felt the rough texture of his palms against her skin. He smelt of a pungent aftershave, and had a bulbous red nose from his years of dedicated drinking, in the middle of a kind, warm face.

He was like a grandfather to her. An eccentric, wonderful man, who had stepped down to give her a chance, years after she had started at the restaurant as a Saturday girl, in her teens. No one had ever understood her potential quite like Mauro did. No one seemed to have so much patience with her. He'd never disciplined her, or shouted at her; even when she had managed to screw up the opening of a champagne bottle so badly that a customer had gone to hospital with an eye injury. Instead, he had merely chuckled quietly to himself in the corner of the kitchen, before writing out an accident report note.

A warm feeling built up inside her when she thought about this man, who had always believed in her.

Sara had never really thought she would go far. She was a quirky, unusual woman, with short, dark hair. Her skin was so pale it was almost translucent, and her eyes were a striking blue. She was hauntingly beautiful, with a slight and graceful frame. She was an alternative soul, with a beautiful, clipped voice that would melt into something altogether earthier in the right circumstances. A social chameleon, she could fit in anywhere, but it often left her wondering who she was: she could be the girl at gigs, with dark eyeliner highlighted like tiger markings in the strobe lights, and yet she could be a no-nonsense businesswoman in a suit and high heels when she wanted to be, too.

Sara had a strange, dry sense of humour, but most of all she was quick to temper. She was known for her fieriness and it had got her into trouble in the past. Being different, there came difficulties. She often wondered if she didn't have an off-kilter attitude to life from all the violently different reactions she had provoked in people over the years. Men either fell obsessively in love with her, or found themselves in blazing arguments with her over the foundations of feminism because they'd dared to utter the term 'bird' or 'slag' to a friend in the queue of a nightclub. She was outspoken, but quiet. Strikingly attractive, but prone to slip into the background.

And while her parents hoped she would step into a law career as they had, running The White Rope was bigger than anything she had ever imagined for herself.

The Maccabees were playing at a low volume through the sound system. She sang quietly along to the song, as she made her way to the back of the restaurant to start shuffling through the paperwork in the small office booth there, which was still very much part of the restaurant floor.

It was quiet, the only customer an elderly man who sat on a table near the back of the room, drinking coffee and staring at the back of her neck, remembering what youth was and a wife he was once lucky enough to love. He always sat near the back in quiet moments just so he could be close to someone.

The White Rope fitted snugly in the high street, nestled between a quirky coffee shop and a posh bakery, which was usually bursting with honey-blonde-highlighted, pram-wielding women in groups that would bubble with laughter.

It emitted a warm, romantic glow in the winter, transforming into a fresh, open eatery in the summer, which had such a genuinely Mediterranean feel to it that people often felt pangs of regret for ever coming home from their holiday in France as they passed. It was perfect all year round. It felt like home.

Sara had something in common with Mauro: she, too, had wanted to run her own restaurant since she was five years old, setting one up in her room with plastic doll's-house chairs and musty flannels for tablecloths. And here she was.

She thought about the task at hand once again, and talked to herself quietly under her breath, trying to sum up the manager inside. She continued to sing to herself, a little louder now. The elderly man – who was so weathered by his years – started to chuckle to himself.

'Hey, missy! I'm trying to have a quiet coffee here,' he said, his voice gravelly and deep. As he smiled, there were gaps where teeth used to be.

'Oh, sorry, John!' Sara replied, throwing her head

back with a laugh and spinning round in her chair, revealing a smile so bright and wide it often startled people. 'I forget where I am sometimes,' she said, turning back around and thinking who she could call on to take over her shift.

John continued to chuckle under his breath before turning and staring out of the windows at the front of the restaurant, admiring the usual bustle of the town centre; a homeless man outside Waitrose begging for change; a group of kids bouncing footballs and shouting. Sara had always been a 'nice person' – a push-over, some even said, who usually put the needs of others before her own.

The only person who saw this as wholly good was her husband Tom, a twenty-nine-year-old wildly creative artist who said that it was Sara's honesty and understanding of the world around her that had made her so attractive to him in the first place. He was the only person who had never let her down. They had only met three years ago, but Sara had known he was the one from the moment she had set eyes on him at a party of mutual friends.

As Sara pondered her replacement problem, she noticed with satisfaction that the tables were being set for the evening, when the restaurant would have a completely different atmosphere. Waiting staff shuffled around, adorning the place until it dripped with sparkling silverware and crisp, white napkins, reserved for the glamorous and often more demanding late-evening guests. The 6 p.m. diners would soon be filing in, holding hands under and over the tables. Most of them would grab a quick seafood linguine or risotto special before heading into town to watch some passionate wannabe belting out show-tunes.

Within half an hour, the candles were lit. The music was on low. The atmosphere was beautiful. Just how she wanted it.

Sara stood at the back of the room taking in the calm before the storm, but was distracted by the thought of her curvy and strikingly gorgeous best friend, Tanya, sitting at home on the sofa, watching the music channels and obsessing over whether or not it was too early to crack open a tub of Ben & Jerry's. Tanya had been more than a little heart-broken of late, so Sara had vowed to introduce her to the world of internet dating. As far as she was concerned, it was acceptable now. No longer a place where the gorgeous 'Jed' you were talking to via email usually turned out to be a ninety-year-old hermit from Arkansas who had last trimmed his toenails when his wife died twenty years before. Sara knew a few people who had met 'the one' on dating websites and considered that pretty good odds.

It was time for Tanya to meet someone she would never normally bump into. She needed to avoid the usual guys who were attracted to her perfectly toned hourglass figure and striking eyes. The ones who would swagger up to her in a bar, leaving the nice guys staring into their beer, wondering quietly why they hadn't plucked up the courage before.

She hated changing shifts . . . asking people to take on duties at dangerously short notice. She slid over to the small office booth at the back of the restaurant where the phone was, looking around quickly to check there were enough staff at the bar and on 'foot patrol'. She swelled with pride at the happy team she had built up. She picked up the phone and dialled.

There were four rings and then the call was answered. 'Er, yeah, hello?' came the deep, earthy tone of Simon's voice.

'Hi, Simon,' Sara purred down the line. She caught a glimpse of herself in the reflection of the computer screen: her pixie crop had grown a little too long for her liking. She tugged at her fringe and cursed herself for not getting it trimmed earlier that day.

'Oh, oh, er, hi, Sara. You all right? I mean how are you?' Simon asked, audibly trying to stand to attention.

'Yes, great, thanks. Look, I have to be quick – do you fancy taking over my shift tonight? I can trade with you so I'll cover your day shift tomorrow; and you know what that means, don't you?' she asked, with the same 'blink and you'll miss it' tone of voice as a highly skilled car salesman. She doubted he'd even had time to correct his wedgie.

'That means I can go to Pacha tonight and not

work tomorrow, doesn't it?' he responded, a smile in his voice.

'It certainly does . . . do you think you can be here in half an hour?' she begged, knowing that his flat was a two-minute walk away. It was a strange, rickety little box-like dwelling, wedged above a newsagent that still sold troll pencil toppers and penny sweets for a penny.

'Yeah, all right. Give me twenty-five minutes,' he muttered, before ringing off.

Sara hung up with a sigh of relief and grabbed her mobile phone. She tapped a message quickly, telling Tanya she would be round shortly with a bottle of Pinot Grigio.

That done, Sara set about quickly tidying the office before she left. Her wedding ring flashed in the dim light thrown by the computer as she moved a dangerously high pile of paperwork into a box file. The sight of it still made her glow inside. Every time she looked at it, she almost couldn't believe it had happened.

She had married Tom Wilson a year ago, and became Sara Wilson, née Peabody. She loved Tom more than anything in the world, but one of the best parts of marriage, she had to admit, was being able to finally cast aside her surname, which had been more than enough for teasing fodder at school. Most school bullies have to look for the usual target points: knock knees, rickets, food in braces, unfortunate hair, crooked glasses, but with Sara's surname, it had been there on a plate.

Tonight, Tom was at some art event that would probably involve endless trays of canapés, and small foodie 'sculptures' comprising dollops of fish eggs and grilled goat's cheese balanced precariously against each other. It sounded great, but she had been to enough of the things, so was leaving him to it – more often, lately. He was understanding about it, and Sara certainly didn't demand his presence at her special restaurant events. It was the parts of their lives that stayed relatively separate. Healthy, she reckoned. Tom's career had rocketed in recent months, with the pop-up Mulai Gallery on Tottenham Court Road agreeing to exhibit his work. It had been a big deal; a huge deal, in fact.

She saw clearly the contrast in her love life and Tanya's. While Sara returned home to her scruffy but gorgeous husband, Tanya had been having her heart swiftly crushed again and again by the next bad boy in her life.

Simon eventually materialised before her wearing a black shirt and grey trousers. His blond hair was as she expected: perfect.

'Hi, Saz,' he said, sashaying around her and tying a burgundy apron around his waist. 'Where are you off to?' he asked with a grin, finishing the knot at the back before placing both hands on his waist confidently.

'I'm off to look after a friend. Man problems,' she said, throwing her notepad onto a pile at the back of the desk and untying her own apron quickly, her straight nose crinkling a little with her expression of concentration.

'Oh, right, good luck with that. I'll call you if the place burns down, yeah? Or would you rather not know?' he called after her as she walked out of the door, rolling her eyes and grinning.

Tanya lived in Finsbury Park, just near the tube station. Sara dived into a branch of Tesco Metro and picked up a bottle of wine, a super-size chocolate bar and a packet of Marlboro Gold before jumping on the bus. It was going to be one of those nights, she could tell. Tanya was heart-broken by the sound of it. Sara pondered this on the short bus ride, as it chugged up hills and blundered clumsily around corners. Neither of them were heavy drinkers, but she thought that tonight they might need a glass or two.

Within fifteen minutes the bus had pulled up at busy Finsbury Park station and Sara jumped off, clutching her bag of goodies. Tanya's flat was near a pop-up bar that had never quite managed to pop down – they had spent a few fun nights in there dancing to indie bands on sweaty nights.

'Hello, sweetheart,' Tanya said now, opening the door slowly. Her sudden appearance revealed not only a significant loss of weight for the two short weeks they had been apart, but also a wild change in hair colour. Her normally dark brown afro-curls had been bleached blonde, and she'd had her nose pierced. Her usually curvy body had lost several inches: it was a bit of shock.

They weren't kidding when they said heartbreak is the best kind of diet, Sara thought. *She didn't need to lose weight in the first place.* 'Wow! Look at you!' she said, putting as much false cheer into her voice as she could. Pulling Tanya into a cuddle, she could feel more ribs and elbows than she normally did when embracing her, and the image of a xylophone popped into her mind. She grimaced to herself while stuck behind her friend's ear, her face full of newly coloured hair. It was a bad sign.

'Come on in,' Tanya said, shuffling through her hallway in her slippers. She was wearing a pair of black skinny jeans and a tight grey T-shirt, giving her that sexy, girl-next-door look that seemed to attract all the wrong men.

Sara followed her, wine bottle in hand, wishing she were a little more glamorous.

Tanya had already ordered an Indian takeaway, which had been their favourite for years. They had discovered their joint love for curry at university when they were dumped together like unwanted gifts in the same halls of residence. Tanya's hair had been a full-on wild bunch of curls when they had first met, and Sara had always been envious of that. Tanya was full of the sexy, beautiful and confident traits of her Jamaican heritage. She had been the cool girl at university, and Sara had looked up to her ever since.

The order arrived five minutes later, complete with a sweaty delivery guy at the door, slightly out of breath from the five steps he had had to tackle, his moped quietly sputtering away behind him.

They poured out the wine and dished up the food, before retiring to the sofa to enjoy it all.

'So, what's happened, then?' Sara asked, lifting a forkful of rice to her mouth.

Tanya's face was instantly clouded with sadness, her brown eyes looking down at her plate piled high with curry. 'Well, I thought everything was going amazingly well, you know. I'd met his friends; he'd met mine. It was early days, but all very promising. And then it just went wrong. The whole thing just collapsed like a house of cards,' Tanya finished, swirling her fork in the sauce and staring at it with the expression a child adopts when they don't want to even try to eat any more.

'What do you mean by "went wrong"?' Sara probed gently, staring at the pretty freckles dotted all over her friend's face.

A small tear welled up in Tanya's eye and ran down her cheek.

Sara put her plate down and shuffled a little closer to her, shocked. Tanya never really cried – she was the tough one out of the two of them.

'I'm so sorry,' Tanya said now, wiping her face as more tears followed.

'Don't be sorry, Tanya, we all get sad. And this is what I'm here for, isn't it?' Sara asked, rubbing Tanya's arm gently.

As she put her plate down, Tanya laughed a little, despite her tears. Sara had that way about her.

People often crumbled around her, but she put them back together so well.

'Well, he just stopped calling, and then every time I rang him, he would just cut off the call. And at first I thought he must just be busy or something. But then, after a few days of this, he just sent me a text – a text message, for fuck's sake! – and all it said was, "Sorry, I don't think I'm ready for a relationship." And that was it. And I'm confused, Sara!' Tanya said, looking at her friend with utter despair. 'I don't understand. I did everything by the book – we didn't sleep with each other too soon, I wasn't jealous, or posses- sive, or clingy. I didn't say "I love you", the sex was fabulous . . . I just don't get it.'

Sara didn't know what to say, so she took a large sip of wine and looked into her best friend's reddened eyes. It was hard to know how to react in these situations, Sara realised. She was twenty- eight now and had done her fair share of dating in her early twenties, and, until she had met Tom, it had been exactly like this. You never really felt safe, she remembered. Men blew hot and cold like dodgy heaters in student flats: they lied, they cheated, they confused you; and never once had she ever really understood why she hadn't been good enough for them. And then she had met Tom and everything had just clicked. It had made sense.

Tanya pushed open a large window next to the sofa and lit a cigarette. Little raindrops were starting

43

to gather on the glass, and the smoke curled out into the evening air. She had a beautiful apartment, and Sara loved popping over to see her for nights in as much as she loved sipping cocktails with her in expensive bars.

'Well,' said Sara now, 'I don't know why he disappeared. But all I can say is that it's a blessing it happened sooner rather than later, and you just have to hang in there, and think positive, and do *not* blame yourself. Promise me?' Sara was aware her plea came at the end of a long list of rather worn-out advice, but she did know how much these things could affect a person's confidence. She lit a cigarette, too, cradling her glass of wine in her other hand and pursing her lips in thought.

Tanya smiled bravely, eyeing her dinner like she still couldn't face it.

Sara looked at her friend and really didn't understand why a man would meet her and not want to hang on to her for ever.

Tanya looked down at her nails. The colour, her favourite coral shade, was starting to chip a little, Sara noticed.

'Oh, well. I'm really happy on my own. I'm just getting a bit paranoid because nothing has properly worked out for, well, a long time, really,' Tanya said, a look of defeat on her face.

'I've had an idea, Tanya,' Sara said, perking up, her eyes wide with enthusiasm. 'What do you think about internet dating?' She dropped it into the conversation as if she had only just thought of it, when she had actually been plotting for a few days about how she could introduce the idea to Tanya.

Tanya grimaced slightly before laughing, her familiar giggle turning into a slight cackle; she had a naughty laugh that only really came out when she drank wine. It reminded Sara of nights out in their early twenties. It was the defining sound of that time, along with the DJs they used to listen to at The Relic, a music venue converted from Victorian public toilets.

'You're joking!' Tanya shrieked now, leaning back in her seat, her hair bobbing around her softly.

'No. No, I'm not. If I were single, I would be on there, no question. It's not weird any more, honestly!' Sara protested, holding on to Tanya's arm tightly now, as she laughed, too.

Tanya was unconvinced – Sara realised she was going to have to use evidence. Real, hard evidence. 'OK, er, you know Chloe and Greg? You know, the ones who were at mine for dinner the other month?' Sara said. 'They met on PlentyofFish.com,' she continued, folding her arms and nodding her head with authority.

'No way! I thought they said they met at a charity gala?' Tanya asked, looking confused.

'Charity gala, my arse. That's just what they tell people, but Mark told Tom all about it in the kitchen that night.' Sara smiled, and started to eat again.

'Wow,' Tanya said, her perfectly kept eyebrows

45

raised so high they looked as if they might jump off her face.

'Come on, get your laptop out and we can just have a look. See what's on offer . . .'

Tanya jumped up from the sofa and got her MacBook Pro, which was starting to show signs of overuse, the letters on its keys fading slightly. She settled back into the sofa and pushed the computer onto Sara's lap.

Sara opened up a Google search page and typed in 'Dating'. Within seconds, there were thousands of entries to choose from. Dating for professionals, for members of uniformed public services – for geriatrics, even. The list went on and on, but she was looking for something that would suit her friend.

Tanya smiled and took another sip of wine and stuffed her cigarette into an ashtray, looking more than a little bit apprehensive.

'Right, let's just check out one of these sites and see what there is out there,' Sara said, clapping her hands together excitedly.

'I suppose we can do some window shopping,' Tanya muttered, slipping on a pair of thick-rimmed glasses and leaning in towards the screen.

Sara clicked on one of the first sites advertised. Immediately, they were greeted by a bright background and a search bar, allowing them to look for men in categories according to age and location. *Yes, this looks OK*, she thought.

'Right then, Tanya, tell me, how old?' Sara asked,

adopting a game-show-presenter voice and sitting up tall on the sofa.

'Hmmm . . . he would have to be between twenty-five and thirty-five. I would say twenty-five is the absolute minimum age,' Tanya said, looking up to the ceiling for inspiration with a naughty smile.

'OK. And just men from London?'

'Yes, just from London.'

Sara hit the return key and the screen was soon taken over by dozens of little thumbnail photos of men in all shapes, sizes and styles. It was a little like Topshop.com, she realised, but with hundreds of potential love interests as opposed to knitwear and handbags.

It only took about five minutes before giggling ensued. Soon, both Tanya and Sara were shrieking with laughter over some of the profiles, and cooing longingly at others. 'Oh, not him, he looks like an axe murderer! And not him either, he looks like he's on drugs,' Tanya said, pointing first to a man who had an exceptionally creepy vibe about him and another with advanced red-eye. 'Oh, click on him,' she then said, gently putting her index finger on the face of one exceptionally gorgeous man.

'Right,' said Sara, double clicking with the mouse. 'So, his name is Alex, he lives in Hammersmith, works in graphic design, and is a hopeless romantic, apparently . . . Cool!' Sara said, turning to Tanya, who was now smiling so widely she felt like her

47

job to cheer her up had been done. Even if Tanya didn't sign up to one of the sites, it was worth looking, just to see the smile on her face.

They kept scrolling through the pages and giggling at the profiles until late in the evening. The combination of alcohol and laughter made the hours pass by like minutes. Tanya had just pointed to one photograph and started to say something about what her type of man was, when they were suddenly interrupted by a loud bang.

They both jumped and looked at each other; an eerie silence falling over them. Tanya heard a lot of noise late at night because she was so close to the tube station, but there was something about this sound that made her react strongly, even though she was never normally shaken by things like that. 'Holy shit,' she whispered, as she moved over to the window and opened a curtain.

'That was a gunshot, surely?' said Sara, who could feel all the hairs on her arms standing on end.

Tanya opened the window and leant out to see up the street. 'I can't see anything but, yeah, that sounded bad.' After taking a last look up the street, she moved away from the window and poured some more wine, concern written across her features.

'Let's hope it was a car backfiring or something,' Sara said awkwardly, before picking up the laptop again.

They were scrolling through another internet dating site, trying to take their minds off the sound outside, which had by now been followed by the sound of police sirens, when Tanya suddenly grabbed hold of Sara's arm, her nails digging into her skin.

'Ouch, what the fuck, Tanya?' Sara shouted, wriggling her arm away from her friend's killer-robot death-grip, half laughing, and half wondering if she'd had too much to drink.

'Oh, holy shit, Sara, don't look, don't look!' Tanya yelled in reply, her legs pulled up to her chest like there was a mouse on the floor.

Sara stared at her, totally confused. The night was taking a strange turn. As she turned back towards the screen, Tanya suddenly leapt onto her like a monkey wrapping itself around a tree branch, a knee on her upper thigh and an elbow in her neck.

'Jesus Christ!' Sara tried to yell, her voice muffled somewhere in Tanya's boobs. They were close, but this was pushing it a little.

Tanya stayed still and held on to Sara, who couldn't see anything past her armpit. 'OK, Sara,' Tanya said carefully, 'I'm going to let you go, but just don't look at the screen, OK? When I get off you, you need to let me take the laptop to the other side of the room and just look at something first, all right?'

'Yes, yes, all right!' Sara laughed, totally confused by Tanya's behaviour. 'Just get off, you mad cow, you're hurting me! You're bonier than you used to be!'

As Tanya climbed off her friend with an enviable agility and gracefulness given the amount of wine she'd had, she managed to keep a hand clamped over Sara's eyes, while picking up the laptop with the other hand and whipping it out of her sight. She carried the laptop over to the kitchen counter and clicked on what Sara assumed was a profile.

Sara looked out of the window, waiting for Tanya to snap out of this utterly strange behaviour. But when she looked back, there were tears in Tanya's eyes and both hands were clamped over her mouth. Sara stood up abruptly and started walking over to her. 'Tanya, what the hell? You're starting to freak me out now!' But what she saw when she walked behind her friend and peered at the screen freaked her out much more than her friend's erratic behaviour.

There on profile number 456 was a photo of a man she recognised.

Tom. Her husband. Smiling back at her. His dark blue eyes were staring out of the screen at her, smouldering away for all the women of the world to enjoy. His hair was waxed so it looked messy, and he had on a blue checked shirt he'd had for ages.

Her heart stopped, and she unconsciously put her hand out until it found Tanya's, her fingers slipping between hers. Sara felt dizzy. Weak. Confused. She had been with him for a long time. They'd got married less than a year ago. And there was her husband, Tom. 'Generous', 'loyal' and 'sexy' were the words he'd used to describe himself.

The arrogant shit, Sara thought.

She stormed back to the coffee table, grabbed her wineglass and tipped its contents down her throat, wondering how on earth she was going to handle this.

CHAPTER 5

SHE HATED CABBAGE.

Thursday 12 March 2009
Ealing, west London
9 p.m.

'Can you pass the salt, please, Mum?' asked Rachel, sitting at the dinner table. Her lovely, clipped accent – the product of an expensive education – contrasted with her elbows crooked carelessly on the flawless wooden tabletop, which was so shiny she could almost see every ripple of the old-fashioned plasterwork on the ceiling reflected in it.

'Elbows off the table, please,' responded Rita, curtly, ignoring the question.

An onlooker might almost not have known that Rachel was ballet's Next Big Hope, unless they had looked under the table at her feet: battered toes wrapped in neat, white bandages; and the perfect curve of her left foot, reaching out for some imaginary stage in an imaginary block shoe whether she was eating, sitting or simply at rest.

People could just tell she was a ballerina by looking at her feet – the way they naturally went into fourth position when she waited for the tube, for example – but her face gave away other signs, too, usually overcast as it was, with worry and exhaustion from training. Her posture, too, was so beautiful it made her a striking sight whenever she walked around in public places. She stuck out like a sore thumb among angry commuters, their backs slumped from the weight of backpacks and bottomless handbags. Her frame was slim but muscular, and often covered in rock band T-shirts that topped the everyday black leggings of her profession. That evening, her beautifully sculpted arms were hidden underneath a giant, baby grey jumper.

'Rachel, elbows. Don't make me say it again.'

Rachel sighed hard. She pulled the offending body parts from the table, scooping her long, blonde hair into a neat ponytail as she frowned. She then leant forward and grabbed the salt herself, and started shaking it onto her food.

'You don't need that much salt, Rach. It's a bad habit,' Rita Matthew said quietly, her jet-black bob shining in the light of a huge lamp shaped like a hot air balloon that was suspended from the ceiling, in the centre of the room. She drew her hands together and pushed them up in front of her pursed mouth so she looked for a moment as if she was praying. Her light green kaftan set off her rich, gold jewellery – it was a look that complimented her dark olive skin tone. Her black eyelashes fluttered as she studied her daughter's face, at the same time whipping the saltcellar out of Rachel's reach.

'I do. I've been getting cramp lately. It's a lack of salt,' Rachel growled, her nose wrinkling with annoyance. In contrast to her mother, Rachel was fair, like her father, Edward, with pale skin that burnt easily in the sunshine. Although she looked tired, her skin was, as always, totally flawless, stretched over delicate, almost sharp features. Rachel was a tall, blonde dancer and she was strikingly beautiful.

'Well, if that's the case, you need to let Anneka know about that, and soon. Don't put it off,' she said, her voice warming a little as she slid the saltcellar back over to her daughter. Anneka was Rachel's go-to person at her ballet company, a spindly ex-ballerina with dark hair always scooped into a chaotic, nest-like bun. Everything had to go through Anneka, from medical advice to those dreaded sick day phone calls.

Rachel and Rita shared a relationship like many other mother–daughter partnerships. They bickered. They fought. But, most of all, they loved each other very much.

Rita was aware that Rachel should have moved out of her parental home by now, but her circumstances were pretty unusual. Things had been particularly tense recently in particular, with all the pressure on Rachel, who had impressed so much with her dancing that she had found herself being invited to try out for a role with The Royal

Ballet. Added to this, the press had found out about her, a twenty-three-year-old from Ealing who was set to tread the boards of the global stage.

Everything about it was unusual, unexpected, unprecedented. And while she looked untouchable on stage, Rachel's reality was wracked with early-twenties angst and personal insecurities.

This week, Rachel was waiting to find out if she would be chosen to play the lead role of Swanhilda in *Coppélia*. Hanging around for news like this made her particularly irritable.

'So, how's Richard?' Rita asked, hoping they could sidestep their usual dinner-time argument surrounding how much sleep/salt/vitamins/rest time her daughter should be getting.

'He's a dick.'

'Rachel! Don't use that word around me, please,' responded Rita, who had almost swallowed a whole new potato in shock. She was a prudish woman, who had tried to instill in her little girl the importance of being a lady.

While Rachel had grown into a graceful woman on stage, when the curtain fell it was a somewhat different story. Her time-off attire comprised scruffy navy Converse hi-tops, bright red lipstick and black, black and more black. She often shrugged off the pressure of her day-to-day life by going clubbing with friends, drinking and smoking too much, and generally behaving like every other young person in London. But she wasn't like every other person. She had pressures and responsibilities that required her to behave differently, and this was a huge issue in the Matthew household – on the morning of a key audition, she was often found trying frantically to scrub off layers of charcoal nail varnish. Gone would be the dark make-up from around her eyes and her heavy jewellery. It was as though she lived a double life, but she somehow got away with it.

Her mother was concerned, though. While her daughter's movements on stage made the hairs on the back of her neck stand on end and a pride swell within her greater than anything she had ever personally achieved, she was exhausted with worry when she watched Rachel fiddle with her hair nervously in interviews and respond to phone calls with roars of laughter in quiet, formal moments. She was concerned that she wasn't quite up to the public side of her role; unable to answer questions the right way, or give the right impression of herself in a world so fiercely judgmental.

Company magazine had interviewed her just last week for a picture special. They had picked up on her beauty and how it was juxtaposed with a grungy style and unusual attitude. They had printed a splash of images of her wearing her delicate, peach satin ballet shoes, teamed with Rolling Stones T-shirts, torn jeans and lots of kohl. They had put her in a £1,500 embellished leather jacket, and a hair stylist had transformed her thick, blonde locks into a sixties-style curly creation, which had tumbled over her collarbones like water. She had looked incredible.

'So, um, why is Richard a . . . erm, an . . . idiot?'

Rachel shovelled some peas into her mouth and started to say something.

'Mouth closed, please, dear, while you're eating,' Rita whispered, an impish smile on her face to take the sting out of the words, almost bracing herself for the backlash, the tirade of swearing, the slammed door.

Rachel chewed fast and irritably before opening her mouth to speak, frustration brewing inside her. 'He forgot my birthday,' she said, raising an eyebrow.

Rita looked down at her hands, which were wrinkled and covered with little brown spots where her skin had seen too much sun over the years. She thought back to Rachel's first birthday and shivered a little at how fast time had gone, and how far she felt from the young woman she called her daughter.

'Well, that's dreadful, sweetheart,' she said, shaking a light sprinkling of salt onto her own meal and ruining the example she had previously tried to set. 'Has he tried to make it up to you?'

'Yeah – he bought me a Disaya necklace but I threw it at him and slammed out of the apartment. We haven't spoken since,' she replied flatly, unflinchingly, as if it wasn't a big deal.

Like many mothers, Rita was not delighted

with her daughter's choice of partner, but at twenty-three there was little that could be said. Richard was a stand-up comedian, a trendy type, who wore huge, chunky glasses and the latest preppy clothes that made him a style icon, a huge part of the geek chic wave that was so in fashion. His career had started with a bang three years ago: reviews in the *Guardian*, photos in *Time Out* and glamorous parties. He was the young, fresh face of UK comedy, and the media had latched on to him in a way publicists could only dream of. But things weren't looking so funny any more.

He was the son of a wealthy investment banker and had his life taken care of, financially. This had enabled him to really push his career in comedy, even managing to get himself a respectable agent. But he had handled his financial security and sudden rise to fame badly, and had been unable to turn down the drinks, drugs and wild nights out. He had been seriously spiralling down into trouble for the past twelve months, and it showed in his work: all the important meetings and events he was late for, and the new material that would sink like lead among restless, unimpressed audiences.

Word had got out about it. No one had the proof to make it public, but the press waited in the wings for a scandal. Watching. Finally, critics had panned his last gig at a small Camden comedy club. He had been drunk on stage, and those who were waiting for his fall from the dizzy heights of success knew that it had arrived. They had their headlines.

His agent had advised him on the best way to handle the situation, to try and turn it all around, but he had to be careful now, Rita knew.

'Wow, that's pretty brave of you. I would have kept it and then shut the door,' Rita said with a giggle, standing up to clear the plates, bracelets clattering together. A few moments later she returned with dessert: two modest piles of fresh fruit, glistening on dark blue plates.

Simba, the family cat, waltzed confidently towards the table. Rachel threw a grape on the floor towards the tabby, but he wasn't interested.

Observing her daughter as she stared at her plate again, she decided to change the subject. 'We need to get your driving licence copied for the DVLA,' she said.

Rachel poked at the pudding with her fork, chasing a piece of melon around the edge of the plate but failing to actually spear it. She couldn't give a toss about her driving licence; she was quite happy being ferried around in the taxis her ballet company provided for her. She wasn't remotely interested in buying a car and taking herself anywhere.

'Can you stop poking at your food, please. Either eat it or leave it alone.'

Rachel suddenly snapped. 'For fuck's sake, Mum,

can't you just lay off me for one second?' she yelled, standing up and charging into the large, sprawling living room. She huffed and puffed while flicking through the channels on Sky, tears pricking at her eyes.

She was jaded, tired – exhausted, in fact. The day's training had been so intense: she had ached, sweated, and even bled until it had felt like she could give no more. And every phone call made her heart race because it might just be *the* phone call, the one to seal her future for ever.

The big launch. The leap. The *grand jeté*.

Rita left her to it for a while, and then walked through into the living room, guilt hitting her for interfering. But she cared so much. That was all it was. She sat next to her daughter on the sofa, watching her as delicate tears ran from her eyes, and she considered for a moment just how beautiful her profile was: a cute little nose and long eyelashes. She was naturally blessed, but she couldn't help but wonder where those blessings came from . . . Then Rita noticed the purple bags under her daughter's eyes.

'I'm sorry, sweetheart,' she said, trying to smile a little but feeling slightly frustrated that they kept having the same arguments again and again.

Rachel continued to look at the screen, embarrassed by her emotion yet so desperate to let it all out.

'What's wrong?' Rita asked, breaking the silence once more.

Rachel had put a music channel on but the sound was off. The screen flickered with the images of women gyrating their bony hips around Ibiza swimming pools, draiping themselves over handsome rappers emblazoned with fun-size diamonds. She wasn't paying attention to any of it. She couldn't really see properly, anyhow. Not through her tears.

'Give me your feet,' Rita said, putting on her softest voice.

Rachel continued looking at the screen but swung her legs over, onto her mother's lap, not quite forgiving her just yet. Her toes were red raw from all the pointe work, the muscles so tight Rita could almost feel each and every one. Rita had always done this, ever since Rachel had first started to dance, wearing a scratchy tutu so small it would fit on a teddy bear. As Rachel had shown more and more promise, and her ballet slippers had graduated from a size one to a size five, Rita had studied this kind of massage. Now, she pulled the balls of Rachel's feet up and stretched out the muscles, digging her thumbs into the arch of her foot and working all the way up it.

Rachel flinched a little, a few more tears falling from her eyes. 'I'm sorry,' she started, wiping her cheeks with her thumbs. 'There's just so much pressure. And it's so horrible waiting to hear about this role. I love this so much, it means so much . . . I, I just . . .'

61

The pair was interrupted by Edward, who, just back from work, waltzed into the room in a pristine black suit, his slight middle-age spread creeping over his belt. 'My girls,' he said, in a loud, well-spoken voice, dropping his briefcase gently to the ground. Simba jumped and scuttled away, wedging his body mass into an impossibly small gap in the family wine rack.

Rita turned and gave him 'the look'. 'The look' was well understood in their five-bedroom house on Elthorne Parade. It generally meant that Rachel was either upset, angry, nervous or all three; this last being the worst.

Ed sighed and crept out quietly, helping himself to dinner in the kitchen and a bucket-sized glass of red, knowing it was best to stay away during moments like these. He couldn't handle them. He could cope with banking, the daily commute, the office politics, but he couldn't quite handle the pressures of his daughter's rocket-like rise to stardom. They weren't kidding when they said that when it happens, it happens quick, he reflected now. It had been a shock for everyone. And he couldn't quite believe his daughter, the girl he had caught smoking when she was fourteen, and picked up from parties because she was too drunk to stand, was ready for it all, too.

But he never said so. He had to show, on the outside, unflappable confidence in her. He had to overlook the mood swings, the boot marks on the carpet and the smell of smoke on her clothes – this other side of her life was something no one talked about.

There was a sudden knock on the front door, which broke the quiet moment between Rita and Rachel.

'I'll get it,' Rita said. She released her grip on Rachel's weary feet and walked to the door, her slippers sinking into thick, cream carpet like quicksand.

Rachel pricked up her ears, waiting to hear who it could be: there was no sign of a car outside. She didn't need to listen too hard.

'Baby! Come out here, please!' came the shriek of a posh, male voice. A male voice that was clearly ignoring the instructions of her mother at the door.

It was Richard.

Rachel could hear the muffled sound of her mother attempting to usher him away; she could just about pick out phrases such as 'It's not a great time right now,' and 'Can you come back tomorrow?' echoing in the hallway.

The fact that he was so rudely ignoring her mother made Rachel angry. It was embarrassing, and more fuel to the fire. More reason for her mother to roll her eyes whenever his name was mentioned. More reason for her friends to invite handsome, single men to parties and push them in her direction.

She got up and walked through the living room and out into the hallway, the balls of her feet still aching from five hours in the studio earlier that day. And there was Richard, wearing a classic university outfitters-style cardigan in bottle green and some beige cargo trousers, holding a huge bunch of roses so overwhelming in colour they made the world go black and white for a second.

At the sight of them, she melted a little, but still felt a prick of frustration. Richard infuriated Rachel to her core. He was unpredictable, lazy and changed like the weather, but at the same time he was so funny, handsome and passionate that she had little strength to push him away for long. She knew deep down he was spoilt, and that he wasn't always the man she thought he was when she had first met him. He had also been useless and selfish at Rachel's most important events: press parties, expensive dinners with theatre companies and drinks with directors. They were the most dangerous combination for each other, but could not spend much time apart, even in the wake of a blazing argument.

'It's OK, Mum, I'll talk to him now,' she said, looking at Rita apologetically.

Her mother flung her arms into the air and stormed off into the kitchen.

'What do you want?' Rachel demanded, curling her toes around the edge of the doormat and suddenly feeling self-conscious about her puffy face. All the signs were there that she had been crying just minutes before, and she hated that he might assume it was over him.

'Look, Rachey . . . I know, I know, I know . . .

I'm the biggest idiot going, OK? The birthday thing – there's no excuse for it. I'm aware of this . . . things have just been so busy, preparing for the next show. Come on – you know how it is, surely?' He pouted, crossed his eyes slightly, and pushed his bottom out, his feet pointed inwards like a pigeon's.

Sometimes he irritated her to the core. It was one of his most popular stage positions he adopted, but it was wearing a little thin now. It was a look that had had Rachel crying with laughter when she first met him at a magazine launch party two and a half years before, but now she wanted to slap him across the face and see exactly what happened to the look – which he gave whenever he was in hot water – when she did so.

But she couldn't.

'Will you just come here . . . please?' he said, opening his arms and looking like a lost dog.

Rachel felt that burn. That pang to be enveloped in his arms. She tried to resist. Staring into his eyes and imaging that she could magically turn him into a cabbage. She hated cabbage.

Her eyes scanned up and down his body. She was so attracted to him that even when he was the biggest bastard on earth, it was nigh-impossible to walk away from him. She put one foot forward delicately, and his features softened.

Before she knew it, she was wrapped in his arms, her soft lips touching his neck and taking in the smell of him. She could see the hair on his chest poking out from his top and immediately thought about how he looked naked. He was built like a rugby player.

It made it much more difficult to drag the argument out any further.

'I'm so, so sorry, Rachey. Can you just give me another chance?' he whispered in her ear, in his deep, sexy voice.

A loud tut resonated from the kitchen and a door slammed shut.

'Come on, let's go upstairs and talk,' Rachel said, pulling away from him and taking him by the hand.

Rachel's room was right at the top of the house. She had the whole floor to herself, with an ensuite bathroom and an enviable wardrobe. It was a haven for her, a little bit of privacy. She was blessed, really. She had everything she could ever want; it had been that way ever since she was a child. But as all her friends lived like that, she had never really questioned it: the sons and daughters of artists, architects and bankers – the in-crowd of young twenty-something 'it' boys and girls who had never had to worry about the pennies and the pounds.

Rich propped the roses up against a bookshelf and sank down onto the bed. The room was painted a calm blue, but the contents were less than serene. Rachel had pinned up posters of her favourite bands, beer mats from memorable nights out, and album covers, all over the walls.

The floor was scattered with copies of the *NME*, grungy T-shirts and cigarette tins that her mother naïvely assumed were eye-shadow cases. And amid all this were the telltale signs of a ballerina: satin pointe shoes in a variety of colours; a small box of rosin that had spread itself all over the floor like spilt talcum powder; the remains of a costume she had cut up and tried to make into a going-out top.

Even though she was twenty-three, and most of her friends were living with friends or boyfriends, Rachel had remained at home because it was easy with her manic training schedule. Dinner was ready on time. Her washing was done. It was the ideal support network for a young, overwhelmed athlete.

'So, how's that lift going?' Rich asked, lying back on the white duvet and staring up at the ceiling, being careful not to put his trainers on the covers.

'Not great. We've been practising it a lot but I can't seem to perfect it just yet. Paulo is a bit of a moron, really,' she sighed, staring into the mirror on the front of her wardrobe and playing with her fringe, thinking about her latest training partner with his knobbly knees and inability to support her eight-stone frame.

Her fingernails were nibbled too short, she realised. She hated it when she did that.

'Well, come here, then,' Rich said, rising to his feet and walking into the middle of the room, just like it was routine. As if it was perfectly normal.

Like it was something all couples did . . . He stood on a small wooden board in the centre of the room, which Rachel had had fitted so she could practise pointe work if she needed to. She moved a few steps to the left so she was in front of him, still looking in the mirror. Richard put his hands around Rachel's waist and started to lift her, his hands supporting her hips. It was almost effortless as she gently sprang from her feet and rose up into the air. It was a good job the ceiling was high. Time seemed to slow down as his strong wrists allowed her to sail there, as though she were almost weightless or suspended on string. She pushed her arms out into a dream-like third arabesque and stretched her legs, creating perfect lines and curves. It was the most beautiful yet unusual sight. Rachel Matthew balanced in the air, supported by the strong arms of Richard Moseley, his feet enveloped in a pair of pristine white hi-tops.

After thirty seconds or so, Richard's arms trembled a little under her weight, the veins in his hands rising up visibly under his skin. He gently brought her back down to earth, her feet touching the ground with a soft thud.

'Well, I think that was just fantastic, pookie,' he said, pulling her close and kissing her nose. Richard was no dancer; in fact, his moves in a nightclub were nothing short of disastrous: drunken, jerky twitching, just visible beneath a strobe light. But being Rachel's boyfriend, he had learned a basic lift, and she was able to practise in impromptu moments with him. It was something he was secretly proud of.

An upper hand.

'I need to find my driving licence; hold on a minute,' she said, snapping back into reality, pulling herself away from him.

'Do you have to do it now?' he pleaded, enjoying their sweet reunion and pulling her back towards him with his hands around her tiny waist.

'Yes, I have to send it to the DVLA tomorrow. Mum's been nagging me about it all week – I won't be a minute,' she said, slipping from his grip and stepping out of the room.

Rachel would have normally asked her mother for these things but she didn't want to bother her now. Standing in the dark quiet of the corridor, she could hear the gentle hum of the television downstairs. The lights were out in her parents' bedroom. Rachel stood for a moment. She should ask . . . she *knew* she should . . . *I can sort it,* she thought, stepping into their room. She didn't need to disturb them.

A small, Art Deco lamp sat on a desk amid piles of books. She turned it on and it spilled out a gentle beam. An inadequate one. It was hard to make everything out in the half-light. Deciding to start looking under the bed first, Rachel's eyes slowly adjusted to the shadows. She could see all sorts of things: mail order catalogues. Old accountancy books. A suspicious-looking feather duster. *Hmmm . . .*

She kept feeling around with her delicate hands but nothing seemed promising. Rachel was about to try the old chest of drawers, but then her fingers located a huge box file that she remembered her father going through when he needed some important paperwork. For some reason her parents would never let her near it, and always got things out for her. *This must be it*, she thought, sliding it out and blowing off a thin layer of dust. She moved slightly so she wasn't blocking the soft light and, as she opened the file, she saw a huge stack of documents in neat, regimented order. Tabs had been stuck at the side of dividers in alphabetical order, and she quickly flicked through to R. There was a red label. On it had been penned 'RACHEL' in black biro. *This* is *it*, she thought, quietly pleased with herself.

Her fingers separated the wads of paper until she was clutching her documents. Letters from The Royal Ballet. Bank slips. A paying-in book. There was no sign of a driving licence, so she kept looking. But, before she got to it, a crumpled piece of paper caught her eye. It stood out because it was so old compared to the other things in there. It had her name at the top, and her parents' names. *My birth certificate*, she thought. She stood up and walked over to the lamp so she could see properly. She'd never seen it before.

But there was a word at the top that wasn't right. Her eyes kept flicking back to it. Surely this was a joke? One of those fake forms you get printed up for a laugh, maybe? But it looked too real . . . Too aged.

Her eyes darted back and forth a few more times. Down to her name. Her mother's name. Her father's name. Surely not . . . But, yes, at the top of the form was the line. 'UK Certificate of Adoption'.

Adoption.

'Rachel?' came the sound of her mother's voice from downstairs.

'Shit, shit, shit,' Rachel whispered, shoving the paperwork back into the folder and putting it back where she had found it.

'Rachel!' Rita continued to shout.

Rachel tiptoed out of her parents' room and stood in the hallway, trembling at what she had just found.

'Yes, Mum – what?' she shouted back, down the stairs.

'There's a terribly sad story on the news,' Rita called. Richard came to the entrance of Rachel's room and poked his head out of the door. Rachel sighed, irritably. Her mother always did this. She was always issuing cautionary tales. *Taking everything too seriously*, she thought.

'What's that?' Rachel asked, looking up at Richard and rolling her eyes knowingly. But her heart was still thumping hard in her chest, trying to digest what she'd just found.

'A young, well, young-ish guy has just been shot dead outside a tube station in north London . . . They're saying he was possibly killed in a mistaken-identity gang shooting,' Rita said, her voice fading a bit at the end.

Rachel said nothing, but stared at her feet. She couldn't really hear what her mother was saying. Nothing made sense any more.

'Just goes to show, doesn't it? You never know when it's coming for you . . . Take care, you two, take care when you're out and about, won't you?' Rita said, before sighing loudly and going back into the kitchen.

CHAPTER 6

'I'M HERE TO SEE MY BOY.'

Friday 13 March 2009
Police Station Custody Unit, north London
9 a.m.

In all her days on this green earth, Tynice Hendry had never prepared herself for a thing like this: the night she would get a call from the police to say her son had been arrested on suspicion of murder.

She didn't believe it. Not at all. She was sure there had been a mix-up. Tynice sat on the sofa in her flat, head in hands, trembling. Officers had barged into her home the previous night and searched it high and low. They had gone through everything in Keon's room. Magazines were splayed on the floor in the aftermath of the chaos, and the doors to his wardrobe were like mouths gawping wide in shock.

They had asked her questions. Hours of questions. Had he been in trouble before? Did he suffer from any mental health problems? Where had he been that day? She had had clear and simple answers for everything or, at least, that was what she had thought.

Black boys were always getting the blame for this kind of thing, she had muttered so many times when talking to a neighbour, both cradling cups of tea. The women on the estate moaned about how their sons were hauled into police stations accused of all sorts: shoplifting, gang fighting, whatever. Word travelled fast on the Fairgrove Estate. Just a few months ago, one of Talia's boys had been taken into the police station on suspicion of GBH. It had turned out he wasn't involved. They had simply seen a black guy on the street and taken him in. They let him go within a few hours. Tynice guessed it was just a method to get their arrest figures up most of the time, but the stories and tales, which rattled around the flats, caused a deep-set resentment within the community.

Tynice was *sure* there had been a mix-up. Absolutely positive. So sure, she had decided to wait until the morning to go and see Keon, as she didn't want to leave her daughter, Reb, alone in the middle of the night. She was only thirteen. Reb was in shock, despite everything she had done to explain to her that there had been a mistake.

Tynice knew someone had been shot dead. She had read it on the local paper's website as soon as she was told about Keon. A twenty-eight-year-old local guy. There was no way her son was involved in that.

'OK, OK, stay calm,' she said to herself, rocking back and forth gently, stroking her own arm just like her mother used to do to her when she was a child. This situation had made her miss her mother more than she had done for a long time. Elsie Lock had died five years ago of a heart attack, and Tynice had cried until she feared she would run out of tears. Only recently could she look at a photo of her mother and smile, genuinely feeling at peace with the situation.

Tynice imagined now how Elsie would have handled this. She would probably have come straight round in her green Nissan Micra, wearing one of her usual floral dresses, before taking charge of the house, making a huge dinner with a roll-up in her mouth at all times, and ensuring Reb was OK; all with her own style of bolshie management and love – the perfect blend.

Keon hadn't been at home the night before, but he often wasn't home now. He was eighteen. Keeping tabs on him was impossible. He had told her he was going to Westfield with his friends to get some new trainers. She'd given him £40 for them ahead of his birthday. 'I need new kicks, Mum,' he'd said, storming around the house, drinking orange juice from the carton. Although it was fairly minor, the orange juice thing had made her worry. None of her friends' children walked around so brazenly drinking from the carton. It was a small thing, but it had always bugged her. It showed a level of defiance, almost a middle finger thrust in her direction, because she asked him time and time again to stop doing it.

As a mother, something had kicked in when she had got the call. Denial.

Standing, she knew it was time to go to the station. She would leave Reb with their neighbour, Jackie. She wouldn't tell anyone where she was going. *There's no need for it*, she thought, *not when it's all just a misunderstanding.*

Having dropped Reb off with Jackie, Tynice realised her heart was racing as she got on the bus, much more than she had expected. All she could think was that she had to get him out of there. How she had to be a good mother to him and sort this out. This crazy, silly mess.

Tynice's heart sank when she noticed that Fiona from the hairdresser that she went to was at the front of the bus, wearing a navy hooded jumper and a pair of black leggings. Tynice tried to blend in, to sink behind the modest crowd of people standing up. She didn't want her friend to see her now. She didn't want to have to explain where she was going. It would bring shame on her family. Shame that wasn't needed or deserved.

All the possibilities starting running through her mind again as the bus crawled along. What if Keon was wrongly convicted for something he hadn't done? What if it had been one of his friends, and he was just in the wrong place at the wrong time, and had got the blame? What would everyone at church say if they got wind of this?

Never once did she imagine that he was responsible.

Tynice smoothed down her navy blue dress as she stood, propped up against the bright yellow pole near the exit doors at the back of the bus. She slicked on some lip balm while looking in her pocket mirror, inspecting herself. Her thick, curly hair had been pulled back into a bun. She noticed that she looked a little tired, but had managed to cover it up pretty well with make-up. She looked OK though, despite everything. A young, respectable mother, who had brought her boy up to be a good man.

The bus driver kept braking too sharply and it irritated her already frayed nerves, so she got off a couple of stops early, turning her head away from the direction of the bus, hoping Fiona wouldn't spot her and come bounding up behind her like she usually did. She walked quickly, as it had started to rain again. Within a few minutes she was at the police station.

It was at this point that Tynice started to feel sick to her stomach. Sick that Keon was inside there, behind bars, like an animal.

Tynice walked up the steps to the entrance of the police station, and walked blindly through a small reception room. She was dimly aware it was full of other people, but she concentrated solely on getting to the reception counter in front of her.

Her motherly instinct started to show as soon as she reached it. The feeling suddenly over-whelmed her, making her breath so fast it felt like she might faint. It was as if someone was standing behind her, squeezing her ribs, constricting them. 'I'm here to see my boy. Keon Hendry,' she said, breathlessly, feeling a bead of rain trickle down her forehead. She brushed it away with the back of her hand, her stack of bracelets bashing against each other.

The officer behind the counter was deathly pale. She looked like a vampire under the artificial lighting, her face like putty against the crisp white shirt she was wearing.

'Name, please,' she grunted, dead in the eyes. Tynice wondered if she had any idea at all how she was feeling. It seemed there was nothing human or compassionate in her expression. It scared her.

'Tynice. Tynice Hendry. It's flat 12, Fairgr—'

'Stop there. I don't need your address at this stage; just your name,' the girl said, typing into her computer and failing to make any eye contact with the woman in front of her.

Tynice felt an anger rise up within her, but she knew she had to control it. She had to stay on top of this situation. Keon had done nothing wrong, after all. This was all just a big mistake and it would be sorted out very soon, she told herself, praying to God all the time.

'Right, Tynice. If you would like to go through

the doors to your left, Inspector Rusbin will come and find you.'

Tynice was so nervous and overwhelmed by all of this that it had become difficult to walk. She shuffled through the room full of people; it felt like they were all staring at her. Red, sad eyes beneath baseball caps. Equally mortified-looking parents. Magazines left untouched – she doubted anyone had the concentration for the antics of the rich and the famous here.

She pushed the door but it just rattled in its frame. Frustrated, she pushed it again, her nerves going up another notch or two. *Please, God. If you'll just help me sort this all out I will do more for you – anything*, she thought, her body pressed against the heavy, cold door.

'You pull the door, love,' came a gruff voice from one of the chairs behind her, a tinge of sarcasm in the comment.

Tynice didn't even turn round to acknowledge or thank the speaker. She didn't want anyone to recognise her. To see her. Instead, she pulled at the cold, silver bar that was arching over a panel clearly labelled 'PULL'.

The policeman was waiting for her in a long corridor that was painted half eggshell white, half bottle green. His legs were set shoulder-width apart and his hands were clamped together. 'Hello, Mrs Hendry,' he said, as soon as the door swung shut behind her.

Tynice nodded some kind of acknowledgement,

unable to find the words to address the situation. She knew right away from the inspector's face that it was bad. The questioning she had been subjected to the night before had been calm, non-accusatory, like it was part of a routine the officers had had to go through.

'I think you should follow me, Mrs Hendry. Cup of tea?' he asked.

She nodded and a young, female officer who she hadn't noticed until that point rushed away. The policeman was tall and imposing. His dark hair was broken by intermittent grey, his skin puckered with scars from a youth blighted by acne. He had rich brown eyes. Eyes that had seen it all.

She tried to sit down on a chair in the small white interview room she was shown to, having to steady herself first. The room resembled the inside of a shoebox, bar a tiny window, covered by metal mesh in case some hooligan smashed it. There were no pictures, no notice boards, no posters using fancy wordplay to deter kids from buying guns and growing their own cannabis forests, only a lone clock, high up on the wall above Inspector Rusbin's head.

'Mrs Hendry, I am sorry to tell you this, but we have decided to charge your son in connection with the murder of a twenty-eight-year-old local man. Officers apprehended your son within an hour of the crime – he was found in an alleyway. He had been quite sick . . . but I am sure you have heard all this already.'

She hadn't known that Keon had been in such a state when he had been found. She had imagined arriving at the station and being told it was all a mistake, and that she would be able to take Keon home.

Her stomach convulsed and she took a deep breath in, lifting her hands to her face. She imagined a young man, trembling in an alley, holding on to the brickwork with sweaty fingers and unable to speak as he was handcuffed; but his face was not Keon's. It couldn't be. Tynice took a few more breaths so she could be calm before she spoke.

The female officer came in and carefully placed a mug of tea in front of her. She would never forget that mug, even as an old woman. It was red, and it said 'Just Keep Smiling'. She wanted instead to throw it against the wall, but she kept her cool.

'Mrs Hendry? I imagine this is a great shock for you,' said the inspector, reaching an arm out across the table. She pulled her own away so that he couldn't touch it; because if he did, she would know that somehow this situation was real. That somehow she was in an interview room at her local police station, being told that her baby boy was the prime suspect in a murder investigation.

The clock ticked loudly.

'Listen,' she said now. 'I think – in fact, I'm *sure* – there has been a huge mistake here. My son is a good boy. He's not like those lads that run around our streets at night, in gangs. Carrying

81

knives and guns and whatnot. I go to church, sir, if you don't mind me respectfully saying. I brought him up better than this. I said all this to the officers who came round last night. He just wouldn't do something like this . . .' She tried to carry on speaking, but noticed a wet sensation on her face.

Tears. She hadn't even noticed them slipping from her eyes. She hadn't noticed that her breath was now so fast it was audible. She hadn't noticed the tissue bunched up between her fingers, covered in charcoal mascara.

The inspector shifted uncomfortably in his seat. 'Look, I can't discuss all this now,' he said, 'but you can visit Keon, and then afterwards we can explain the next stages of the inquiry. We have a room where you can see him, but there will be an officer there. Do you want to see your son?' he asked, his voice echoing a little around the room.

'Yes, yes, of course I do,' Tynice replied, not even having to think about it. She wanted to do more than just see him. She wanted to rescue him. Take him away because this had all been a horrible mistake and this was no place for her little boy to be. Her mind flashed back to when he was just a baby. The first time he was placed into her arms in the hospital, screaming so hard his whole body was shaking. She remembered loving how fat he was, elbows and knuckles just dimples, buried under a healthy mass of young flesh. She remembered holding his tiny little socks, and the first time she dressed him up in a little blue suit for a cousin's christening. She remembered his first day at school, and how his knees had looked so funny under his grey woollen shorts.

And then her mind scanned all the way past his first disco, his first driving lesson and exam results day. Then it went back to his eighteenth birthday, and how he had brought his girlfriend, Charlotte, to a barbecue at hers and looked so grown up. She had thought they had made it then. They had got through it all. Together.

'When you're ready, go to the room next door on your right and he'll be there, waiting for you,' Inspector Rusbin said, before standing up and smoothing his jacket down. He nodded to her and left the room.

Tynice sat still in the silence of the room, staring at her cup of tea. She was shaking so much she couldn't even lift it to her mouth. After three minutes and thirty seconds, she stood up and left the room. She knew and would remember exactly how long it was because she had timed it by the clock in the room, telling herself that in that time, she would be strong enough to cope with the situation.

She was greeted again by the dark, dank corridor of the police station. The female officer came forward and led her into the room next door, a hand on her back as they walked through into yet another shoebox.

And there was Keon, sitting at a white table, with handcuffs on his wrists.

Tynice rushed to him. She ran the tiny distance to the table and held his face in her hands, pulling it towards her body. It had been a long time since she'd held his face like that. He usually ducked away and flapped his arms about whenever she or his aunties tried to kiss him.

'Don't hold me, Mum. Don't hold me,' he said, looking up at her and gritting his teeth together. He looked like he hated her, but she would know later that he hated himself.

She pulled her hands away from his soft skin and sat down slowly. 'And why, Keon, why can't I hold you?' she asked, looking into his eyes and hoping the truth was written there in the limpid brown irises he had. Those eyes that mesmerised all the girls and had them annoying her, knocking at the door when she had just put tea on the table. 'Why can't I hold you?' she suddenly barked, her worry and fear suddenly twisting into madness and frustration.

The security guard in the room with them cleared his throat, and Tynice suddenly felt very aware of his presence. He was standing far enough away from them that he wouldn't hear a word if they whispered, so she lowered her voice, leaning her face towards Keon's until she could smell the faint traces of last night's after-shave across the table.

His breathing was quick, too. The skin around

his eyes was puffy. 'I've done something terrible, Mum,' he said, water dripping from his eyes and landing on the table. He didn't even try to wipe it away.

'I swear to the Lord, boy, if you've done it, if, if, if you've taken this man's life . . .' She gripped Keon's forearm tightly, wishing that this was all wrong.

He looked down at the table, more tears falling fast and landing in the puddle that was collecting there. His body started to shake. 'I didn't mean to do it,' he whispered. 'I never fucking meant to shoot, Mum. Never, ever,' he continued, his shoulders so hunched now and his head so far down Tynice could see the bumps of his spine on the back of his neck.

'Oh God, oh God, oh God . . . *why*, Keon? Why?' she asked, struggling so hard not to scream this out across the room. So loud that maybe someone could hear and help them; turn back time and make it all undone.

'Mum, I don't *know*. We – me and Steve – we were just going to scare this bloke we know. I got hold of a gun but I didn't even mean to pull the trigger. I still don't know why I pulled it, Mum. I don't know why . . .'

Her blood ran cold, and she felt unwell. She imagined a gun in his hands. But he was still her son.

'But, you see . . .' – Keon could hardly get the words out now, and Tynice had to lean further in to make out what he was saying – '. . . what's worse is that we didn't even scare who we meant to scare, anyway. I shot someone, by mistake, someone completely innocent,' he finished, looking back up, snot running from his nose and down his lips.

Tynice had never seen such fear in a face.

'And now, this guy, whoever he is, he's *dead*, Mum. And it's all my fault . . .' he said, starting to weep again.

'Stop crying, Keon. Please, just stop crying,' Tynice growled over the table.

Keon flinched as she did so, looking so afraid of her. Afraid of what she might say or do. Like this alone would be the worst kind of judgment he had coming. He hadn't looked scared of her since he was ten. After that, any telling-off she had given him had been greeted with laughter or rolled eyes. And she had known she'd lost control of him then. But Tynice felt a fury now. Fury because not only had he ruined his life, her life and his sister's life; but someone else's life, too, and all those who knew and loved him. The man could have been married, he could have been a father.

'I'm going to admit it, Mum. And I will go down for this,' Keon said, his tears now slowing a little. As he swallowed she could see his voice box move up and down.

The room started to spin. 'I'm sorry Ke— I've got to . . .' Tynice said as she rose to her feet.

The chair screeched loudly against the floor as she stood. She had to go, had to be out of there.

'No, Mum. No, Mum, please! Mum, *please*,' he begged, rising a little too, trying to call her back to him.

Things started to go white. Brilliant white speckles clouded her vision and everything went blurry. Then she hit the floor.

CHAPTER 7

HE HAD TO MAKE TODAY WONDERFUL. THE BEST DAY EVER.

Saturday 24 August 2002
Brighton beach
2 p.m.

Bryony had bought a black, fifties-style swimming costume especially for the date. She looked so beautiful Max couldn't believe he'd finally managed to persuade this woman to come out with him.

The sun was out and it made the sea glitter. The air was crisp, fresh, miles away from the smog of London, whipped over the sea from France and carrying the scent of a thousand love stories.

Max was nervous, it was tickling his stomach. Every time he thought of her, he could barely focus on anything else. *The flowers and the pestering worked*, he thought for the umpteenth time in amazement, holding the cricket ball tight in his hand and feeling the sun beating down on his back. He was a lucky guy.

A girl walked past and smiled at him, tucking her thick, blonde hair behind her ear and glancing away playfully. He looked away. Nothing else and no one else interested him any more, which was unlike him, he realised, because when it came to women he usually had the attention span of a goldfish.

Max knew he was a typical man in his early twenties, running around town, chasing girls. He'd developed a reputation as a guy who had little time for love; someone who went through the local female population as quickly as he went through pairs of socks, and he'd regrettably hurt a few feelings on the way, too. But this, this was different. He'd never wanted something or anyone so much in his life, and when he looked back on the girls he had dated and the excuses he had made, he realised that he had never really been as into them as he'd convinced himself he was. This was a new feeling for him.

He continued to stare at Bryony, who had her back to him, standing some distance away. He could barely make out her movements, but she seemed to be staring at the pier.

Max wondered if he would ever be good enough for a girl like her. He had to make today wonderful. The best day ever. Especially after the spilt beer and dress incident. But he was worried that karma might come back and bite him in the arse now that he'd finally found someone he wanted to spend every waking moment with.

He looked down at the red ball with its white stitching, feeling a flash of mischief suddenly take over. 'Now, Weaver, now! Catch it!' Max suddenly screamed from the far end of the beach, pulling a muscular right arm back and hurling the cricket ball as hard as he could. Several people were disturbed by his shouting and watched the ball soar through the air, expectant grins on their faces beneath sun hats. A little girl in a pink and white swimming costume clapped excitedly and shouted 'Wheeeee' as the ball spun and turned through the air. Time seemed to slow down, though, as Max followed the ball's trajectory and, frame by frame, his face fell from a wide, excited smile to a look of utter horror, as Bryony turned around.

Thump.

At least ten people gasped in horror. A group of teenage girls started laughing and a little boy who'd been standing near Bryony screamed and ran into the waiting arms of his mother, whose mouth was hanging open in horror.

'Oh God, oh God, oh God!' Max cried, starting to run across the pebbles towards her. His slim, muscular legs skidded furiously as he approached her with desperate speed, his wet, navy blue shorts slapping against his legs. From a distance he looked a little like a broken windmill.

The ball had hit Bryony square in the face. She lay on the ground, motionless. 'Holy shit, fuck, why?' he muttered under his breath, picking up his pace and almost breaking his ankle en route. He realised with dismay that a good-looking guy had already run over to Bryony, effortlessly navigating the bumpy landscape to rescue her. 'Oh, for fuck's sake, piss *off*,' he gasped under his breath, hot humiliation soaring up his neck and painting him a lobster pink. By the time he arrived, huffing and puffing, the guy had already started looking after her.

As Max bent over to catch his breath, he considered all the possible injury outcomes as a result of his ill-thought-out tomfoolery. Bryony would probably have a very sore face, and a bump, and that was if he was lucky. She could have both of those things and a bad bruise. Or if the ball had hit her in the *mouth* . . . he shuddered at the thought of it.

'Hey, are you OK?' the man asked, a hand on Bryony's back.

Bryony sat up shakily and spat, first into her hand and then onto the ground. The fleck was tinged with blood.

Oh shit, Max thought miserably, his hands now on his hips in the posture of the hopelessly embarrassed.

Bryony looked down at the tooth lying in her palm, but didn't say anything.

'It's OK, mate, I've got it,' Max said, mortified as he realised the injury was far worse than he'd imagined.

'You're a douche, man. Why'd you do that?' the stranger asked, looking at him like he was something he'd found on the bottom of his shoe. He had an American accent. Max felt even more irritated. A *douche*.

The stranger ran his hand over his stubbly chin, eyes squinting as if in an attempt to comprehend this disastrous date.

'It's OK, it's OK, he didn't mean it,' Bryony said, flapping her spare hand but tilting her head down so her mouth was hidden.

'Yeah, all right, mate – obviously I didn't intend for that to happen, yeah?' Max growled, tears of frustration filling his eyes.

'Calm down, Max,' Bryony said, still looking down at her lap.

The man turned around and left, muttering to himself. As he joined his friends, he gesticulated wildly in their direction. Max watched him and tutted, realising that they were probably talking about how much of a wanker he was.

He slid down into the sand behind Bryony and put his arms around her, squeezing her tight. 'Oh, shit. I am so, so sorry,' he said, sweeping her hair behind her neck and holding her face gently. She had tears in her eyes and blood around her mouth. She was squinting in the sunlight as she clutched the tooth in her right hand and placed her other hand over her mouth self-consciously. He wondered at which point he should find out just which of her teeth he'd managed to knock out with a cricket ball. He desperately hoped it wasn't one of the front two – that would be an utter disaster.

'It's OK,' she lisped. She sounded like she'd just had a brace put on.

Max could see the smile in her eyes and he kissed her forehead, his legs wrapped around her. They sat for a moment. Alone. Together.

'I don't know what to say, Bryony. I'm a prat, a total and utter dickhead. I ruin everything I touch,' he said, pulling her hand away from her face gently and pulling up her top lip.

It was one of her front teeth.

This was bad. Really bad. Women did not appreciate this stuff. Teeth were kind of important. Bryony was beautiful and now she looked like a pirate.

Did she realise it was one of her front teeth?

Max couldn't believe it, and looked up to the sky, wishing he was someone else. He was sure he'd blown it now. 'Come on, we need to get you to hospital,' he muttered, starting to stand up, worrying about how much pain she was likely to be in and wondering how this was going to be explained to her family and friends. He'd be the laughing stock of Shoreditch.

'No, wait,' she said, pulling him down, back into the sand. 'I'll be OK, just give me a minute.'

Max settled down behind her again and pulled her head to his bare chest, looking out at the sea and wondering how she would feel about him after this gaffe. A seagull soared over their heads before lurching suddenly to the ground and pecking aggressively at a discarded bag of chips.

Then, the miracle happened. Bryony started to giggle. Max felt her shuddering against his skin, the muscles on her back expanding and contracting violently. He traced a finger from the bottom of her spine all the way up to the top of her neck, a frown still plastered on his features.

'Bryony, are you delirious? I don't think this is funny, really,' he said. More tears filling his eyes, he bit down on his bottom lip. Hard. Maybe girls like Bryony *were* too good for him, he decided. Maybe this was a sign from the gods that he should not be messing around with her. *Get the hint, Max.*

In reply, Bryony traced her fingers over the blond hair on his legs, and gripped on to his thigh as the laughter continued to swamp her. Her body was shaking so hard with the hilarity of it all, Max feared she might be concussed. A huge tear rolled from his eye and dropped onto her dark brown hair.

She looked up, her mouth still covered, her giggles falling out like bubbles. 'Are you crying?' she asked, laughing even harder now.

He quickly wiped the tear away with the back of his hand and pulled his face into an expression of serious concentration.

'Are you seriously *crying*?' she shrieked, totally losing control of herself now. Max tried to compose himself, and Bryony thought how silly he looked, but how she still adored his face. She still worshipped the ground he walked on, despite the fact that he'd just knocked out her front tooth with a cricket ball on their first proper date.

He was absolutely gorgeous.

'I'm so sorry. Listen, I'll take you to the hospital and I'll pay for the best dental work you can get, Bryony. I'm just such a dick,' he said, looking down at her face.

'The thing is, Max, we all make mistakes,' she said, her laughter stopping and her eyes suddenly totally serious. She was still covering her mouth, so her words were slightly muffled.

'So you don't hate me?'

Bryony emitted a loud sigh, and stroked his hair with her free hand. She'd never seen him look so vulnerable.

'No, of course not. You didn't mean to do it, did you? I think it's kind of funny. And it can all be fixed,' she said, standing now and starting to gather their things.

There was a level of understanding and forgiveness in her heart that he'd never experienced before. And that was when he knew Bryony was the one.

CHAPTER 8

'HE'S REALLY GONE,
ISN'T HE, MUM?'

Friday 13 March 2009
Finsbury Park, north London
1.10 a.m.

The buzzer kept sounding. Over and over again. Bryony lay there, paralysed in a half-sleep, wondering if she was dreaming it.

Beep.

Beep.

Beeeeeeeep.

Maybe it's another flat, she thought, as she lay with her long legs tangled in the sheets. The sound seemed to get louder, however, infiltrating her coma-like doze and bringing her into reality. She rolled over and squinted at the alarm clock on the bedside table – 01:10 in sharp neon green. Groaning, she double checked the time on her mobile phone. Yup, ten past one in the morning.

She was still trying to take in what was going on – she had only been asleep for a couple of hours. But as the buzzer kept sounding, she realised it would probably keep on going until she was fully awake. *None of our friends would call on us at this time, and ring the bell so persistently,* she thought. She wondered if there was a nutcase trying to get into the flat. With this thought, she sat up sharply in bed and felt around for the lamp, considering again for a second if she should ignore the buzzer or not. She ran a finger over the cool, metal base and then flicked the switch, a gentle light spreading across the room. Her eyes were stinging. There were so many weirdoes out there . . . Nor would it have surprised her, either, if it was some student tanked up on rum and coke, swaying back and forth and wanting to get into the wrong building, having tried to use a mascara wand as a key.

Typical that this is a work night for Max, she thought. Still, she'd have a good story to tell him in the morning, when he was back.

The buzzer stopped for a second and she lay back down on her pillow, totally confused. She rolled back over and started to drift off again, despite the fact that the lamp was on. Her right foot twitched a little as she slipped away . . . But then it started again.

Beeeep.

Beeeep.

Beeeeeeeep.

Bryony jerked back into life and threw the duvet away from her body, cool air tickling her legs. She swung her weary limbs off the bed and plodded through the bedroom doorway, past the small open-plan kitchen and living room, and towards the intercom, growling a little to herself at this terribly rude awakening. She was preparing to shout at the idiot, who was still pushing the buzzer like a lunatic. Something along the lines of 'Sod off' would be appropriate, she reckoned, with more colourful language to be deployed if the buzzing continued; followed by a quick call to the police as an emergency back-up plan.

'What?' she said flatly, her breath hot against the plastic square of the intercom mounted by the front door. A small green light flashed to show that she was connected with the outside world.

'Hello. This is PC Reynolds from the Met Police. Is this Bryony Weaver?' came a voice from the other end.

'Yes . . . yes it is.' She didn't know what this could mean. Bryony didn't know why this even involved her.

'Can you let us in, please? We need to talk to you.'

It sounded serious. There was a tone there and Bryony didn't like it. She told herself that she must be calm. That it was probably just a routine visit, but police always made her nervous for some reason . . . she didn't trust them.

'Oh, sorry, yes, of course. Come up the stairs – flat four.'

She moved her finger over to another, smaller button and heard a click as the door downstairs was released. She suddenly felt self-conscious. Bryony was wearing a T-shirt with no bra, and hated the way that looked, but there was no time to get changed now. She could hear heavy footsteps coming up the stairs.

Before she even had a chance to check her breath against the back of her hand, there was a knock at the door. She opened it slightly and was greeted by two officers, one male, one female, in their traditional black and white uniforms. They looked young. Young and tired.

Her heart sank a little further when she saw the serious expressions on their faces. But there was no need for drama, she was sure of it.

'Hello, sorry. I was asleep. Can I help you with anything?' Bryony asked, still reluctant to open the door properly.

The same officer she had heard over the telecom spoke to her. He had a deep voice, with a London twang flowing through it. *The quintessential London copper*, Bryony thought.

'We need to come and speak to you, inside,' he said now, taking his hat off and holding it against his chest.

Bryony's stomach suddenly plunged with fear. Her mind raced as to what might have happened, adrenaline starting to creep numbly into her legs. She realised they were shaking involuntarily. This made no sense at all.

Bryony switched the hall light on and let the two police officers in, forgetting all about the way she looked. She led them into the living room and stood there, wanting some answers.

'I think you need to sit down, Bryony,' said the second officer, who was a stocky woman with short blonde hair.

'Would you like a cup of tea or coffee?' she asked instead, automatically wondering if there were any of those nice chocolate rounds left in the cupboard after Max had raided the tin the other night. But she figured from the look on their faces this would be no tea party.

'No, thank you, Bryony.'

The first officer gestured with his hands for her to sit down, so she sank into the single chair and let them have the sofa. The material felt scratchy against her legs. Bryony immediately felt the urge to call Max and tell him they had the police round. She wished he was at home now. *He'd be great in this situation*, she thought. *Cool, calm and collected.*

The two parties sat opposite each other, a sickening silence enveloping them. The first officer cleared his throat and started to speak. She noticed his hands were shaking.

'Bryony. I am dreadfully sorry to tell you this . . .'

The room started to twitch before her eyes. Bryony realised this was very serious, and affected her directly. With stark clarity, she suddenly realised, too, that her phone had not been flashing when she had looked at it the first time the bell rang, meaning that Max had not contacted her. She realised suddenly that maybe this involved—

'Max Tooley died this evening outside Finsbury Park tube station. He was shot.'

And that was it.

The words came from the policeman's mouth like water, slipping and sliding into her world and instantly diluting everything she ever knew that was happy and joyful. A sharp twinge of sickness shot from her stomach into her throat. She blinked several times, taking in the enormity of what he'd said.

'Bryony, I'm so sorry. Is there anything we can do?' the policewoman asked, leaning forward a little, the shuffle of her uniform loud – a slight rip of Velcro and a squeak of plastic on plastic.

Nothing could come out of her mouth. Bryony nodded pathetically, unable to see through her watering eyes. The policeman's voice was muffled, far away, as if he was trying to speak to her from beneath the sea. She felt like her legs had been carried away from her, and although she wanted to run away, it would be impossible because they weren't there any more.

This has to be a nightmare, she thought. *Maybe I'm still asleep* . . . Bryony stared at the police officers, open-mouthed. Her breath had started to quicken, faster and faster until she realised that she was not saying a thing but just sitting, looking at them and hyperventilating.

The second officer walked round and knelt down beside her, tears brimming in her eyes, too. *That's unusual*, she thought, numbly. *She must be a rookie.*

'He had passed away by the time our colleagues

arrived on the scene, but there was a woman with him. She'd found him shortly after he'd been shot, and we are currently speaking to her about the events. We also found the man we think is responsible for the shooting, in an alleyway nearby. He has been taken to the station for questioning.'

Her breathing was coming so fast now she was rasping. This reaction was something that would normally have humiliated her completely, but now she didn't care whether these police officers, these strange people she'd never met, watched her implode. Watched her melt down into a single atom. Smash into a trillion little pieces.

But then doubt began to cloud her mind. This couldn't be right. She started the denial process, already knee-deep into the first of the five stages of grief: 'But, he was working tonight. He wasn't due home till the morning, he told me that. Work would have put him up in a hotel. You've made a mistake. There's no fucking way! I think you have the wrong man,' she said, pleading desperately, leaning so far forward in her seat it made her back ache, her whole body shaking now.

Then she was begging. Begging some higher force to let her talk them out of this. Talk them out of this silly connection they had made and got so wrong.

The second officer got up from her side and walked over to the kitchen behind her. She heard the sound of the tap running.

'These were found in his bag. This is how we

found you,' the first officer said, pulling out, as if from nowhere, Max's work card and his driving licence. He pushed them across the coffee table between them and there, in front of her, was the face of her man. Max. A cheesy little grin. Beautiful dimples. Those eyes.

'Oh, *shit*,' Bryony said, pulling herself back and sinking into the chair. She tucked her head down towards her knees and started to cry. But they weren't slow, melancholic tears. They were tears of fury.

She heard the soft sound of a glass of water being put down in front of her as images flashed before her eyes: Max just a few days before, coming out of the shower with a towel around his waist. Alive. Droplets of water dripping down his warm skin, his blood rushing around beneath it. His heart beating.

And then the hysteria hit. She would recall, weeks later, one of the officers – she couldn't tell which one – holding her still, pushing her arms against her body so she couldn't lash out. But Bryony didn't remember much after that point apart from screaming. A lot. And the screams had sounded like they were coming from elsewhere, from the throat of some other heartbroken woman. They were so loud that they split and scratched in her throat like dry reeds.

The next thing she knew, her mother had arrived and the police were gone. And her mother was lying with her on the kitchen floor, holding her

103

from behind while she cried so hard it hurt. Bryony could feel every rib, every muscle in her stomach and chest expanding and contracting. The tears themselves felt like razor blades after a while.

Her mother held her tight but said nothing, so she imagined those arms belonged to Max and that they were anywhere other than on the cold tiles of the kitchen floor that smelt faintly of disinfectant. She was a whimpering mess, snot pouring down her top lip, angry fists rubbing out her own eyelashes like they were a mistake in a drawing. A vile sickness washed over her body as though she had a fever.

Bryony was so consumed by grief that she eventually forgot she was there at all.

And then she was back in bed, holding in her arms seven of Max's shirts, pulling them against her face. Red cotton, blue stripes, white starched collars and soft seams. She'd fished them out from the dirty linen basket, wading through the socks and pants until she could find something he'd worn that had picked up a hint of his life – the living smell of a human being, his aftershave, the unique fragrance of his soft skin she had never smelt on anyone else. The kind of smell that would fade. A smell she knew she couldn't bottle for keeps.

Bryony was scared that if she inhaled it too much she might draw it away from the fabric: if she was greedy she might use it all up, or become immune to it, so she swapped the shirts round in rotation.

It was as if she was the most drunk she had ever been, except she hadn't touched a drop. All she knew was that someone had stolen Max, the light of her life, from her; the only true love she had ever known.

A palpable desperation swept through her, an urge to turn back time; change something. Why had he come back early? She couldn't understand.

The pillows were wet with her tears, her skin sticking to the damp surfaces. Yet, somehow, at some crazy hour, Bryony slipped into a fitful sleep. Lying in a sea of Max's clothes and imagining he was with her, pushing his lips against the back of her neck and kicking her gently in his dreams by mistake. And, as she slept, her own voice kept circulating around her head, that it was all a dream. That maybe she had fallen ill, in the head, and that when she woke up she would be in hospital and tall men in white coats would give her some tablets in a paper cup and she would realise that she had lost it for a while. Just temporarily. Her brain was on vacation – that's how they would describe it, so she didn't feel ashamed. And everyone would smile at her with that half-pitying, half-fearful smirk that you see in the soaps whenever someone's lost his or her mind.

And Max would visit her and she would understand that everything was OK . . . really.

Bryony woke up the next morning at 7 a.m., the long sleeve of a dark blue shirt gently wrapped around her neck, a pearlescent button gripped between her teeth. She had such a strong headache it felt like someone had thumped her around the back of the head with a plank of wood.

There was a feeling of dread in her stomach, but she couldn't work out why. And she couldn't work out why Max's clothes were all around her.

At first she thought she was hung over, that maybe she and Max had got drunk together and done something silly – he'd put his trainers in the freezer for a laugh once when he was pissed and they'd forgotten all about it until the next day when she'd gone to get some chicken out of it to defrost for their dinner. She wondered if it had been 'one of those' nights. One of those wild, lost nights of reckless abandon. But he wasn't there.

Then she remembered. And suddenly she was going through it all over again.

'Mum. Mum. Muuuuum!' Bryony called out with desperate urgency, sitting up in bed and pulling the shirts onto her lap, more tears rolling down her cheeks. She heard fast footsteps come from the kitchen and into her room, and there was her mother, silently looking at her like she was a scary film.

Her mother's eyes held huge puddles of tears that were on the verge of spilling onto the floor like overflowing bathwater. She put her hands up to her face and leant against the doorframe. Her wiry blonde hair was scooped up into a messy bun, and she seemed older than Bryony had ever seen her. Bryony started to shake her head, faster and faster, pulling the shirts up around her like she was looking for Max underneath them all.

'Bry, I'm . . . I'm so . . .' her mother started, but didn't finish her sentence, rushing over to her daughter and pulling her into her arms like she was a tiny little girl again.

'He's really gone, isn't he, Mum?' Bryony said, more tears flowing from her eyes. Her face felt like it was made from rubber.

'Yes, baby. He is,' her mother said, gripping on to Bryony, her own tears now dampening her daughter's greying T-shirt.

'But, what the fuck, Mum? How? *Why?* Who would shoot him? Why would anyone shoot Max?' Bryony whispered, suddenly feeling a pang of agonising guilt. Guilt that she wasn't there when it happened. That she wasn't there to hold him in his last minutes of life, and tell him that he was the most beautiful thing that had ever happened to her. Bryony thought that maybe if she'd been there, she could have made him comfortable in the last few moments, those vital seconds, as they slipped away into an inky abyss. She could have pushed her lips against his and felt his last breaths, warm and moist, seeping away from him.

And then, when he was dying, he would have known that he was loved, more than a girl could ever love a boy.

And Bryony could have told him that she didn't really care that he wasn't keen on getting married.

107

And that she had really and truly forgiven him for the time he'd accidentally knocked her front tooth out with a cricket ball on their first proper date. And that her aunty didn't really hate him like he thought she did, that she was just a bitch . . .

And that, maybe, in all the agony of this crazy, dark world, he would know in his last moments that he was everything to her.

CHAPTER 9

THIS WAS NO TIME FOR HEAD TURNING.

Friday 13 March 2009
Finsbury Park, north London
10 a.m.

S ara made sure her outfit was nondescript. Greys, blacks, charcoals . . . a pair of sunglasses she hadn't worn for years.

For today's task, she had to be someone who blended into the background. Somebody whose eyes could only just be recognised over the top of a newspaper by a close friend, and only if they looked carefully enough . . . This was no time for head turning. No time for bright red heels that clicked down the tube station platform and made men turn their heads around like barn owls to get a better look. No time for plunging necklines and flashes of those trademark pins she had, after years of stomping the restaurant floor.

She stood in front of the wardrobe mirror and inspected her choice of attire for the day. She was aware that her unusually short hairstyle might betray her, but a headscarf or an elaborate hat would have potentially drawn even more attention, and given the game away. Instead, she wore a pair of black office trousers, a grey and white shirt, and a black cardigan hanging limply around her shoulders to hide her subtle curves. The curves that had first prompted Tom to shuffle over next to her, slide an arm around her waist in a crowded bar and whisper into her ear.

The moment she fell in love . . .

The sunglasses sat in a box in her handbag, nestled between a pink leather Filofax and a cheque book. She could tell just by looking out of the window that it would be a pleasant day – March had been surprisingly humid.

Tom thought she was working at the restaurant today, but she had again changed the rota around, plucking up the courage to really do this; to stalk her own husband and try to catch him in the act. To try and catch him stealing a forbidden kiss in some dark London alcove, running his hands over a strange, new body. A body that wasn't hers.

When she had arrived home the night before, after finding his dating profile on the internet, she had struggled to keep the knowledge to herself. She had thought surprisingly calmly about the best way to handle it, and had wondered quietly if she was in denial. But it *was* so unlike him. Such a huge shock. Nor was there any other indication that he could be out dating; it was beyond him and all that she knew about him, and for this reason it seemed so disconcerting. She wondered if she shouldn't set up a profile too, with a fake picture, and arrange a meeting to actually catch him in the act.

Sara had struggled to bite her tongue as Tom quietly snored in bed, when really all she had wanted to do was scream and shout and hit him with pillows until the feathers came bursting out of the seams.

She and Tanya had agreed that she should keep what she knew about Tom to herself for the time being, and try and find out more before making any rash accusations. She hoped that maybe she had got it wrong, that it wasn't what it seemed. She hadn't been able to get the image out of her head all night: his face beaming back at her from the pages of an *internet dating site.*

Denial had arrived almost instantly. It was like paracetamol on top of a headache, a little mask to get her through the short-term. A plaster over a wound that wouldn't stop bleeding. But, deep down, she knew she had to catch him at it, because otherwise she would spend the rest of her married life chewing her nails and fighting her negative gut feeling.

She almost wished that she hadn't seen it in the first place. *Ignorance is bliss.*

So, here goes, she thought, looking at the bright green clock on the kitchen wall and picking up her bag. It was 10 a.m. Tom had left an hour before, peeling himself out of their warm bed and

111

heading to the Mulai Gallery because his exhibition had finished. He had to pack up his work and load it into a van. She knew that if she could sneak around town for a while, and be in the right place at the right time, she might see something, anything. A flick of a fringe, or possibly the fluttering of eyelashes, which might give the game away if he was seeing someone else. Even though she knew that the odds were remote. He was more likely to cheat at night when she was working at the restaurant, she reckoned, but it was worth a shot.

She stepped into the dark hallway of her Finsbury Park home and opened the front door, brilliant sunshine greeting her immediately. The rows of houses opposite always reminded her of the traditional streets of New York, with their big steps leading up to the front door, and she always felt that they should be littered with crowds of young people, rapping over a beat from a tin boom-box.

Sara slipped the sunglasses over her eyes and took a deep breath, the door clicking closed quietly behind her. She was nervous. If she did see something . . . did she *really* want to see it? To know for sure? Did she need to have her husband's potential infidelity rubber-stamped to begin the inevitable fallout? Rows over dividing up the Le Creuset pots and pans, and who should have the pick of the DVD collection? They had been married for twelve months. It would be soul destroying.

Her modest heels hit the ground purposefully as she walked past the small, bedraggled-looking trees planted down the street that led to the tube station. To shirk this would be cowardly.

Despite the warmth of the early spring, there was a nice breeze, which flapped through her cardigan as she walked. But it did nothing to calm her down. A child walked a few metres ahead of her, kicking an empty Coke can along the street. Everything seemed louder and sharper, the sound of tin against concrete grating in her ears. A bus drove past, its suspension hissing loudly, making her flinch and an angry heat rise in her cheeks.

She picked up her pace, aware that if she timed this wrong she would miss him. She overtook the child and narrowly missed the can as it was kicked towards her feet. The boy, dressed in shorts and a bright blue T-shirt, spat on the ground and scowled at her.

When she got off the tube at Tottenham Court Road she felt even more nervous. Was she doing the right thing? She had already trawled through their joint bank statements online, looking for something incriminating, but there was nothing apart from the odd binge in Topman, the usual Oyster card top-ups and late-night Tesco Express visits. There wasn't even a subscription charge for his internet dating profile. She had checked the statements thoroughly, going back months and months. His suit jacket pockets had failed to shed any light on the matter either, which suggested he must be resorting to clever tactics, and this worried her even more than any kind of blatant foul play. It was more calculated. Colder.

She weaved through the crowds of people moving along the pavement like ants. There was so much *variety* in them – it was what she loved about London – but now everyone seemed to act as an obstruction: walls of people, hiding her perfectly, but preventing her from progress. Tourists irritated her as they suddenly stopped in her path, craning their necks at the stunning cityscape.

Eventually, she reached the gallery, pausing for a moment a few yards away from its glass doors, looking down at her feet and forcing herself to breathe slowly. A pigeon shuffled around by her shoes, its head twitching back and forth frantically.

She felt slightly guilty for a moment that she was resorting to such measures. She was effectively spying on her husband. But that guilt didn't last long as she began to tiptoe down an alleyway to the side of the gallery, listening for any voices she might hear through its open windows. She stepped lightly so the sound of her heels would not give the game away, her hands gripping the cool tiles on the wall: the warmth of the morning sun had failed to reach this quiet, dark tunnel, which smelt of damp.

It was difficult to hear anything other than the fast beating of her heart in her ears, so she took a few more deep breaths to calm herself down.

The hum of the street behind her was barely audible now as she strained to hear anything that could be going on at the back of the gallery, where cars and vans were loaded and unloaded with art and installation equipment. There was nothing, of course . . .

She realised it was more than likely that Tom would be inside and this could be a wasted trip. And even if he was inside, he wasn't likely to be carrying on with some other woman there, was he? *Maybe I could go inside*, she thought, *and surprise him*. She could tell him that she had taken a day off and had just wanted to come in and say hi. *I'm just being silly*, she thought, suddenly feeling rather foolish for resorting to such measures.

But her plans were suddenly interrupted by the voice of her husband at the end of the alleyway, echoing so much that it was hard to make out the words. She pressed herself as flat against the wall as she could, and a little closer to the sound, but far enough away to be well hidden.

An engine started, and Tom's dark blue van appeared in the small box of vision at the end of the alley. She prayed that she wouldn't cough, or sneeze . . . it would totally blow her cover, and having to explain to her husband why she was hanging about in a dank alleyway next to the gallery would be somewhat difficult.

The gentle hum of the engine stopped and was replaced by the click of door handles, the opening of the back of the van, and the shuffle of feet against concrete, every sound magnified by the depth of the alleyway.

And then a man's voice. Not Tom's; someone he worked with that she'd never met, perhaps – she didn't recognise it. 'So, how's married life then, mate? It's been so long since I last saw you – it was before the wedding, wasn't it?'

Sara held her breath.

'Brilliant, thanks, yes . . . We're so happy, it feels like we only got married yesterday,' Tom replied, the sound of strain in his voice as he spoke, as if he were lifting something heavy.

Sara sighed deeply in silent relief, thinking yet again that she might have overreacted about all this. But there *was* that dating profile. It just made no sense.

'What's it like, you know, to actually be a married man, then?' came the voice of the stranger.

There was a pause. 'Well . . . er, it's not much different, really . . . but good! I love Sara so much, I was completely bowled over when she said yes, so I've just been kind of pinching myself ever since . . . You spend years dating people who aren't right for you, and when it clicks, that's it. It all just makes sense.'

Sara's heart melted a little, and she experienced the familiar pang of love in her stomach that she hadn't felt since last night. It was as if all the tension and paranoia was seeping away from her. Maybe there *had* been a mistake?

But again, the internet dating profile didn't just appear from nowhere.

'Do you not ever get freaked out, though?' came the voice again. *He must be young – he shouldn't be asking Tom questions like that*, she thought, smarting a little at the tone of the question, which by default almost demanded a controversial answer.

'By what?'

Sara could tell by the tone of Tom's voice that he wasn't too impressed with the question, either.

'Well, that Sara is *it* now. You can never be with another woman, for the rest of your life. That's a huge commitment. I admire you for it . . . I sure as hell don't think that I could do it,' the man said, from slightly more to the left and a little more muffled than before.

There was the sound of a can of fizzy drink being snapped open.

Sara felt a spurt of anger, and just about held herself back from running out and giving this man, whoever he was, a good talking-to. *It's this kind of man-talk*, she thought, *that is the biggest problem with relationships today.* The idea that a guy's choice to marry is like cutting off a whole range of experiences that he simply *must* have, and that without them he is somehow less of a man. Castrated somehow. She certainly didn't feel a desire to be kissed by someone else ever again, so why should it be the case the other way round?

What was wrong with them?

'No, mate, not at all. I'm just really happy,' Tom

replied, a shift in his voice implying he was lifting another painting into the back of the van.

Sara let a deep breath out, careful to be absolutely silent.

'Hey, look, I'm just really young and silly, I'm happy for you, Tom,' the other voice said, as though finally realising that his questioning was a little off the mark.

'So, are we all done here now?' Tom asked, still a little sharply.

'Yes, mate, all packed up.'

Tom walked back into the gallery, wiping a few beads of sweat from his brow with his forearm, which was covered in thick hair that was already turning blond from the sun. His baggy jeans hung over a pair of white Converse trainers, and he undid the first few buttons of his green checked shirt, revealing the hairs at the top of his chest.

The white walls were almost as pure as they had been when he and his exhibition first arrived, bar a few scars here and there – marks from industrial tape and some new nails banged into the surfaces. Wires hung from the ceiling, where his paintings had hung in the centre of the room in clear glass frames.

Outside the gallery, a banner was covered in clever wording in some fancy typeface, with promises of a new exhibition to come. A new artist. Someone better, perhaps . . . And soon that new artist would be in there on his or her opening night, schmoozing the national press in a crisp shirt and brand new suit, or dress, paired with a megawatt smile full of promise and excitement.

Tom realised that he was up against it again.

The display had been a massive boost for his career, but it had gone by so quickly. The reviews had mostly raved, but there had been a disappointing number of follow-up calls from those interested in commissioning him, or even displaying his work. The offers that had been made were certainly not overwhelming. He had greeted them with polite thanks, but kept them at arm's length, just in case something better came along . . .

'I can't believe this is over,' he whispered to himself under his breath, feeling the heat of his physical exertion continuing to rise to the surface of the skin on his face despite the fact that he was standing still. It seemed like only five minutes ago that the room had been a bright buzz of energy, full of flash photography, sharply dressed journalists and trays brimming with canapés.

A small wave of panic washed over him as he considered what the hell he was going to do next. He needed to come up with his next exhibition. A new concept, something groundbreaking. He'd had vague plans for some really unusual installations – multimedia features to compliment his work – and something to shock the critics this time . . . An artistic critique on society maybe? Something that would really get people talking. He just didn't know what his theme should be.

He squinted as the stark whiteness of the walls penetrated his eyes, making him feel a little overwhelmed. The whiteness seemed to multiply and brighten until his vision was clouded by hundreds of white dots, like pixels. He eventually shut his eyes, letting the darkness calm him.

He knew he was being paranoid. It would all work out in the end. This was the nature of the business, and it certainly wasn't the first time he had felt like this. He was sure it wouldn't be the last.

His next exhibition needed some edge. It needed to be spectacular.

As he stared out of the window, both hands on his hips, he noticed a woman dash past on the other side of the street who looked just like his wife.

CHAPTER 10

'PEOPLE TALK IN THIS INDUSTRY.'

Saturday 14 March 2009
Ealing, west London
7 p.m.

It was a deathly black. The same shade as a Victorian-school inkwell, the darkest aban-doned corner of a theatre, or the inside of a tomb. A shade so glossy in blackness it reflected the strip lighting in the bathroom like a mirror.

The stuff was dripping all over the bath, running down the smooth, white curves and tainting it with sloppy muck, reminiscent of an oil slick. The eye-watering stench of chemicals filled every part of the bathroom, able only to escape through a tiny window that was slightly ajar.

Rachel knelt in front of the bath looking at the expensive tiles, before flipping her head over quickly, not thinking of the consequences. Drops of vile blackness splattered all over the snow-white wallpaper behind her, up and over the ceiling and back down into the tub again: an incriminating trail that could only be traced back to her. She immediately realised she had probably ruined the bathroom in one head flip, but didn't bother to turn around and inspect her handiwork.

Rachel wasn't sure why she was doing this.

She had hovered in the hair-dye section at Superdrug for all of about thirty seconds; she had known what she wanted. She had to grab some attention. It had to be jet-black.

She switched on the shower, angling the plastic head over her own and letting the water start to run through her hair. The new shade was a shock to her.

The colourant flooded into the bath, starting to fade slightly only after what seemed like gallons of water. Five minutes passed, and then ten, and still there was a charcoal tinge running through the water as it twisted and turned through her hair. The plughole glugged away in satisfaction, like a greedy drunk. This was the most rebellion the house had seen since the Matthew family moved in ten years ago.

Eventually, Rachel slicked some special conditioner over her hair from a small bronze-coloured tube, the lettering printed on it promising world-changing confidence. Words like 'Outstanding shine' and 'Sublimely nourishing conditioner' paired with the sentence, 'For the best colour you've ever had out of a bottle.'

But Rachel didn't really care if this *was* the best colour ever, because to her it was a *shade*. It was black, and it had sunk into the strands of hair on her head and changed her from an angelic

122

creature into a little demon. Exactly as she had wanted.

She kept working away at her hair, rubbing the conditioner into the strands all the way from the base of her neck to the tips. After leaving it in for two minutes, as instructed, she rinsed it out until the water finally ran completely clear. She could feel on the tips of her fingers a plasticky coating that had been left behind.

She stood in front of the bathroom mirror, staring at a girl who almost seemed like a stranger.

Suddenly, there was a piercing scream. A note so high and sharp that Rachel raised both eyebrows as she stood, feet hip-width apart, staring at the reflection of herself. Her ears almost flinched in an effort to shut out the sound. But it wasn't her scream. It was her mother's.

Rita stood in the doorway, her eyes darting backwards and forwards from her daughter's raven locks to what looked like the speedy getaway trail of an injured squid all over the bathroom walls. She wasn't entirely sure which of the two sights was worse, and she certainly wasn't sure which of the two to deal with first.

The colour drained from her face, and tea from the mug she was holding – now almost at ninety degrees – started to drip onto the floor. Her mouth hung open. She suddenly realised what she was doing as she felt the warm drips of liquid splashing up onto her toes and tilted it upright again, too baffled to even begin to address the tea stains at this stage.

'Rachel! What in God's knickers have you done?'

Rachel smiled a little. That was the closest her mother had ever come to swearing.

'Nothing, Mum. Just changing the colour of my hair. I felt it was time for something new,' she said quietly, running a bright red comb down the strands. They were so long they tickled her shoulders. The teeth of the comb got caught in a knot at the bottom of her hair; she tugged it hard until it was free, taking a small clump of jet-black hair with it.

'But . . . but . . . that's *far* too dark for Swanhilda. You look like . . . well . . . you look like a gothic, Rachel, or an Imo,' Rita said, slamming the mug down on the surface by the sink and folding her arms.

'Emo.'

'What?'

'Oh, don't worry. It's fine, Mum,' Rachel whispered, turning to face Rita with a look of contempt on her face. It was incredibly difficult for her to mask her fury.

'No, Rachel, it's not bloody well fine,' Rita fumed.

Another swear word, Rachel thought. *An upgrade from the use of the words 'knickers' and 'God' in the same sentence. This* must *be serious.*

'And, look, you've got it all over the back of your neck, and there are spots on your face. What are we going to do with you?' Rita yelled, tumbling relentlessly into angry hysteria.

'I can cover up the spots. That's fine,' Rachel said calmly, starting to try and walk around her mother, but stopped by her as Rita sidestepped to get in her way. Rachel sighed, her elegant shoulders slumping forwards, and she placed a delicate hand on the sink to steady herself. The chemicals had gone to her head somewhat.

'Why now? You have your first run through of *Coppélia* on Monday. I don't understand!' Rita shrieked, throwing her hands up towards her face, her pupils almost dancing in incandescent rage as she strove to take in the sight of her daughter's new hair.

'I just felt like it, OK?' Rachel said, her voice bearing more than a little bit of an undertone.

'Well, you just wait and see what the company says. They are not going to be impressed!' Rita said, as Rachel pushed her gently to the side and ran up the stairs to her room with natural agility.

She had not told her mother or Richard about the document she had found. It was too much to handle. Too big a subject to broach. She had stuffed the papers back into the file and put everything back into its rightful place, so Rita would never know that the secret had been revealed.

Rachel had stepped into a world she didn't like. She had ventured into a forbidden box, and instead of finding a delicate model ballerina, spinning on a coiled wire to a delightful, tinkly tune, she had uncovered something dark that she couldn't ignore.

Her nights had been filled with ugly dreams, with tossing and turning.

She had started staring at her father's face over the dinner table. Looking at his furrowed brow and bulbous nose, taking a photograph of his face in her mind and then sitting in front of the mirror upstairs and realising that nothing matched apart from the tired bags that had formed under their eyes – and that was more nurture than nature.

She had asked to flick through photographs of her mother as a young woman, and saw nothing in her youthful face or frame that suggested she was a part of this woman. This stranger. And, over time, she thought about her family. Everything that had ever been said to her. The lines at dinner parties like, 'Hasn't she got her mother's cheek-bones?' followed by 'Ohhh, maybe she looks more like her father', and how her parents had smiled politely and changed the subject, holding on to their glasses of fizzing champagne and looking at each other with a certain level of mutual under-standing in their eyes.

Who knew? Did everyone know apart from her? Did her teachers know when she was back at school? Her doctor? Was there a club? A secret handshake? Badges and printed T-shirts, even? And then a whole new can of worms was opened when she wondered where her real mother was . . . if she was alive or dead. If she had babies of her own, a new family to replace the one she left?

Why did she give her up when she was just a

poor, defenceless baby, too young to sin, too young to be unbearably irritating, to be unloved . . . to be *abandoned*. And how had it happened? Was she dumped on someone's doorstep in a wicker basket on a dark and stormy night? Or was she handed into the arms of a social worker by a sobbing teenage mother, who was just too young to handle it all?

On top of the hurt and the confusion, anger had risen, its ugly head like a beast from the bottom of the sea, bearing ferocious teeth. And this would be followed by guilt when she lay awake at 3 a.m. listening to the sound of silence, and considering how Rita and Edward, whoever they were, had taken her in and given her everything, even though she wasn't their own flesh and blood. And how she hadn't always been good to them: the door-slamming, the smoking, the rows audible to their next-door neighbours causing crimson cheeks on school runs and scribbled apologies on the back of crumpled receipts.

Would she tell Rita, her 'mother', that she knew? Or would she keep her own secrets too, just to redress the balance a little . . .

Rachel flicked the switch on her hairdryer and began blowing the water from her hair until her soft, black locks shone through from beneath the damp. Her hair flicked out in different directions, trailing into the air like ribbons attached to a model aeroplane. When she was finished, she could not help but notice her split ends were showing up white. Her hair now looked brittle and dry. It made her already pale face look gaunt and tired.

But she loved it.

She slicked on some dark mauve lipstick and pouted in the mirror, almost forgetting how she'd looked when she was a girl with a lot less knowledge about herself. She smiled falsely and noticed some of her lipstick was stuck to one of her teeth. She rubbed it off quickly with her index finger.

She was interrupted again by Rita, who barged through the door of her bedroom, her dated mobile phone in her hand. Everyone else had BlackBerrys or iPhones, or something similar, but she had stuck to an old-school Nokia because the buttons were bigger and there was less frustratingly complex technology to deal with.

'You look dreadful, Rachel,' she said, tapping her foot on the carpet in the way she always did when she was extremely angry. Her face matched the shade of her hot pink shirt. 'That's it. I'm calling the company. I'm going to tell them what you've done. We need to sort this out somehow,' she continued, unconsciously pulling at her own hair now.

'Well, at least I look a bit more like you now, hey, Mum?' Rachel said, unblinkingly.

A shiver ran down Rita's spine as she pressed the 'call' button on her mobile. She could tell that something bad must have happened to make Rachel behave like this, but she didn't know what it was.

Rachel wondered whether or not she should stop the call. She knew full well she would be in a lot of trouble for this with the ballet company, but it was as if she was in a trance for the moment. Somehow, she had managed to convince herself it would be OK. Fooling herself, just like everyone else had fooled her all along. Maybe if her mother didn't make the call she could go to a top-end hairdresser on Monday morning and get them to change her back to blonde. If that was even possible . . . Swanhilda was usually brunette, anyway. Maybe they would even be pleased with her . . . No. Probably not.

She decided she had to stay strong on this one, her heart starting to race a little.

Rita's left eyebrow was twitching in fury as she stared at her daughter, sitting on the floor, resembling a ghoul but, somehow, still utterly beautiful.

Their eyes were locked as the phone rang and rang, but no one answered. Eventually, Rita hung up and slapped the handset against her palm in frustration. 'This is really *crappy* behaviour, Rachel. What's going on?' she asked after a few moments, softening a little in the last part of her sentence in an attempt to get some answers from her daughter. Her daughter who seemed to be going even further off the rails than she ever had done before.

Rachel rose to her feet without using her hands – an almost impossible manoeuvre for anyone who hadn't had the finesse of ballet trained into them for more than a decade – and casually flung herself down onto her bed with an audible sigh.

Rita had no idea what to do. She looked at the room around her. A glittering tutu, half wrapped in protective covering and ready to be taken to a major London theatre first thing in the morning, hung limply against the backdrop of teenage rebellion. Except Rachel wasn't a teenager . . . she was too old for this kind of moodiness. This was pushing it, even for her.

'I think this could jeopardise your role, Rachel; your whole career, even. I'm sorry to say it, but I think you have made a huge mistake. People talk in this industry,' she said quietly, a certain level of toughness in her tone. 'They have a wonderful understudy, who is desperate for the part. There are other girls who want this, possibly more than you . . .' she added, the last part trailing off quietly until it was barely audible.

Rachel said nothing for nearly a minute, before uttering, 'Well, maybe the understudy should have the lead. Maybe it's fate.'

There was little that could be said to that, so Rita left the room, shutting the door quietly behind her. And while she cried in her husband's arms in some far corner of the house, Rachel was painting her pillow charcoal-black with mascara-laden tears, her fists tightly clenched.

CHAPTER 11

FLUTTERING LASHES AND PROPPED-UP TITS.

Sunday 15 March 2009
Finsbury Park, north London
5 p.m.

Sara's 'stalking' hadn't come up with anything that incriminated her husband. In many ways, this should have been considered successful, but not to her. She *had* to get to the bottom of this mystery. The profile was still on the website and she was furious.

She was heartbroken.

'What are you doing tonight?' she asked Tom now, as she ran a small dab of wax through her hair so it would be neat and tidy for the evening shift at work. She could feel her heart beating hard in her chest. She felt as though she was about to explode.

The small light bulb above the bathroom mirror was flickering a little, and she cursed herself for forgetting to buy a replacement on her recent shopping trip, finding herself instead preoccupied by the romance films in the DVD section of the supermarket.

Tom was lying on the bed, looking at the ceiling. 'Oh, I'm just going for a few beers with the boys. We're probably going to World's End – the usual, I guess,' he said, his hairy legs propped up on a cushion he'd thrown to the far end of the king-sized bed. His legs were muscular; it was one of her favourite things about his body. But he had a thing about keeping his legs elevated when he was 'chilling out', and she suddenly found it an irritating and pretentious habit. Plus, the cushions were expensive and covered in intricate beads. It made her shudder – she heard the scratch of the embroidery under his feet as he shuffled around to make himself comfortable, and flinched inside. All of a sudden she saw all the flaws in him, and none of the things she had fallen in love with.

'I don't really want to go now, to be honest,' he said, running his hand through his hair.

'Why?' asked Sara, gritting her teeth. She dabbed a small amount of Benefit tint onto her cheeks so it gave her the youthful glow she'd lost naturally through years of hard work and stress.

'Ahh, I don't know. I'm tired, darling. But I do have to go . . . I haven't seen them for a while and it is Saturday night, after all. Liam's new girlfriend is coming later, too; apparently she's bringing some friends. I think the lads are looking forward to that,' he said with a smile, both hands now on his broad chest.

Sara realised she was reading something into everything he said and everything he did. Even the slightest twitch of an eyebrow – everything took on a new meaning now. She imagined him in the middle of a pool of attractive women, all fluttering lashes and propped-up tits.

'Are you OK, Sara?' Tom asked suddenly, sitting up a little in bed.

She glanced through the doorway and remembered how handsome he was, particularly in candlelight, and wondered if she could possibly just let go and be in love with him again, just as she had been before she had discovered his internet dating profile. The sweet sound of Norah Jones's voice was curling through the room. It was a total contrast to the reality of Sara's feelings.

She was furious. She couldn't hold it in much longer.

'Yes. Fine. I'm sure you will have a lovely time,' she said flatly, turning back to look at herself in the mirror, and noticing a huge crack down one side of the glass.

She decided now wouldn't be the time to mention the crack. She couldn't be bothered, and her mind was elsewhere. Plus, if she mentioned the mirror, it would probably lead to a soul-destroying Sunday traipsing around IKEA with a wobbly-wheeled trolley. That would push her over the edge.

'Yes, it'll be fine,' Tom conceded, sounding genuinely exhausted.

Sara stepped back into the bedroom and slipped her feet into a pair of neat, black ballet pumps.

'You look beautiful,' he said, tilting his head up

to see her properly. 'Can't you be late? You know, come to bed first?' he added cheekily, sitting up again, his faded red T-shirt crinkling up where his tummy bent at a ninety-degree angle. His face was crunched up in a familiar expression of wanting. He had picked up on how irritable she seemed, but he was hoping to distract her.

She looked at him. He was gorgeous. 'No. I have to go,' she responded.

She didn't want to lose him. This was why she hadn't confronted him about her find before now. She'd so often heard about women who knew their men were straying, but they couldn't face up to it. She could never understand it before, but now she felt some level of empathy.

Tom sighed a little in disappointment before wiggling back down on the bedspread, which was of Moroccan origin. The whole room was themed like that: greens, pinks and blues, with delicate embroidery and small panels of mosaic-style glass here and there.

Tom's phone, which was perched on top of a pile of books, vibrated loudly. Sara never looked at his phone, and he never looked at hers. There was a level of mutual respect and trust between them that made it completely unnecessary. But Sara couldn't help herself this time. She pushed a button on the bottom of the screen to bring it to life.

'What are you doing, Sara? Pass it over here, please,' Tom said, sounding a little nervous.

But there it was. An email from a dating site. 'Caroline has sent you a message,' it read.

Sara felt fire spread inside her. 'Yeah, sure . . . you might want to make sure you read that one,' she said, throwing the phone in his direction.

Tom caught it, and looked down at the screen. His eyebrows jumped up.

Sara stepped quietly out of the room and stood in the hallway. 'Have fun cheating on me tonight,' she said matter-of-factly, before running down the stairs and out of the door, which she slammed behind her hard.

Tom sat up sharply in bed and raised his hand to his hair. Miss Jones carried on purring through the stereo as he ran his hands down his face.

The air was starting to chill now, but pub gardens were still full of daytime drinkers armed with cardigans and jackets, preparing to battle on into the night, freezing-cold pints of cider and delicate glasses of wine in their hands. Loud, boozy laughter could be heard on almost every corner, and several of the cars that drove past her had their soft tops down, with music blaring from speakers that had been abused for so long they rattled.

Sara switched off her mobile phone. She was fuming. She was still shaking from confronting Tom, if she could call it that. The rage she was well known for was dancing around inside her. Tears kept coming to her eyes, and she tried to look at the sky in a bid to stop them flowing so obviously down her face. When that failed, she rooted around in her handbag until she found a tissue and pressed it to her eyes. People walking past her gave her the odd glance, but no one really cared.

Sara started to feel giddy.

Tom had already tried to call her, before she had switched off her phone. She didn't want to talk to him. She couldn't handle her rage and heartbreak.

After navigating a few corners and trying not to bump into people due to her teary vision, she stepped into The White Rope.

Simon was standing by the bar, shaking a card machine like it was one of those maze puzzles with the metal balls inside, or a Nintendo DS during a particularly fraught game.

Sara flicked into work mode automatically, smiling as she walked towards him. 'It's hold Up and then press B, hold Down and press A, and that, my friend, is how you conquer the big bad monster,' Sara whispered into his ear, making him jump.

'Jesus! You scared the shit out of me! Look, the machine won't take this,' he said, pulling a silver Visa debit card out of the slot and blowing on it uselessly like it was a hot beverage. A long line of thin white paper was spilling from the top of the machine, with the word 'Declined' on it. It had been the third attempt and this could no longer be put down to a bad signal. The card was in perfect condition, too. 'Hey, are you OK? You look like you've been—' Simon started, but he was cut off.

'Shall you tell them or shall I?' Sara asked, before waltzing off, not giving Simon the opportunity to take her up on the offer. Her shoes almost glided across the marble flooring, which had been cleaned to within an inch of its life. She loved the way that felt.

Simon sighed loudly as she sauntered away. Before long, he was leaning towards the customer, talking quietly yet earnestly to him.

Sara watched as the man, who was wining and dining a stupendously beautiful young woman with legs longer than the 15.13 from London Bridge to Brighton, went a shade of beetroot, and started shuffling around in his wallet for more cards. She felt embarrassed for him.

The shift went slowly. Tom kept calling the work phone, but she told the staff to tell him she was busy, getting the odd raised eyebrow as she did so. She needed to concentrate on her work. The breakdown of her marriage was not going to affect her career. Now was not the time to deal with all this. Throughout the evening, she found the word 'divorce' popping into her mind. She was trying to concentrate but it just kept thumping away like a headache. She thought of all the cheesy stories in women's magazines about the subject, and had never once imagined something like it would happen to her.

During a brief lull in orders later on in the evening, the restaurant's chef, Carlos, emerged from the kitchen, sweat pouring down his forehead. Diners glanced over, wondering what could have brought the chef out there among the candles and the silver service. There was a trail of blood down his apron from where he had been preparing the steak special.

'Carlos, what are you doing?' Sara cried, starting to push him backwards into the kitchen. To her, it was as if the secret to a coveted magic trick had been revealed and everything else ruined.

'But listen, Sara, it's your husband, he's out—'

'What?'

'Tom is out the back, Sara! He has come in through the kitchen door and wants to speak to you. He's been knocking for ages, but I ignored him because I am so busy,' he said, walking backwards as she pushed him around the corner, her hands flat against his wobbly chest. 'What's going on with you two, anyway? Why won't you speak to him on the phone? You're married, for Christ's sake. In Spain, Sara, in Spain we don't have this in marriage, it is all about the fam—'

'Shut up, Carlos, please,' Sara said, out of breath at struggling with him, starting to sweat now herself.

'Fine, fine, have it your way,' he said, slapping his hands together and storming back into the kitchen as if he had given up on her. A fine mist of flour was left in his wake.

Sara took a deep breath, clamped her lips together and followed him into the kitchen. *I am not going to forgive Tom for this*, she thought, unwilling to let him squirm his way back into her heart. She wasn't going to take his lies. She'd heard so much about cheaters, about how manipulative they could be. She'd seen the evidence; there was no way he could get out of it now.

She turned the corner into the kitchen, catching her leg on a trolley full of vegetables and swearing under her breath.

And there he was. Her husband, juggling three oranges, clearly trying to look casual. As soon as he saw her, however, he dropped one, and it rolled beneath one of the counters.

Sara knew immediately that she would forget it, and it would emerge some weeks later with its own set of legs and facial hair.

'Sara, listen, I appreciate this looks bad but I can explain,' Tom said, placing the other oranges gently on the brushed steel surface of a sink next to him.

'Looks bad? Are you having a laugh?' she asked, her eyes squinting and the heat rising within her chest. The kitchen was hot enough as it was, with five steaks softly sizzling under licking flames, and a million and one sauces bubbling away in giant pans.

Tom didn't seem to be taking this nearly as seriously as he should be, she realised.

'Sara, I don't date women on that site. I don't

even reply to them – it's . . . it's . . .' Tom said, starting to stutter. A look of bemusement swamped his face as he tried to explain himself. His eyebrows were raised, forcing his forehead to crinkle like ripples in vanilla ice cream, while his thick brown hair was stuck to his forehead where he, too, was starting to sweat.

'Oh, come on, Tom!' Sara cried, huffily crossing her arms and her feet at the same time. She steadied herself by gripping onto a nearby work surface. 'You're obviously having an affair, or sleeping around, or, or, *something*!'

Tom looked for a moment like the ground had been pulled from under his feet, tablecloth-magic-trick style. He grimaced to himself for a moment, as if he was trying to speak with a mouth packed full of cotton wool balls.

All Sara saw before her was a flustered, guilty man.

'I don't cheat, Sara . . .' Tom said, squinting now and leaning against the garlic rack.

'Tom, this is not really something you can explain, is it? Or something you can wiggle out of,' Sara spat, starting to pace towards him.

Tom glanced to his right-hand side where a bunch of knives hung from a magnetic strip, their sharp metallic surfaces glinting in the light.

'No, please wait, Sara, listen! This isn't the right place – I want to sit down with you and tell you the whole story. If you give me some time to talk, you will see it's not nearly as bad as it looks!'

But Sara was beyond listening. '*Dating*, Tom! Dating other women, in secret, behind my back. I've found you out!' Sara said, reaching him and planting an accusatory finger on his breastbone.

'It's not like that!' he yelled. Sara winced and put her finger on his lips, hoping the diners couldn't hear the spectacular row unfolding in the kitchen.

Carlos obviously felt the same. 'Shut up, you two, I'm trying to fucking work!' he shouted, before throwing an aubergine in their direction. It hit Tom's arm before landing on the floor with a gentle thud.

'Get out, Tom. Now. I'm not coming home,' Sara said, before pushing him resolutely out of the back door and into the cool night air, among the bins and the mice.

CHAPTER 12

'WOULD YOU LIKE CREAM WITH THAT?'

Wednesday 1 April 2009
Angel, north London
1 p.m.

Bryony didn't know why she had started going to the café so much.

Her rage at Max's death had been near impossible to deal with. She had cried for too long in her bed, flown off the handle in front of too many friends, and distanced herself from most of the people around her by letting an uncontrollable fury take hold of her.

Her rationale was that if she could go to a public place like the café on Chapel Market, she would be close enough to home to make a speedy getaway if she felt herself crumbling, but far enough away to keep the sound of that gunshot from her ears. It would mean that she couldn't sit there and weep until her lungs hurt. She couldn't fester away in her bed and go mouldy. And she couldn't pull out clumps of her hair in sheer, naked frustration, because it was a public place.

The café was a light and airy room, full of the sobering smell of freshly brewed coffee and soft doughy croissants. Plus, there was plenty of inane conversation to distract her. The things that people said to each other were often enough to even make her laugh occasionally, which she didn't think was possible in the midst of all her turmoil.

She sat in the window of the café wearing a huge pair of black sunglasses. Her latest weapon to hide her pain, they allowed her to watch the world go by and let a gentle tear or two fall unnoticed.

Bryony didn't care if people thought she was weird for spending too much time in there. She didn't care about how much money she was shelling out on over-priced drinks. And she especially didn't care about all the calories from the cakes and pastries she was eating, because they were about the only things she ate nowadays.

Cooking at home was pretty much out of bounds. There were too many memories tied up in the kitchen: the Sunday afternoon two months before when Max had spent hours baking a cake and then promptly dropped it on the floor as soon as he pulled it from the oven; or the time he accidentally put a fork in the microwave, causing flashes of light across the room that terrified her even from where she was curled up on the sofa, trying to lose herself in a good book. He wasn't a very practical creature, unless he was handling a video camera.

At the café, Bryony didn't have to worry about

any of those memories coming back and making her sad. She went there to while away the hours several times a week, just watching the cars chasing each other along the road, and the old ladies stooped over their shopping trolleys, maybe feeling just as alone as she was.

The short weeks after Max's death had been the bleakest of her entire existence.

She'd started off with an unbearable pain at him not being around, but that had melted into fury at the man who had done this to her boyfriend.

And hand in hand with the fury was unbearable fear. Bryony had decided that she never wanted to know who it was that had killed Max, and this had become a fixation. It was bad enough imagining the face, or the eyes of a person who could do something like that, but she didn't want the image confirmed. She didn't want to lie in bed at night for the rest of her life with the face of the vile creature who had ended Max's life tattooed on the inside of her eyelids. At least if she didn't know, she reasoned, it was open to question – just a blur of wonderings in her head that could never form any real conclusion.

Friends found it odd that she had made this decision, but she had vowed to stand her ground. In fact, she was so determined not to know the name of the man who'd been arrested for Max's death that she had avoided the papers and the news altogether. Bryony made it clear to her friends and family that she only wanted to know that the man in question had been sent to rot in prison, for how long, and the date the sentence would start. That was it.

When she saw papers piled up on newsstands she felt real fear that she might accidentally see something. A mug shot. A name. Anything. It was tough, averting her eyes from the pages of the local newspaper in shops, suddenly darting away if she ever heard anyone talk about it in the queue for the cash machine, or the ladies' loos at the café.

It had fast become a phobia, and Bryony wondered sometimes if it was normal to have reacted in this way. Usually, it seemed, loved ones huddled together in starkly furnished courtrooms, watching every twist and turn of a case and staring into the eyes of the killer until he was sent down to his own miserable destiny.

But she couldn't do it. She *wouldn't* do it. She needed to be blissfully ignorant.

A reporter had come to see her, just a week after Max died, and Bryony had been scared that she would tell her.

She was a young, shy little thing, who seemed far too inexperienced to deal with the subject matter when Bryony first looked at her. Her skinny frame was almost swallowed whole by an ill-fitting suit, and she had an innocent glaze to her eyes, as if the hardest thing she had had to deal with in life so far was her student overdraft.

When Bryony pressed the buzzer to let her up the stairs to the flat, she had wondered if she was doing the right thing by talking to a stranger about Max: sharing his memory with the whole community in a newspaper that would soon be used to carry the fish and chips of the city's staggering drunks; or newsprint blurring in the rain, tucked under some stranger's arm as they rushed for the tube.

When she opened the door, she had noticed the reporter was trembling a little – a reaction that so many people seemed to have when they met her since that night. The shaking of fingers, the welling of eyes; uncomfortable silences and empty apologies for something they had nothing to do with.

The journalist had short blonde hair, cut into a sharp bob that revealed a long and graceful neck. And, of course, there was the black suit. *Another fucking black suit*, Bryony had thought, looking her up and down with red eyes. She wanted colour and warmth; she was sick and tired of visitors in suits. A pizza delivery guy dressed as Big Bird would have been more welcome.

'Hello, Bryony. I'm so sorry for your loss,' the journalist had begun. *Yada yada yada*, Bryony cursed to herself. *Just like everyone else* . . . She had stared her in the eyes, suddenly jealous of this young girl who had a bright future ahead of her. A girl who would probably one day get married

146

to the one she loved, and not lose him, as Bryony had.

'I heard the dreadful news about your husband.'

'Boyfriend.'

'Oh, sorry. Your boyfriend.' The girl made a note, then continued. 'I'm Kate Walsh, a reporter from the local newspaper. We thought you might like us to print a tribute piece about Max and his life?' She was blinking a lot and looking as if she really wanted to run as fast as she could in the opposite direction. Her notebook trembled in her hands.

Bryony's pulse seemed to slow down at this point as she had visualised how the piece might look. An image of Max's beautiful face staring out from the page, a quote pulled out here and there and made bigger and bolder to break up the text.

'Er, OK, well, I might find it difficult to talk about . . . I might, well, I might cry,' Bryony warned, being horribly honest about the situation. Her emotions were pitched somewhere between raw agony and numbness, and swung between the two almost equally on a daily, if not hourly, basis. In fact, it was lucky this journalist had knocked when she had, because for the moment Bryony was in the right frame of mind to take a chance on it.

'Well, that's OK. I don't mind if you cry,' the hack said, straightening a little, giving Bryony the impression that maybe she would be able to deal with this, after all.

'OK . . . well, come in, Kate,' Bryony had replied, stepping to one side and letting the journalist step timidly into the hallway. There was a massive pile of unopened post to navigate, and having an outsider in the house reminded her how behind she was with the real world.

There was a huge bag of Kettle Chips on the coffee table and a selection of dips, but Bryony hadn't been able to touch any of them. Her mother had left them there in the hope she might be able to eat. It struck Bryony now that the dips had been sitting in the living room for several days, becoming more and more unappealing while she listened to punk bands on the second to highest volume and painted her toenails black. By now, they were making the living room stink, so she overtook her guest and led the way, darting over to the kitchen sink to open a window, and shovelling the rank sour cream and chive paste into a bin.

Kate sat down on the sofa, sniffing a little and making Bryony paranoid that the putrid smell of her own depression was even more offensive to a fresh, inexperienced nose than the smell of rancid dips had been.

Sliding her bag from her shoulder and onto the floor, Kate began, 'So I take it you've heard about the man who was charged—'

Bryony had whizzed round quickly and pushed her index finger up into the air, her mouth open in fear. 'Please don't say anything more,' she said

148

abruptly, shaking her head, a horrible feeling of dread filling her tummy. Did she need to get this tattooed on her forehead? she wondered.

Confusion had etched itself all over the young woman's face, and she fell silent.

Bryony had looked down at her feet, which were encased in a pair of Max's tartan slippers, and realised how silly and possibly rude she looked with her finger in the air. But she didn't care. 'I'm sorry . . . I just don't want to discuss that. I only want to talk about Max,' she said, shuffling over now and sitting on the chair opposite the journalist, whose frame had been reduced to mouse-like proportions by the sudden renewal of intensity in the situation.

'OK. That's fine. I understand,' she replied, brushing a strand of her hair behind a delicate ear.

Bryony wondered if those ears were really ready for what they were about to hear.

'So . . . let's start with Max's details,' Kate said, opening her notebook and pressing her black Bic into the page, scribbling before Bryony had even started talking.

'Max Tooley, as you know . . .' Bryony started.

Kate wrote the letters in capitals across the top of the small, lined page, and Bryony already wondered if she could carry on.

'He was twenty-eight years old. Cameraman for a variety of shows and channels. No children. No siblings. Born in Cork, but never really lived there

149

for long. And, erm . . . my boyfriend,' Bryony had said, starting to feel the familiar heavy ache of emotion in her throat.

Bryony looked away from the coffee shop window now as she remembered sitting there with the journalist. She cradled her mug of coffee in her hands and wondered if anyone would notice as a tear slid from behind her sunglasses and landed in her lap like a solitary raindrop.

'So, how did you meet Max?' Kate had continued, a small smile spreading across her face, as if she was preparing for the story. A positive smile. Like all was not lost. A look that seemed to tell Bryony that she was lucky to have the memories at all, rather than not have ever experienced them. The journalist leant forward, her gaze unavoidable. Her nerves seemed to have melted away, bringing Bryony's to the fore.

'Well . . . I was twenty-one. We were in a pub,' Bryony replied, smiling herself now and gazing at the coffee table. 'He was sitting opposite me, and he told me how bad smoking was for you, yet he was puffing away himself.' She could feel tears rise to the surface again as she chuckled a little. Speaking was difficult when there was a rock in your throat.

'OK . . .' Kate said, reassuringly.

'I pretty much knew then and there that he was a little bit special. I actually went home and discussed it with my housemate at the time, but she didn't like the sound of him,' Bryony said, starting to laugh more now, remembering a young Eliza, who had now grown up to be a sophisticated and successful name in the jewellery industry, just as she'd always dreamt.

'And how did you end up getting together?' Kate prompted, her lips turning up a little in encouragement.

'I saw him at the same pub again, just weeks later, and he spilled a pint of beer all over my dress; by accident, of course. I wasn't too bothered that he did it, actually, but he still spent the rest of the summer bringing me flowers at the shop where I worked . . .'

Images filled her mind: roses and tulips on the till, ready for her to take back to the flat, which had ended up looking like Kew Gardens within just a few days. It had been so beautiful. Bryony would have given her right arm to hear a gentle tap at the door at that very moment, and see Max standing there with a bunch of roses in his arms.

Kate had looked for a moment like all the girls in the shop had done at the time. Like she was going to melt. 'And I assume he was living here with you?' she asked, scribbling away again, her shorthand resembling some kind of alien code.

'Yes, he was,' Bryony said, suddenly unable to say anything more.

'And what was he like as a person?' Kate had

asked, looking up at Bryony once more, but with a raised eyebrow this time. It had held a delicate, silver piercing.

Bryony's stomach felt like it was turning to jelly, so she had taken a few deep breaths. How would she put Max into words? When she thought about his face it was a blur, and sometimes she had to remind herself of it with old photos because, somewhere in the trauma, her mind had smudged her memory of his image a little.

Bryony simply opened her mouth to see what might come out. 'Well, if you can possibly imagine the nicest, warmest, most gorgeous human being on earth, and multiply that over and over again, that was Max. He was intelligent, very funny and incredibly clumsy, and he made me happier than I've ever known,' she had said, feeling more tears slide down her cheeks.

Kate reached down into her bag and pulled out a pink tissue, before placing it in her open hand.

Bryony had pushed it against her face, feeling the paper weaken under the tips of her fingers where it was soaking up her agony.

She was then asked more and more questions: what school he went to, which training course he took when he left school, where his parents lived, and what his hobbies were.

'And do you have any message at all? Anything to say that could maybe reach out to young people, or those who have lost someone in such tragic circumstances?' Kate finally asked, pushing the end of her biro into her top lip.

That had been difficult.

Bryony had known that she couldn't say in a newspaper that she wanted to tear Max's killer apart with her bare hands; that he had not only killed Max, but a huge part of her too, and Max's mother and father, and all his friends. How they were all a little bit less alive than they had been before. How life is so precious that each day should be treated like it is a present. And that really, money and clothes and careers, and all that bullshit, spirals into total insignificance when you lose someone you love.

And how she was scared because there was a hole in her life and she wasn't sure if it was ever going to be filled. Nor the intensely painful, bullet-sized hole in her heart.

'I would just say that more than one person died that day . . . that I'm not sure how I will be able to carry on without Max, but I will have to, somehow. And that, actually . . . how sorry I am for the person who did it, because I will never be able to forgive him.'

Kate's eyes had been wide as she finished writing, and Bryony had realised how dark that sounded. But it had hit her then why she didn't want to know who Max's killer was; at that very moment, remarkably early on in the grieving process. Why she was so terrified of his identity.

Because she was scared of knowing someone whom she knew she would never forgive.

'Are you sure that's what you want to say?' Kate asked, biting her lip a little.

'Yes. Please, quote me word for word,' Bryony had replied, feeling a strange satisfaction course through her veins, hoping that the vile monster, Max's killer, would read her words and turn a dark shade of grey inside.

'Do you have any photos? Maybe a nice picture of you and Max we could print?' Kate said then, changing the subject.

'Yes, of course,' Bryony replied, leaning forward and pulling a big, black photo album from the shelf under the coffee table. She'd been staring at these photos for days now, in mute disbelief. Wondering how someone could be there one day, and not the next.

She chose a photo of Max on his own, taken at a Christmas party. He was wearing a suit with a skinny black tie.

'That's lovely,' Kate had said, leaning over the picture.

'He was . . . he was incredibly handsome,' Bryony replied with a beaming smile and, for a moment, she found some warmth and happiness in the bleakness that had enveloped her in the time since his death.

'He certainly was,' the journalist said, smiling with Bryony.

She had pushed a business card across the sofa with an email address so Bryony could send her the image, and that had been that. After a few minutes of consolatory conversation, more pitiful looks, and an awkward handshake, she had left, and Bryony had been alone in the flat once again.

'Hey, what can I get you?' came a male voice, wrenching Bryony away from her daydream like a child reluctant to leave a party.

Bryony flinched a little as she realised she was staring into the bottom of an empty cup as if it had the meaning of life written there. She straightened her back and tried to compose herself. She could feel the heat of the sun, magnified through the glass of the window.

The guy was handsome. *Strikingly so*, Bryony thought. He had a kind of sexy cheekiness to him that she'd seen in Max. He frightened her because of this. She almost couldn't look directly into his huge green eyes.

He was tall, with a good, strong frame beneath his clothes. He had a small nose piercing, a tiny silver stud. She normally hated them, but it really suited him. He had short dark hair, which was slightly thicker on top. It looked sharp and bushy, like it had recently been cut. He had a nice, open face, liberally covered in stubble. He looked like he belonged in a band.

'Er, hi, thanks. Yes, you can get me . . .' she said, pausing, so it sounded like she needed to think about it – she felt stifled and frightened by his good looks. 'Can I have a decaf latte with one sugar, please?' she asked, politely.

He scribbled away at his notepad, his cheeks flushed. Why couldn't he remember her order? Bryony wondered. It was always the same.

Silly man.

'Cream?' he asked, smiling at her now, with a cheeky grin.

'No, thanks,' she said.

'OK, that'll be right with you,' he said, turning around quickly. His pants were hanging out of the back of his trousers.

Bryony turned to stare out of the window again.

CHAPTER 13

HE WONDERED WHO HE COULD RING.

Saturday 4 April 2009
Islington, north London
6 p.m.

'Fuck, fuck, fuck!' Tom said out loud, a trickle of soapy water running down his forehead. A pink rubber duck slid from the edge of the bath and landed in the water with a splash.

Sara had kicked him out of his home just days ago. In true film and music video fashion, she had thrown him out in a storm of rage and venom, his clothes thrown from the top window of their house, pants everywhere like some embarrassing Tracey Emin work. He was now roughing it. Sofa surfing. He was technically homeless, he realised, visualising himself turning up at a soup kitchen in three months' time, with an advanced beard, smelling of fish and bin juice.

He was lying in the bath at his best friend Mark's house, wondering how on earth this had got so out of control. He'd tried to call Sara's friends to explain himself, but they either didn't pick up or they blocked the call. No one seemed to want to get involved.

Getting hold of Sara was impossible.

The situation looked so bad it made him panic even more. She was right; this would be difficult to 'wiggle' out of. Nor could he blame her – he wasn't sure if he would believe her had the situation been reversed.

He missed Sara deeply.

Sitting in the bath, he even missed the awkward sex he used to have with his wife in the tub, all squeaking arms and legs and violent slips. He missed lying in bed with her and feeling her breath against his nose. He missed her singing in the shower. He missed it all.

'You all right, mate?' came Mark's voice through the bathroom door. 'You've been in there for, like, an hour and a half or something. And I need a wizz, if I'm quite honest.'

Tom sat up with a start, the water lapping around him violently. He noticed it was nearly cold.

Mark was a single man with a good sense of humour, and his flat had seemed like the perfect place to go. It was a haven for the scorned man, with a 42-inch television and enough computer games to stock an Amazon warehouse. A four-bedroom bolt-hole in Exmouth Market, it was decked out with the finest furniture. The corners of the flat, those that weren't draped in women's clothes and make-up, were minimalist and smooth.

There was that one problem, however: Mark shared the flat with three women, and the last thing he needed right then was the probing and sad looks from a group of attractive young ladies who probably secretly thought he was a scumbag, too.

The only thing that was remotely out of character in Mark's home was a baby blue plastic container in the corner of his bedroom, from which there came the odd rustle. Ryan was Mark's hamster. A tiny, brown lump of fur, it had been named by one of Mark's ex girlfriends after Ryan Phillippe, the sulky one in *Cruel Intentions*. Tom wasn't sure what the actor and the hamster had in common apart from a strong desire to hump everything that moved. The damn thing had been keeping Tom awake at night, spinning in its wheel as he lay on a camp bed on Mark's floor, desperately trying to tune out the regular snoring coming from his friend.

Mark had been left with the fractious, overweight pet when his ex had moved to America to enjoy the high life.

Tom had been wondering if he could take the wheel out when Mark fell asleep, or even put the cage out into the garden 'for some fresh air', when Mark knocked on the door.

'Yeah, yeah, sorry, I'm fine. I'll be down in a minute,' Tom said, stepping out of the bath and leaving a trail of lukewarm water all over the floorboards.

He eventually emerged, clean and dressed, plodding into the kitchen, where Mark had a cold beer waiting for him.

'I've got to warn you, by the way – the girls are having a night in tonight. They're inviting others, too,' Mark said, looking excited at the prospect.

'Are you kidding?' Tom replied, taking a long pull on his beer.

'Nope.' Mark paused, looking hard at Tom. He had heard his outburst in the bathroom earlier, and had decided he needed to give Tom a few home truths. 'Look, do you want to sort this out or not? If so, you're going to have to do a bit more than moping around here . . . yes, you're my best mate and of course I've got your back, but you do realise you're going to be asking a lot of Sara for her to just go back to you now, don't you?' he said.

Tom sighed. He'd been expecting this. 'Yes, of course, I understand. And I'm feeling gutted about it. But it's like she's blocked me out so I can't even explain myself. This just isn't Sara. We've always talked through everything,' he said, mournfully.

Mark shrugged. He had done his bit, he reckoned. 'Right, well, you can make yourself useful, then.' He warmed to his theme. 'We're in this for the long haul. The girls will be here shortly and it's going to be a long, tough night. You may need earplugs, mate. Go and get us a takeaway, and get some fresh air . . .' he finished, sliding a £20 note from his pocket and over the kitchen countertop to Tom.

'Yeah, all right then,' Tom said, taking the money and folding it into the pocket of his jeans. He grabbed his phone, threw on a waterproof jacket and headed out of the door, quietly thankful for an escape.

The warmth of the early spring day had melted into tropics-like rain, and it was chucking it down. Great sheets of water were being wrung from the clouds over Tom's head. Alone now, he could feel the recently-all-too-familiar panic rising in his chest as he walked, his trainers making a slapping sound against the wet concrete of the pavement. An old lady shuffled past him slowly, wearing a large mac and a pink rain hood; her dog, a small, brown terrier, was looking decidedly miserable. Tom felt that he could relate to the dog, with its look of sheer melancholy painted across its damp, furry chops.

As he walked down the two long streets that lead to the Chinese takeaway, he wondered what Sara was doing that evening. Was she alone in bed, feeling sad and angry still? Was she at work, commanding the floor in the restaurant she loved so much?

Tom ducked into the takeaway shop and was more pleased than he had expected to be on being greeted with the familiar smell of Chinese food. It made his mouth water and he felt secretly glad that they had resorted to takeaway – yet again

– rather than attempting to cook something properly. He couldn't focus on cooking at the moment; he couldn't focus on anything, not even his artwork that he loved so much. Comfort food was what he needed.

He placed an order and took a seat, wondering whether or not he should try and call Sara again. An overweight man in his mid-thirties was sitting in the shop too, with a teenage boy Tom assumed was his son. They were wearing Manchester United shirts and looked like clones of each other: the boy had the same piercing blue eyes as his father, and they both had thick brown hair, which had been gelled back.

'When are you seeing Mum again next?' the boy asked, wiping his nose with the back of his hand and looking down at his feet.

The man shifted uncomfortably in his seat and dark clouds seemed to consume his features. A small TV in a corner of the room was showing a fuzzy soap but a connection kept going, resulting in the screen flickering every few seconds. *It's infuriating*, Tom thought. He felt helpless, utterly helpless.

'I don't know, mate. When I drop you off on Monday after school?' the man said, shrugging his shoulders and focusing on a huge fish tank installed behind the till.

'No, I don't mean like that, Dad. I mean properly seeing her. She's sorry, you know; she really misses you,' the boy added, starting to tear up a page of the *Sun* newspaper, which was sitting on the small coffee table in front of him along with a few women's magazines full of articles about 'Your summer wardrobe' and 'What he wants in bed'.

The father's face softened a little, but he still hadn't looked his boy in the eye. Tom was looking on, furtively, struck by the conversation playing out before him.

'Ah, well, she should have thought about that before, shouldn't she?' the man replied, before clearing his throat.

The boy looked crestfallen, and kicked the table gently with his foot before looking at Tom. Tom turned his head away, embarrassed that he had been caught staring at them and listening to their conversation.

Seeing the three of them there, Tom reflected, there was nothing that they appeared to have in common apart from the fact that they were all lads, in the same, strong-smelling takeaway shop. But there was something in their dialogue that had struck cold fear into Tom. And it was a look, a look on the father's features. The look of someone who cannot forgive.

Tom pulled his phone from his pocket and hovered his finger over the speed dial key Sara's number was assigned to. He loved her so much that her name almost burned his eyes. He couldn't lose her. It would be the end of him.

He'd been on the dating website to read the

messages for titillation really . . . some of the ads had genuinely made him laugh. The site was free to use, so it wasn't costing him any money. He'd never replied. He'd never acted on any of it. Was that something that warranted the end of an incredible marriage?

It was humiliating, too. He knew that many of his friends would probably jump to the same conclusions as Sara. He couldn't believe how stupid he'd been.

Tom stared at her name on the screen for a minute or two, wondering what he was even going to say to her. He pressed the 'call' button and held the phone to his ear, dread filling his stomach in anticipation of what might be said.

But it turned out he wouldn't get any kind of reaction at all. The number was dead. Sara had disconnected her phone, moving on from him yet further by taking on another phone number.

Tom came back to absolute chaos. In his state of panic and turmoil, he had forgotten he would have to negotiate a house full of noise and giggling.

It was a bad sign when he walked in at the front door and heard laughter. Not just one laugh, but an assortment of laughs. Female ones. High-pitched shrieks, combined with low, dirty giggles and wicked, loud cackles. It was the sound of a gaggle of women winding each other up into absolute hysteria.

Tom was terrified.

Standing at the front door, he was frozen to the spot as he realised fully what Mark had meant when he said they were in for a rough night. And, now that he thought about it, all the signs had been there in the kitchen that morning. Six bottles of white wine, twenty-four posh and intricately decorated cupcakes, six super-sized packets of Doritos and some dips. A whole range of DVDs from Play.com had plopped onto the doormat during the course of the week, too. Tom reckoned they would all feature revoltingly handsome men with daft speech impediments, floppy hair and/or massive packages: Hugh-floppy-fringe-Grant, Jake Gyllenwhateverhisnamewas, and Colin fucking Firth.

'Bollocks,' Tom whispered under his breath, suddenly missing home more than ever. He'd hoped that if he could stay away from their home for a while, give Sara space, and concentrate on his art, the whole silly episode would be over in a matter of days.

Tom stayed where he was for a while, half his body in the doorway, the other half still protruding into the street, unwilling to commit to the house but too scared to spend the evening alone in the local drinking cheap beer. Even though Mark had been moaning about the stampede of women, Tom knew deep down that he wouldn't be able to persuade him to escape.

A moment or two later, Tom darted through the corridor and locked himself in the loo, pulling his phone out of his pocket. As the smell of Chinese takeaway swamped the bathroom, he sat on the edge of the toilet, trying to come up with a get-out plan. He wondered who he could ring.

As he scrolled down the names on his contact list, he was interrupted by a loud cry of, 'Ohh, but you should have seen the size of it!' It was Dina, one of Mark's housemates, who, he assumed, was running down the stairs in a dressing gown, her face covered in pale green moisturising gunk as she finished some tale that he very much doubted was about the latest offering from Honda or a pizza she had ordered the night before.

Tom realised he would get busted, so popped his head out of the door to see if he could find Mark.

'Oh, Tom, hi. You all right?' she asked, standing, frozen, a pair of huge, blinking eyes peering out from – oh yes – gallons of alien-green slime on her face.

'Yes, er, sorry. Don't mind me, I'll just be in the kitchen,' Tom said, unable to meet her gaze. He had decided a long time ago that women in face masks were actually quite scary.

'Mark's in the shower, love – he won't be long.'

Tom grabbed for the takeaway bags at his feet and shuffled into the kitchen. Plonking himself by the breakfast bar, he wondered what to do next.

Dina quickly poured herself another plastic flute of 'champagne', picked up the bottle and darted back up the stairs again, a pair of seemingly endless legs trailing from beneath her dressing gown.

The laughter commenced once more and, as The Smiths starting pumping from the speakers upstairs, Tom picked up his phone again, went through to his contacts list and started at A.

Andrew.

Yes, Andrew from the old football team might be around, he thought. *Good old, dependable Andrew.*

Tom called him. It went straight to voicemail.

B.

Bernie.

Bernie from uni – he would probably be about. He always seemed to be at a loose end.

Tom called him.

'Hello?'

'Mate, you need to rescue me.'

'Why?'

'Women, women everywhere.'

'You lucky bastard!'

'No, seriously. I'm not fucking kidding.'

'Dude, you sound traumatised.'

'I am. Just tell me, are you free tonight?'

'No, sorry, pal, I'm with Shell tonight; we're having an Indian takeaway and watching the *24* box set.'

'You lucky, lucky bastard,' Tom said, before hanging up in frustration.

As he kept making his way down the list, it slowly dawned on him that most of his male friends were from the era of him and Sara.

Scrolling on, he got to F.

Frederick. Frederick from the first ever gallery where Tom had exhibited his work. A fellow artist, definitely the most bizarre of all his friends, with a penchant for emulating the style of Andy Warhol, smoking cigars and drinking whisky during daylight hours. Basically, he was an alcoholic, but covered it up with all his 'Pain is art' and 'I'm such a sexy tortured soul' stuff . . .

Tom called him.

'Hello, bud. Can't talk now, painting . . . sorry.'

'Are you pissed?'

'Yes.'

'Oh, sod it,' Tom said, before pressing the red 'end call' button irritably.

He stared up at the ceiling in frustration and quietly cursed Mark for taking a shower.

'Go on, then, Claire, your turn – best sex you've ever had,' Tom heard from upstairs, despite the fact he was trying his best to block out the snippets of conversation he could hear.

S.

Simon Taylor, another uni friend. He was single. Tom knew he would be around. He called him.

'What's up?'

'Si, hello. I have to be quick. What are you doing tonight?'

'Date, mate.'

'What, a *date* date?'

'Yes. With an actual, real woman. A fit one, too.'

'Shit. Good luck,' Tom said, before ending the call.

Fuck. *OK*, he thought, *I'm getting down to the reserves now.*

W.

Will Poole.

He was in a serious relationship, or he certainly had been the last time Tom had spoken to him, which was ages ago. Maybe his girlfriend was busy covering herself in gunk and talking about penises as well, and he needed rescuing, too?

As soon as Will answered his phone, Tom's ears were assaulted by high-pitched laughter. Maybe his prediction had been right.

'Er, hello?'

'Hi, Will. Listen, mate, I know it's been a while . . .'

Laughter turned into crying. That of a small child.

Hold on a minute . . .

'Ah, Tom. Look, I'm kind of busy with the little one right now.'

'Little one?'

'Yeah . . . Emma and I had a baby, mate. She's two tomorrow, actually,' Will said, sounding a little pissed off.

Will and Emma had a baby. She was two years old . . . Tom imagined himself standing there, holding his daughter and being, well, complete.

'Fucking hell, Will. Congratulations. So sorry we haven't spoken for so long, we must catch up soon. I'm gonna go, OK?' Tom said, reaching for the 'end call' button, but he was interrupted.

'Listen, don't be a stranger, yeah?' Will said.

Tom hadn't bothered to speak to him for so long now, it just seemed weird.

There was one more option. Chris Black. Sara's friend Lea's husband. They hadn't really spoken for a couple of months, but he'd sent Tom a couple of texts quite recently saying he was keen for a beer.

'Oh, hi, Tom, you all right?'

'No. Not really, pal. Are you free tonight?'

'Ah, sorry. Not really, I'm taking Lea to the airport,' Chris said, sounding apologetic.

'Oh, right. No worries, it was only on the off-chance, really. Sorry to have bothered you, and my love to Lea, yeah?' Tom said.

'Hold on a minute, Tom . . . Sorry, darling, just on the phone to . . . er . . . Tom, actually . . .'

There was a pause and Tom heard a crackling sound he could only assume was Will putting his hand over the microphone so he couldn't hear the next bit. But he did. Unfortunately.

'That bastard? Tell him to fuck off,' Tom heard Lea say, in the background.

'Look, sorry, gotta go,' his friend said, before hanging up abruptly.

Tom turned to look out of the kitchen window as the girls upstairs started to sing, badly, to Leona Lewis, and felt the lowest he had ever been. Frightened that what had happened had ruined his relationship. Frightened that his friends had, well, grown up. They were all getting on with their

170

lives by the sound of it. While his had mysteriously collapsed. This was rock bottom.

It got worse, though. The next thing Tom knew, the ladies were stampeding down the stairs, sounding like a herd of wildebeest, clutching on to glasses of cheap booze and bottles of nail varnish. Shit. *Shit.* There was no escape now.

'Owww, hello, trouble,' came the cockney purr of Lucy, by far the 'worst' of Mark's housemates. She sauntered across the small, carpeted space from the stairs to the breakfast bar and planted a huge, pink, lipsticky kiss on Tom's cheek. He could feel the layer of gloss on his face remaining there as she pulled away, and wondered if it would be rude to start frantically wiping it off then, or whether he should wait a few moments and desperately squirt himself with washing-up liquid at the sink while her back was turned.

The other girls stood looking at Tom shyly, managing to pause for a moment from their aggressive sex questioning and comments about celebrity thighs and Spanx. Eventually, however, one of them spotted that week's *Heat* magazine on the table, and the women were soon deeply back in their former conversation.

Mark had followed the girls downstairs. He was in his pyjamas, a pair of large, checked things that he knew women loved. He fell on the Chinese takeaway bags with delight and started dishing up, only looking up at the sound of a large sigh from Tom.

Mark narrowed his eyes. 'Listen, Tom, just chill out for a moment, will you? You've been silly, mate, if you don't mind me saying, but I'm trying to help,' he said, sounding decidedly unimpressed with his friend. He'd been initially excited at the idea of having another man around the house, but Tom was not the Tom he had known. He was, he realised, turning into a bit of a drag to be around.

'Oh, great, thanks for your support . . .' Tom muttered sarcastically.

'I still can't really understand why you would need to read those messages,' Mark said. 'Sara is a pretty cool woman. If there are problems in your relationship you can tell—'

'Listen! Mark! Do you think you could be a good mate and just try and take my mind off this?' Tom suddenly yelled, prompting an immediate silence from the women, who all turned around and stared at them, their mouths open.

Mark was shocked into a statue-like state by Tom's outburst, sweet-and-sour sauce dripping slowly and apologetically from a spoon dangling from his right hand. Ever the professional around women, he quickly snapped out of it, however, saying, 'Carry on, ladies,' as he smiled easily at them.

A low murmur of female conversation began again.

Mark pushed a plate of food towards his friend. Tom was now slumped over the breakfast bar after his eruption of rage.

'I can't eat, mate,' Tom said, feeling sick and rising to his feet.

'Oh, come on, pal, stay. I'm sorry, I just think it's . . . I just think . . .'

'Yeah, you do. And so does Sara. I'll be back later,' Tom said moodily, hurriedly putting his jacket back on. He darted out of the front door, mobile in hand. As he strode down the street, he thought about Sara again, and what she might be doing that evening.

And then it struck Tom – the perfect place he could go in his turbulent emotional state. He needed to escape. He jumped on the tube, took the Northern Line to Moorgate, the Circle Line to Liverpool Street, and then boarded a bus.

It was dark, rain still tipping from the sky as he got off the big dilapidated vehicle, which was spitting out clouds of dark, dusty crap into the city air. Tom walked quickly to his studio in Shoreditch. It was positioned above a sandwich shop and a newsagent, the entrance down a small, narrow alleyway. It gave him the creeps a little to be walking down it in the dark, as London's drinkers and delinquents started to spill out into the street, making their way from bar to bar.

Tom quickly shoved the key into the thick, metal door and heard the familiar crunching sound as it turned. It needed a slight wiggle to the left, one to the right, and full body shove to make it open. 'A door with quirks,' was how the elderly landlord had described it when he let Tom in on the first day, his breath smelling like sour milk. Sour milk had been something of a theme inside, too. The place had stunk.

It wasn't the most glamorous of studios, because Tom had somewhat downsized his budget, and it had taken a good few days of deep cleaning – he had even found a pair of size 18 industrial white knickers from Primark in there – before he was ready to use it. But he had made it his own somehow, using funky lamps and furniture from independent, second-hand shops, and brightly coloured prints from his favourite artists. It was an escape for him, though the inspiration hadn't been flowing recently – even if the beer certainly had. A small pile of cans by the door greeted him, making him feel a little guilty.

Tom shut the door behind him and threw off his jacket, switched on some lamps and sat down to work.

It was then that the flash of inspiration hit him.

He had discussed ideas and themes for his next exhibition with his agent, and other artist friends, and was looking at 'the human condition' in whatever form it would take shape in within this concept. It was a huge topic that could encompass a whole range of work; feelings from love, to guilt, to anger. The freedom had left him a little nervous, if he was honest.

He had sketched out various ideas for feelings, trying to encompass the emotions that were felt by everyone who lived and breathed on earth, whether they were Joe Bloggs in an office in London, or a tribesman in the Australian Outback. But he had struggled, lost his way: the task seemingly too big, nothing had felt right to him.

But there it was, right in front of him now. The thing he wanted the most.

Forgiveness.

Forgiveness for something he had only half done. He knew he would never cheat on his wife; the prospect was impossible. But he had to accept that his curiosity had got him into this mess. No one seemed to believe that he wasn't cavorting with other women behind her back, not even his best friend.

Sara wasn't taking his calls, so he had to catch her attention somehow.

He pressed 'play' on his old, paint-spattered CD player, and for at least four rotations of the *Colour It In* album by The Maccabees, he sketched, wrote and planned. He sharpened pencils and brushed wood shavings from the desktop onto the floor. He sipped cold beer and felt proud when he managed to throw the empty cans straight into the bin on the other side of the room. He wrote hurried notes on Post-its and stuck them on a draft proposal sheet, downed the occasional shot of coffee, and ran his hands through his hair, staring at the things he had created.

It was all there, all the images and feelings and ideas. Tom felt alive, as if he was about to burst with excitement over what he could create.

Just before 3 a.m., he switched on his laptop and composed an email to his agent. It simply read, 'I've got it. The theme for the next exhibition . . . but it needs to be done quickly. I need this up and running ASAP. Will have some plans over to you within the next forty-eight hours. There isn't much time to put all this together, I know, but I'm pretty sure I can give it my best shot.'

Tom decided, too, that it was time to delete the online dating profile. It was long overdue, in fact. He logged into an old email account he hardly ever used and, from it, deactivated the account. Within seconds an email appeared in his inbox: 'Confirmation of account deactivation: Congratulations, your account has been successfully deleted.'

He stared at the email in the half-light and prayed that Sara would one day understand.

CHAPTER 14

'PLEASE BE SEATED.'

Friday 17 April 2009
Blackfriars Crown Court, London
11 a.m.

Silence descended on the courtroom.

A young black man in handcuffs was led up into the dock by two security guards, who were about as stereotypical as it got: shaved heads, the edges of tattoos poking out from beneath blue starched shirts.

The defendant was *her son*. Her baby boy. Tynice had sat through the trial, listening to him try to explain that it was all a mistake, that he hadn't meant to do it. And while his crime repulsed her to the core, he was still her son.

His head was bent, and she wanted to slap him and hold him in equal measure. He had the look of a young man who knew what was coming. And what was coming was not good for him at all.

Her boy in prison. Only God knew how she was going to explain this all to Reb. And the family. And the church. *His granddad would have turned in his grave*, she thought, running her hands over the cold wood of the bench on which she sat.

Keon didn't resemble the usual half-wit thugs who would come up with some crazy web of lies to get out of their drink-drive charges. Tynice had done jury service before – she knew how this went, and all the bullshit that would come from their mouths: how they had fallen into the car after having one too many and accidently started the engine with their elbow. Or the men with red, coarse noses from too many years of hardcore drinking, who said that the guy in the pub simply walked into their fist during a game of darts . . . Bullshit, bullshit, bullshit . . .

Everyone in the room stood up as the judge came in, his wig looking as if it was glued to his head at all times. He had a thin, sharp face, with features like razor blades. He cleared his throat and, suddenly, her stomach plunged as if she was on a rollercoaster, the blood rushing in her ears. This was judgment day.

Distracted, Tynice noticed that the woman with the straw-like hair, blonde, all scratchy and springing away from her face, was staring at her again. Looking and waiting for a reaction. She was the one that had found Max Tooley's body as he lay on the pavement bleeding, and she looked old beyond her years. Tynice wondered suddenly if finding his body had added to this; how she had been a stranger holding the hand of another stranger while his life ebbed away from him, and how it was the kind of experience in life that would haunt your dreams until your own death.

The court usher nervously eyed the journalists, searching for contraband: cameras they shouldn't have in the courtroom, phones set to record, any sign of contempt. Tynice wanted to push them out, to stop them covering the trial, reporting on it. To bring some kind of damage-limitation to protect her family.

'Please be seated,' the judge said, and the room almost collectively sighed with the sound of creaking seats and papers landing on tabletops and laps. The reporters sat with furrowed brows and pens in their hands, waiting to scribble at the speed of lighting before taking their notes back to the office and cursing themselves for not concentrating more during the arduous hours of shorthand training.

The case had been going on for all of three days. Keon Hendry had pleaded guilty from the word go, but there was still evidence to be heard, formalities to go through.

Emotion swept over Tynice, just has she had expected. She pressed her face into a hanky, trying not to sob loudly. She looked up and met the eyes of her son.

She had never seen so much fear.

They had all heard the statements, Keon's defence solicitor explaining that it was all a horrible mistake. Tynice had heard all the reasons, all the excuses, how every part of him was sure he wouldn't pull the trigger. How the whole thing was a fright tactic.

How he heard the sound of a gunshot and couldn't believe he had done it, and what unfolded next . . . Tynice hadn't been there. She didn't understand. She thought she would never understand. She was still so angry at Keon. Furious.

She wondered if it was her fault for buying him computer games with gun simulators, and that maybe she had inadvertently trained him into the natural way a finger should move when there was a cold, hard trigger beneath it.

But then, she had never expected him to go out and actually get a gun.

'Keon Hendry. Can you look at me, please,' said Mr Justice Layner, his thin cheeks shiny in the bright light of the room. He had cold, glassy eyes that looked as if they took no prisoners.

Tynice suddenly wanted to show him pictures of her little boy when he was growing up, tell him all the challenges he went through, all the hurdles he faced. Humanise him somehow. But at the same time she felt guilty for feeling like that, for wanting people to see the good in Keon, like she used to. She was a religious woman, and believed in rightful justice. But she still held a candle of hope somewhere.

'Keon. I repeat, will you please look at me?' the judge said again, glaring at him.

Although it was more of an order than a question, it was loaded with the usual tired cynicism of a high court judge seeing another young boy in front of him, about to throw his life down the toilet.

Keon raised his head, his frightened and defeated eyes darting nervously across the courtroom. But there was something in his body language, his frame, which showed he was big enough to take this like a man. That his crippling sentence would not be met with rolled eyes and huffs and puffs. For this, Tynice felt just a second of pride. That maybe she had done something right, bringing him up to be a man who took responsibility for his actions. She instantly felt bad about feeling this, of course. How could she ever feel proud of her son who had taken another's life? It went against everything she believed in. Whether or not he was facing up to his sins, he didn't deserve the 'pride' of his mother, she thought.

'Keon Hendry. The court has heard over the past few days the full details of your case. In deciding your sentence today, we have taken into account your defence and the fact that you have pleaded guilty from the start, but sadly we cannot get away from the fact that the life of an innocent man has been cruelly taken from him, his friends, family, and all who loved and knew him.'

Tynice felt sick.

The sound of pens against paper seemed loud in the quietness of the room, which was filled with no more than twenty people. She had no idea who the others were. Maybe friends of Max Tooley, family members? There was little support for Keon: just her.

'So, Mr Hendry, today we are sentencing you to

fifteen years in prison. Do you have anything to say?' the judge asked.

The silence was interrupted by the sound of Tynice crying into her tissue, her body shaking violently. And then suddenly she was on her feet, shouting. 'Keon! You stupid, stupid boy,' she yelled, smacking the back of the bench in front of her with her fist. She realised how hysterical and strange she was being, but she couldn't hold back. It was like she was outside her body, watching this madwoman losing control of everything she ever knew and understood.

Keon had inspired this rage in her because he'd wasted everything she'd invested in him. All the love she put into his upbringing, it was all for nothing.

A few members of the jury looked down at their laps awkwardly as Tynice felt someone gently pull her down to her seat.

Keon barely reacted physically, but did open his mouth to speak, which was a surprise to everyone in the room. His voice was trembling as he spoke, the deep voice of a boy who had recently become a man, but for all the wrong reasons. 'I'm sorry to Max and his family, and also to my mother. I hope you can all find a way to forgive me one day.'

CHAPTER 15

HIS MATES COULDN'T HELP BUT WATCH AND GRIN.

Sunday 19 April 2009
Finsbury Park, north London
2 a.m.

'So, give me coffee and TV . . . History,' came the loud wail of a young man's singing from the speaker system, which squealed sharply with feedback every now and then.

His black Vans trainers thumped the wooden flooring. He was super cool. Max's eyes were 'drunky' – that was what Bryony liked to call them. His fringe flapped backwards and forwards and, as he spat out the lyrics, a sly smile spread across his features. He was utterly gorgeous. Even the barmaid stood captivated for a few moments, smiling coyly behind the beer pumps. Bryony looked up at her half-pissed boyfriend on the small stage and, rather than cringing, thought about dragging him home as soon as possible for some cocktail-fuelled passion.

It was his twenty-fifth birthday and a handful of his best friends were gathered around him in a karaoke bar in the depths of Soho, clapping their hands as he screamed almost unintelligibly into the dented microphone. Some feeble lights danced over his face and body from a dangerous-looking set-up that was balanced precariously on some scaffolding. A DJ who must have been in his early thirties and wearing a flat cap stood in front of a laptop, sneering slightly as he watched Max take on song 14,065 from the library he had stored on his hard drive. The lyrics were coming up on a small TV screen, and a small buzzy bee cut-out danced over the top of each word as it was time to sing it.

The guitar in the backing track had so much positive energy, it made people twitch their legs to the beat with hysteria, despite the dubious vocals. 'Coffee and TV' by Blur was infectious. Delicious.

Perfect for Max, even though the sober might have found it unbearable.

A fat man **was** propped up against the bar, looking thoroughly miserable with his head resting on his hand, rolls of cheek-chub spilling over his knuckles. But he was barely noticed by the twenty-somethings, to whom the night was young and full of promise. It could lead anywhere, a nightclub, a lock-in, a house party maybe . . .

'I've seen so much, I'm goin blind, and I'm brain dead virtually,' Max continued, smiling at his friends who were whooping with joy. A tiny bead of sweat trickled down his forehead, and he wiped it away with the back of his hand. He grabbed the microphone from the stand and started stomping around the stage, the black wire that trailed from the mike curling around his feet and turning his performance into a potentially dangerous stunt. Sociability, it's hard enough for me; his smile, his energy, was like a drug to everyone around him. His mates couldn't help but watch and grin.

The next line was for Bryony, so he leant forwards over the stage, almost toppling over, but managing to keep it together. Her glossy dark hair looked shiny in the glow of the bar and she blushed a little. Max held out his hand and grabbed hers, threading her delicate fingers with manicured nails painted aqua blue, between his own.

'Take me away from this big bad world, and agree to marry me,' he yelled, staring into his girlfriend's eyes, making her melt a little more in her heart . . . even though she knew it was just a line. Words from a song. He pulled away and she held her hands together in front of her face, worshipping her rock-star boyfriend, even if it was for one night only and purely brought on by Dutch courage.

Eliza squeezed her arm and smiled. She no longer had dreadlocks – it wasn't appropriate any more. They had been replaced with a stunning set of golden curls, instead. 'You two are bloody perfect for each other. Even if he did knock your tooth out,' she said, downing her glass of wine and slamming the glass on top of a speaker.

Bryony raised her index finger to her front right tooth and ran it over the replacement that Max had paid for, just like he had promised.

Eventually Max jumped off the stage and into her arms, a sweaty mess. His friends ruffled up his hair and jumped around him. It looked like he felt a million dollars. As a small, wiry man with thick glasses timidly stepped onto the stage and began to massacre a Bob Dylan song, Max whispered in her ear, 'You are my world, Bryony Weaver.'

This was followed by a high-five with Ben, which entirely ruptured their short-lived, but deeply intimate moment in the midst of a raucous night out. She kissed him on the cheek, feeling his warm skin and stubble against the soft surface of her lips . . .

And then she woke up with a start.

Panting.

Alone.

Darkness.

Bryony felt like she was missing something, so frantically thrashed her arms around in the bed, running her fingers through the pillows and the sheets, looking for Max. But he wasn't there.

And then she remembered.

CHAPTER 16

A CRIMINAL.

Wednesday 6 May 2009
Prison Wing A, High Elms Prison, south
west London
1 p.m.

It was just a few days into Keon's sentence that he started to put pen to paper.

He was surprised at how much comfort there was to be found in the glide of a ballpoint pen against the scratchy paper they gave him. He decided that his favourite pen was a black Bic, medium point. He was starting to pay attention to these small things, locked up like an animal with nothing but his own self-loathing and a handful of violent oafs for company.

But pens were hard to come by in prison, and the inmates could only buy them from the shop once every few days. People asked to borrow them and never gave them back. They were quietly pilfered from the pockets of others, and stashed away under pillows and mattresses. Keon was amazed at how many fights started over pens.

He was lucky because he had a pack of them in

different colours, and he looked after them like his life depended on it. It was a small thing but indicative of how vulnerable he was when it came to his feelings. He didn't, he now realised, know how to deal with his emotions. He'd received some therapy in prison, and his therapist was dredging up all sorts of things from his past.

It had started when his father walked out when he was little. After watching his mother cry loudly while curled up in a ball on the sofa, ten-year-old Keon had decided that he would be strong and never indulge his own feelings, just so he could get his mum through it all. There was no room for his tears; that was the assumption he had made, on his own. As a result, he was bad at dealing with the regular emotions of everyday life. Love and fear were now dehumanised products, trapped beneath his skin but cooking up a storm inside.

But now things were on a totally different level. He actually had problems. Incredibly serious ones. Ones that made the departure of his father seem like a walk in the park. Problems he had brought entirely on himself. He had fucked up his life, and the lives of many others, too.

His mother had always tried to make him talk to her about 'feelings' and it had made him cringe; made him angry with her, even. And now he saw that she had been trying to stop stuff like this happening. Stop him from growing into a moron.

A criminal.

A *murderer*.

There were several other emotions he was living with now too, taking over his ability to think straight. The worry, the sadness, the guilt – they were so strong he couldn't even be alone with himself in a room. He couldn't concentrate on anything. They just buzzed around his head like a swarm of angry bees.

His first few nights had been spent in utter terror. He had experienced a constricted feeling in his chest when the enormity of his actions had kicked in and he had finally realised that this was not a dream. This had all actually happened. He was, actually, his own worst nightmare.

He remembered the assemblies they used to have at school in year 7, 8 and 9 about violence: knives and guns and stuff. He hadn't listened. He had never thought it would affect him, and so he just used to play with his shoes until the laces were frayed. And that would piss his mum off.

'Oh, for God's sake,' she would say when she spotted them. 'I'll have to go into town tomorrow now and get some more.' And she would sigh loudly. She'd always been a perfectionist when it came to things like that, saying how Keon and Reb needed to look and behave like a 'proper' family, a good one.

Now he was locked up with all these feelings, and he needed a way to cope with them.

His therapist had encouraged him to imagine his emotions rushing around his body, each one an individually coloured truck on a congested road. That way he could try and separate them, visualise them, make sense of them. But they kept getting in each other's way, crossing each other's paths and, at times, crashing together in the central reservation, leaving nothing but sharp, agonising carnage that he had no idea how to unscramble.

So he had started by simply drawing the straightest lines he possibly could on the paper they provided, imagining those lines were markings in the road, trying to keep the trucks from colliding. It was the only way he could have a relatively clear head.

From there, the idea had progressed. He had lots of time to think in prison, and he wondered if, as a flawed human being, it was possible to draw the perfect straight line. The kind of straight line that only a computer could produce. No bumps. No mistakes.

Once he'd started trying, he had kept drawing those lines: sometimes they went well, and sometimes they went badly.

Kinks in the road.

Almost naturally, he progressed to curves. He thought about what it would take for him, an entirely imperfect person, to draw, freehand, the most perfect curve. The kind of curve you would find drawn by the design equipment used by a top architect. But, eventually, even that wasn't enough to keep his thoughts at bay, and the trucks just kept rushing through his mind, no matter how much he tried – and kept trying – to concentrate on the impossible task he had set himself.

First there was the blue truck, and that represented sadness. Sadness for the man he'd killed, his girlfriend, his family, and his friends. And then for his mother and his family and, dare he admit it, himself. A sadness that filled his stomach with such overwhelming depression he didn't know what to do with himself. It was like an ache all over his skin, and there was nothing he could do to dilute it.

Then there was the red truck. Red for anger. He was angry with Steve. Furious, in fact. He'd never come to visit him in the time before the trial, and he'd fled like a coward from a situation that Keon was convinced would never have happened if he hadn't been putting so much pressure on him. Keon felt that Steve was more than partially responsible but then, he had to admit, everyone inside was looking for a scapegoat. Then there was anger at the man who had sold him the gun. His sly features haunted his nightmares: the scuffmarks he had noticed on his knuckles from a recent fight and his chipped front teeth. How he greedily took the money from him and never thought about the consequences. And then, finally, his greatest anger was aimed at himself. He had grown to detest himself. He hated his face, his feet, his legs and, particularly, his hands. He couldn't even look at himself in the mirror any more; he always kept his eyes down towards the sink when he was washing his hands in the prison bathrooms.

Next came the green truck. Jealousy. Jealous of all the good boys who had done what they were supposed to do from the beginning, jealous of their brilliant futures, the beautiful weddings they would have, and the first cry of their newborn children. He was so hungry for freedom, for the challenges of the outside world, that even the sound of a police siren in the distance made him twinge with envy, because it reminded him of life on the outside. In the past, that noise had pissed him off when he was lying in bed and trying to sleep the night before an exam. Now that noise was for ever connected in his mind to the night he shot Max Tooley. He was jealous of all the people who would hear a police siren scream past, and know it was nothing to do with them, wonder what it could be, and then carry on with their lives.

He just kept drawing those lines, all day long.

'Nice lines, mate,' a voice startled Keon as he shuffled his hand further along the paper to complete his latest masterpiece.

It was a deep voice, and it originated from behind him. It shocked him both because the person was being quite nice, rather than threatening to wedge his feet up his own arse, and because he didn't think anyone appreciated the creative side of life in here. If he could call this creative . . . In fact, Keon half expected this kindness to be followed by some level of sarcasm or violence, so he turned around slowly in his chair, almost wincing, waiting for the inevitable smack in the face, or spit-wad in his eye. He'd had that a few times already because he was the newbie. Bullies love a newbie, and prisons are full of bullies.

There was a tall man standing behind him, a bald-headed person who must have been in his late teens or early twenties. He had skin so pale it was almost see-through, while spots were dotted around his chin and forehead. His frame was painfully thin, and the bones of his forearms jutted out like knives. The man had a very kind smile, but his teeth were dreadful. Uneven, sharp and chipped, as if they'd been carelessly thrown into his mouth like darts.

A kind smile, Keon thought. For a moment, he realised that he had never really got that saying before, but it was the first thing that came into his head when he saw the man standing there. He still wasn't going to let his guard down, though . . . He wasn't that naïve, not any more. Keon kept his free hand under the desk and scrunched it up into a tight fist, ready for the first swing of self-defence. 'Oh, right. Thanks,' he grunted, pushing the body of his pen down onto the notepad and feeling the plastic roll under his fingers like a six-edged wheel.

The man was still smiling, though . . . there was

no hidden right hook waiting to be unleashed from beneath his standard issue uniform, no surprise smack to the jaw.

'What are you doing, anyway? I don't get it,' the guy in front of him said now, crossing his arms and leaning forward a little. It was some comfort to Keon that he could see where both his hands were.

Keon suddenly felt a little embarrassed. He thought he wouldn't share the motorway thing with the guy. It was a bit weird. 'Erm, well . . . I'm trying to draw the perfect line, or curve, as if it's been drawn by computer,' he said, clearing his throat and realising how stupid it sounded.

'WANKERRRR!' came a loud cry from the desk behind Keon's, confirming what he'd been thinking.

'Fuck off!' snapped the man, defending Keon. *Keon* of all people . . . Keon felt a little twinge inside. This was the first display of kindness he'd seen since he had arrived in the prison. But he quickly flattened the smile that had automatically appeared on his face – it was early days yet.

'So, are you, like, a bit of an artist or summat?' the guy asked.

Keon was trying to figure out which part of the North his thick accent could be from. He loved northern accents. The Hendrys had gone on holiday to the Lake District as a family a good few years ago, and Keon couldn't get enough of the local dialect – he'd been practising it in the back of the car so much that Reb had pinched his arm and drawn blood.

'Oh, no. Not at all. It's just something I do to make time go quicker,' Keon said, thinking how much there was of it. Seconds dripping into minutes and hours: none of those counted for anything any more, apart from the timer counting down the days until he could get the fuck away from here.

Fifteen whole years. 180 miserable months. 780 hideous weeks. 5,475 shitty days.

'Can I have a shot?' the man now asked, rubbing his hands together eagerly, his brown eyes glinting a little like he'd been offered a test drive in a brand new Ferrari. It was amazing how the value of things changed once people were stuck behind bars.

'Yeah, sure,' Keon said, shuffling along the bench a little so there was space for the guy. His pumps squeaked on the floor as he did this and he felt like a kid again, trying to work out who was who in the playground. Who would look after him, who would go for him? Who would steal his lunch money and who would push his head down the toilet? He slightly reluctantly pushed his pens along the wooden tabletop, still concerned about this.

What if the guy went for him and jabbed one in his eye? Or wedged one up his nostril? Or, even worse, took them away? They were Keon's pens and paper. He really needed them. They were all that he had left, really.

The man almost jumped to sit down next to him, making Keon bob up and down at one end of the bench as he landed on the light blue plastic with a thud.

'Where do I start?' he asked, turning to look Keon in the eye. Keon noticed he was covered in stubble. It gave him an earthy, almost rugged quality, and he touched his own chin, angry that he'd never been able to grow any decent facial hair himself apart from a few sprigs of bum fluff. The strange man continued looking at Keon, and he pulled his hand away from his face self-consciously.

The human contact scared Keon because, in a way, now that he had him, he didn't want him to go. With this thought, he smiled, genuinely, for the first time in a long time, and didn't cut it short this time. He let it mould his features, pushing his cheeks into small apple-like bumps, making his eyebrows shift up a centimetre or two, his eyes smiling as well.

He watched intently as his new friend drew the black ink across the stark whiteness of the page. He was doing fine until about four centimetres in when a muscle in his finger must have twitched, causing him to wobble a little.

'Bollocks,' he said, slamming the pen down in frustration and looking at Keon again. 'That fuckin' twitch of mine,' he continued, starting to smile to himself.

'It's hard, isn't it?' Keon said, pulling the paper

back to him, hoping he could wow him with his new-found skills. To impress someone, for the first time in a very long time, rather than drawing expressions of half disgust, half fury.

He started drawing again.

'By the way, do you know if there's anywhere to get books around here, pal?' the man said.

Keon stopped drawing and looked up at him. The guy was squinting a little as he said this, almost in embarrassment. The volume of his voice had dropped significantly.

The question surprised him a lot, and Keon wondered for a second whether or not he was kidding. A man in this place asking for books was surprising. No one seemed to be into that sort of thing. The kind of people in this prison were down for extremely serious offences. Most of them had never previously been interested in literature because they were caught up in gang life, trapped in corners of the world they should have avoided. If they were into books, they certainly kept that hidden now.

'Sorry, I hope you don't mind me asking . . . you just look a bit more intelligent than all the shit-for-brains morons in here, and I only arrived yesterday,' the guy said, starting to laugh a little into a closed fist, which he had placed over his thin lips in order to stop himself being overheard.

'I have no idea. Sorry,' Keon said, trying to ignore a yell of 'Geek corner!' that had been thrown in their direction.

'Shame,' the man said, also ignoring the insult. *Water off a duck's back* . . . 'Are you struggling?' he continued, leaning towards Keon a bit more now.

This was direct.

Struggling? He had to be joking, right? This was an appalling state of affairs. While Keon knew he belonged there for what he had done, at the same time, he felt like he really didn't. He was in denial still. He should have been looking to his future now: education, a career, whatever. He knew this, but he didn't know how honest to be. Was this something that warranted a simple yes, or should he spill his guts? Tell the guy how he cried on his first night into his scratchy pillow, desperately trying to muffle his pathetic sobs so no one would hear and twist his arm back until he felt the bones moving inside? He was almost at breaking point.

'Of course I am,' Keon said now, abandoning his straight lines and drawing little embarrassed hash tags all over his paper.

'Have you tried writing letters?' the guy sitting next to Keon said, gazing down at the paper again, his own cheeks going a little red.

'No. I haven't,' Keon responded – he hadn't given it any thought at all. 'Who would I write letters to?' he asked, realising he didn't really have anyone in the world apart from his mum and Reb, and neither of them had come to see him since he had been locked up. Not once.

'The people whose lives you affected, maybe? I

did the first time I went to prison, when I was eighteen. Sometimes I sent them, sometimes I didn't,' the man replied, looking a little embarrassed, like he wished he hadn't mentioned it.

'What's your name, anyway?'

'Eddie. What's yours?'

'Keon,' he replied, ashamed of his own name. Ashamed of himself. He suddenly thought that he didn't deserve a friend – one person in this shithole who didn't want to see him hurt in some elaborate way he'd never thought possible. The guys here had a lot of time to consider the most painful ways to fight, and it normally involved positions that resembled some fucked-up game of Twister. Keon also resolved not to ask what the man had done to be sent to prison, either. It was best not to ask. He'd learned that.

It was that night Keon wrote his first letter.

It was for his mum.

He never sent it.

CHAPTER 17

SHE KNEW IT WAS FROM TOM.

Monday 11 May 2009
Finsbury Park, north London
7 a.m.

The first letter dropped through Sara's letterbox with a gentle thud, followed by a flurry of others.

She crawled out of bed and thumped moodily down the dark wooden stairs in a pair of black French knickers and a thin, grey vest top. Her short hair was ruffled, sprigs of it sticking out in different directions.

She shuffled through the small pile. A letter from HSBC, which she knew she wouldn't open because she did her banking online; a scam letter promising her a holiday in Barbados; a letter from the council; one from the gas board; and, finally, a small, white envelope with her address in shaky capital letters.

Her eyes narrowed and she felt a flash of anger. She knew it was from Tom. He hadn't put her name at the top – probably to pique her interest and make sure she opened it, she realised. And changing his handwriting, too? That was a smart move. But it hadn't got past her.

She clutched the letters as she stomped up the stairs again, making her way back along the hallway and into the kitchen, keeping the one from Tom in her right hand. She sat at the table staring at the envelope, set against the background of the table's fifties-style, flowery tablecloth.

She was so tempted to open it, but she didn't want to read his words right now. She couldn't do it at a time when she was so confused. There was no way her husband could explain this.

Sara stashed the letter away before showering and getting ready for the day ahead. She had to be at the Covent Garden office of the restaurant's account manager for a meeting. It was a standard get-together over delicious cups of coffee and croissants Sara bought from a nearby patisserie – she needed something, anything, to make the drudgery of going through figures a little more enjoyable. She was prone to daydream while Christopher went through the numbers, finding herself staring longingly at handsome strangers walking past the window, going about their business when she should have been concentrating on hers.

She was feeling troubled and she knew this wouldn't help her focus levels at the meeting. The Tom situation was plaguing her every thought. She'd cut all contact with him. She missed him, of course, but she couldn't get over what had happened. Her husband had been dating other women. There was no way he could explain it. There was no easy way to get over this.

The tube carriage was packed with people, suit after suit dotted everywhere. It felt like there was hardly any room for another being: sharing every breath and moment in a strange sardine tin of forced intimacy, before everyone would exit and go their separate ways and forget the journey, which would soon merge into the thousands of others they had already taken. Most people would never be able to recall the faces they had studied in idle moments on their day's journey to and from work. Sara found herself oddly depressed by it all.

She managed to get a seat next to a pregnant woman, who rested a book on her bump. Sara briefly caught her reflection in the glass of the tube windows as she sat. Her husband's infidelity had taken its toll on her, and she noticed she looked gaunt and pale. She'd dyed her short hair a much darker brown just the night before as she had noticed a few grey hairs appearing in her fringe, so had decided to buy some cheap dye and do it herself at home. She wondered now if it was too dark a shade, and if she'd only exacerbated her drawn features.

A stray copy of the *Finsbury Ad* was on the ledge behind her. Sara twisted round and picked it up, feeling several vertebrae in her spine click as she moved. She knew she was carrying most of her tension and misery in her shoulders. She got back to thinking about all the things she needed to do as she flicked through the first couple of pages of the paper, unable to focus on the stories.

There was a long list of things that needed to be organised by the end of the day: the menu review, the cocktail glass order she needed to complete, the napkins that needed to be changed for new ones because they were fading after so many visits to the dry cleaners, the light bulb in the bathroom that needed replacing . . .

She looked up suddenly, and noticed a young woman glancing at a page in the same paper, and then directly at Sara's face, as if studying her. The young woman's glances went back and forth from the paper to her face several times. Sara felt a shiver as she turned the page, laughing a little inside at how paranoid and on edge she had become.

But the moment her eyes settled on the next page of the paper, she was greeted by the sight of her own face smiling back at her. She looked away from the page and then back down again, in total disbelief, wondering if she was going crazy. She quickly scanned the headline: ARTIST'S HEARTBREAK EXHIBITION GOES PUBLIC

What?

She felt nauseous as she looked again at the photo, which was captioned IN HAPPIER TIMES. There she was, in a plunge-neck dress, her beaming smile and bright eyes staring back at her. She had her arms around Tom – the photo had been taken at the opening night of his Mulai Gallery exhibition, which had caused such a huge stir among the critics. He was wearing a brand new designer suit, and looked so gorgeous she wondered for a moment if it was the same person. The man who had hurt her so badly.

Sara's eyes stung with tears as she looked back down at the page and tried to read:

Local abstract artist Tom Wilson has unveiled a new exhibition, inspired by his heartbreak over a rift with his wife.

Mr Wilson, of Finsbury Park, who won five awards for his Mulai Gallery exhibition in March this year, has dedicated his latest work to 28-year-old Sara Wilson, a restaurant manager, in a last-ditch attempt to win back her heart.

The exhibition, 'Broken', was installed last night in the gallery of Words café, Crouch End, and will officially open this Thursday.

Mr Wilson told the *Finsbury Ad*, 'I have never been in such an awful situation in my life, and felt so inspired by my feelings of agony that I had to turn it into art. I love Sara more than anything and needed to capture these feelings, which I am sure others will be able to relate to.

'What has happened between my wife and me is something I want to keep private. I made a huge mistake and I hope she learns to see the real me once more.'

It is thought that the restaurant manager is unaware of the exhibition.

Local critics have so far labelled his latest work as 'stunningly moving' and 'a raw, heartbreaking depiction of the need for forgiveness'.

'Broken' will open on Thursday evening at 6 p.m. It will remain on display until 31 October 2009.

Sara felt as if she couldn't breathe. She shoved the paper into her handbag and jumped off the tube at the next stop. She ran up the stairs, and walked the steps on the escalator rather than just standing there, daydreaming as she usually did. Her head was spinning as dozens, if not hundreds, of people passed her by in a strange blur of umbrellas, newspapers and handbags, while the adverts positioned on the walls seemed to stare and sneer at her.

As she neared the tube station exit she felt around in her bag for her Oyster card, her fingers running over the bag's contents frantically as she felt more and more lightheaded. As soon as she was out and into the fresh air, she checked her voicemail.

She had received a few calls from numbers she didn't recognise the day before, but she'd ignored them, thinking they were Tom trying a new way to get her to answer. She knew there were voice-mails waiting but she hadn't wanted to hear his voice.

Her hands were shaking as she hurriedly typed in the code for her voicemail inbox. She pushed the phone up to her ear and tapped at the ground frantically with her right foot as she listened.

'Hi Sara. This is Greg Jones from the *Metro*. Just wanted to have a chat with you about a story regarding your husband that we spotted in the local paper's website. Can you give me a call back, please? We go to press in a couple of hours. Thanks.'

'Hello there, I'm Lisa Stavlos and I'm calling from *The Times*. We are running a story tomorrow about Tom Wilson and his new exhibition after we saw it online in the *Finsbury Ad*. Can you give me a call straight back, please?'

'Hi, Sara. This is Ryan Young calling from the *Finsbury Ad*. Can you call me back within the hour, please? I need to talk to you about a new exhibition by your husband. Thanks.'

The messages went on and on. There were frenzied messages left by at least ten journalists on deadline, desperate to get her side of the story. The *Finsbury Ad* story seemed to have sparked something, and she had a feeling it was too late to stop it.

CHAPTER 18

'MORON.'

Tuesday 12 May 2009
Angel, north London
2.30 p.m.

S he was back. Yet again.
Oh, wow, Adam thought, running a hand over the stubble on his chin.
Her black, square-neck dress looked like it belonged in a posh office, and her hair was loose and tumbling about her shoulders. She had a kind of fifties, retro look about her. He didn't think she had worn her hair down before, and today she looked even more beautiful than normal. If that was possible, he considered.

'Adam, mate, seriously, I need some help out here, it's getting proper busy now,' came his colleague Zach's voice. He was talking to Adam as if he was the big boss, but had only been working at the small Islington café for a week and a half.

They had been getting on quite well that day until Zach said that.

'Moron,' Adam said, under his breath. He felt riled at being ordered around, but also a little bit embarrassed that he'd caught him looking at the girl through the shelves again, like a creep.

'Yes, yes, all right,' Adam sighed, swinging himself around the partition where the sink met the main floor of the coffee shop. He kept a hand on the cool metal divide, and tore his eyes away from her.

Adam had been tired, lately. Studying for his masters was really taking it out of him, and he kept finding himself slipping into daydreams for a means of escape. She was the perfect escape.

'Who are you looking at anyway?' Zach asked, standing next to him so he could try and work out for himself who Adam had been staring at so intently. Zach's blond fringe flopped over his face and he brushed it away with his hand in irritation.

The café *was* busy. There was a posh-looking guy wearing neatly pressed chinos, a blue checked shirt and a navy gilet; and a rather large woman with a brood of three equally large children who were almost entirely covering a table in chocolate cake and crumbs. Two blonde girls giggled away behind huge cappuccinos – they looked like clones, with their on-trend indie-style clothes from Urban Outfitters or Topshop, over-sized gold earrings, and long hair, deliberately messed up. Then there was an elderly couple, huddled together, reading the same page of a newspaper and holding hands. Along with the seated customers were the take-out hordes, calling in regularly for their usual coffee and tea orders.

And then there was her. The girl. Whatever her name was. Adam still hadn't found that out.

'Ohhh, the blonde chicks,' Zach said, pursing his lips and nodding his head.

One of them caught the boys staring and smiled cheekily. The other one laughed loudly and flung her head back.

Adam suddenly felt a little embarrassed. Yes, granted, they were attractive. But, no. He wasn't interested. They weren't his type.

'Not them. The other girl.'

'Where?'

'Just behind them.'

'I can't see her.'

'Oh, come on – the one in the black dress.'

'Holy shit. I hadn't noticed her before,' Zach said, gulping in a comedic manner and pulling his head back in an exaggerated startle, almost as amazed as Adam was by how damn gorgeous she was.

'Right, that's it. I'm going to ask her out,' Adam said, pulling his apron off speedily and throwing it behind him onto the till. *Zach is not getting there first*, he thought. *No way*. 'Woah, woah, woah! Now, come on, mate. No offence but . . .' Zach said, as he pulled on his right arm to hold him back.

As Adam turned around he noticed that Zach had an expression on his face that basically said, 'She's a million miles out of your league.' He raised an eyebrow, feeling a little insulted by the implications of what the face before him was saying. 'But what?' Adam asked, puffing out his chest.

'Well . . . I'm not sure she . . . you know . . .'

Adam suddenly felt deeply inadequate and insecure. He never usually had problems talking to women, but he struggled even asking this one how many sugars she took in her coffee. Plus, he normally felt quite confident about his looks – not arrogant or self-obsessed, but just happy with himself. A 'rugged but handsome face', that was how his ex-girlfriend had described him, and he had thought it was a good thing at the time. Now Adam wondered if he looked like a creature that had scuttled sideways out of an ancient rock formation. Craggy. Interesting. Fucked.

'Ah, well . . . go on. You never know, right?' Zach relented, giving Adam a glimmer of hope.

He didn't even know why he was listening to him. Zach had all the grace of a giant sloth, while his belly hung over his waistband and was only just contained under the black, standard-issue shirts they were given.

'Bollocks to you,' Adam said, half joking, half serious. 'I'm going over there,' he added, moving off abruptly in a flash of bravado, without looking first where he was going.

He walked straight into Carla, who was carrying a tray of hot drinks in the other direction.

Uh oh.

Carla, thankfully a skilled and experienced waitress, managed not to drop the tray. Instead, she rocked back and forth violently, like an anti-stress executive desk toy that had been pushed a little too hard, the tray wobbling and the cups on it starting to slide off to one side. It all seemed to happen in extra slow motion. Instinctively, Adam put out his right hand to steady the tray, but misjudged the angle and ended up flipping it in the air, like the clumsy, cack-handed idiot that he was.

The mugs jumped upside down, covering everyone in a one-metre radius in warm, chocolatey liquid. The room fell silent after the ear-splitting sound of china crashing to the ground and smashing into a million tiny pieces. It was so loud it made Adam grit his teeth hard and his ears ring.

Everyone looked around and stared as they stood there, covered in various drinks. Adam wiped a great slop of cappuccino froth from his shoulder that looked as though he had had a run-in with a particularly large pigeon, admiring as he did so the neat moustache Zach had acquired, from a streak of hot chocolate, on his upper lip. With his blond hair, the effect was rather startling. Carla seemed to have escaped unscathed, apart from a large damp patch on her backside that Adam was not inclined to tell her about. She could be a bit fierce, and would no doubt discover it for herself when she next went to sit down on her break.

Carla went into emergency mode. She grabbed great swathes of blue tissue from an industrial-sized roll and starting to mop down the bedraggled-looking customers who had been unfortunate enough to get caught in the crossfire. Adam saw

211

grimaces and angry shifting of feet from some of these customers, who had been waiting patiently in line for their take-out orders. He was aware of a small but palpable air of tension and irritation, as if one of the customers was about to kick up a massive stink over it.

But then Adam heard laughter. A woman's laughter.

Loud.

Genuine.

Lovely.

A sound that pierced through the tension and brought about a feeling that was altogether happier.

Adam looked over to where the laughter was coming from and realised it was her. The girl. She was bent double, flapping her right hand in the air apologetically and trying to cover her mouth with the other. Her face was beautifully covered in happiness, and it was wonderful to see. Normally she looked, well, really down. Adam was glad to know that not only was she capable of smiling, but also of emitting a range of high-pitched, bubbly giggles. There was something very naughty about her laugh, he realised.

He smiled as he looked at her, feeling the warm coffee against the skin of his shoulder as it seeped through his shirt. Some of the 'injured' customers looked at her in disgust, which only seemed to make her laugh more.

Adam liked this girl. He liked her even more.

'I'm so sorry,' she said now, getting to her feet

and starting to help with the clean-up effort, but still giggling away.

She was at Adam's Converse-trainered feet now, on her hands and knees, her expensive-looking black dress trailing in the mucky mess on the floor. He crouched down beside her, smiling as the room hustled and bustled around them with the effort of the clean-up.

'Look, don't worry, you don't need to get all dirty,' Adam said, putting his hand out in a bid to pull her back up and away from the slop all over the tiles. She reminded him of Zooey Deschanel. Her beauty was in her eyes, in her skin, in everything about her. Her hair was a tempting shade of auburn, thick and sprawling now that it had been released to cover her shoulders. She was a naturally beautiful woman. Strikingly different, and impossible not to stare at. Her ribs were moving in and out as she laughed – he could see it through the delicate material of her dress. She arched her back like a cat in a stretch, and got even more coffee over the bottom of her dress. She was wallowing in the moment. This happy moment born from Adam's ultimate clumsiness.

'No. No, it's OK. I'm sorry. It's just that was the funniest thing I have seen for a long time. It just, you looked like such an *oaf*,' she said, before collapsing again into laughter as if she was drunk.

That made Adam laugh, too.

And then Carla.

And then the table of chunky children. Even their mother started giggling as well.

Eventually she calmed a little, wiping up the last bit of drink from the floor, before getting up and brushing herself down. She seemed a little embarrassed now, but he was just glad she had been there to diffuse the situation with her own brand of quirky behaviour.

'What's your name, by the way? I've, um, seen you in here a few times now,' Adam said. He was trying to sound casual, like he'd only just realised who she was. Chilled out, as opposed to how he really felt. Deep down, he wanted to beg for a few minutes of her time so she would let him take her for a drink somewhere.

Her cheeks were pink with happiness. *It really is good to see*, Adam thought, given her usual deeply melancholic demeanour. It made her even more attractive.

'Bryony,' she said, suddenly looking a little bit wary of talking to him.

Adam wondered if she had a boyfriend or something by the way she reacted. It was almost as if she felt guilty.

'Well, nice to meet you properly, Bryony. I'm A—' but he didn't get to finish his sentence, because she had flashed him an apologetic look, darted back to her table, grabbed her handbag and coat and rushed out of the door. It slammed behind her hard, causing the vintage Open/Closed sign to rattle noisily.

Silence spread over the café again.

'Damn,' Adam said, deflating.

Zach rolled his eyes at him in an, 'I told you so' look, and went to get on with the washing-up.

CHAPTER 19

THE SWEETEST THING.

Thursday 14 May 2009
Crouch End, north London
7 p.m.

S ara was not sure what it was that prompted her to walk into the café on the High Road and face up to this utterly bizarre display of public remorse.

How did she feel about it? Was she angry? Touched? Humiliated? In love?

Would she respond to her husband's very naked plea for her heart in the way that he, and probably the rest of the newspaper-reading public, wanted her to?

The story had gone viral. Sara wasn't completely sure how she felt about this, but humiliation was the overriding emotion. Irritating newscasters dressed in their starchy suits had read out the story on the six o'clock news, before smugly turning to their co-presenter and making some light-hearted joke about the situation. Bored office workers had forwarded links of online newspaper items to each other, while others tweeted their opinions in a seemingly non-stop flow of gooey-eyed drivel.

Sara was also surprised. Tom wasn't a particularly famous artist. And certainly no one knew who she was. The breakdown of their relationship was not that unusual – romance died all the time. She knew that love was transient, impermanent, a delicate flame, so easily snuffed out too soon. But something about their story had caught the attention of the whole city, even if it would be forgotten about, like all the other breaking news stories, in just a few weeks', or even days', time. Everyone seemed to love the idea of the breakdown of a marriage, and the artist husband – a sad, waif-like figure – trying to paint his way back into his beloved's heart. What was even more intriguing to the public was the mystery that surrounded the falling-out. As yet, that hadn't been explained. In the end, Sara had felt that she had to be at the opening night.

It seemed like a lot of other people had, too. A queue of at least fifty people had gathered outside the café, chattering away loudly, smoking cigarettes and holding coffees. A few tourists were even in the line. They were clutching maps and cameras and, for a moment, Sara wanted to laugh.

Her stomach had plunged in horror as she walked past the queue, a few people spotting her and lowering their voices. No one questioned her when she pushed to its front and walked into the café.

She had dressed appropriately for the evening, she reckoned. She was wearing a lightweight leather jacket over a delicate black vest top paired with black skinny jeans. Her shoes were simple black ballet pumps. Black. It was the colour of mourning for the end of their relationship and her husband's deceitful double life. The only thing that gave a flash of anything other than raven darkness was a gentle sweep of light green eye-shadow on her eyelids, and a silver necklace, shining bright against its inky backdrop.

Tanya had come with her for moral support, but promised to stay calm and quiet. She was furious about the way Sara's business had been splashed all over the press, and particularly angry at how Tom was now turning it into an opportunity to get the crowds in to see his new show. She walked behind Sara, a few steps away, so Sara knew she was there.

The owners of the café had not been at all prepared for the interest the exhibition would attract. The quiet of the café – usually only ever broken by a quiet hum of conversation, the scrape of a fork on a plate and the careful setting down of coffee cups – had been ruined by a noisy burst of unprecedented attention. A tanned man with slicked-back hair – one of the owners, Sara presumed – was darting around, muttering to himself and frowning, while shuffling papers and clearing tables.

Sara saw Tom standing in the middle of a modest

opening-night media scrum, holding a sparkling flute of champagne and twitching nervously. He caught a glimpse of her and suddenly seemed to zone out of his conversation with the people around him, but she just nodded at him to carry on and leave her be for the moment. They still knew each other so well that a simple nod was worth more than any words.

The lighting in the area of the café where the exhibition was displayed had been dimmed just a little. The first thing Sara saw in front of her was a small bath on the floor, with a mobile phone in the water. It was so simple, obvious even, but it brought back the fury she had felt when she had discovered Tom's secrets. She had wanted to destroy everything. She had wanted to tear pictures from the walls, cut up the bed sheets, and cover his clothes in paint. Sara had wanted to destroy him inside, as he had done to her.

Along the wall on the left side of the room was a series of paintings and collages of Sara. That was weird to see, she realised, running a hand through her hair and letting her fingers rest at the base of her neck. They did not show large sections of Sara, but the arch of an eyebrow, her back when it was turned at a party. The way he depicted her made her look so much more beautiful than the image she had of herself in her mind.

Another part of the exhibition was a laptop, which had been taken apart. Keys had been pulled out, rearranged to spell 'I'm sorry' and attached to the main keypad section with invisible wires to look like they were flying from the computer. It took a little artistic licence considering there was only one 'R' on a keypad, but it worked somehow.

In a large frame was a photograph of Tom, with white labels next to different parts of his face, the wording in classic typewriter font. They read 'I was foolish', 'I made a mistake' and 'I'm human'. It really was pretty stunning, Sara thought, feeling a tide of love wash over her again, just like it did when they were first dating and she knew she was onto something special.

On the far back wall a projector screen showed what looked like a male model covering himself in shiny, black tape and singing something. Sara could see some headphones by the installation.

A few people were milling about, standing in the ruins of her past and Tom's present, cooing at how painfully beautiful it all was. Some of them looked at Sara and realised who she was, nudging the person they were with and whispering in their ear.

But Sara wasn't embarrassed.

She had, in that moment, realised just how much Tom loved her, and it hit her like a bolt of lightning, sending chills down her back. She was touched to the point where she could have cried on the floor and made herself the final, missing part of Tom's exhibition. A live display of the agony that heartbreak brings. Did it really have to come to this?

Part of her wanted to rush over to him and kiss

him passionately and to make everything OK again, but it was still difficult to get over what had happened.

Should she forgive her cheating husband? Did cheats ever stop playing the game? She'd asked herself these questions unceasingly while lying awake in bed at night, listening to drinkers stumble home from the local watering holes.

Tom kept looking at her nervously, glancing away from the people he spoke to every now and then as if to assess the damage. To see how she would react. Would there be drama? Would there be tears?

'Hello, are you Sara?' a voice came from behind her, accompanied by a tap on her left shoulder; strange fingers making contact with her skin.

Sara turned around and saw what could only be a reporter standing there, looking slightly nervous, notebook in hand. Tanya came over to be by her side, and Sara felt her hold on to her arm and pull her a little closer, just to make it clear she was there.

'Yes, I am. And who are you?'

'I'm Ryan from the *Finsbury Ad*,' the man said, reaching out to shake her hand.

Sara shook his, noticing how sweaty his palms were. This was certainly awkward. She remembered his voice as one of the many that were on her phone's voicemail, pleading for a comment on what should be a beautiful, moving, human-interest story. But she hadn't known if she could

221

give any of them the follow-up they wanted, and had rung none of them back.

'Hi, Ryan. How can I help?'

He shuffled nervously, running a hand down the front of his jacket. Sara noticed a few more reporters turn around and look at him with envy for attempting to secure the first interview.

'I want to talk to you about this exhibition, really. I guess what I want to know is if you will be taking Mr Wilson back into your life after his gallant display of remorse?' he asked, with a raised eyebrow, looking more and more confident as he reached the end of his question.

There it was. The question of the night from the mouth of a handsome young journalist.

But she wasn't going to be forced into anything. Or rushed. This was not about saying, 'Yes, yes, I still love him,' loudly until the paintings shook on their hangings and the people around them fist-pumped the air and smiled. While it was a beautiful and romantic idea, Sara knew that after the champagne flutes had been collected and the lights of the gallery switched off, it would be she who was left with the reality of the man she believed had let her down, and could do so again. But she loved him so much . . . 'I don't want to comment on that just yet,' Sara said, calmly.

'Well, look, please, when you are ready to talk, call me . . .' Ryan said, reaching into his pocket and handing her a business card. He turned around and walked away from her slowly. He must have given some subtle gesture to the pack of journalists who were watching their conversation because they all looked suddenly crestfallen, before dispersing to get more coffee and champagne.

'What are you going to do?' Tanya whispered in Sara's ear.

'I don't know. This is all so touching, and it seems so real, but I just don't know if I can trust him again,' Sara replied, looking at Tanya and seeing her sceptical look, one she had worn ever since the whole affair was discovered.

Tom looked over again, and Sara again gestured at him to stay away. He stepped back into a shadow in the room, where she could see him watching her over the top of his glass, his gorgeous face partially hidden in the darkness. He looked sad; desperate, perhaps.

Sara asked Tanya to give her a few moments alone. Tanya looked hard at her before moving off and staring – arms crossed and a scowl over her face – at the paintings of her best friend that adorned the walls of the café.

Sara made her way to the video projection and slipped the headphones onto her head. Goosebumps covered her skin as she heard the music – U2's 'Sweetest Thing'. She mouthed the words as the thin, pale man on the wall still wrapped himself in tape, staring desperately at the camera as he sang them, too . . . That look, that desperation she saw in Tom's eyes that evening. He'd somehow captured it perfectly.

As she sang along the hairs rose on her arms.

The tape had completely covered the model's legs and stomach now: the clip had been sped up so the process of covering himself was quick, but the movement of his mouth to the lyrics was in sync, creating a strange effect that reached right inside Sara and made tears well in her eyes.

As the lyrics of the song spoke of sewing up tears, she couldn't help but think that was the point. You could stitch these things up again, cover them with something, and pretend that everything was OK . . . *But you would still see the scar, the join and the tear where everything was ripped apart,* she thought.

A tear slid from her eye and she saw a flash to the side of her as a photographer took the liberty of capturing this moment of raw, emotional nakedness.

The model was up to his neck in tape now and, as she stared at the image, something about his crazy behaviour struck a chord with her that gathered in her throat like a stone.

Suddenly she felt a soft touch on her arm. She knew immediately it was Tom.

Sara turned around slowly, and looked at him. Her face was completely still, the muscles not moving and contracting the way they usually did when she tried to hold back her tears. They were just flowing from her eyes.

Tom reached out and held her chin, tilting her head slightly. 'You are so beautiful,' he whispered, wiping her tears away. 'I'm so glad you're here, so I can just tell you finally what I've done and what I haven't done . . .' he whispered. He shuffled her slightly into the corner of the room away from prying eyes, turning her to look at him. 'Oh, Sara, when did you learn to doubt me?' he said, pleadingly.

Sara kept her face dead still and her mouth tightly closed as he searched her eyes for the answer.

'Listen, Sara. To begin with, I'm sorry this went as big as it did. I had no idea it would be picked up by all the nationals when the local paper got wind of it, but it seems you can't really put the brakes on all this stuff once you've said something. It's a bloody nightmare. But you need to know that I *haven't* cheated on you . . . you shut me out, and I've had no chance to tell you what's happened. It's been awful . . .'

Sara glared at him as the model flickered on the screen beside them, singing to himself, now almost totally covered in black tape. 'I just don't feel like I can trust you any more, Tom – how can you even try to get out of this? You have a profile on a dating site, and it is being used,' she said, through gritted teeth. She pulled her face away from Tom's hands and wiped it dry before folding her arms and looking at him once more.

Tom sighed. 'Listen. I know this doesn't look good. I know that. I set up a profile years ago, before we met. I was dating then, of course. When we got together, for some stupid reason, I was still intrigued to read the messages I was being sent.' Tom looked down at the floor, his face pained. 'Some of them were very funny, some weird – it kind of became an amusement to me . . . I appreciate it was incredibly foolish of me, and dishonest in many ways, and unkind to the women contacting me . . .' Here Tom looked at Sara, saw the look on her face and hurried on before she could say something. 'But I can wholeheartedly promise that I never went on any dates since being with you. I've never even replied to the messages. Not once. I love you, Sara, more than you will ever understand. I know I've been an idiot, but you are the best thing that ever happened to me . . . I couldn't bear for what we have to end over this.'

Sara bit her lip and looked down at her feet. She knew him so well that she believed his argument. She could see it in his eyes. He was right about his stupidity. But as stupid as he had been, he hadn't cheated on her as such . . .

She was going to have to take a huge leap of faith.

'I love you, Tom,' she said, slowly.

Three little words.

'I love you so much. I miss you deeply. I just need to know you aren't going to hurt me again,' she said, tears welling in her eyes.

'I would never hurt you, Sara. What we have is true love – it's rare. We can't let something like this keep us apart, not for a second longer. But I do know that it's you that needs to make the decision whether or not you believe in me and whether or not you can forgive me for this . . .' Tom's hands were over his mouth now, like he was praying.

Sara's heart rate felt as if it had slowed right down. She had to take the leap right now. She had to jump.

She couldn't imagine a world without him and, as she looked at him now, she realised she could feel sorry for him, in some ways. She reached forwards, pulled his hands away from his mouth, and kissed him softly.

He put his hands around her waist, pulling her close to his body. 'I love you, Sara. I'm so sorry. I just need you back with me, in my life, by my side. Every day—'

'Shhh,' Sara whispered, pushing her finger to his lips before kissing him once more.

The room burst into applause.

CHAPTER 20

'JUST MAX.'

Saturday 16 May 2009
Finsbury Park, north London
7.30 p.m.

'It was a cracking night out, Bryony, you should have come,' Ben said, gazing up at the ceiling.

Bryony thought it was the last place she would have wanted to be: in some sweaty Soho bar, fighting her way to get a drink and being letched over by strangers.

'I just don't feel ready.'

'Of course, I understand.' Ben suddenly panicked as he realised the story about his latest drunken exploits had come to an end and he would have to distract Bryony with something else.

He was starting to understand why their friends were finding it so difficult to be around her. It was as if the usual bubbling conversations had been covered in glue, which seemed to set them, hard and solid, with no room for any movement.

There were a few moments of silence, as they lay on their backs on Bryony's bed, wondering how to fill the void. *Shit, shit,* Ben thought. What could he talk about? What could he ask her? What could he do to distract her for just a few short minutes?

He'd come round specifically to tell her something, but it was too hard to say and he'd wimped out. All he could see on the ceiling was Max's face. It seemed to be everywhere: in the foam of his morning coffee or the sauce left on his plate after a bacon sandwich; he could see it when he shut his eyes. His best friend. Dead. Gone. Tragic.

Painful.

'Erm . . . what can we talk about next? Oh, yes, I know, tell me your funniest memory from primary school,' Ben said completely out of the blue, before kicking himself mentally for the game-show-like delivery of the horrendously obvious conversation starter.

He was amazed at how useless he was.

'OK . . . so that came out of nowhere!' Bryony laughed despite herself, turning to look at him. She knew what this was all about. She knew what he was trying to do. He might as well have asked her what star sign she was, or her favourite colour. And it was ridiculous because she'd known him – through Max – for years now. 'Hmmm . . . I'll have to think about this one,' Bryony said, humouring him. Her long, dark hair was pulled back into a loose bun and a few tendrils, which had freed themselves from a tight hair band, were now resting on her beautiful face. She stretched her legs out over the thick, white duvet in the style

229

of a starfish. Her beige cropped trousers revealed thin legs and ankles, her toenails painted black.

This is all such a farce, she thought, avoiding the elephant in the room that was Max.

Ben put his arms over his chest and pushed his feet into the bedcovers, feeling the buttons at the bottom of the duvet cover under his toes. Their shoes sat side by side at the foot of the bed: a pair of vintage Adidas Gazelles and some tan leather pumps from French Connection.

The room was dark apart from the light of the small bedside lamp, which dimmed every now and then before returning to full strength. Summer rain was pummelling the window as if a thousand tiny ghosts were knocking to be let in. Thick, grey clouds had boiled up to disguise the previously bright blue sky, and it felt like a winter's day inside the flat.

'Oh, I know! I had this really weird project as a kid. I was in year 4, I think, and for some reason I decided it was my God-given mission on earth to save worms,' Bryony responded, smiling widely at the thought of her own youthful stupidity. 'So, basically, every lunch break I would bolt down my sandwiches and then take my lunchbox out to the playground and fill it with all the worms I could find on the grass at the edges,' she continued, shuddering at the thought of handling worms; a prospect she would find unbearable now.

'And what did you do with them once you'd taken them away from their happy place, you know, their natural habitat?' Ben asked, desperately trying to speak between his deep giggles.

'Then, I would put them in my locker for the rest of the afternoon before setting them free in our garden at home,' Bryony replied, shrieking out loud.

'The poor fuckers!' said Ben, rubbing his right eye with a chunky fist. His thick blond hair had grown the longest it had been since he was a skateboarding teenager. His legs were thick like tree-trunks from years of rugby practice, and he looked like a giant compared to Bryony. His nose had been broken twice, thumped by a knee or an elbow on too many occasions to count. He'd tried to get Max involved in the game but, when he had glanced at him standing on the sidelines, a handsome, slim rocker dude reading Kerouac and sipping Diet Coke, he had just known it wouldn't work. Max had been too 'pretty' for rugby. Too arty. Too creative.

'Yeah . . . I doubt they appreciated being stuck in a sweaty lunchbox that smelt of stale corned beef for two and a half hours,' Bryony said, suddenly feeling bad for her rescued worms, trapped in a hot locker, with leftover chunks of her sandwiches to contend with.

'I'm going to report you to the RSPCW,' Ben replied, pulling his green T-shirt down over his belt. It had ridden up in all the hysteria, revealing a toned stomach with a snail-trail of blond hair.

'What's that?' Bryony asked, turning to face him with a puzzled expression.

Ben cringed at the lameness of his joke. 'Um, The Royal Society for the Prevention of Cruelty to Worms?' he said, before clearing his throat.

There was an awkward silence as they both quietly acknowledged the shockingly poor levels of their banter. But then a smile began to creep across Bryony's face before she yelled, 'Hey! I was trying to be a good person!' She pulled a pillow from under her back and hit him square in the face with it.

Ben hadn't had time to block it and spluttered underneath the fabric, which had gone straight into his mouth.

'Go on, then. Your turn. What did you do?'

Ben thought for a moment, and realised that his funniest primary school moment had involved Max. Like most of the funniest moments in his life. He wondered if it would be a bad idea to discuss him. The whole point of his visit was an attempt to cheer Bryony up.

'Well, it's do to with Max, actually, Bry. Is that OK? I think you'll like it, though . . .'

Bryony's face was suddenly overcast. Ben turned his head to face hers and saw sad vulnerability flicker in her eyes once again.

'Yes. Please tell me.'

'OK,' Ben started, fiddling with the corner of the duvet and looking up to the ceiling, feeling a lump in his throat. 'Well, basically, I was the king of kiss chase, Bryony. I must admit, I really was. And as funny as Max has always been, he had that hilarious fear of girls as a kid that so many little boys have. It used to make him cry at nursery school if a girl even went near him, or asked for a biscuit or something.'

Bryony chuckled, and shuffled a little closer to Max's best friend. A person who, if she was honest with herself, had possibly known him better than she had. Someone who'd shared the sandpit with him as a toddler and stolen cups of milk from his lunch tray. Someone who had carried him home, over his shoulder, after overindulgent nights out, and then drawn on his face in permanent black marker while he was sleeping. She knew that Ben was worried about talking about Max, about making Bryony sad, but she wanted to hear all these stories – she wanted to fill in the gaps and feel like there was nothing she didn't know about the man she loved.

Ben was smiling. 'So, I finally persuaded him to play kiss chase with us. He'd been hiding in the hallway outside the canteen every lunch break to avoid it, but I finally got him to agree to take part. And then, when the most "popular" girl at school, Sonya Lockhurst, I think her name was, went to kiss him, he, he . . .' Ben couldn't finish his sentence due to his laughter.

'He what? Come on, tell me!' Bryony said, tugging at the sleeve of his T-shirt, desperate to hear the end of the story.

'He wet himself!'

Despite being a manly man, Ben was shrieking with laughter, collapsed in a heap on the bed.

Bryony laughed so hard she snorted, and then felt a little embarrassed that she had.

'And he never really lived that down, Bry. He was wearing these little beige shorts and it was so obvious,' Ben said, calming down suddenly and feeling the usual tears start to rise to the back of his eyes. He fought them back. He had to be strong for her.

'Ahhh, that's so sweet,' Bryony said, feeling a familiar shift deep inside. The hungry ache that would materialise whenever she missed Max.

It materialised a lot.

'It carried on into his teens, too. Not the wetting himself, of course, but the nerves around women. Spin the bottle was an absolute no-no.' Ben was deadly serious now as he remembered what Max would look like at their sixth-form parties, clutching a red plastic cup full of beer and trying desperately to hide his teenage insecurities with his trademark cheeky grin. The ironic thing was that his cute shyness had just made girls like him more.

Ben had watched him change from a little shy boy into a young man who had a kind of radioactive confidence.

Bryony cast her mind back to the first time she and Max had kissed. And it *was* she who kissed him first. In the kitchen at a house party, among a sea of beer bottles, bowls of stale cheese twists and the streamers that had splurged from inside a party popper. She suddenly remembered that as she had kissed him, she had held his hand and noticed it was trembling. It had been as if he was terrified.

Bryony felt like there was still so much to learn about Max and, yet again, she felt that sickening longing for him in the pit of her tummy. 'God, I miss him so much,' she said now, shuffling even closer to Ben, hoping she could absorb just a little of Max's youthful energy from him.

Ben was trying his very best to wrestle silently with the monstrous emotions that were gathered in his throat, forming a lump that made it hard to swallow or speak. 'I do, too, Bryony. I understand completely,' he said, as he raised his arm and put it under her neck for her to lie on. She moved so that she could put her head on his shoulder. Ben was so big and muscular that it was a slightly uncomfortable angle, but she just needed to be close to him. To someone. Anyone. Close to anything that was a part of Max.

As she lay there, she remembered how Max's shoulders had been the perfect fit for her. She dreaded the day she would have to find a way to fit into someone else's body. To put her arms around a different frame. To run her lips over skin that could never smell as sweet as Max's did.

Ben said a few words in his head for his lost best friend.

He told him that he was there with Bryony, and that she was safe and well. And he told him how she hadn't lost too much weight, and that everyone was making sure she ate enough. He told him that

235

they missed him more than anything in the world, and that nothing had been right since he'd been taken from them. He told him that he missed his most treasured friend, and didn't know how he would ever really recover from the magnitude of losing him.

'What are you thinking about?' Bryony said suddenly, letting her tears slip onto Ben's top, not even trying to apologise for them or hide them.

'Just Max.' Ben lifted his hand to Bryony's face and swiped a tear away from her cheek. He wondered for a moment if he should tell her what he'd been wanting to tell her for so long. He'd asked Max about it in his prayers a few times, but never seemed to get his consent or his blessing. And it always seemed like the wrong time to mention it to Bryony. He was worried that it was one of those things you should never say to the girlfriend of your late best friend. But he didn't know what the right thing to do was any more. This thing he wanted to say, *needed* to say, wasn't going away.

So he just kept asking Max, hoping that one day he would give him a sign.

CHAPTER 21

WHITE PANTS GONE GREY.

Monday 25 May 2009
Hackney, north east London
6 p.m.

'I think you're making a massive mistake.'

Richard's voice crackled down the line. Rachel pressed her phone harder against her ear as she slid along the red bench at the bus stop to allow an elderly woman some more room. It was a mild day. The sun wasn't out, but the warm rain of the last week had died down, and there was a small interlude of dry weather.

Rachel looked down at her black, knee-high riding boots, which had conveniently come back into fashion, trying to fight back the tears of nervousness that were welling in her eyes. Tears of fear. But she also felt anger creep through her. She was always frustrated at Richard's inability to really be there for her, and she needed him with her today. The fact that he'd quietly declined had maddened her.

She felt herself explode. 'Look,' she whispered angrily, not wanting to be overheard. 'I'm sodding well here now. It's taken a lot to get to this point, Rich, can't you be a bit more supportive? In fact, where the fuck are you today? Couldn't take time out from your busy schedule to be with me? No, of course not, because you're a selfish wanker.'

Rachel suddenly realised she had caught the attention of the elderly lady by her side, who tutted under her breath and shook her permed hair in disapproval. Rachel cringed at the expletives that were tumbling from her mouth, and smiled an apology at the lady.

An articulated lorry roared past them, followed closely by a small motorbike with an engine that sounded like a broken hairdryer. 'Wait, I can't . . . I can't hear you,' Rachel said to Rich, plugging her ears and frowning. 'Say that again,' she added, standing up quickly and starting to pace the pavement behind the bus stop with angry energy.

'I can't be a part of this, Rachel,' Richard's voice came through again, clearly. 'Fair enough, you've tracked down your real mother, that's fine. But you haven't told your mum. It's going to crush her when she finds out,' he said, from the comfort of his favourite pub in the centre of town.

'But, but, she's *not* my mum, and she kept this all from me! What about how *I* felt, when I found out?' Rachel cried, flinging her free hand in the air in utter frustration. The tails of her black jacket, nipped in at the waist, flapped in the breeze as she walked. Her hair, which had been dyed back to blonde, was pulled into a tight ponytail; her skin was free of make-up. Her eyes were puffy because she had been up all night, worrying.

'Well, that's a horrible attitude to take, Rachey. Come on,' Richard said, taking another swig of his pint. Rachel could hear the distinct sound of the glass against his teeth as he gulped.

'OK, OK, I know that sounds bad. But a big part of me doesn't want Mum . . . I mean Rita . . . God, I mean Mum . . . to know, because I want to protect her – don't you get this? Don't you understand that my feelings are conflicting?' she said, crushing an abandoned crisp packet under the toe of her right boot. It made a satisfactory crunching noise, as there had been a few crisps left in the bottom of it.

'Look, I don't know what else to say apart from the fact that I think you should go home, darling. Speak to your mum first, for goodness' sake – you're being really selfish,' Richard said, anger showing in his voice now.

'Oh, oh . . . you know what? Fuck off,' Rachel said, before hanging up on her boyfriend and throwing her phone into her Mulberry bag.

Her stomach plunged in terror. Maybe he was right. Maybe the least she should do was tell Rita about all this. Didn't she owe it to her? But then she imagined her face, the disappointment she would inevitably feel; maybe the anger, even . . . There was a reason that her parents had decided to keep this quiet and she didn't want to interfere with that, despite her fury at learning about her adoption in the way that she had. When she was at home, she locked herself away in her bedroom, trying to fight all the confusion and questions she had, while listening to her favourite bands on repeat.

Getting hold of her birth mother had been surprisingly easy after she had made the decision to do it; it was the decision itself that had been difficult. Rachel had scoured the internet, reading other people's stories; she had scrolled through what felt like hundreds of chat-room discussions and reams of articles from all over the world. She heard how some people regretted finding their real parents because they were rejected by them, or even hated them, causing a whole new level of confusion to add to the already crowded melting pot of emotions. On the other hand, she also read about people who felt it was the best thing they could have done. People who said that finding their real parents had answered all the questions that had troubled them and kept them awake at night. Some people had even managed to form some kind of positive relationship with the parents who had given them up.

Why did she want to find her real mother? Was it to find her real family, to know what they looked like, to find out why she was put up for adoption? Or was it out of spite? She wasn't really sure.

Rachel had started by taking the adoption papers from under the bed again, when Rita and Edward were away for a wedding in Spain. She'd walked down to the local post office and photocopied them, before sliding them back into the filing system, never to be touched again. She had then got in touch with an adoption support agency through a government website and, after being passed from department to department, she had finally been put through to the right one for the area where she was born. She had learned quickly that her birth mother had made it clear that she would be willing to meet her daughter in the future, should she come looking.

Now that time had come.

Rachel knew just a few things. She knew that her mother was called Lisa Reid. There was no mention of her father: the authorities didn't seem to know anything about him. She was given her birth mother's address, which she Googled and realised was a social housing flat in a tower block owned by the council. Her first thoughts were that her real mother was clearly not well off, that maybe her life was a struggle in many respects. It was a bit of an assumption, but a pretty safe one, she reckoned.

Rachel had sent her birth mother a simple letter, explaining who she was, and leaving her mobile number.

Lisa had not called the number for a fortnight, leaving Rachel wondering if she'd had a change of heart. But then, the Sunday before last, a message had come through on her mobile that had instantly made her cry. But they were not tears of happiness, or sadness; more disbelief that this was real. It had simply said, 'HI RACHEL, THIS IS YOUR REEL MOTHER YES. WANT TO MEET UP SOON?'

And that was it. A badly spelled and punctuated message from a stranger. No kiss on the end. It almost seemed too casual, but then what had she expected? Some kind of grovelling apology? Some emoticons, maybe, showing an embarrassed face?

This might all be new to Rachel but, she realised, her birth mother had clearly moved on long ago. She was amazed at how much those few words had told her. Her mother was clearly not well educated, which was fine because not everyone had had that advantage, but it wasn't what she had perhaps expected. She had imagined someone glamorous, someone glossy, who would come over and pick her up in a soft-top BMW and say how it had all been a huge mistake that she really regretted now. She had also thought that maybe her mother was some crazy career bitch, who had given up her child to chase her business dreams at a young age. Or, again, she thought that perhaps her mother was a deeply intelligent woman who she would become friends with; she imagined them taking holidays to Italy on long weekends, shopping, giggling and being really close . . .

But the message she had received painted a different picture. It had struck fear into her soul, and made her think about how different life could have been. She had just assumed she'd been born into the world of Rita and Edward, with their posh cars, nicely decorated house and gold and silver trinkets dotted around the place. They had pushed her to get the most out of her education, her dancing; everything she put her mind to, they had supported.

Did she really want to explore the pathway that could have been hers?

Would she have ended up a professional dancer? Would this Lisa lady, her real mother, have driven her up and down the country to auditions, and even slept in the car overnight when she took part in training sessions at prestigious day schools that often carried on into the early hours of the morning, as Rita had done, time and again?

Would Lisa have even encouraged her to dance?

Rachel turned back to face the bus stop and noticed that everyone who had been waiting had gone. Possibly long gone. She looked at her watch. She had been standing staring at the pavement for fifteen whole minutes. She looked up at the sky. It was now overcast and threatening.

'Right. Come on, let's do this,' she said to herself quietly, unsure of who she was talking to. She was so nervous she was struggling to do basic things like cross the road – she stepped out in front of a cyclist who swerved violently to avoid her, and then nearly crashed again as he threw a series of insulting hand gestures her way as he departed.

She felt around in her bag for the map she had printed to help her find her mother's flat. It was times like these she resented the trend for large handbags. She could feel a ridiculous assortment of useless items at her fingertips: an emergency bottle opener, a pack of Marlboro Gold, a tube of bright blue eye-shadow, six pens, a pack of hair bands, five lighters, the cork from a bottle of celebratory champagne and a miniature, stuffed three-legged donkey given to her by Richard as a good-luck charm. Rachel started to feel her anxiety levels rise as she rummaged around inside her bag, wondering if she'd managed to leave the map at home. Eventually she gave up, and then remembered that she'd tucked it into her purse.

It was only a five-minute walk from the bus stop, but it was a difficult one. She was so nervous that her legs were shaking. Soon enough, she reached Chestnut Court. When she'd first read the address, she had thought it sounded like a pretty place with large lush trees, horses and a gaggle of small girls making daisy chains and smiling.

It wasn't.

She stood at the bottom of the main block of flats and looked up, feeling small. The building was huge, and looked as if it had hundreds of tiny little windows belonging to hundreds of tiny little flats. It was a world away from the life she knew. Some of the windows were smashed, and clothes hung, sagging, from makeshift drying lines as if they had been left there for weeks, in wind and rain. White pants gone grey. Bras with the under-wire missing.

She could make out what sounded like ten different babies screaming in ten different rooms, their cries carrying in the wind from separate flats, along with the laughter of young girls and the thud of music from the bedrooms of rebellious teenage boys. The smell of weed hung faintly in the air.

Rachel looked down at her riding boots and suddenly felt a million miles away from it all.

She was no snob and, in a way, feared that she would be ridiculed by people here; for the way she carried herself and for the way she spoke. She was scared that she might accidentally offend someone, or get herself into trouble.

Her thoughts were interrupted by the scream of a police siren, which hurtled past her on the main road. She felt sick. Plastic bags and empty Coke and beer cans were littered around the estate. As they were dragged over the ground by the wind, they made gentle scraping noises against the concrete. The sky seemed to have suddenly turned a dark grey.

A group of five little boys walked past her, towards the main door at the entrance to the flats. They were wearing tracksuit bottoms made of thin fabric and T-shirts, despite the threat of rain, but they looked and sounded happy as they chattered about their day at school, thumping a football to the ground as they walked, the noise echoing loudly.

'Carl!' came the loud shout of a woman who was leaning from the balcony of a flat on the second floor, her hair scraped back tight against her skull.

'Yeah, Mum, I'm here!' shouted one of the boys, whose body language had stiffened somewhat. His friends stopped bashing the ball against the ground and looked down at their feet, trying not to get involved.

'Get inside now, please. Where 'ave you been?' she screamed.

The boy didn't reply, but just high-fived one of his friends before running in through the main door.

The car park, Bryony noticed now, was full of dated BMWs and gas company vehicles emblazoned with brightly coloured writing, but all in dire need of a proper wash. A young man who must have been in his late teens was sitting in a van to Rachel's left, filling in some forms with a biro. Judging by his frustrated scratching in the margins of the papers, it was running out. He shook the pen in frustration before throwing it out of the window; it rolled across the ground, stopping at her feet.

Rachel stepped back, wondering if maybe she could just go home and forget about all this. She imagined Rita's face and found it difficult to proceed. Then she imagined her father Edward's features crumpling in horror at the fact that she had discovered the family's huge secret.

She took another step back, and then another, her legs twitching, urging her to leave.

CHAPTER 22

IT WAS UNTHINKABLE.

Tuesday 26 May 2009
Angel, north London
2.30 p.m.

'Come with me.'

That was all he said as he stood in front of Bryony, his black apron covered in chocolate dust and with a large smudge of the same across his left cheek, all caught in stubble and magnificence. His body language oozed confidence: a sexy grin, arms slightly out, legs shoulder-width apart, palms open. The stance of the self-assured.

But there was something in his eyes, a flicker of fear, because she might just say no.

'Where to?' Bryony asked, looking up from the tattered pages of her book, a blank expression on her face.

'The kitchen,' he said, the fear now spreading slightly into his limbs. It was amazing how much the body could express without using the mouth.

'Why?' Bryony asked. Still no expression on her face.

'Because I'm making cookies, oh and my name's Adam, by the way,' he said, his voice squeaking like a broken accordion in the middle of the word 'Adam', causing a violent crimson to spread across his cheeks. 'Adam,' he repeated, clearing his throat and saying his name in a much deeper voice this time, smiling to himself, eyes averted to the floor. A look of embarrassment.

Bryony didn't know what it was about this guy. She had been dragging her sorry self to the café several times a week since Max had been killed, gulping lattes until she trembled and pretending to read dozens of books, when actually she just re-read the same lines of *Pride and Prejudice* over and over again.

But he kept coming back, offering her cream she didn't want, chocolate eggs at Easter, and now, he was bothering her with cookies.

'Sorry . . . don't worry about it – I can see you're busy,' he said now, a crestfallen expression on his face.

Bryony suddenly felt bad. Here was someone trying to reach out to her, someone who actually wanted to spend time with her despite all the misery, moping and crumpled tissues. Her eyes met his and she wondered what to do. She wondered if maybe it was time for her to start connecting with the outside world.

He started to turn around to walk away.

'Wait.'

One word. It just came out of her mouth.

He turned around slowly to face her, and there was a sparkle in his eyes.

'Can I help?' she asked, putting her book down on the table.

'Yes, that's just what I hoped,' he said, reaching down, grabbing her hand and whisking her away to the kitchen.

It was so sudden, and exciting, that she left her bag right there under the table. She didn't care about stuff like that any more, anyway; after losing Max, a phone or a wallet going missing seemed like pointless things to worry about.

'Won't your boss mind?' Bryony asked, walking under a row of pans hanging from a rack at the entrance to the kitchen, a huge smile on her face. She pulled a band from around her wrist and tied her hair in a loose bun, looking down at her black smock dress and wondering how messy this could get.

'She's not around,' he said, his cheeky grin returning yet again.

Bryony felt bad all of a sudden. Here she was connecting with another man, even in this small way, and it felt awful. Would Max be angry at her if he could see this? *Jealous, even?* she wondered. She tried to push the thought out of her mind because she knew it wasn't rational. Bryony would never get involved romantically with another man. She knew this, just like she knew there were 360 degrees in a circle. It was unthinkable. She had resigned herself to a lifetime of romantic barrenness, because nothing and no one would or could ever be, or measure up to, Max. *So this is fine*, she reasoned. She was just making a new friend. *Although he is pretty good looking,* she thought, dismissing the idea from her mind as quickly as it had entered.

'Right, stick these gloves on,' he said, lobbing a pair of thin, see-through monstrosities at her, the fingers of which stuck to her light pink lipstick as they rolled off her mouth.

She looked unimpressed again.

Bryony picked them off the top of her dress and put them on.

'What are the cookies for?'

'Just wanted to try something new – it's a bit of an experiment, really. I'm a bit bored today, surprisingly enough,' he said, rubbing his hands together and staring hungrily at a huge pile of pre-rolled dough.

Bryony looked at a tray of heart-shaped cookies; it reminded her of Valentine's Day. A sharp pain rose inside her: *Valentine's Day* . . . She wondered if she could leave, make some kind of excuse. Last Valentine's Day, Max had taken her out for her favourite food, a curry. They had drunk beer and eaten until they were bursting, and then stumbled home at 2 a.m. It had been another blissful night in a patchwork of stunning memories they had made. And neither of them had had a clue that in a matter of weeks he would be gone. For ever.

'Are you OK?' he asked, looking at her and then

down to a heart-shaped cutter in his hand. He ran his fingers over the metal of the instrument, and turned it around in his rough-looking palms, pouting slightly as if in thought.

Bryony had to be strong. *Life must go on*, she thought. For the rest of hers there would be Valentine's Days and Christmases, and Easters, and weddings that weren't theirs, and baby showers for other people's growing families, and somehow she was just going to have to cope with all that.

This would be a good place to start.

'Yes. Yes, I'm fine. Thank you. So what do I do?' Bryony asked, flexing her fingers in the gloves and faking a smile.

'Could you cut out heart shapes in this bit of dough, please? I'm going to start icing the ones that have just come out of the oven,' he said, pulling a tray of delicious-smelling cookies from a shelf.

OK. I can do this, Bryony thought. She pushed the cutter down, deep into the dough, shaking it a little when she felt it hit the greaseproof paper beneath so the edges would be clean and neat.

'So, tell me about yourself. You've been coming in here a lot – what do you do?' he asked, leaning close to a row of baked cookies and starting to pipe on some icing.

'I work in PR for a charity. I have this week off though, just to spend some time relaxing.' *Bullshit*, Bryony thought. She had this week off because she'd been really low again, so had been signed off. She'd hardly been back to work since Max died anyway, certainly not for more than a day or two in a row; it was almost a farce that she was still a member of staff there, but she appreciated how understanding her boss was.

Still, while she had been sobbing into tissues he probably thought she'd been lunching with friends and visiting museums, going to the pub and having fun.

'OK, PR sounds cool. Do you live round here?' he asked, accidentally squirting too much of the red icing onto one of the cookies and tutting under his breath.

'Not really. I live in Finsbury Park.'

'Really? Why do you come to this café so often, then?'

Shit, here we go, she thought . . . 'Oh, erm, my grandmother lives nearby so I visit her and then come here, or come here and visit her, whichever way round . . .' Bryony said quietly, hating the dishonesty. She didn't even have a grandmother. Her father's mother had died before she was born and her mother's mum had passed away right in front of her when she was eight years old and talking to her – literally to death, as it turned out – about a Barbie she had wanted but didn't get for her birthday. Bryony had always felt bad that her grandmother's last seconds had been accompanied by her selfish whining. So often she had reluctantly visited her grandmother's cigarette-smoke-filled flat as a child, frustrated by how tired she was all the time and the patches in her memory that stopped Bryony from getting the things she asked for at Christmas. Guilt filled her heart every time she remembered stealing cupcakes from her grandmother's plate while she dozed off.

'Oh, right. That's nice of you,' he said, looking at Bryony like she was an angel.

She cringed inside. 'How about you?' she quickly changed the subject.

'Well, I'm studying for a masters in chemistry, and working here, obviously. I live just a few roads away,' he said, casually, like studying for a masters and dealing with the everyday moaning of the public was no big thing.

Bryony suddenly felt very small. 'Wow, that's amazing,' she said.

'Who do you live with?' he asked now, stepping behind her and ushering her to his left with a gentle hand on her waist. It made Bryony jump a little, but she obliged and swapped tasks with him. She was now facing a huge pile of new cookies that needed icing.

'Oh, I live alone,' she said.

'That must be really nice,' he replied, raising his eyebrows in envy and passing the piping tool to her.

Nice. It wasn't *nice*. 'Nice' was not the word to describe the nights she spent lying on the sofa and aching for Max to come back, wishing that he would just knock on the door and tell her this was all some kind of sick joke. 'Nice' was not the word to describe the night terrors she'd experience, when she woke up clawing at the sheets and panting violently into the humid air of the bedroom she and Max used to share, taking in huge gulps of her own stale breath.

'Yes, it's lovely,' she said, pushing her fingers into the tube and feeling the red icing shift and move beneath her fingertips. 'What do you need on these?'

'"I love you", please,' he said, going red.

I love you.

I love you.

Flashbacks surged in Bryony's mind. She had to push them away – *Ask him a question, any question,* she thought, anything, anything to stop her mind rushing away from her. Pulling her back. Back. Backwards.

'Who do *you* live with?' Bryony asked, her voice wavering dangerously. She leant forwards and started drawing the 'I'. It came out terribly. *A wobbly, shit, fucking mess,* she thought. Max had told Bryony he loved her for the first time in Tesco. She would never forget it.

'I love hummus, Max,' she had sighed, staring longingly at the stuff piled high in plastic tubs and twisting a lock of her hair thoughtfully in her hand.

He had been clinging onto a basket full of wine, beer and pasta. 'And I love you,' he had replied.

'What?'

'I said, er, I love cheese.'

'No, you didn't.'

'No, you're right. I didn't.'

The sick feeling returned to Bryony's stomach. Panic started pushing the blood around her veins, her heart pumping faster and faster.

'I live with a couple of housemates,' Adam said, breaking her spiral of hysteria as she kept piping out wobbly letters that would be totally unsellable to the public. They looked rubbish.

'Good fun?' she gasped out, clinging to the normality of the conversation.

'No, it's crap, actually. Neither of them know how to use a vacuum cleaner or have any idea where the sink is located. It's hard work,' he said, moving the pre-cut cookies onto a baking tray and eyeing up Bryony's disastrous attempts to write romantic messages on foodstuff. Then he steeled himself. 'Well, with all this sloppy bullshit,' he asked, 'I have to ask, do you have a boyfriend?'

'No,' she said, breathing more easily – the panic was letting go of her. 'How about you? Got a girl-friend?' she asked him, continuing with the mechanical motion of conversation. Back and forth. Ping pong.

'Oh, no,' he said sternly, leaning over the counter and squinting again at the treats. His arms were lithe, but strong. Little muscles twitched and flexed beneath his skin as he started to cut dough again.

There was an awkward silence.

'I mean, I've had girlfriends,' he said hastily, 'but I've just had so many bad relationships. Disastrous, actually. I'm on leave from women, signed off for the foreseeable future.' He laughed, standing up straight again and looking flustered. A hot redness was tickling the skin of his cheeks. 'Sorry, that makes me sound like a bit of a bastard. Basically, I fear relationships because as soon as things get serious, they go wrong . . . I just want good friends around me for now,' he said, starting to relax as he explained himself better.

Bryony was quietly relieved. *He must have gone through some shit,* she thought. 'No, I get it. Completely,' she said, picking up one of the cookies and taking a small bite.

CHAPTER 23

SHE KNEW THAT HAT WELL.

Sunday 24 May 2009
Finsbury Park, north London
8 a.m.

Tynice Hendry was dressed mostly in black. She wore a black pencil skirt that ended below the knee, with a black blazer, cream blouse and a small, formal, petrol-blue hat. She'd always made an effort for church, but this was the first time she had been since early March. Her thick, dark brown hair was pulled into a neat bun. She looked a little like she was attending a funeral.

Father John Dewry stood in front of her. She was perched nervously on a pew right at the front of the huge church, blazing sunshine hitting the stained-glass windows and filling the place with the majestic light she had missed so much.

It was just over an hour until the usual members of the congregation would flock into the room: beautiful, giggling, suited and booted children, elderly ladies in their Sunday best, younger men and women draped in finery, all ready to have their weekly celebration with God.

Tynice didn't want to see any of them. She needed to have this meeting away from the prying eyes and ears of the community. And, she hoped, away from judgment . . .

'Hello, Mrs Hendry. I'm glad to see you this morning,' said Father Dewry now, his hands clasped together in front of his long black robes.

Tynice bowed her head a little, as if in shame. She moved her foot forward, and the heel of her shoe made a sharp, scraping noise against the dark red tiles on the floor. She flinched a little, somewhat apologetically. 'I am so sorry I haven't been here for such a long time, Father,' she said, unable to look him in the eye. She pulled the knee of her tights nervously with her fingers, as she had used to as a teenager.

Father Dewry paused briefly, as if considering what he was going to say, smoothing down his short, grey hair with his right hand. His face was thin, pale and drawn, his eyes a cool shade of grey. He seemed to look even older than he had back in March, but maybe that was just the way she looked out on the world now. Everything had changed.

'I understand that circumstances have been somewhat unusual for you, Mrs Hendry, and I can assure you that you, Reb and Keon have been very much missed in the church community,' he said matter-of-factly, his voice dancing with its own gentle meaning in the enormity of the nave.

Its sound gave Tynice the strength to raise her

head. Summer flowers, which had been arranged beautifully by dedicated volunteers, stood proudly on top of plinths. They gave comfort to her; she didn't know why and, all of a sudden, a tear fell from her eye. She mopped it up quickly with a white, starched handkerchief. Her emotions had risen to the surface – far too quickly for her liking – but Father Dewry's words had cut right to the core of her. There was a level of kindness and forgiveness in them that was bigger than she was, and all she could ever imagine giving to humanity.

Tynice had avoided church ever since the shooting. The Sunday community, which once had felt like a happy family, had seemed a dark and foreboding place. Everyone knew what had happened, from the postmistress to the local barber. Her little boy's face had been plastered all over the papers, both local and national. In fact, most people now knew who he was – but for all the wrong reasons. And while no one had outwardly berated or criticised her as she had feared, when she saw acquaintances in corner shops and super-markets, they hadn't come over to say hello, either. Her local area had, all of a sudden, become jam-packed with strangers who had once been friends.

Her daughter had the same problems at school, too. The girls in her class had turned their heads away; the friends who used to chatter away tire-lessly with her suddenly had nothing more to say. In shops they averted their eyes and focused on something else – cereal packets, cigarette lighters, shampoo bottles – whatever they could look at so they could pretend they hadn't seen Reb – someone they had always been proud to call a friend. Until 'that' had happened.

It had been a painful reaction.

'Thank you for your words,' Tynice said, gathering herself together just enough to be able to speak clearly and coherently. 'I don't think you will ever know how much they mean.'

'I was so dreadfully sorry to hear about what happened,' Father Dewry said, moving around the end of the pew and sitting next to her, so they were equal. His robes sank down heavily, like a last breath. He hadn't wanted to stand over her, like some judgmental figure. He was well respected in the parish, and he was quietly aware that the main reason for that was because he knew that he was human too, and must be a friend on the same level. He placed his palms on the cool wood of the pew and listened to the sound of her crying.

He'd offered to go round and see her just after it all happened, but she was too ashamed to take him up on it.

'The thing is . . . the thing is . . .' Tynice said, her face sinking into her handkerchief again and screwing up into what seemed like the dozens of new wrinkles she hadn't had last year, 'I just can't forgive my son,' she blurted, between heavy breaths. Her chest rose up and down, as if she was trying to swim against a heavy tide, battling something bigger and much more powerful than herself. 'I haven't been to see him. Not once. I can't, Father. I'm *scared* of him, and what he did,' she finished, her carefully applied make-up now running down her cheeks, leaving sooty smears.

Father Dewry ran his thin, dry hands down his face, pulling his cheeks even further towards the ground. There was a look of desperation in his eyes, but Tynice didn't see it because she still couldn't look into them.

'I can't be OK with him, I can't be around him, or even look at him,' she added.

An elderly lady, whose back was hunched, scuttled out of a small back room clutching a cup of tea on a saucer, which rattled as her hands shook. She limped towards Tynice, hesitating slightly as she saw the woman's outpouring of emotion, before proceeding and placing the tea down on the bench beside her with a loud clatter.

'Thank you,' Tynice said, bobbing her head in thanks before the lady made quickly away, ducking in between a pair of huge, red curtains to some mysterious part of the church where people didn't usually go. Keon had always asked about that part of church when he was a child, and Tynice had never known what to say in response; brushing his questions off and not feeding his curiosities. She felt bad for that.

It was one of the many thoughts she'd had while lying awake at night, wondering if all that had happened was her fault. Keon had been an exceptionally inquisitive child up until the age of ten, asking so many questions about the world that she had felt exhausted by it and shocked at her own lack of knowledge. When he asked about how the moon 'hung in the sky' at the age of five, she had found herself consulting library books to come up with the answer. Her cheeks had reddened on the bus when he had shouted out for the answer to seven times nine, and she hadn't known. 'Shh, Keon, baby,' she had whispered instead, staring out of the window and ignoring the question, while fellow passengers had tilted their heads to one side and smiled at him. He had been beautiful as a child. She could still remember staring at him as he watched Saturday-morning TV and being so overwhelmed with pride that it had hurt. Everything had been a mystery to him to be discovered, and she had thought that this could be a sign of a unique intelligence and thirst for information that had never really presented itself in the family before. Their family was from a humble background and no one had ever gone on to university or to have big careers or posh titles; she had thought that maybe Keon would be the one to break that mould. However, she had found herself quietly disappointed when this had all melted away in his early teens, and her efforts to get him to do his homework after school had been met with loud protests and slammed doors.

'Accepting what someone has done, especially in this case, is very difficult, Mrs Hendry, and I imagine your situation to be a deeply challenging one, to say the least. I think you need time, I really do.'

'But it's been a long time now, well, for a family – many weeks. Have I done wrong in not supporting my son? I just keep thinking about the poor man, Max Tooley. He was a good man . . . I can't get his face out of my mind. It's there all the time. It's just dreadful. I just don't know why Keon did it – I don't feel like I know anything, any more.'

'And you haven't tried to visit your son?' the father asked, gently.

'No. I'm too angry at him, and I'm afraid of what I might say to him, and how I might feel afterwards.'

'Do you think maybe you can try?'

'I don't think I want to, not yet. Can you actually forgive your own family for doing something so monstrous? Do you think that it's possible?'

'Well, yes, of course, Mrs Hendry. That's the thing about family, and friendship, too. You would be surprised at how cleansing it can be to cast aside that anger and hurt, and forgive. I feel it would be very good for your son, too . . .' He trailed off.

Tynice suddenly found herself almost angry at how simple he made this sound. At how much he seemed to be sympathising with Keon. At how bad this all looked on her, when all she'd ever tried to do was bring Keon up to be a wonderful young man.

264

She felt ashamed that she had not done it yet.

She took a deep gulp of her tea, and felt the hot, sweet taste soothe her conflicting emotions. Tynice had seen Keon's ex-girlfriend Charlotte in the post office last week, smiling and joking while talking on the phone. She remembered this now, and was taken back to the first time Keon had introduced Charlotte to her, and how beautiful she was. Tynice had really thought he might grow up to be a good man . . .

Her thoughts were interrupted.

'Do you think you can start coming back to church, Mrs Hendry?'

She thought about this for a moment. Would people leave huge gaps of empty pew space either side of her in the congregation? Would they ignore her in the coffee morning after the service? Would they be cold to her, like she'd been to her own son?

'I'm not ready yet. I'm sorry. In fact, I have to go before everyone gets here,' she said, looking down at her small black watch and feeling a sense of dread and urgency.

'How about Reb? Don't you think this would be good for her?' Father Dewry probed further.

'Perhaps. I'll speak to her this evening and see how she feels about it,' Tynice said, knowing that Reb probably wouldn't go back, not without her. This tragedy had taken its toll on her, too. She was half the young lady she used to be, and that in itself was a huge challenge for a mother to face.

'Look, I should get going—' Tynice said, starting to rise to her feet.

'Before you go, you are always welcome here, always. As for forgiveness, that may come in time, and I hope very much for you that it does,' he said, his voice deep, quiet, each word beautifully pronounced, in the style of a man who speaks truth and wisdom to people who may or may not be willing to take it on board.

'Thank you. And thanks for your time this morning, Father. I hope I will be back soon,' Tynice said. She walked delicately through the small space in front of the pew and towards the back of the church. Her heels clicked loudly, getting quieter and quieter as she exited the building.

Father John stayed seated for several minutes, quietly thinking to himself.

Tynice thought she had got away without being spotted by any of her old friends, but the sight of a pink hat in the street outside the church made her stomach plunge suddenly.

She knew that hat well. She'd even admired it and tried it on herself.

It belonged to Maggie Brewster, a forty-year-old woman who had been one of her best friends at church. Just the sight of it made her hurt deep inside – Maggie's was one of the faces she most resented not turning up at her door to offer her some kind of friendship and support.

The hat bobbed up and down energetically as

Maggie walked, saying so much about the wearer's demeanour. Maggie had seemingly boundless energy. They had sung together in the church choir for years, arm in arm.

Tynice froze on the spot. She had to turn around and go another way, she realised. She had to leave. She spun around quickly and started to walk in the other direction, but a loud call stopped her in her tracks.

'Tynice! Tynice, is that you?' shouted Maggie, now jerking her head up and down, squinting her eyes and trying to get a better look through the small crowd of people milling about on the pavement by a bus stop.

Tynice turned around slowly. She didn't know how to feel.

Maggie broke into a gentle run, her light pink skirt trailing behind her, the fabric of her jacket flapping. Her expression was one of happiness, steeped in serious concern. *It's lucky that she's alone*, Tynice thought; she couldn't have dealt with seeing all the other women from church as well. All the other people she felt had let her down so badly.

Maggie barged through the people and bounded towards Tynice, grabbing her arms with both hands and pulling her close into her ample and somewhat overpowering chest so that there was no escape. Tynice turned her head away, and stared at the road.

'Oh, Ty, you have no idea how pleased I am to

see you!' Maggie's wide smile was encased in bright red lipstick, while her eyes were flickering with sadness and concern, despite the smile.

Tynice turned to face her, tears rolling down her cheeks.

'Why haven't you come here, why? We've missed you so much, Ty – we want you here,' Maggie said, shaking her arms a little to gently reassure her of the fact.

Part of Tynice wanted to melt into her embrace, let bygones be bygones and believe what she wanted to believe, but her anger was boiling in her chest. She had come to realise how little the values of church must have meant to her friends, who had slunk away into the undergrowth; and also to her, as she'd abandoned her son in his greatest hour of need.

'You know where I live, right?' Tynice said now, her sudden fury making her voice tremble.

Maggie looked down at the ground and bit her bottom lip. 'Well, yes . . . of course I know where you live,' she said, quietly.

Tynice stared at the soft skin of Maggie's eyelids, her whole body starting to shake with the reality of her anger. 'Well, where the hell were you, then?' she shouted, before yanking her arms free of her friend's strong grip and storming off.

CHAPTER 24

WICKED GAME.

Saturday 30 May 2009
Screen on the Green, Angel, north London
8 p.m.

'Why are you wearing your sunglasses inside the cinema, Bryony? You look like a prat,' Adam said, laughing and flicking a puff of popcorn at her face.

The chunk sailed through the air, hit the edge of her Ray-Ban Wayfarers, bounced off and landed on the scratchy carpet of the vintage cinema.

'I'll do what I like, thank you very much,' Bryony said, staring at the screen, which was playing the trailer for a new Pixar film.

There were only about twenty other people in the cinema, stretched out like sleepy cats in the large, worn seats, scruffy feet rested casually on the headrests of the rows in front of them. The gentle clinking of glasses could be heard from the bar behind them, and there was a low hum of conversation and laughter.

'No, seriously, Bryony. It's weird. Why are you doing that? You wear those bloody things everywhere,'

Adam said. He sat up straight and started squeaking away in his mock-woman voice, his right hand flapping through the air in front of him. 'Hello. I'm Bryony. I'm a celebrity and I'm far too cool for full vision,' he babbled, making Bryony laugh.

'Stop that!' she yelped, looking at him through the darkness of the lenses. She smiled a half-grin that gently pulled at the corner of her mouth as if it was lifted by invisible string.

Adam tried to pull the sunglasses away from her face but Bryony slapped his arm gently and slid them back up her nose, focusing on the screen again.

'OK, well. Suit yourself. Be weird,' Adam said, shovelling a handful of popcorn into his mouth. 'Next time we go out I shall humiliate you too, by wearing a cow outfit complete with tail. We'll be the coolest kids in town . . .' he muttered, between mouthfuls of salted corn.

Bryony sighed inaudibly. She couldn't tell Adam the real reason why she wore the glasses so often. That she was prone to tears at random times, and this was the only way to stop people gawping at her, or offering her the tissues they found languishing at the bottom of their handbags, smelling of cigarettes and Chanel Number Five.

When it came to Adam, she needed to escape her troubles, and if he knew about Max she would never be able to do that. He would start pussy-footing around her like everyone else did, tilting his head to one side over coffee and talking about how sad it all was. Granted, she needed that sometimes, but she also wanted a friendship that wouldn't be tainted with the tragedy of her past.

'Right, Bryony, we're going to play a game,' Adam said, whispering in her ear now as the curtains started to open.

She slowly moved her head closer to his so she could hear what he was saying.

'Seeing as you insist on being so damn mysterious, we are going to pretend we don't know each other. A little make-believe. Use your imagination . . .'

'Is this some kind of lame and gross attempt at picking me up, Adam?' she said, raising an eyebrow above the frame of her sunglasses.

The lights dimmed.

'Hell, no. I don't trust women who can't make eye contact,' he said, squeezing her arm gently. He smelt of delicious aftershave, which danced through the small space between them, tickling her nose with spicily sexy notes of wood and citrus. 'So when I come back from the toilet, I am no longer Adam. OK?'

'Fine, whatever,' Bryony said, suddenly starting to panic that she might not be able to make up an exciting enough identity. Which was ironic, she realised, as she was already pretending enough with him as it was.

The three minutes that Adam spent in the toilet felt like an eternity.

She could be a secret detective, but that seemed a little too clichéd. She could be a world leader, but she was pretty sure she didn't have the political knowledge to back it up.

The first scene of the film was playing out on the screen. A woman was singing into a microphone in a glittery dress.

That was it. Inspiration. She didn't have to search too far.

Adam shuffled quietly back into the cinema, and made his way back to his seat.

'Well, hello there. You seem to be sitting in my seat – there has been a mix-up of some kind, no?' he asked, leaning down and whispering into her ear.

A man sitting behind them cleared his throat, irritated by all the shuffling around and muttering.

'No. I do believe this is my seat. You are sadly mistaken,' she said, still looking at the screen. Adam watched as the light flickered on her face, her perfect nose set against the inky darkness to her right. 'You may sit next to me if you wish, but do be prepared for the rumours that could start. If we are photographed together, we could be in all sorts of trouble.'

Adam sank into his seat, putting the popcorn on his lap again. 'Rumours? What rumours?'

'Do you not know who I am?' Bryony gasped, sliding her glasses down her nose elegantly, staring at Adam with faux disgust.

'No. I don't believe I do. Who are you?'

Bryony put the glasses back on. 'I am Leila White, the Grammy-award-winning singer with five platinum albums under her belt and a well-publicised addiction to sleeping pills. In five years' time, I will be admitted to hospital for that very reason, before throwing in the towel on the career I worked so hard for, and buying a zoo,' she whispered.

'Oh, good lord, Miss White. How could I have not recognised you? You look so much more beautiful in the flesh. Clearly the camera fails to capture you at your best,' Adam said, extending a hand to shake hers.

She snubbed him.

'And who are you?' she asked.

'You might have heard of me. I am Tyson Row, bodyguard to the stars. Beneath my T-shirt is a bulletproof vest, and underneath the jeans? A pair of custom-made, bulletproof pants,' he said, deadpan. He was beautifully well spoken, and his tone of voice just added to the comedy of it all.

Bryony started to giggle at the imagery, but composed herself again.

'Excuse me,' came the voice of the man behind them.

Bryony and Adam turned around in unison.

The man had leant forward in his seat. 'Would you mind possibly shutting the fuck up, please?' the stranger said, before calmly leaning back again.

They turned around and stayed silent for a minute or two.

'Well, Miss White, this film looks shockingly bad already, and I believe you have a gig tonight. Is that correct?'

Bryony silently agreed that the film was failing to hold her attention in any real way, and leant down to grab her bag.

'Well, yes, you're right, and I'm running late,' she said, looking down at a £15,000 diamond-encrusted watch that wasn't there.

The man behind them moved forward again, and cleared his throat. 'Yes, all right, mate, calm down, we're leaving,' Adam growled, before he had time to open his mouth.

The man looked affronted but shuffled back down into the depths of his chair, his neck disappearing like a tortoise withdrawing into its shell.

Adam and Bryony tiptoed out of the cinema and into the gentle night. It had been a warm day and the heat still danced in the air, doing a tango with intermittent currents of a cooler breeze.

'So, will you be my bodyguard tonight? Mine's off with gout,' Bryony asked, crossing her arms and smiling.

They faced each other in front of the cinema, the huge red neon sign behind them reminiscent of fun and fairground rides. Taxis and buses chugged past them, and laughter and cheering trickled from a nearby bar.

'Well, of course – I will be by your side at all times,' Adam said, straightening his jacket and puffing out his chest. 'First of all, does the lady need any filtered water before the big show?' he asked, as they started to walk, gesturing towards a newsagent in the near distance.

'Yes, certainly. Take me there.' The pair strutted down the road, full of their own fictional importance.

Bryony, in particular, was loving every moment, and pulled her thick, grey cardigan over her shoulders. Luckily she was dressed for the occasion, with a classy black top underneath her jumper and a pair of black skinny jeans and silver heels.

The shades went back on.

The couple walked into the newsagent and was greeted by the sight of a small queue at the till, comprising three grumpy-looking teenagers, a woman who was so drunk already she was tottering around in her heels, and a short, fat man with big, round glasses.

'Excuse me . . . sorry, guys. Celebrity coming through. The limo broke down, she's on the way to her show and we're running late,' Adam said, gently ushering the people out of the way, and spreading his arm so that Bryony could waltz through.

She felt more than a little embarrassed, but the reaction was priceless. Bryony had the kind of classical beauty that could easily have seen her gracing the pages of magazines and, paired with the shades, was clearly enough to make these people wonder if indeed she could be a star.

The teenagers studied her carefully, trying to find a hint of familiarity.

'A celebrity! Who is she then? I can't tell 'cause of the glasses,' the drunk woman started to shriek, staggering forward and grinning wildly, almost knocking over a rack of cereal bars.

The shopkeeper started to smile, and stood to attention.

'Now, calm down please – we'll only be a moment,' Adam said, in the poshest voice he could muster.

'I think it's that bird off the telly,' one of the teenagers said, his hand on his chin.

'Which bird?'

'Oh, you know . . . er, that singing programme,' the boy said, starting to nod his head in some kind of recognition.

Bryony wanted to laugh out loud. She secretly thought that people always believed what they wanted to believe.

The fat man piped up, 'Oh, come on, seriously? I don't recognise her, and none of you seems to be able to name her,' he said, shifting his weight irritably.

'Yeah, but to be fair, she's got some massive shades on. Who are you, love?' the woman chimed in.

Bryony stayed silent while she pushed a bottle of

water over the counter and reached into her handbag to pay. Adam was standing behind her, protectively, his hands on his hips and a serious expression all over his face.

'Oh, no, madam. You don't need to pay,' the shopkeeper said, all starry-eyed and excited.

'No, no, I insist,' Bryony said, before handing him a pound coin.

The shopkeeper leant back and shouted in the direction of a small door at the back of the shop. 'Hey, Rashid. There's a bloody celebrity in here. Come out now,' he shouted, before suddenly realising how inappropriate his reaction was. 'I'm so terribly sorry, madam,' he amended. 'Please do come back soon.'

Bryony turned to leave, but too late. A young man she could only assume was Rashid came dashing out of the back room with a camera.

'Where are they? We need to put this on the pinboard!' he yelled.

Bryony was really struggling to hold it together as the shopkeeper gave her her change, his eyes studying her face. 'I do definitely recognise her, Rashid!' he said, as his colleague came screeching up to the till, totally out of breath.

As soon as Rashid put the camera up to his face, however, Adam shouted that no photos were permitted, and ushered Bryony out of the shop, leaving the customers in a state of bewildered excitement.

When they had turned the corner of the street,

Bryony started to laugh so hard she had to stop walking. Adam was hysterical, too.

'Right, back into character, Bry, back into character,' Adam said, gasping. He straightened up.

Bryony managed to compose herself, and started walking again, with all the mock authority of the celebrity she'd become.

'Oi, can I have an autograph or something!' came the high-pitched cry of the woman who'd been in the shop. Bryony turned around to see her swinging out of the door, clutching the frame and waving wildly with her free hand.

They scuttled off down a side street, hand in hand.

'OK, to the gig,' Adam said, becoming Tyson the bodyguard once more.

They walked past a small row of expensive-looking flats, painted the most perfect shade of white. Soon they joined another road, which was lined with a few bars and small restaurants. There, Adam marched Bryony to a bar nestled between an old pub and a clothes shop. Outside was a sign that read 'Open mic tonight'.

'Oh, no . . . oh, no . . .' Bryony said, grabbing Adam's hand and starting to pull him in the opposite direction.

'Do you have stage fright? I'm surprised, considering your extensive experience performing to huge crowds such as this,' he said, gesturing, leading Bryony's line of vision towards the window.

The bar looked absolutely dire. It was painted red inside, with a few miserable-looking punters seated near the window, staring into their drinks and fiddling with their phones. Posters were hanging limply off the walls. The faint drone of a shockingly bad vocalist was seeping out through the doorway.

Bryony's heart started to thump in her chest. She didn't know Adam well at all – she didn't know how far he might take this.

'Come on, I believe your audience is waiting for you. Look at them, look at the longing in their eyes.'

Bryony peeped through the window again, as a woman who had started to fall sleep, her head resting on her chin, slipped off her own support and awoke with a start.

She took a deep breath. 'OK. OK, I'm ready. Let's do this,' she said, flinging her head up, her heels striking the pavement loudly and storming into the bar. She was pretty sure she could get out of it once inside.

Adam raised his eyebrows, grinned and followed her in.

They sashayed their way through the small sprinkling of people, sticking out like sore thumbs in their trendy clothes and the well-heeled stances of their new identities. The 'singer' had just finished his rendition of Ronan Keating's 'When You Say Nothing At All', and a feeble round of unenthusiastic clapping slowly died down. 'YMCA' came on the sound system.

Bryony found herself struggling a little with the prospect of karaoke. It was something she had always done with Max. But her thoughts were soon pushed away when she noticed a man dressed as a vampire, with a small keyboard hanging around his neck. He was clearly itching to go on next. He kept nervously tapping at the keys with bony fingers, his red cape draped over his slim shoulders. She was intrigued.

As Bryony waited at the bar, Adam went over and whispered in the ear of the event organiser. He was animated, and pointed towards her with passion and persuasion. The man first of all looked confused, before nodding and smiling at her. 'YMCA' had finished, and he made his way to the microphone. Bryony's stomach plunged.

'Ahem . . . ahem,' he said, through the microphone. No one was paying any attention.

Bryony suddenly felt a deep fear rushing through her limbs. Adam turned towards her, rubbing his hands together and laughing mischievously.

'Er, guys?' the man said, the microphone squealing loudly, causing several people to put their hands over their ears and wince. The man tapped the microphone in frustration. 'Hey, listen, yeah?' he said, his cockney accent ever more apparent.

The quiet room actually managed to hush some more.

'There's someone special here tonight, um, apparently. A famous singer from abroad or something

280

– Leila White. I've never heard of her but you might have done. She's gonna sing for us. Thanks.'

The man was socially useless, considering his job.

The words 'famous singer' had managed to rouse the attention of at least half of the bar, and people started clapping and whistling, even though they clearly had no idea who she was.

Bryony suddenly wished she wasn't there. She didn't even know which song she could choose. Song names started rushing through her head as she timidly walked to the small stage set up in one corner, totally forgetting who she was supposed to be.

The organiser was waiting for her by the edge of it.

'Er, can I have a backing track or something?' she whispered.

He looked confused. 'Your mate over there said you were doing this a cappella, love.'

'Aca-what?'

'No backing. Enjoy,' he said, before plodding off to the bar.

'Come on, Leila!' Adam shouted, as she timidly stepped up on the makeshift stage, which looked as if it had been fashioned from unwanted milk crates and gaffer tape.

A few people joined in, and more claps and whistles were heard.

Bryony was so terrified she felt like she might faint. She tried to think of something she could sing. This was going to be terrible.

The lights went down again, and a spotlight was cast in her direction. A tattooed woman, who sat on a tall stool chewing gum and playing with her hair, was operating it.

Bryony's mind went back to all her favourite musical memories: the first time she and Max had danced together at a wedding; the songs she'd sung with her friends into the end of a hairbrush in her early teenage years. And then it came to her. 'Wicked Game'.

She'd once sung this to Max, in the bathroom. He was in the shower and she was sitting on the closed toilet, painting her toenails pink. Bryony hadn't even realised what she was doing. She was relaxed at the time, and he had been bowled over.

'Hi,' she said quietly into the microphone, holding on to it for dear life and smiling.

The room was silent.

'How are we all tonight?' she said formally, too awkward for her own liking. She suddenly detested the sound of her own voice, and wondered how singers got up on stage and had any kind of coherent banter with a crowd of more than fifteen people.

'All right,' a man grunted.

'Great, hey, glad to hear you're all right, yeah?' Bryony said, giving him the thumbs up, desperately trying to warm up her audience. But they remained as cold as the object that had sunk the *Titanic*. Out of the corner of her eye, Bryony saw

282

Adam melt into silent laughter, his hands over his mouth. He was rocking back and forth and shaking.

There was some more silence as Bryony shrivelled inside, blinded by the light glaring in her face and totally unable to cope with this moment of 'fame'. She could feel her knees sweating. *It's always bad when your knees perspire,* she thought.

'Can you get on with it, please!' the vampire man shouted now, obviously desperate to get on stage and do his act.

''Course, yeah, so this is "Wicked Game",' Bryony said, before clearing her throat and taking a deep breath. She closed her eyes, and held the microphone with both hands. She imagined she was in a candlelit room, and that Max was sitting on a chair before her. She imaged his handsome face, and the way he smiled. She imagined she was singing for him.

The first line came out OK, a little wobbly perhaps, but she had a sweet timbre to her voice. She took a deep breath before singing the next line, her eyes still closed. She felt an ache as she saw Max in her mind, smiling and tilting his head to one side, lost in his love and all the admiration that brought.

Her voice started to warm to the song. The notes were perfect. People started craning their necks to see her, and putting their phones down.

The Max in her imagination grinned, and put

his hand up to his face, gently running his fingers over his stubble.

There was a deep, sexy quality to her voice, yet it was sweet and innocent. Adam was no longer finding the situation funny; in fact, the hairs on his arms stood on end.

People nodded to each other and smiled over their pints.

As she sang of love and loss, images of Max's funeral suddenly appeared in Bryony's mind, and she felt a lump of emotion gather in her throat. The black cars, the flowers, the desperate pain of it all.

Adam could feel something in the way she sang. There was something so knowing about the way she was expressing emotions, especially for such a young woman, that it was like she'd been somewhere, or experienced something truly remarkable. Good or bad, he couldn't work it out yet.

Bryony's mind flickered back to the candle-filled room, her eyes still closed. Max was slowly walking towards her as she sang, both hands in his pockets.

Her voice gently hit the high notes, with a beautifully jazzy waver.

She breezed her way through the song, singing in a way she had never thought possible. When she had finished, she opened her eyes, where tears had been forming, not quite big enough to spill onto her cheeks.

She swallowed hard and Max was gone.

People started to cheer and clap. When she looked over at Adam, he was wiping his own tears away with the back of his hand.

CHAPTER 25

SPLIT ENDS.

Friday 5 June 2009
Hackney, north east London
7.30 p.m.

'Who's this?'
A middle-aged woman had answered the door. As she did so, an eye-watering smell of ancient cigarette smoke had tickled Rachel's nostrils.

She stood almost open-mouthed, shocked by what she saw.

Lisa was nothing like the woman she had visualised, in hard-shouldered eighties business suits, sporting a perfectly preened bob. She was short and plump, with lines under her eyes; lines that told their own stories of sleepless nights, stress and worry. Her shoulder-length blonde hair was frizzy and unkempt; Rachel thought of dry grass. Reeds. Split ends. In her hand she clutched a sad-looking roll-up. Her fingers carried the telltale signs of years of smoking; there was a strong yellow tinge to her skin and nails, and her teeth told the same story.

Rachel stared at the woman, taking in her eyes, her nose, her lips, wondering if maybe there had been some mistake. She had just seconds to make a decision, to try and work out if they had anything in common but the blood running through their veins. But she couldn't see anything in this woman's face that resembled hers, apart from the eyes, which were an almost mirror-image reflection.

Rachel's heart sank in disappointment, while a feeling of coldness shot through her body as if she'd plunged into a tank of freezing water.

'Listen, love, I don't take sales callers, all right?' the woman said moodily, reaching for the door-frame, a great drape of fat wobbling beneath her upper arm. Her pink T-shirt was sagging around her stomach, doing nothing for her at all.

'No, wait,' Rachel said, impulsively, pushing her boot out so she could stop the door if she needed to. *People always do that on TV*, she thought fleetingly. But this seemed like an inopportune moment to be doing it: the day you meet your real mother.

The woman opened her door a little wider. She couldn't make out her caller's face because it was shrouded in darkness; the lack of light in the hallway was making it impossible to see clearly. Her own features were locked in a grimace of suspicious hostility.

A toddler suddenly ran out of the room behind her towards the back of her legs and peered through them at the strange girl. She looked sad and sulky and was gripping a giant yellow play-brick. Rachel felt a wave of confusion spread over her. Who was this little girl? Could she be a sibling she'd never met before, or a child her mother was simply babysitting?

The woman stared too, at what she could make out of Rachel: a tall, slim, almost sculpted figure in skinny jeans and a long, grey cardigan.

She watched as Lisa studied her and suddenly felt self-conscious about her expensive-looking boots. They were real leather and cost £600.

'I'm sorry, darlin', but you're going to have to help me out here,' she said, sliding a cigarette between her lips, then leaning down and holding her daughter's podgy hands in her own, squeezing them gently.

'Hi, you're Lisa, I take it?' Rachel asked, feeling nauseous and suddenly guilty. Rita's face flashed before her eyes and she suddenly wanted to call her, and tell her everything. But it was too late.

'Yeah, that's me,' Lisa said, her stomach suddenly plunging with full realisation.

'It's me, Rachel.' She stepped forward, into a shard of natural light that spilled from a hole in the roof of the balcony upstairs, and Lisa suddenly recognised her.

A minor celebrity. A dancer. Her *daughter*.

Lisa's face went pale and she let go of her little girl's hands, pulling her cigarette away from her mouth.

Rachel was unsure if hers was a face of happiness or horror.

'Well, you'd better come in, hadn't you?' Lisa said, smiling weakly and opening her green, cracked front door wide for the daughter she'd never met.

Rachel wondered if she could leave now. Run away again. This wasn't a warm reception. This wasn't the picture she had built up in her head of tearful cuddles, the start of something wonderful. But she knew she had to do this: the curiosity had been eating her alive.

As she looked beyond the doorway she saw a dark flat, full of cigarette smoke; a small, magnolia-painted corridor opening up into what looked like a living room, packed full of mismatched furniture. The edge of a floral sofa was dog-eared, the stuffing spewing out of a corner where the seam had burst under the pressure of the years. It reminded her, sadly, of this woman's face.

This wasn't Rachel's world, but she'd been brought up well enough not to judge. She stepped into the flat timidly, and bent down to remove her boots. The flat was surprisingly cold despite the time of year, and there was a certain dampness in the air. It reminded her of the ageing church halls she had used to dance in as a child, doing spins and turns in a chunky jumper to avoid getting a chill.

'No, don't worry about it, love, there's no point doing that round 'ere,' Lisa said, urging the toddler into the living room ahead of her. The little girl crawled clumsily on her hands and knees, dressed in pink and white stripes and smiling broadly.

Lisa ushered her into the living room, too. As she stepped through the doorway into the room, Rachel was greeted with a shocking mess. A small coffee table was covered in bills and receipts. Four mugs of coffee were balancing precariously on its edge, and a giant TV flickered in the corner, on mute. The floor was littered with packets of baby wipes, stuffed toys with various limbs missing and random shoes.

'Sit down, love,' Lisa said, sinking into the largest sofa herself and swinging her legs around so she was sitting comfortably.

Rachel perched in a creaking armchair, too afraid to sink into it for what might be lurking in its nooks and crannies.

Just as it seemed like they were going to settle down to chat, a sudden look of panic washed over Lisa's face as she looked towards the coffee table. She got up suddenly and moved some paperwork over something Rachel didn't have the time to identify properly. Lisa turned around, put on a fake smile and was seated again.

Rachel thought this was strange, but was too distracted by meeting her real mother for the first time that she soon focused on other things.

'So, you finally came, then?' Lisa asked, with a positive tone to her voice, running her hands through her hair in an unconscious effort to smarten up. Her eyes darted from left to right as she surveyed the carnage she lived in, but there was nothing she could do to make it better now.

'I wish you'd warned me first, I would have at least . . . you know, tidied the bloody place up,' she said, abandoning her scruffy hair for the moment and gesturing at the scene around her.

It was a world away from the clean lines and rich textures of the home Rachel came from. 'Yes, sorry. I've found it difficult to, well, pluck up the courage,' she replied, realising that her hands were resting primly in her lap. She unclasped her fingers.

'Does your mother know you're 'ere?' Lisa asked, with concern.

'Yes, of course she does,' Rachel lied, feeling her cheeks turn red.

'OK, good. It's important she's OK with this. So, what do you want to know?' Lisa asked, in an almost business-like fashion.

It had become apparent to Rachel that this woman was a powerhouse, but just not the kind she had envisaged. Lisa clearly took no shit. There seemed to be no emotion in her, like she was made of the same hard materials that had been piled up high to create this tower block. It was unnerving.

'Well, I would like to know more about you,' Rachel started, suddenly aware that she hadn't even been offered a cup of tea. Tears started to sting her eyes, and she told herself to get it together. To be strong.

'OK, so, I'm Lisa. I'm thirty-eight . . .'

Rachel did the maths in her head, numbers spinning around on a frantic abacus in her mind. *Fifteen. She was fifteen years old when she had me,*

Rachel thought, unable to get her head around the magnitude of that.

'I'm a carer. I have one daughter, Claire – well, sorry, two including you . . . And I'm single, of course,' Lisa continued, looking out of the window at the drab cityscape.

'Ahh, Claire looks lovely,' Rachel said, turning her head towards the child, who was now leaning up against the bills and the paperwork and smiling still. She was amazingly well behaved.

She felt an ache of something. Sadness? Jealousy?

'Well, what I am is pretty boring, really, love. But you . . .' Lisa said, her face suddenly illuminating with some kind of human warmth, 'When I found out your full name, I instantly thought you might be *that* girl . . . I know it might not look like I know anything about ballet, but I've read about you in the magazines. I want the little one to go when she's old enough, if I can find a way to afford it,' she said, her eyes looking down to the floor, before flickering up again and meeting Rachel's with a mix of admiration and awe.

Lisa had changed, suddenly, and Rachel wondered if her initial coldness was because she had been holding all this back.

'It's amazing, really, Rachel . . . I've been hearing about you, reading about you in the papers and stuff, and I never realised you were my . . .' She was unable to finish the sentence.

'You must tell me how you came to be this

dancing girl,' Lisa said, leaning forward and brushing a tear from her cheek.

Rachel's mind scanned back through the years: it was a blur now. A wonderful blur that she felt grateful to have experienced every time she got out of bed in the morning, despite the huffing and the puffing, and the anger. 'Well, errr . . . Mu . . . Mum's always taken me to ballet classes ever since I was old enough to realise I wanted to go. And I loved it – she couldn't drag me away, actually. Every time she came to pick me up I used to go and hide in the dressing room of the halls we danced in, because I didn't want to leave.'

'That's sweet,' Lisa said, pulling a pre-rolled cigarette from a gold tin and lighting it.

'Ever since I was young, really, I was performing good roles in all the productions I was in, and then the next thing I know I was in my early teens and trying out for The Royal Ballet. When I got in, I thought that would be the end of it, but it wasn't, and I just kept going from there,' Rachel said, excitedly now.

'It's incredible, Rachel.' Lisa smiled bravely. 'Your . . . your parents must be so proud of you,' she said, blowing a plume of smoke from her lips. There was a deep longing in her face. But there was a flicker of gratitude, too.

Or was it regret? Rachel wondered, trying to read everything into the woman's demeanour.

'Yes, thank you. They've been amazingly supportive.' Rachel looked down at her lap and hoped she wasn't rubbing salt into Lisa's wounds. Because she must have felt wounded, surely? No one *wants* to give up their child, do they?

As if reading her mind, Lisa said, 'I suppose you want to know what happened.' She turned her head towards the window again, the June evening sun finally coming into the flat and warming her face a little.

'Yes, I would. That would be nice,' Rachel said, bracing herself for what she was about to hear.

Lisa took a deep breath. 'I was fifteen. I was young and stupid, and I got pregnant by this boy – your father, Nigel. And I will tell you this now, because you need to know – he isn't around any more.'

There was silence, only broken by the shuffling of the baby, and a slow, loud ticking from an ancient-looking clock hanging on the far wall.

Dead. Her real father was dead. Rachel just felt a numb haze spreading through her body. Lisa's voice seemed like a far-away echo.

'He was into drugs, he drank too much, and he died when he was twenty-three after an overdose. I'm sorry you had to find out this way. He wasn't a good man, darlin' – I'm not one of those sorts what glorifies people after they're gone,' Lisa said, bluntly. 'If they were good in life they're good in death, but they don't deserve it if they weren't. Do you get me?' she finished, her eyes suddenly narrowing with emotion that was clearly still very close to her heart.

Rachel knew what she meant, however awkwardly it was phrased.

'OK. But what about you? What happened?' Rachel asked, her palms almost dripping with sweat, she was so nervous.

'Well, your father did a disappearing act when I got pregnant, so my mother, your grandmother, Elaine, said we would do it together. The months went by so fast, and I was scared, Rachel. I didn't feel like I could look after you, do you justice and, you know what? I was right, because look at you,' she said, turning back to the beautiful young woman sitting opposite her, tears now streaming down her crinkly cheeks. 'Do you really think you would be all that you are now, love, if I'd brought you up?' she asked.

Rachel didn't know what to say. She had thought about this often. Was it the nurturing and unflappable determination of her parents that had led her to do what she did? Or would she have been discovered anyway, dancing quietly to herself on the balcony of one of these flats, by some ballet talent scout who'd broken down on the road and come knocking for help? It didn't seem likely, but she knew anything was possible. She wondered briefly about paths in life being determined.

'I can't answer that, Lisa. Claire looks beautiful, and I have hope for her,' she replied, looking over to the little girl that could have been her, and who was now shoving a chunk of chocolate cake into her chubby face.

And Rachel *did* have hope for her. There were plenty of people in the world who'd broken the mould. People who had pushed away their barriers and emerged as something totally unexpected.

'When you were born, Mum and I made the decision to have you adopted to a family who could make your life better, and they clearly did,' Lisa said. She was looking glad, but obviously hurt at the same time. 'We didn't have a pot to piss in, and I still don't. I'm knee-deep in debt since the little one's father left me,' she said, gesturing towards the paperwork and grimacing a little. 'It wasn't an easy decision, though, and I've thought about you a lot. And I was nervous about you coming here, because I'm embarrassed,' she added.

Rachel didn't say anything to this, because it was a hard thing to respond to.

'So how did you find out you were adopted?' Lisa asked.

Rachel looked down at her lap. She didn't know what to say.

CHAPTER 26

SHE HAD GONE TOO FAR.

Monday 8 June 2009
Hammersmith, west London
9.30 a.m.

Nora was sniffing again. A lot.

It grated on Bryony's nerves. She knew she couldn't help it, the poor girl. It was a 'perma-cold', that was how she described it. The 365-day-per-year snots. But as she sat at the desk opposite Bryony taking great, sharp, bubbling inward snorts through her nose every twenty seconds, it made Bryony's blood boil.

Bryony looked towards her screen and told herself to stop being such a bitch. She had been a real nightmare lately, she realised, staring at the mouse pointer as she idly traced it over the icons on her desktop. Bryony's mother had been amazingly supportive ever since 'that' day, but even she was growing tired of Bryony's mood swings. Her friends were struggling to handle it all, too. They had tried to get her to go out for a night on the tiles, the kind she used to rally all her friends together for. But they couldn't have been more wrong about a night of vodka-fuelled abandon supposedly making her feel better, she had realised on the first drunken escapade, which had ended with her crying for two hours in the toilet of the club they had been in.

'Right . . . where were we . . . Oh, yes, the organic farms campaign,' Bryony whispered to herself, finally selecting one of the folders and double clicking.

SNIFF.

Oh, there it goes again. Sniffedy fucking sniff, she thought. 'Right, come on, Bryony, concentrate . . . Spring 2010's schedule for promotions should be in a folder on my desktop, if I can just find the damn thing,' she whispered again.

SNIFF.

For fuck's sake, she thought. *Surely no one actually needs to sniff that much? Just focus . . .*

She reminded herself to email Mr Webb about the posters because he hadn't liked the font last time . . .

SNIIIIFFFF.

She was Going. Slowly. Insane.

Must. Not. Flip. Lid, she repeated, in her head.

SNIIIIIIFFFFFFFF.

Right, that's it. 'Nora, *would* you care for some tissues?' Bryony asked, slamming both hands on her desk, aware that she possessed all the subtlety and grace of a one-legged rhinoceros there was such an aggressive tone in her voice.

With the force of her hitting her desk, a model

origami duck that had been taped to the top of her computer screen fell off and landed in her half-empty cup of coffee.

Nora, her cute nose all red, flinched a little. She was the kind of girl who baked cakes and brought them into the office on Fridays, and said 'Oopsy daisy' and 'Fiddlesticks' a lot. Her eyes narrowed and her cheeks flushed a deep pink. Nora was blonde, very blonde, with pale, freckled skin and as a result, whenever she was angry or upset, it really showed on her cheeks. She had once told Bryony that her skin was so sensitive she resembled a supermarket rotisserie chicken within just minutes of sunbathing on holiday. It had made Bryony laugh at the time, but nothing seemed very funny now.

Bryony felt sick as she realised she was being rude to her, but was unable to stop herself.

'I have some, thanks,' Nora said bravely, clearly trying to diffuse the situation, but Bryony could see tears coming to her eyes already.

She was a sensitive type.

But this didn't stop, couldn't stop, Bryony. 'Really? Where? Because you don't seem to have made use of them yet this morning,' she said, fury still coursing through her veins. The almost palpable despair of losing her boyfriend had developed into something altogether more obnoxious and vulgar. Destructive even. It was a toxic rage that Bryony didn't know what to do with.

Nora went quiet and continued typing, while the

rest of the office tried to act like it hadn't heard the outburst. A small radio playing Wham! had been turned down drastically; whoever did it must have known the psychologically damaging effects of exposure to 'Club Tropicana' when (some)one was already in a rage.

Then, a miracle. There was a moment where Nora almost broke into a sniff but stopped herself from carrying it out properly.

Ha! Took care of that *situation*, Bryony thought, starting to compose a new email.

But then David piped up. David, who never, ever, ever made the sodding tea; just expected everyone else to do it. All the time. It was a petty thing that had bugged Bryony for months, way before she had become an irritable monster. She had always found herself slinking into the kitchen to make a round, slamming the cups down on the counter and cursing under her breath about his utter laziness. She'd tried everything: swamping his drink with dozens of sweeteners so he might find her tea so repulsive he would hopefully stop asking, re-using day-old teabags to make his tea, and even over-squeezing the teabags so leaves escaped and floated around in the top. But nothing ever worked. He was one of those hippy-type blokes who thought he was all 'different' and 'cool', but Bryony always found him deeply pretentious. His beard had grown so out of control now he resembled a tramp.

Bryony's rage sparked again as David leant to

his left so he could see around her computer screen. 'Bryony, love, fancy making the tea?' he asked in his deep voice, moving back to type casually as if it was just fine.

But it bloody well isn't, Bryony thought. Today was not a good day to piss her off.

'No, David, I don't. Why don't you fucking well make the tea?' she yelled, typing hard at her keyboard, and pressing enter with wild, angry enthusiasm. She was so fed-up she could burst into tears at any moment.

Bryony knew that people in the office had started to notice she'd been behaving rather strangely lately, collapsing into fits of giggles at inappropriate moments, followed by periods of unbearable fury and sadness. After these would come the unbearable embarrassment at her own behaviour, which would take hours to leave her. But at the time of these episodes, Bryony always felt well within her rights to behave that way, as if the world owed her something and she was perfectly entitled to throw her toys out of the pram.

'Pardon, Bryony?' David asked in his flat voice, which remained a monotone despite his obvious shock.

A few of the girls who sat near them started clearing their throats uncomfortably. One of them darted out of the room to 'make a phone call'.

Nora sniffed again, and then quickly exited before Bryony exploded.

Wise, Bryony thought.

'You heard me,' she said *EastEnders*-style, leaning forward and gritting her teeth.

David's mouth was gaping open now, as if someone had punched him in the stomach. 'Bryony, is everything OK?' he asked finally, after collecting his bottom jaw from the tabletop and composing himself.

Bryony looked over at him. He had a look on his face, a look that said he wouldn't take this kind of shit from anyone else apart from Bryony, because she was damaged goods and this was the kind of thing damaged people do.

This only fuelled the fire. The anger was pulsing inside her now. She wanted to break things. Scream. PMT had nothing on her.

'No, actually, David, of course everything isn't "OK",' she shouted, standing up and leaning over the desk aggressively, pointing a finger and catching the expressions of half horror, half amusement all over her colleagues' faces. Her hands were shaking.

Nora had by now walked back into the room and was standing awkwardly near their block of desks, clutching a roll of toilet paper so she could have something to blow her nose with at all times. Bryony looked up at her, and noticed that her body language was that of fear and upset. She experienced a twinge of guilt, but it still wasn't enough to stop her. She was making a scene and it was too late to do anything about it. A U-turn wasn't an option. She had gone too far.

Cheryl, who normally worked in the accounts

office next door, had also walked into the room. Bryony assumed she'd heard her furious ranting and wanted to come in and check out what was going on. She was nosy like that.

'Hon, I think you should take some time out, you know. You're being quite unreasonable,' she now said in her high-pitched voice, stepping slowly towards Bryony like she was an unexploded bomb.

Hon. *Hon?*

I'll give her Attila the Hun if she isn't careful, Bryony thought, looking at her trembling hand and feeling like an Incredible Hulk-type monster about to burst through her own skin in a patchwork of green fury and bubbling smoke. She then looked at Cheryl's hand and noticed her sparkling engagement ring, and felt another firework go off in her head.

She realised she was so unhappy with her life. With everything. She missed Max too much to function properly and it wasn't getting any easier.

They had promised it would, all those people who told her it would take time and that she wouldn't always feel like this, but they had lied, she realised. She couldn't seem to get any answers to the questions that continued to rattle around in her head, any closure, and yet the answers she needed scared the living daylights out of her. Answers to so many questions. Had this really happened? Why Max? Would she ever feel normal again? She couldn't sleep properly, or eat properly. She couldn't really connect with her friends and family, and it was all building up into a vicious circle she couldn't see any way out of.

Bryony saw herself standing there, wearing a pretty vintage floral shirt and some high-waisted black trousers she had got from Zara on a recent shopping trip, the first since Max's death, trembling like a lunatic with her finger pointed. It was not how she had imagined wearing the outfit when she had stood looking in the changing-room mirror, peering round to see if her bum looked OK. She had pictured herself at work, looking super happy.

'Screw the lot of you,' she said, before storming out of the room and into the corridor.

Screw the lot of you? That's mature, she thought, leaning back against the wall and breathing hard. She imagined everyone in the room eyeing each other. What had they done to deserve that? Nothing.

She tried to make her way to the toilets, her eyes twitching as a result of her emotional outburst. It was hard to walk in a straight line. It was terrifying to be this out of control, so angry that she could trash everything around her, humiliate herself, and scare away the people closest to her. Her anger had come from nowhere. And now all the humiliation was poking at her eyes in the form of tears, trying to find a way out of her body and wash some of the desperation away. More bloody tears. Sloppy, wet tears, running down her face, today and every day since Max had been taken away from her by that scumbag.

She threw the weight of her body into the big wooden toilet door and it swung open all too easily. Bryony nearly tripped and fell into the room, and then felt angry at the door for nearly causing her an accident.

Thankfully, there was no one in the toilet. Each footstep she took created an echo. She found herself leaning over the expensive-looking sinks and staring at her reflection in the mirror. There was a certain wildness to her eyes, and it scared her. The reflection looking back at her seemed to be that of a stranger, so she kept staring, trying to understand the girl in the mirror that she was meeting more and more of late.

She must have been there for a good ten minutes, just staring at herself, until the handle on the main entrance door to the toilets moved slowly, creaking a little.

Bryony flinched.

'Bryony? Can I come in?' came Nora's sweet voice.

The door was ajar slightly. Bryony could see her small face almost wedged against the frame; wisely, she was not committing her body to the situation just yet. Her eyes were darting rapidly from side to side.

'Yes, of course you can,' Bryony said, peeling her hands from the posh marble sink and looking down at her palms, which had lines on them from the sharp edges she had been holding on to so tightly.

Nora stepped in quietly and closed the door behind her, locking it slowly.

Bryony's fury had now melted into something else: exhaustion, sadness. She felt bad looking at Nora now. So bad. It wasn't her fault that she was unwell.

Nora had chosen to wear a light blue smock dress to work, which complimented her eyes, and was gripping on to her brown leather handbag like it was a security blanket. *She's so sweet*, Bryony thought.

'Bryony. I'm really worried about you,' Nora said, letting her bag slide from her fingers and land with a gentle thump at her feet.

It was as if a trap had been disturbed by the soft, nervous paw of a mouse, lost in a winding world beneath the floorboards. Bryony felt more tears sting at her eyes, felt the threat of a crying bout that, once started, wouldn't stop. *This is so embarrassing.* She started pacing the room, running her hands through her long, thick hair. It felt as if there was no escape. The main door to the bathroom was locked and she was trapped.

Bryony knew Nora – she really liked her – but she didn't know her well enough for all this. The closest they had ever got was organising an executive luncheon, failing at the catering side, and then finding themselves wedged tightly together in a queue at Pret A Manger during a mad panic-buying session.

'I'm so sorry,' Bryony said between tears, starting

306

to plead with her but still unable to look her in the eye. 'I don't know why I behaved like that; everything has just got so overwhelming.' She really regretted her actions. She didn't know how to face the office again. *What if they sack me?* she thought.

Nora was looking at Bryony intensely. She had tears in her eyes, as if she was sorry she had upset her, but also as if she was feeling just a little of what Bryony was feeling. As if the pain was rubbing off on her. She bent down and reached into her bag, pulling something out of it and walking to the far end of the room. She opened a large window and perched on the windowsill. Bryony couldn't work out what she was holding until she smelt it, because the tears in her eyes were making everything blurry. The smell had followed a clicking sound; she realised Nora was smoking.

Bryony walked over and sat down next to her, and within thirty seconds there was a cigarette in her mouth, too. Bryony didn't know if she put it there or not, but it was there and it tasted wonderful. She blinked hard and the swelling of tears, which had rendered her temporarily blind, spilled over onto her cheeks.

And there they were. Like naughty schoolgirls, smoking in a place they knew they shouldn't be smoking in. Breaking the rules. But together. A pact.

Nora leant out of the window, blowing the smoke out into the rain, which was tipping down beyond the warm, dry room they were in, rushing down the gutters like a river.

She was one of those people who looked OK smoking. Bryony, with her clumsy fingers, had already nearly dropped her cigarette twice with all her shaking, and looked awkward holding it; like some men do holding a baby.

'I know I have my friends and family,' she said now. 'I've made a friend called Adam and he has been such a good help . . . But, this feeling, this rage, it's something I've never felt before,' she finished, rubbing her free hand self-consciously over her cheeks in a bid to remove any make-up that might have dripped from her eyelids and onto her pale skin.

'Do you still not know who did it, Bryony?' Nora asked, squinting at her.

She knows, Bryony thought . . . she could tell. *Everybody knows.*

It seemed like no question was out of bounds any more between them and, secretly, Bryony was sort of glad to be interrogated.

'I don't. I haven't been able to cope with the idea of knowing who did it. Do you understand why?' she asked, hoping Nora might but knowing she probably didn't.

'I do, actually.' Nora looked away as Bryony stared at her, surprised. 'I've had my own experience with something like this; years ago, though . . . My mother was killed by a drunk driver. She was walking along the pavement with some shopping, and this guy mounted the kerb and hit her. It was unbelievable, so ridiculous, Bryony, that she was in the wrong place at the wrong time like that. I was in a tailspin for a long, long time, and I found that the only way I could piece my life back together was to face up to this person, and forgive him.'

Nora's words threw a whole new concept into Bryony's life that she'd never considered before. *Forgive* him? Actually forgive the man who had killed Max? In that way they always preached about in churches and in films? The thought made her feel ill, like she was betraying him by even entertaining the idea.

The automatic room freshener suddenly emitted two sharp sprays in close succession, making the girls jump. Their nostrils were greeted by the tangy scent of orange, intertwined with nicotine. Briefly distracted by it, Bryony turned back to Nora when she suddenly realised that her legs were tingling with some kind of new feeling. Release.

'But how? How did you do it?' Bryony asked Nora, desperate to know what she'd gone through all those years ago, but in a way not ready to take in the details. It was too scary.

Nora smiled at her. 'I started by going to a group that was in my local area. I don't know if they do stuff like that any more. It wasn't self-help or anything; it was actually based around the idea of forgiveness and coping with traumatic life events, minus the bullshit,' she said, laughing to herself a little.

Bryony had never heard her swear before.

The old clichés filled her brain. The idea of figures in a room, sitting on sharp-edged, uncomfortable wooden chairs, spilling their guts and announcing themselves as society's biggest victims. Alcoholics. Cheats. Liars. The unloved.

Unfortunately, the way Bryony had pictured this image – thanks largely to films and the like – had created an incredibly negative image in her mind, even though Nora had clearly said it wasn't 'group therapy'.

Nora's earrings rattled a little as she smiled again at Bryony, imagining the cogs going around in her brain. 'I don't think he would mind, you know,' she said, glancing down at her knees and then back up again. There was a depth in her facial expressions Bryony had never seen before.

'Mind what?' she asked, as she threw her finished cigarette out of the window into rainy oblivion, watching it tumble away from her fingers.

'I don't think Max would mind you forgiving, trying to move on . . . If you like this Adam guy, it's OK, you know . . . Your face lit up for a moment when you said his name.'

Bryony shuddered inside. Being romantically involved with anyone else was out of the question. That's why her arrangement with Adam worked so well. He was on leave from women – he had said as much.

She pictured Max and it filled her with warmth. She remembered what it had felt like to hold his hand as they walked around London on their 'Max and Bryony Adventure Days Out', trawling Camden Market or a new art gallery. She ached for those days.

Bryony suddenly felt a breeze rush in through the window. It curled through her hair and sent shivers down her spine, and she wasn't sure if it was the cold, or something else.

CHAPTER 27

'YES, THIS IS SHE.'

Wednesday 10 June 2009
East London
7.30 p.m.

The phone rang three times before Bryony's mother picked it up. She leant against the hallway wall, twiddling the white cord between her fingers.

'Hi, is this Sylvie Weaver?' came the voice of a young man on the other end of the line.

'Yes, this is she.'

'Hi. This is Ben. I don't know if Bryony has told you who I am, but I'm – I was – Max's best friend. I'm really sorry, I had to talk to you, and I found your number on directory enquiries,' he said, quietly and nervously.

Sylvie released the cord from her hands, turned towards a dimly lit mirror and started poking gently at the bags under her eyes, a thick drape of dark brown hair threaded with silver sliding over her forehead. Sadness crept across her face as she wondered what she was about to hear. Was Bryony a lot worse than she thought? Was she not eating? Taking drugs?

'Hello, Ben. I certainly have heard of you, and thanks so much for keeping Bryony company. I know it has meant a huge amount to her and, please, don't ever worry about getting in touch,' she said, warmth radiating from her voice, despite her desperate need to know what was wrong.

'Oh, it's been no problem. It's obviously been a very difficult time for her, so it's the very least I can do,' he responded.

'How can I help you?' she asked, leaving her eyes alone now, and just staring at the lines around her mouth. She felt like she'd aged years with worry about her little girl, in a matter of months.

'Listen, I know this is going to sound strange but there's something I want to tell Bryony, but I don't know if it's the right thing to do. I need to talk to you about it, to see what you think . . . whether it would be right or wrong to tell her. It's something I can't really ignore any more, but I don't want to confuse or upset her, or make things worse,' he said, his voice cracking a little with nerves.

Sylvie took a deep breath, and drew up a chair. 'OK, go ahead. I'm all ears.'

CHAPTER 28

'IT'S POSH IN 'ERE, ISN'T IT?'

Saturday 13 June 2009
Covent Garden, central London
7.45 p.m.

The theatre was sold out, again.

Coppélia had gone down a storm, and the papers had made sure the message was out that Rachel Matthew was one of the best Swanhildas to ever grace the London stage. She'd blown people away with her performances and, tonight, Rita was ready to watch, once more.

She had not seen much of her daughter recently. Rachel had flown the nest. She spent most nights staying with Richard now, who lived closer to the centre of London, closer to the action, and closer to the stage.

Rita now felt that the only way she could be really close to her daughter was by sitting in the theatre and watching her. Most of the time she didn't even tell her she had been, but she wondered if, as her daughter danced, there was a movement in her eyes as she performed her turns and leaps – a flicker to scan the audience for her mother.

Rachel would come home every weekend where she would hurriedly collect some of her clothes, and drop others off to be washed; breezing in and out, leaving Rita with nothing but a kiss on the cheek to hold on to. That was OK, though . . . it was natural. She had prepared herself for it.

The usual buzz was spreading through the air in the auditorium, feet shuffling in aisles, handbags landing softly on the thick carpet, keys spilling out of purses. Rita heard people moan about the cost of the bar snacks, how they couldn't see in front of them because there was a man with huge hair, and argue about where they had parked the car. Sometimes she heard people talk about Rachel. They would point her out in the programme, trace their fingers over the image of the stunning young woman with a neck like a swan and legs like candy canes, and she would feel good inside, because everything *was* OK. Really, it was.

The house lights were still bright as a scruffy-looking lady, dressed in badly matched double denim, made her way along the row towards the empty seat next to her. She was so odd looking, in fact, that Rita could not help but stare at her as the lady made her way past lifted knees to get to her seat. After a few moments, though, she realised she was being rude, so opened her programme and pretended to read, despite knowing the whole thing almost word for word.

The woman sat down heavily in the seat next to hers, bringing a strong odour of cigarettes with her, which made Rita wrinkle up her nose. The woman looked strange, uncomfortable, out of place. Nervous, even. She was a far cry from the usual crowd of people who lined the seats of the theatre, decked in diamonds, tulip-skirted dresses and brightly coloured shirts. However, although the woman looked untidy, it was apparent that she had made an effort. A small sparkling clip had been placed in her hair just above her ear, and red lipstick was smeared over her lips.

Rita looked around her, left and right, wondering if she might be able to make her excuses and change seats, but then she told herself off, warned herself against being a snob and judging people. Hell, she used to smoke in her twenties.

Suddenly, a mobile phone rang. It was loud, and the strident ring tone was awful: a tinny recording of a chart song. 'Fuck's sake,' the woman said under her breath, sighing loudly and rooting around in her bag roughly until she found the phone – an old and scratched Nokia with a pink Winnie-the-Pooh case. 'Wha—?' she said loudly into the mouthpiece, her cockney accent clearly audible in the one word she had spoken: the dropped 't' said it all for Rita. Rita, who was particularly pedantic about diction.

A woman in front of them turned around and tutted loudly, expressing her disapproval at the call. She was met with a glare that could have slain an entire army.

'Look, I'm at the ballet, all right? Can't you just

change her?' the woman yelled, one finger in her phoneless ear. Her fingertips were as yellow as her teeth, which had turned a canary shade from what looked like years of smoking.

Rita was trying not to stare, but it was near impossible.

The woman eventually put the phone on silent and threw it back into her bag. 'It's posh in 'ere, isn't it?' she said suddenly, looking towards Rita, a vulnerability in her eyes.

'Yes, it is rather. Have you been to the ballet before?' Rita asked.

'No, I haven't. I've got a few DVDs at home, though,' the woman replied, blushing a little and fiddling with a large gold ring on her index finger.

Rita looked down at her dark green suit and suddenly felt bad. Bad that she'd been so cold and judgmental without even knowing who this woman was; bad that she was sitting there, decked out in Jaeger, a glass of cool white wine in her hand and casting aspersions, when all she had ever known was comfort, culture and privilege.

'Oh, that's nice. Well, I bet you are very excited about seeing it for yourself.'

'Yeah, I can't bloody wait. My daughter is in it, actually,' the woman said, visibly swelling with pride.

'Really?' Rita asked. She turned to face the woman properly now, so that they were eye to eye.

'Yeah,' came the reply, as the lights dimmed and the orchestra started to warm up.

Rita wondered who her daughter could be: she'd met a lot of the cast members' families at the opening night party . . . maybe she was working behind the scenes, or in the lighting department, and that was what the woman meant by 'in it'.

'Oh, lovely, is she helping backstage?' Rita asked, lowering her voice for the benefit of the people around them, and lifting her wineglass to her lips.

'Oh, no. It's amazing, really. She's the lead. She's Swanhilda,' the woman said as the curtain started to rise, her smile widening to reveal a gap where a premolar had once been.

Rita started to choke, promptly spitting her drink all over the coiffed hair in the row before her. As Rachel gracefully walked onto the stage, Rita looked at the woman in horror.

Her hand was pressed against her denim chest, her craggy face youthful again, her expression one of overwhelming pride and love.

CHAPTER 29

'SHALL I TAKE MY SHOES OFF?'

Friday 19 June 2009
Angel, north London
6 p.m.

'Welcome to my humble abode, lovely lady,' Adam said, opening the door, a huge smile on his face.

Bryony hovered on the doorstep, clutching a bottle of white wine. Her stomach churned. He was so handsome. She always knew he was good looking, but tonight he looked particularly gorgeous. She wondered fleetingly what it would be like to kiss him, and then felt guilty just as quickly. She wondered if he could see it in her face.

'Shall I take my shoes off?' she asked, looking down at her feet. She was wearing a red vest top, a pair of black skinny jeans and some brand new hi-top white Converse trainers.

'No, don't be silly. Come in, make yourself comfortable,' he said in a funny voice, pulling the door open a little wider and gesturing enthusiastically with his arm, like a circus ringmaster. He was radiating nervous energy.

Adam was dressed casually but somehow still 'together' in a grey, chunky-knit jumper with a pair of black jeans. Bryony noticed that the waist-band of his pants was on show again; this time a white pair covered in green dots. Her heart was beating fast but she couldn't quite work out why.

'Oh, the pants,' he said, noticing where she was looking and pulling his jumper down.

'Sorry, was I that obvious?' Bryony asked, step-ping past him into the hallway.

Adam grimaced and yanked his jeans up while her back was turned, then smoothed his fringe, which had grown yet again at an annoyingly fast rate. 'Come this way,' he said, overtaking her and leading her into the living room.

One of his housemates was sitting on the sofa, tongue hanging out, trying to create an epically large roll-up and failing miserably. He'd dropped a significant amount of tobacco onto his lap and there were three papers stuck to various parts of his hand. Soft rock music was playing in the back-ground, and the white walls of the room were covered in framed album covers that included Pink Floyd and David Bowie.

'What the hell are you doing?' Adam asked him, looking embarrassed.

'What do you think I'm doing? I'm trying to make the world's longest cigarette,' the housemate replied flatly. He had thick, curly hair, which sprung awkwardly from around his slim face, and he was clearly very tall – Bryony noticed how his knees nearly hit the table in front of him. He looked arty and affected, and instantly reminded Bryony of the boys in Shoreditch. He had an aura of the twisted comedian about him.

'Right, OK . . . Salem, this is Bryony,' Adam said.

'All right, gorgeous?' Salem asked, looking up now and winking at her. His teeth and mannerisms reminded her of a strange mixture of Spike from *Notting Hill* and Noel Fielding. She suddenly felt a little uncomfortable.

'Hey,' she said, quietly.

'Are you actually going out tonight?' Adam asked, staring at Salem and wondering if it would be another one of those evenings that would involve him watching box sets while picking at a microwave meal, filling the room with the stench of stale socks.

'Yes, don't worry, geek face, you two can have your romantic evening,' Salem replied, rolling his eyes and smiling. He seemed to have finally had some success at slicking down one of the papers as he looked away from Adam and admired his handiwork with a look of almost pathetic pride.

Bryony turned towards Adam. He had gone a deep shade of lobster.

Adam responded by picking up the nearest cushion and throwing it at his housemate's head, full pelt, crushing the cigarette he'd been so painstakingly crafting.

'Right, that's it. You asked for it,' Salem said,

standing up calmly and walking over to Adam, who was laughing.

Bryony cowered in the corner, clutching on to the bottle of wine.

'And one, two, *three*,' Salem said, before jumping into the air and taking Adam down to the floor in one swoop.

Bryony gasped and stepped backwards again. 'Er, guys?' she said, a little concerned at the level of violence that seemed to be escalating in the small flat.

'S'OK, love. I'm just giving our little friend here what he deserves,' Salem said, leaning his considerable frame down onto Adam's midriff.

Taking advantage of Salem's momentary distraction, Adam swiped at his face, hooked his fingers at the side of his mouth and pulled at one of his cheeks.

Bryony winced. That looked painful. It was cartoonesque play-fighting, and she wondered how far it would go. *But something about it is funny*, she thought, staring at the mass of thrashing limbs and arms, unsure of which bits belonged to which guy. She wondered if she would have to step in at any point.

'Shall I tell Bryony about the fact that you – *arrrgggghhh*,' Salem shouted, interrupted by the amount of hand over his mouth.

'About *what*?' Bryony asked, raising an eyebrow and crossing her arms now. She hadn't been expecting so much entertainment.

Adam looked genuinely panicked.

'About the fact that he – *gufffeww*,' Salem tried again, but his mouth had once again been frantically covered. In retaliation, he started to hold Adam's nose and mouth closed, playing dirty in an attempt to get his own mouth back. Adam's eyes started to bulge.

Suddenly, the fight just made Bryony want to cringe. It was funny, but reminiscent of all the immature men she'd met in her life. 'I'm just going to, er, go to the loo,' she said now, still watching them as she edged into the hallway. She knew where the loo was because she'd seen the door gaping open on the way in, a huge pile of laundry sitting by the bath. She had guessed that it had probably been there for a long time.

'No, Bryony, wait!' Adam shouted, despite the fact that Salem was rubbing the side of his head against the thick carpet and cackling loudly. His hair was sticking up from the static.

She disappeared into the bathroom and shut the door, staring at herself in the mirror. She wondered what she was doing there.

All of a sudden the door opened. She turned around quickly, gasping as she met eyes with whom she could only assume was Adam's other housemate: a plump, blond man, who was waving his arms frantically, as if he'd just discovered an escaped lion in the bathroom, or Lord Lucan.

'Oh, my God. Oh, my God, there's a *girl* in here!' he yelled, so loudly it made her wince, before slamming the door shut again.

'I'm in a mad house,' she whispered to her reflection, before locking the door and sitting on the edge of the bath.

She felt wrong for being there all of a sudden. She could still hear thudding coming from the room next door, along with the sound of shouts and fight-related gasping. She rolled her eyes towards the ceiling. Maybe she had got this guy wrong; maybe he was just another idiot. Bryony felt herself pining for Max again.

Then the thumping stopped, and she could hear low whispering. She stood up and pushed her ear to the wall to listen. She could just about make out what Adam was saying.

'. . . Listen, yeah, I know she's absolutely gorgeous, but will you just piss off, please? Go out or something?'

Bryony felt a flash of fear. Her stomach flipped, and not in a good way. She didn't want this. She didn't need it.

'Come on, you have to tell her . . .'

The end of the sentence was muffled. Bryony pushed her ear even harder to the wall, putting both hands against the cold tiles.

'She doesn't, you know, I . . .' she heard Adam again.

Bryony wondered what on earth could be going on. She heard more whispering; this time it was unintelligible. Then Adam said more loudly, 'Please, lads, come on. You're humiliating me. Just go out.'

Bryony pulled her ear away from the wall and wondered how she was going to be able to escape. She moved over to the bathroom door, unlocked it and walked back into the living room. The men, huddled around each other, suddenly stopped talking, looking up at her with guilty expressions on their faces.

'All right, Bryony?' Salem said, standing upright. 'Phil and I are going out, aren't we, Phil?'

'Are we?'

'Yes, we are. Get your coat.'

'Owww, but I don't want to go out!'

'Tough.'

Phil sighed loudly and picked up a camel-coloured duffle coat from the sofa as Salem grabbed a leather jacket that was hanging limply from the back of a chair.

Adam seemed to sigh with relief as he saw this, his whole body relaxing a little. The red flush on his cheeks was slowly draining away. The lads went into the corridor; Salem pushing Phil towards the door, one hand on his back. Phil's body language screamed 'reluctant, angry teenager'. Adam followed them anxiously. Salem opened the door, letting Phil out, before walking out himself and closing it until just his face was poking through the gap.

'Bryony, er, you should know that Adam . . .'

Bryony's mouth dropped in horror. She didn't want this friendship to end. She didn't want to have to walk away from Adam if Salem said he had feelings for her.

'No, no, no!' Adam yelled, before pushing Salem's face through the door and slamming it hard.

'Wow. What the hell was all that about? You guys are a real comedy trio,' Bryony said, raising an eyebrow and leaning against the wall.

'Oh, erm, nothing . . . I did warn you that they're pretty annoying,' Adam said, leading her by the hand into the kitchen, which was off the living room. It was a pokey space, full of plates crying out to be washed up and empty beer cans.

Bryony suddenly felt grateful that she had her own space, and missed being there now. She decided there and then that she would avoid letting Adam see her flat. He would know immediately what had happened just by taking one look at the place: it still gave the impression that it was inhabited by a real, living man, and not just the memory of one she loved so deeply.

'You know, sometimes, when you feel like you don't belong somewhere . . .?' Adam asked, taking two wineglasses from a cupboard.

'Yeah, I know what you mean,' Bryony replied.

'Right. But as for this evening, it's just that I want to get to know you more. It sounds strange, but we've been hanging out for weeks now, and there's still so much I don't know about you,' Adam said, a cheeky grin on his face.

Bryony felt herself melt inside a little, before more guilt swamped her tummy.

'Follow, follow . . .' Adam said, turning out the kitchen light with his elbow and striding into the living room, putting the glasses on the table with a gentle clunk.

He turned the lights down by dimmer switch, and for a moment Bryony started to freak out again. Adam didn't know about Max. It would be perfectly reasonable, if he did like her, for him to make a pass at her. He was single, and she was . . . single. But maybe she had misheard them; misunderstood Salem's comments. She hoped she had.

Adam poured generous helpings of wine into the glasses, and passed one to Bryony. She accepted it, her dark red nail varnish glinting in the low light. She sat down on the carpet.

'You can have a chair, you know. I won't charge you,' Adam said.

'No. I like it here,' she replied, crossing her legs and taking a sip of her wine.

'OK, then,' Adam conceded, crouching down and sitting opposite her.

He was direct. More confident than she originally imagined. He would be just the kind of man she would have gone for in the past, she realised, studying his chiselled face. And he was blessed in the looks department, for sure.

There were a few moments of silence, and Bryony thought that the night could well go wrong. It could be awkward and stifled, and forced. It could end with a desperate kiss, and she wasn't sure who would initiate it. But she just needed him to be her friend. That was all.

In the end, she was pleasantly surprised. Two hours went by like seconds, and before she knew it she had relaxed completely. They were singing along to Hall & Oates tracks while Adam played his guitar so badly she nearly choked on her wine. The sound of the eighties was jangling around the flat, and she found herself strutting around the small living room, clutching on to her glass and singing loudly. They looked like a pair of fools, but it was just the kind of fun Bryony needed. Adam didn't take himself too seriously, and he had a good singing voice, even if his guitar playing left a lot to be desired.

It had been a long while since Bryony had truly laughed like this and in the space of several hours, she only thought about Max once or twice. When she realised this, it was a shock to her, considering how she usually lived her life with an imprint of him in her mind everywhere she went.

She realised it was tiring to miss someone so much.

When the next song had finished, Adam breathlessly leant his guitar against the wall. 'So, tell me,' he said, a wicked glint in his eye, 'it's time to get onto the juicy stuff. Exes,' he said, and rubbed his hands together.

Bryony suddenly realised how much she'd had to drink, as the room swayed gently in front of her. She hoped she wouldn't give her secret away. The music in the background seemed to get quieter suddenly, and Max's face flashed before her eyes. 'Oh, you know, just the usual. I've been in a long-term relationship and dated a few guys. Things just never . . . erm—'

'Worked out?'

'Yeah, I guess so . . . But tell me more about you? It all sounded so dramatic when we last spoke,' Bryony asked, realising that she had somehow got away with revealing virtually nothing.

A large candle placed between them on the floor flickered gently, and Adam took a gulp of his wine. 'Well . . . I haven't really had much luck with relationships,' he started, pulling a face. 'I've been cheated on a couple of times, and since then I've found the whole trusting thing a little tricky. It's amazing how much it really affects you, possibly without you even realising it.'

There was a look of naked honesty on Adam's face. She loved that about him. He was down to earth, truthful; a real person who wasn't ashamed to admit the realities of his past. Bryony wondered who would be silly enough to cheat on someone like him, and she wished for a moment that she hadn't just had her heart broken into a million little pieces. She wished she was just a regular single girl who'd met him in a bar.

She wished the love of her life hadn't been shot randomly outside a tube station on his way home.

'I'm sorry to hear that,' Bryony muttered, pushing her hand through her hair, which rippled beneath her fingers before falling loosely to her shoulders again.

Adam could think of nothing to say, and ran his finger through the flame of the candle, quickly enough that he didn't get burnt.

'Right. This is officially depressing,' Bryony said, standing up suddenly. 'Come on, I challenge you to giant Jenga!' She pulled the box she'd spotted earlier into the centre of the room.

They played until 3 a.m. When Bryony woke up the next morning on the sofa, the birds were singing, and she was nuzzled against Adam's chest.

CHAPTER 30

SHE WAS THE VICTIM.

Saturday 20 June 2009
Ealing, west London
11 a.m.

'I can't believe you did this to me,' Rita said. She was sitting opposite her daughter, holding a pink tissue to her eyes. Her thick, black mascara was bleeding into the soft skin of her cheeks, only to be poorly smudged away by shaking hands.

Edward was perched on the edge of the sofa, still in his running clothes, his well-fed stomach hanging over the band of his expensive tracksuit bottoms. Saturday-morning television flickered in the background, muted – the fresh-faced presenters speaking about the latest singers and soaps but making no sound.

The run had been long and hilly. He had known he would need to get rid of some tension for when Rachel returned. This was the day that he and his wife had been dreading. *An inevitable one*, now that he thought about it. He almost couldn't believe how naïve they had been to assume that this truth would never be revealed. It seemed now as if it was some dirty secret, when actually all that had happened since the day Rachel had arrived in their home as a baby had been done with nothing but the best of intentions.

Rachel sat on the thick carpet in the sitting room. She had just slid her feet into a pair of brand new pointe shoes that she'd been trying to break in by wearing indoors, with a thick pair of socks over them. Edward knew the process was an almost military mission. Even when she visited friends for dinner, the shoes went on as soon as she got through the front door. She would flex her feet in them all the time, under the table, during supper.

'I didn't do anything to *you*, Mum,' Rachel said. She could feel her eyebrows quivering under the stress of the situation. It was a reaction that only happened in the most intense situations, like waiting for a casting call-back, or arguing with Richard about why he smelt of Armani Code when he came back from a party.

Even Simba had picked up on the tension and had fled to the garden, trying to find some poor, hapless rodent to bring in as a gift to glue the family back together.

'Why on earth, *why*, would you invite her to the ballet without telling me? In fact, why wouldn't you tell me this in the first place? I'm very, very hurt,' Rita continued, the skin around her eyes delicate and puffy.

Rachel felt something shift inside her. This was

not how this conversation was supposed to go. It was meant to be full of apologies from her adopted parents for lying to her, and fucking up her life at such a crucial time. But she tried to be calm. She really wanted to be calm. 'Listen, I didn't even know you would be there. The fact that you ended up sitting next to each other – what are the odds of that? It's crazy. And *I'm* angry at you both for not telling *me* about this,' she continued, irritably pulling at the ribbons of her shoes, which were wrapped tightly around her ankles. Fury seemed to be bubbling away in her soul again, and she wanted to explode with rage. But she knew she couldn't, that she had to try and stay level-headed for once.

Edward slumped back on the sofa, wiping beads of sweat from his forehead that had continued to trickle from his receding hairline after his run.

'To be fair, Rita, darling, I don't think Rachel did this on purpose—'

'Oh, shut up, Edward,' Rita snapped, pushing him out of a conversation that was rightfully his to have as well. His bushy eyebrows jumped up several centimetres, and then slowly sank back down.

'When, and *how* – just *how* on earth did you find out?' Rita asked, squinting down in disbelief and fiddling with the stitching at the bottom of her shirt.

'Did someone tell you, sweetheart, someone in the family?' Edward asked calmly, trying to diffuse the anger in the room.

'No. No one in this fucking so-called family told me,' Rachel suddenly yelled, giving just a small snapshot of her resentment that everyone else *had* known about this all along. 'I went through the stuff under your bed to find my driving licence and came across the paperwork. No wonder you were so funny about your filing system,' she said bitterly, her eyes narrowing and her own tears rising to the surface. 'You have no idea how much this has messed me up,' Rachel finished, gritting her teeth.

Rita bent over at this, cradling her head in her hands, suddenly bursting into fresh tears under the strain of her fears and embarrassment. 'You don't understand how hard we worked to keep this quiet, so you could just live a normal and wonderful life. This was all for you,' she said, between her sobs.

It was unclear to Rachel why her adopted mother was angry or even upset. It was hard to find any empathy when everything she ever knew had been turned upside down. Added to this, it had all somehow been preventable, if only they had just been honest with her in the first place. *If anyone should be angry, it's me*, she thought again, feeling the stress multiply inside her and translate into physical signs: deep, heavy breathing and trembling hands.

'So, this explains why we haven't seen much of you recently,' Rita said, her voice tearful, still unable to look her daughter in the eye.

'I've needed some time to think. To get to know my, well, my mum, actually,' Rachel said, resentment in her voice.

Rachel recognised in Rita's face a stab of jealousy she must have been feeling deep inside. Jealousy about a woman she would normally turn her nose up at in the street. The kind of woman who would serve her in Poundstretcher if Waitrose were out of paper cups and plates were needed for their next summer garden party.

'Why, oh, *why* didn't you just tell us?' Edward intervened again, this time unhindered by his wife. He was a man of few words, but he was prepared to use them now, despite the pressure on him to remain a bystander.

'Because I was *angry*, Dad. And I was scared that if I tried to talk to you about it without working this stuff out for myself, it would come out wrong. So I'm not OK about this,' Rachel said, finding yet more hate coming out of her mouth, even though she'd spent a decent proportion of time recently in awe at this couple, and how they had taken care of her like they had.

None of that seemed to be coming out now.

'Listen, I need to go, OK?' Rachel said, suddenly unable to deal with the moment. She started frantically untying the ribbons on her shoes, tugging at ends, fraying the silk, not giving a damn because she just needed to escape.

'Look, Rach, come on,' Rita said, lifting her head up and revealing a face etched with regret and desperation. 'I don't want to lose you. You just don't understand how humiliating, how upsetting it was to have her just turn up like that . . .' she added, staring at her daughter, who was now pulling the shoes away from her twisted toes and replacing them with a pair of brown Ugg boots.

'Please stay, Rach – we need to sit down as a family and talk about this,' Edward pleaded, sitting up, easing his constricting waistband.

'We aren't family,' Rachel said bluntly, rising to her feet, leaving the room and storming up the stairs.

And that was when the situation ignited. A lit match had hit fuel.

'Oh, come *on*! Don't be so selfish, Rachel, we've done *everything* for you,' Rita yelled, as she chased her daughter up the flights of carefully painted stairs.

Edward remained in the living room, his head in his hands as he listened to the frantic footsteps, which started out muffled and hard and turned into echoing banging as the two women in his family chased each other to the top floor of the house.

'Do you think you would have had this career, all this, all these opportunities, if we hadn't done the things we did for you?' Rita cried now, standing at the entrance to Rachel's bedroom and watching her daughter frantically shove her possessions into a large laundry bag. 'Your mother was a *teenager*, Rachey. A bloody teenager!'

It was difficult for Rachel to think about what she needed to collect together in what could be the last few minutes in her old life. Her old world. A world that didn't belong to her. A lot of her things were already at Richard's, but she knew there would still be possessions here that she would want.

She packed as much as she could fit in the bag: her GHD hair straighteners, three trays of Mac eye-shadow in a multitude of colours, her *Scrubs* box set and a pack of thin hair bands. Her arms moved quickly and frantically as she scooped up as much as she could.

She was the victim. *She* was the hurt party here. That's what she thought, anyway. She felt tears sting her eyes as she packed Lamb, a toy she had been given 'when she was born'. *But who by?* she thought now. Rachel had originally assumed it had come from one of her wealthy BMW-driving aunties, but the reality of the situation was that it was probably paid for by her grandmother, who had lived in poverty on a council estate just off the M25.

Her world was falling apart. Flashbacks played out before her eyes; her earliest memories of falling over in the garden, cutting her knees and crying out for her mother, and it was Rita who'd been there. Rita who had come running, scooped her up and applied the bandages. All her memories tied up in the house, all this confusion; it was ebbing from her now in the form of vulnerable tears.

337

And then there was guilt and anger. Guilt. Anger.

'Look, please, please don't go,' Rita started to plead now, holding on to the doorframe for dear life. She realised that she could be about to lose her daughter. 'I'm so sorry we didn't tell you, but there's so much you need to know about why we made that decision, it was all for you,' she said, wiping her eyes with the back of her free hand. Her emotions were turbulent, swinging from humiliation and shock, to anger and now fear. Fear of losing the most precious person to her in the whole world.

But that person was packing to leave, and had no real tie to her any more.

Adopted children stopped talking to their parents sometimes . . . there was less obligation there. Or at least that was what Rita feared. It had been her fear ever since she had carried home her adopted baby daughter one rainy March morning. It had never really gone away, and now it was coming true.

'I just don't know why you lied to me,' Rachel said, her voice wobbling as she shoved her foot on top of the bag, trying to stamp down and somehow compact the items, which were bulging out of the top. The sound of glass smashing somewhere underneath the hair straighteners could be heard. A pair of knickers fell from the top, but she couldn't be bothered to stuff them back in.

'Can't you forgive me for that, after all that we've done? At least *listen*, and try to understand why this all worked out as it did, won't you?' Rita asked, stepping into the room fully now, in an effort to physically obstruct Rachel with her frame, which felt as though it was crumbling under the stress.

'Not now. I need to go – this place, this world, I don't belong here,' Rachel said dramatically, almost squaring up to the woman who had taken her in all those years ago. She knew that the words coming from her mouth were a little excessive, silly even, but they kept coming anyway. 'Just let me past,' she said, quietly, trying to stop herself from screaming at the top of her lungs and losing the last bit of control she had in her possession.

'No, please, Rachel, just stay,' Rita said, crying hard again, her shoulders heaving.

'Let me go,' Rachel whispered, tears sliding down her own face.

Rita stood still for a moment, breathing hard. Her chest was rising up and down beneath a navy blouse, a diamond pendant at her throat glittering softly in the light. And then she took two gentle steps to the right, making the way for Rachel's exit. 'It's your choice, Rachel,' she said. 'Just don't think you can come swanning in and out of our lives from now on,' she said, shocked at the bluntness of her own words.

Rachel didn't even hesitate. She rushed past Rita, who collapsed to the floor, pulling an unwanted top towards her face and crying into the scent of the daughter she might never see again.

Rachel rushed down the stairs as quickly as she

could, with what looked like a burglary haul. The bag kept catching on the banister, but she roughly pulled it away, taking chips of paint off the woodwork. When she had finally made it to the front door, her father was waiting for her, hands on hips.

'So, that's it then, is it?' he asked, angry now. 'You're just going to go. Run away?'

Edward and Rachel stared at each other, locking eyes. They stayed that way for a few moments. Just staring. Trying to make sense of one another, but unable to find the connection and understanding they had once shared.

Rachel moved round him, opened the door, stepped out and slammed it hard behind her.

A huge, framed family photo rattled on the wall in the hallway, before falling to the ground, the glass smashing to smithereens on the marble flooring.

CHAPTER 31

HAPPY PEOPLE.

Monday 22 June 2009
Drayton Road Community Centre, north
London
10.30 a.m.

Rules. Bryony hated rules.

'I know most of you have seen these before, but could you just read this sheet? It has a few guidelines. Not rules, just guidelines. Although I will have to ask you to leave if you don't adhere to them, OK?'

So they are rules then, Bryony thought, biting her lip angrily. Rules packaged in a 'guideline' disguise. She wasn't going to fall for that. Sighing, she wished she was at work, but the company, being the small, family-run operation that it was, had agreed to allow her time off to attend counselling once a week.

'The Grief and Loss Forum'. That was what the session was called, and it was run by Sol Milderdale, a bereavement counsellor with umpteen years' experience, a strong faith in God and an almighty spring in his step. His smile was akin to the kind found on children's-TV-show hosts: adults dressed as blueberries, raccoons, elves and the like, bouncing around on space-hoppers and singing about love and respect as if they are on MDMA. It was exactly what Bryony had dreaded about coming along to the session. People like Sol. Happy people. Positive people.

'When you've had a good look at the guidelines, our new members can introduce themselves. Does that sound OK?' asked Sol, who was standing in the middle of the circle, looking happier than anyone or anything to have ever graced the room. Ever.

It wasn't a question, however. Not really.

Misery was hovering and moving around the room like a suicidal ghost, Bryony realised, as she pulled her jumper over her knees. Even the cleaner she had seen shuffling around with a mop in the minutes before the session had begun had looked like she wanted to run away from life.

There were a few grunts in response to Sol's 'question'.

There were eleven people in the room, ten of whom were sitting in a circle on wooden chairs that were so hard Bryony could feel the bumps of her spine against the back of the one she had been given. Added to this, it had one dodgy leg, which looked as if it might give way at any minute. Bryony secretly hoped it would; at least it would raise a laugh.

Everyone studied their guidelines, as she covertly studied them. There was a chubby, sweet-looking man, who had sadness etched all over his face. It

342

was in his eyes, in the way the skin sagged below them as if they carried the weight of a thousand unshed tears. Then there was a kind-looking elderly lady, who kept smiling at Bryony because she was clearly the baby in the room. Next to her was a miserable, middle-aged woman who looked like someone had slapped her around the face a hundred times with a wet fish; and next to her was a black woman in her late thirties or so, who was neatly turned out and seemed overwhelmingly nervous. A grey-haired man who was probably in his early fifties was also there; he looked terribly middle-class, having donned yellow cords and a dickie-bow tie, which clashed somewhat with his moustache. He was sitting next to a woman with a sharp, ginger bob and a face so gaunt she could have been mistaken for Edvard Munch's *Scream* painting. Next to her was a man in his late twenties or early thirties; he was in his work clothes, and a mechanic, Bryony suspected. There was also a reluctant-looking Chinese man who looked like he'd been forced to come – just like she had – and a desperately beautiful Asian girl who said nothing to anyone. *And Bryony Weaver, of course,* she thought, *who really isn't sure if this is a good idea.*

She looked at her piece of paper now. The rules . . .

1. Do not speak over each other. Give everyone a chance to speak before offering your thoughts.

343

2. Do not be afraid to cry.
3. Everything said in this room must be treated confidentially.
4. Please respect the privacy of your fellow group members and refrain from recording conversations or taking photographs of any kind.
5. Do not reveal exact details of criminal cases, such as names of defendants, suspects and victims. This is a small catchment area, and it is best to talk about feelings here, rather than individuals involved/to be involved in criminal proceedings.
6. Do not shout at, or abuse other group members. Be respectful of other people's thoughts and opinions.
7. Drinks cartons and food wrappers must not be left in the hall. All chairs must be stacked away at the end of each session.
8. If you do not want to give your name, you don't have to. You are welcome to make up a name; no one needs to know.
9. The consumption of alcohol is not permitted during sessions.
10. No pets.

An interesting set of 'guidelines', Bryony thought, then wondered who on earth would bring their pets. This place was too depressing even for dogs, and they were always happy.

She looked around at the room now, which had

probably last been decorated in the Victorian era, and had a smell of disinfectant, mothballs and gone-off milk. Paint peeled from the walls, and the glass that made up the largest window, which looked out onto an equally drab street scene, was cracked, repaired temporarily with yellow tape.

Bryony had agreed to attend the group after her mother had spent five weeks pestering her to go. Now, reading the sheet, she had to concede that rules 5 and 8 seemed helpful. They fitted perfectly with her refusal to know anything about the man who had killed Max and, considering that everyone knew about the case thanks to the national press, they would work well for her. She guessed that no one would realise who she was, despite all the coverage, especially if she gave herself a new name. None of the papers had published a photo of her, so she was pretty safe, she reckoned.

Bryony felt bad to admit to herself that she was only going to appease her mother, who was convinced she had developed a drink and drug problem. Which was ironic, the furthest she'd ever gone with drugs was a few spliffs one night back in her early twenties, and even then she had had to run out of the room because she had to be sick.

Bryony's mother had put her recently increasing weight loss and tired eyes together and got junkie, whereas Bryony just wanted to pull her duvet over her head and wait out the rest of her life. It all seemed a bit pointless now.

'OK, are we all ready? Let's start with you. Please

introduce yourself,' Sol said, an open hand aimed straight towards Bryony. It wasn't a pointed hand, but an open one. *Probably some psychology mumbo-jumbo stuff he was taught to make people open up and blah blah blah*, she thought, rolling her eyes to the ceiling and smiling. But, shit . . . She suddenly felt very nervous.

Sol stared at her expectantly and encouragingly, like he was tempting a cat down from a high, slippery gutter. His other hand was slung casually in his right jeans pocket, and his T-shirt read, 'Work hard, canoe home'.

Moron, she thought, fiddling with her hair.

She tried to speak but the words got caught in her throat. For something she didn't care about, Bryony suddenly felt very daunted. She looked down at her lap; all eyes were on her and she couldn't handle it. She wondered if she could climb inside her white French Connection dress and pretend to be a misshapen cushion.

'Hello, everyone.' The sound of her voice took her by surprise.

'Hi,' everyone responded in unison, making Bryony jump a little in her seat. It had sounded like a chorus of beings from another planet.

'Right, er, well, I'm B— I mean, Mel, and I live in north London,' she said, changing her name at the very last minute, just to be on the safe side.

'OK, hi, Mel,' Sol said, fanning his arms out with joy and doing a little hop and skip on the worn floorboards.

346

Ergh. Bryony said nothing and stared at him blankly.

'So, can you tell us why you're here? What brought you here?'

Oh, wow, she thought. They weren't going slowly here, were they? Next thing she knew, she would probably be discussing her medical history and bra size. But she took a deep breath; *here goes,* she thought, mentally shuffling her feet to the edge of the precipice and preparing to jump. 'Well . . . my boyfriend died; actually, he was murdered, and I'm struggling a little despite the fact that it has been quite a while. Mum said it might be a good idea to come here,' she said, looking back down at her lap and feeling like a child. *Mum said.*

'OK. Thank you for sharing that with us. Welcome from everyone. It's great to see you here, Mel,' Sol said with a glittering smile, before spinning on his heel and presenting the same question to the Asian girl.

Bryony wondered if she even had a voice. When she was passed a chair, she had said nothing; there was just a mere nod at the offer of a cup of tea; and more silence when the posh man had accidentally stepped on her toe, apologising profusely to a very quiet victim who managed a simple watering of the eyes rather than the frustrated range of expletives the pain really warranted.

The ticking of a large white clock hanging precariously above a worn-out piano could be heard as the girl swallowed, before suddenly trying

347

to speak, but finding the words caught in her throat just like Bryony had.

'I'm Mai. I'm here because my mother was killed in a car accident five years ago.'

Eyes were squinted in sympathy as she spoke, fists clenched through tension, backs locked rigid. Bryony instantly felt bad for her 'quite a while' comment to refer to a loss that had occurred within the past twelve months. This was followed by the sudden realisation that five years down the line, a person could still feel so appalling that they would eventually resort to coming somewhere like this. It was chilling. It made Bryony sickeningly frightened of her future.

'OK, thank you for sharing that with us, Mai. It's lovely to meet you,' Sol said, before spinning a few degrees to his right and addressing the last new member, the neatly turned out black woman, who was dressed in a light blue shirt and black jeans.

'And now, can you tell us about yourself, please?' he asked, gesturing towards the woman, who was already wiping tears from her eyes with a tissue.

Oh, for God's sake, Bryony thought, wondering if this had been a bad idea after all. She had too many tears of her own to be giving a shit about other people. *Must. Stop. Being. Selfish. And. Cynical*, she told herself.

'I'm Sharon. I live in Wandsworth. I, erm . . . I actually don't feel ready to talk about what has happened to me.' There was a pregnant pause. 'I just want to be here to listen to everyone else and try to work things out for myself. There is someone I need to forgive, but I can't – I'm able to say that much,' she muttered, between tears, clutching on to the tissue like it was a blanket she could hide behind.

Shivers ran down Bryony's spine, and suddenly her bad attitude and cynicism melted away to be replaced by something new. Fascination. She leant forward and looked closely at the woman before pulling back quickly, realising how obvious she was being. Her interest was cut short, anyway, when attention was drawn away from the woman and back into the middle of the room.

'OK, Sharon, that's fine. You won't be expected to discuss anything you feel uncomfortable with,' Sol said, rubbing his hands together. 'So we have welcomed our new members. It's great to have you here.' He sat down on the dusty floor, so he was now a level below them.

Probably another thing he's been taught in nut school, Bryony thought cynically. *Some kind of method to make it easier for us to talk to him, or something like that.* She rolled her eyes impatiently again, but was caught by Mai, who scowled at her, which surprised her a little. Bryony realised that maybe she had a bit of an attitude problem about all this. She quickly switched her face back into neutral mode and tried to concentrate.

'It's an interesting thing that, forgiveness,' Sol began, staring into his open palms as he spoke.

He was quite charismatic, really . . . 'What do we all think about forgiveness?' he asked, throwing the thought back to the group so they could hold it and study the notion, examine the concept.

Sharon cleared her throat, and suddenly she had everyone's attention again. 'Well, if you don't mind me starting . . . I think forgiveness is very important. So important that I am disappointed I can't do it,' she said, looking up to the ceiling and breathing deeply, as if she was trying to keep something under control.

'I don't think it's important at all,' a voice boomed out, suddenly cutting the silence like a blade.

It was Bryony's voice. Bryony's words. She was shocked by this. She certainly hadn't planned to say it.

Sharon looked at her sternly, her eyes wide and tearful. 'But why?' she asked simply.

'I'm sorry . . . I'm not being rude. I just . . .' Bryony started, but realised she wasn't sure where she wanted to take the argument. She hadn't even known she had felt like this before the sentence came out. 'I just think it's a pointless concept,' she said slowly, feeling her way. 'Someone killed my boyfriend, and there's nothing that can be done now to make it better. He's gone, for ever, and me wrapping my arms around the person who did this . . . it won't help anything because it's too late. Nothing will bring him back,' she finished, her voice echoing in the room.

All the hairs on her arms suddenly stood on end, as if something or someone had stepped into her body and moved her somehow, deep inside. An all-over tingling sensation swamped her, and she was flooded with a strange energy. She'd been feeling this a few times recently and just assumed it was a side effect of anxiety.

'But how about spiritually?' Sharon asked. 'How about for you? Don't you lie there at night and require some closure? Because that's how I feel,' she continued, gently fingering her puffy cheeks. Bryony noticed her fingernails, which were painted a shade of mint green. She also looked painfully thin.

Did Bryony lie awake at night wanting closure? All she wanted was Max. Her old life and all that came with it.

'I don't think I do want closure. Honestly.' Bryony spoke from her heart. 'My world has been torn in two; I can't imagine genuinely enjoying my life ever again. Even when I'm happy for a fleeting moment, the sadness creeps in, haunting me. How can I turn around to the person who did this to my boyfriend, and to me, and give him some kind of comfort, when the rest of my days will be full of pain, and my boyfriend, well, he has no days left?'

Bryony realised she was crying as she said this, and that it was as if it was just Sharon and her there; and that Sol, and the mechanic, and the posh man and all the rest of them had quietly left the room.

'So why can't you forgive?' Bryony asked Sharon, feeling a sickness rise in her chest, but pushing it away. For some reason, she desperately felt she needed to connect with her, to be challenged by her.

Sharon bowed her head, before looking up again and scanning the faces that were now all turned in her direction, waiting for some answers and some guidance.

'I'm not sure . . . I just know I can't . . . Well, not yet, anyway.'

'Well, I haven't forgiven the man who killed my dog,' came the deep voice of the posh man, who was rubbing his palms up and down his brightly coloured trousers, his moustache twitching a little. His cheeks were almost dog-like, Bryony realised, with great jowls that were almost on a level with his pendulous earlobes. It reminded her of the start of the old *101 Dalmatians* film, and how Pongo stared longingly down into the street at the dogs and their startlingly similar owners, all pointed noses and sharp tails. She smiled inside.

'Is that why you're here?' asked Mai, who was clearly feeling more confident now.

'Yes. I know – I know it's silly, but he was all I had left, really, after my wife died. And then one day, a man hit him with his car and just left him in the road. He didn't even try to knock on my door. My phone number was on his collar, for God's sake,' he said, in sad disbelief. He looked a little unstable, but for the first time all morning,

Bryony felt a jerk of emotion tug at her. She knew they were talking about a *dog*, for goodness' sake, but she suddenly realised that loss didn't necessarily amount to scale, and that the loss of this man's dog meant the same to him as losing Max did to her.

Her gorgeous Max. His face flashed before her again, his cheeky grin, a cigarette hanging from his lips as he had laughed that first day at the pub. The ache returned.

'Would you forgive the man who killed your dog if he knocked on your door tomorrow?' Bryony asked now, nervously, asking the question to chase away the lump in her throat.

The man straightened his dickie-bow tie, which was covered in black and white polka dots, and leant back in his chair. 'Hmmmm. Yes, I believe I could, if I tried hard enough,' he said, with an almost Victor Meldrew-like tone to his voice.

'Why?' Bryony asked.

'Because it would make me feel better.'

'So, basically, are you saying that forgiveness makes the sufferer feel better? That it could help to heal, even?' she probed, raising one eyebrow and feeling a lightness dance around her chest as she started to make new links in her thought processes. Thought processes that had previously been lost in a dark murky cloud.

'Yes, good point, Mel,' Sol said, clapping his hands together loudly, the sound reverberating around the room.

It made her flinch. It reminded her of a gunshot. She took a deep breath.

'Sharon, have you seen this person? The one you want to forgive? Have you seen them recently?' Mai piped up. There was an instant flicker of something across her features, which made her look guilty for accidentally taking her questioning a little too far.

Sharon looked down at her lap again. The sound of children playing outside could be heard for a few seconds.

'No.'

'When was the last time you saw them?' Mai asked, looking nervous.

'The last time I saw them – him – was before he was sent to prison,' Sharon replied. 'I haven't been to see him in prison. He's been locked away for what feels like a long time now . . .' She trailed off, starting to weep again.

There was another pause, the roar of a distant bus disturbing them this time.

'Do you think it would make you feel better to—' Mai continued, but was interrupted.

'Mai, sorry, but Sharon, do you mind being asked these questions?' Sol asked her, stepping into what was becoming a heated situation, while smiling at Mai as if to say 'You aren't doing wrong, I just need to double check'.

He's good at this, Bryony thought, understanding now why he was there. There was a reason he did this stuff, and it was becoming clear.

'No. No, I don't at all. What were you going to say?' Sharon said, looking Mai straight in the eyes, an expression of fear on her face. They were all facing demons, and it wasn't always a comfortable process. Bryony could see it behind everyone's eyes.

'Yes, I was just going to say, do you think it would make *you* feel better to forgive him?' Mai asked, her bottom lip trembling a little as if she was scared of what she might say.

'Yes,' said Sharon, slowly. 'I have thought recently that it would. I can't seem to find peace without forgiving him. I just need to work out how – I feel like there is something big missing from the process of being able to cope with all this, and that could well be it.'

'How about you, Mel?'

Bryony continued staring at the floor, lost in thought.

'Mel?'

Thinking . . . thinking about how this affected her and her situation. She didn't even know who . . .

'Mel? Are you OK?'

Shit. They were talking to her, she realised, snapping back into the room. 'Oh, sorry, I got a bit lost in thought there . . .'

The question had come from Dave the mechanic, whose wife, it came out, had been killed by a speeding policeman on an emergency call. He repeated his question to Bryony. 'Could you forgive

355

the person who killed your boyfriend?' he asked, his brow furrowed as he stared at her.

Bryony unconsciously ran her fingers through her hair for comfort – she had kept it loose so she would be able to fiddle with it. She felt the soft strands trickle through her fingers like water. She imagined a man in front of her, the person who had done this to Max. All she wanted to do was scratch his face, and claw at his body until he felt pain. Until he cried like she had. *How am I going to put this . . .*

'I actually don't know who did it,' Bryony said, her fingers meeting a clump of knots at the end of her hair.

'Wow, really? Wasn't the murd—, um, person caught, then?' Dave replied.

Bryony shook her head. 'No, it's not that,' she said. 'I didn't, I *don't*, want to know. I don't want to picture him, don't want to know the person who killed my boyfriend. It's just . . . easier that way for me.' She nodded calmly. Except inside there was a storm. Her heart was beating fast, and she had started to feel lightheaded. The faces of everyone in the room started moving in and out of focus, as though she were on a fairground ride. She hated talking about this side of things. It terrified her. She could feel her pulse thudding hard in her neck. 'Yup . . .' She trailed off. 'So, listen everyone, I'm going to have to go now; I have a doctor's appointment,' Bryony said with fake positivity, standing up suddenly and grabbing her bag.

The contents clunked loudly as she lifted it from the floor.

'Really, Mel? Are you sure you're OK?' Sol asked, rising to his feet again as she shuffled around the chair, her head spinning faster and faster. Tea cups. House of horrors. A ferris wheel. No vision.

'Yup. Yup, just, er, a routine thingaling, you know, just a check-up, with the whole blood pressure vibe going on . . .' Bryony said, walking out of the hall as quickly as she could, still speaking as she exited through the large double doors that lead out onto the street.

She walked over to a bus stop, and perched on the red plastic seating. Once she was settled she asked Max a question. She hoped he could hear her somehow, and tell her the answer.

'How can I make this better?'

CHAPTER 32

. . . HE TRIED TO SPEAK TO GOD.

Thursday 23 July 2009
Prison Wing A, High Elm Prison, south
west London
11.30 p.m.

He still hadn't heard from his mother or his sister.

Keon had been locked away for a few months now. He was saddened that his mother hadn't been in touch, and wondered if it was because she no longer wanted him as family. He'd questioned everything he ever knew about his relationship with his mother, whose forgiveness and extraordinary patience usually knew no bounds.

Was she scared of him? That thought was the most frightening of all.

The evening had been, without a doubt, one of the worst Keon had experienced inside. He had tried going to sleep at ten to get an early night but all the noise in his head had kept him wide-eyed, like a barn owl, as he shuffled his legs around in the scratchy sheets. It was only 11.30 p.m., but he had a feeling he would be awake for a while yet. He could have been having an ordinary night at home that night, with his family, if things hadn't worked out how they did.

Now that he didn't have the option, Keon was thinking about all the things he would do if he was at home.

It had been his mother's thirty-eighth birthday a couple of weeks ago. He realised he was starting to forget what her voice sounded like. But he could remember her hands. His mother's were delicate, dainty. If he had been home . . . he would have bought her as many David Attenborough box sets as he could get his hands on. She loved them.

Keon had realised, in his quiet isolation, that he'd always been a bit selfish when it came to presents. Year after year, his mother had broken her back trying to get him whatever it was he wanted, even though she couldn't really afford it. Games consoles, expensive but ugly trainers, shirts he ended up leaving at the bottom of the laundry basket until they stank. He had never really understood the meaning of her actions, until now.

And his sister . . . she had most likely changed so much since he last saw her it would probably scare him. He remembered her really long eyelashes – he had always called her 'Giraffe' because of them, and she had hated it. She was so pretty, his sister, and it used to make him angry when she cried over boys, because boys were foolish and she was better than that. Much more ready for the world than stupid, teenage boys. Now there was nothing he could do for her. Lads would be able to hurt her, give her the run-around: he couldn't be a brother to her locked up in here.

He vowed that if he could transport himself back home, he would help with dinner too, instead of sitting in front of the TV in his tracksuit bottoms like he used to, stuffing his face with chocolate, ignoring his mum's shouts for help from the kitchen. He would go to the corner shop when she realised she had forgotten something she needed, something she used to do quite regularly. And Keon would go and visit his nan on his father's side, because she got lonely and sad some-times. Despite the breakdown in his relationship with his dad, Tynice had always encouraged him to visit his only remaining grandmother. 'It's not her fault, Keon, just remember that . . . you are still her grandson,' she had told him, time and time again. He would take his grandma her favourite treat – custard tarts – and give her a big cuddle, feel her frail body in his arms and try to understand what growing old was about, and whether he could make it better somehow. Keon realised he would never see her again now. Never. He would never see her nose again, covered in dark brown freckles, or hear her lecture him about treating women well.

He would do things for other people and listen to what they had to say. Just fucking *listen* to something other than his own selfish voice telling him what to do for himself, to do what made him happy. 'Me, me, me,' he whispered now, gripping his hands together. The dry skin on his fingers pulled over the bones of his knuckles, creating sharp, sore lines.

He would babysit for his Aunty Leah as well, so she could go out with his mother and actually enjoy herself for once. He imagined them giggling in a bar somewhere, commenting on how they felt old now and laughing at men and their cringe-worthy dance moves.

All the things he would do . . .

And he was thinking about Bryony, too, and how long she had been without Max for. Was she with friends and family, or was she alone, staring out of the window and wondering why this had all happened to her?

Oh, God. He couldn't even think about it . . . it was unbearably painful.

He felt panicked suddenly, lying on the stiff bed. The panic tingled through his body, all the way down to his toes. It gathered at the pads of his fingertips like the most painful magic. He tried to concentrate on something else.

The bed . . . it was hard. Uncomfortable. He had thought he'd get used to it but he couldn't.

Keon had taken Eddie's suggestion of letter-writing to heart. He'd sent a few now, to Bryony, but she hadn't replied or come to visit. Her and Max's address had been read out in court several times, he was pretty sure he remembered it.

They had started off short, but then Keon had wondered if maybe she needed to hear more to understand him. He sat up in his bed now and positioned himself so his back was pressed against the cold, white bricks of the wall, his legs slanted at just the right angle so he could use them as a desk to write on. Keon had lost weight since he had arrived at the prison, and could feel each bump of his back against the hard surface. It was uncomfortable, but it didn't matter any more. Life was uncomfortable now.

A little while later, Keon wrote Bryony's address neatly and clearly on the front of the envelope, just like he had with all the previous letters.

It was late. Having finished his letter to Bryony, he tried to speak to God. *Hi, I know you haven't heard from me in a while*, he thought . . . *Not properly anyway . . . I'm new to all this . . . I hope you don't mind me calling on you so late. I hope I haven't woken you* . . . Keon prayed to God that Bryony would open his letter. He prayed to God she would read it, and keep reading until she reached the very bottom line. And he prayed to God, that in some small way, it would help.

Keon was interrupted by a shadow suddenly falling on the bars to his cell. The light was just so that he could only make out the figure of a man accompanied by a guard, standing there, looking sad. The man said nothing, yet everything in his body language said so much.

He turned his head to the side and Keon could see that it was Eddie.

'Try to go to sleep, mate,' Eddie whispered, in the saddest tone Keon had ever heard.

There was silence because he didn't know what to say. 'Yeah, you too, man. What are you doing up, anyway?' Keon asked, rolling over and stretching out, feeling a little better now that another letter to Bryony was written.

There was another silence, longer than the first. 'I'm really depressed, Keon . . . Keon?'

But Keon didn't hear Eddie's reply. He had fallen into a deep sleep.

CHAPTER 33

'HOW DID YOU MANAGE IT?'

Monday 3 August 2009
Drayton Road Community Centre, north
London
10.30 a.m.

Bryony's close friendship with Adam still left her riddled with mixed emotions, and all too often found herself in the middle of a vicious fight between guilt and yearning. They sat in almost deserted cinemas on rainy summer afternoons and watched films about love, while she chewed fizzy sweets, wiping tears from her eyes that were still hidden behind her Ray-Bans. When the sun was out, they'd head to London parks and enjoy picnics, splayed out together on tartan blankets as the world moved calmly around them.

Adam still didn't know what had happened to her, as Bryony still needed him to be her escape. Despite being attracted to him, she didn't really care if it was just a passing thing: a friendship that had a limited shelf life but one that would do something tangible and miraculous for the both of them.

And it was miraculous, in its way. They would make origami animals in his flat and listen to their favourite bands, drinking neat whisky and smoking Lucky Strikes. He'd never once tried it on with her, but the conversation she had overheard in his flat still plagued her.

Bryony decided she had become his project. She didn't mind at all . . . she needed to be saved, and knew he was the one to do it. She needed him, really, but she secretly hoped he would get a girl-friend one day so their friendship would come to a natural end, and stop hurtling down this confusing path.

'You're quite a sad, brooding sort of person, aren't you?' Adam had asked one afternoon, as the rain trickled down the kitchen windows.

'Yeah, I always have been,' she had replied, lying through her teeth.

Even with her Eeyore-like posture and general moping, Adam seemed to enjoy being with her. It was as if he was carrying a stuffed-toy version of the Winnie-the-Pooh character round the funfair with him, while it frowned and stared emptily at all the rides and the lights. Despite this, he seemed to want to see her as much as he could: she didn't know why, as she imagined it would be a little like hanging out with a rain cloud.

Bryony was thinking about Adam as she sat in the community hall waiting for the Grief and Loss Forum session to start. She was thinking about the things they had planned to do, including travelling around Europe, and finally ditching the jars of sauce and making a curry from scratch.

'Mel. How are you feeling today?' Sol asked, breaking her train of thought and making her jump slightly in the chair.

'Not good,' she responded before she could stop herself. She looked around at the faces she had studied a couple of times now, and no longer feared. They all had something in common, after all.

'Can you tell us why?' Sol asked, sitting on the floor, cross-legged. Today his T-shirt said 'A smile is good'. Bryony resented him for it, and its simple message.

'Erm, I would rather not say exactly why, but I'm wondering about something that I wanted to bring up today . . . That is, is it *strange* that I avoided, I mean, *completely* managed to avoid, finding out any details about the person who killed my boyfriend?'

There it was, all coming out again. Bryony hadn't planned to say it, but it seemed to be the general trend in there. People came in closed like an oyster, and yet something in the air made them spill the secrets they had kept so close to their hearts in the outside world. In that dull, moth-eaten room, the things they hid behind a long fringe or a newspaper on the train just rolled from their mouths like a ball of sad, unravelling string.

Mai piped up, 'How did you manage it?'

Bryony took a deep breath and wondered for a

366

moment how she *had* managed it. It hadn't been easy. It had involved long, drawn-out, puzzled conversations with loved ones, fingers pushed onto lips in coffee shops when the information she feared most had threatened to come out and find her.

'I just didn't read the stories about it. I told my friends and family I didn't want to know, and the police, and the caseworkers, and the journalists. I made the rules and people respected them. I gave one local paper an interview, a tribute story, and I avoided the court case. And then I hoped I would be in this blissful place where my boyfriend isn't etched on my memory and all I can focus on is his legacy . . . But *is* it weird?' she asked.

Bryony had thought a lot recently about the fact that not many people did this. What she had done. Developed a fear of the person who had taken everything away from them. A fear so strong it had become an obsession to keep him out of her mind, and that then, as a result, this person *was* always on her mind . . .

'It's unusual,' Sol said, shuffling a little on his bum to get more comfortable.

'I'm amazed by it, really. Don't you want to have someone to hate, someone to blame for all this?' Sharon asked.

'I hate the person who did it, don't get me wrong,' replied Bryony, with a tired smile. 'But I can't know what he looks like, or sounds like, or how he acts – it's too scary for me. I feel like if I saw him, or even met him, I would implode with fury. There's too much hiding beneath the surface, if that makes sense . . . He has become my greatest fear,' Bryony finished, distantly aware again of the sound of children outside the centre: the neat thump of a ball as it was bounced on the hard surface of the pavement.

Her greatest fear. A blurred-out face that haunted her in her nightmares, when the foxes were busy raiding bins and the homeless shivered inside layers of yesterday's newspapers. *But then the imagination often works without us,* Bryony thought, *leaving us behind in its wake as it paints pictures and creates stories that may or may not have happened in the real world.* And hers had already created an image of the man. She saw him as being in his thirties, rough-looking, a degenerate, a drug user perhaps. He had pale skin and blond hair, and he showed no remorse as he was sent down for what he had done to Max.

Sometimes Bryony would dream that the man, the monster, was out and about in the real world, shopping for cooking oil and loo paper in Tesco, or picking up a copy of the *Sun* in the corner shop. She would try to ask him questions, to hit him, and punch him, but he dissolved or faded or melted into the background, and none of her questions were answered.

Sharon started speaking again; her throat sounded gravelly, like she was a little unwell. 'Do you think maybe it's time to find out who he is?' she said. Her cheeks had a rich pink shade to them today, matching her bright fuchsia shirt, which was tucked into a pair of smart black trousers.

Bryony wasn't ready. *Heart. Beating. Fast.* 'No, I don't think it is.'

Sharon didn't say anything to this, but she closed her lips tightly.

Sharon herself still wasn't ready to give anything away and, for this reason, Bryony was still even more fascinated by her than she was with anyone else.

The session passed quickly, partly because the conversation seemed easier and less guarded, and partly because Bryony couldn't wait to go over to Adam's and play rum Scrabble.

As she was leaving, a voice called to her.

'Mel?'

Bryony turned around immediately, used to her new name and persona now. 'Yes?' Bryony saw Sharon standing there, one hand rooting around in her handbag, the other holding onto its eighties-style gold chain strap. Her thick hair had been straightened and glistened in the small beam of sunlight that poured from a skylight.

'Listen, just say no if you don't feel comfortable with this, but I find it helpful talking to you and I wondered if maybe one day we could meet for a coffee – you know, away from, well, you know, all this?' Sharon asked, looking nervous and vulnerable. She pulled out a mobile phone from her bag, as if in the hope that she could soon fill it with the number that would connect them.

Bryony thought about it. Would this be good for her?

Sharon's eyes were filled with a certain level of desperation.

'Yes, of course,' Bryony said, smiling. She reached out, took Sharon's phone and typed her number into it.

'Thank you so, so much,' Sharon said, tearfully, before turning around and exiting quickly, as if overwhelmed.

Everyone had left by now and Bryony stood alone at the back of the hall, her eyes scanning piles of leaflets offering help to people on a variety of subjects, from debt, to abuse, to drugs . . . Where was the leaflet for her? she wondered. The one that would tell her the answers to all the questions she still had? Where was the booklet for the people who were now lost without their loved ones, who had had them taken away from them by a cruel, sudden and untimely death?

Bryony couldn't see one, so she pushed her weight against the heavy door, crossed the street and jumped on the 259 bus, her breath building up in sad condensation on the dirty glass of the window.

She wrote three letters in the cloud of steam with her index finger.

M
A
X

CHAPTER 34

SHE WONDERED WHERE SHE BELONGED.

Tuesday 11 August 2009
Soho, central London
9 a.m.

'I don't think I'm very funny any more,' Richard said, curled up into the foetal position in his double bed.

His Superman-themed duvet cover and pillow-cases smelt fresh and airy, something that Rachel had loved about Richard ever since she had first slipped beneath the sheets with him after a night of cocktails and laughter. He was a scruffy man, and a disorganised one at that, but his sheets were always washed and ironed, to an almost military standard.

But while his sheets had stayed the same, things were different now.

His white T-shirt and Calvin Klein pyjama bottoms were creased from a night of tossing and turning; his thick-rimmed glasses were pushed up against his nose, which was squashed to the pillow. Rachel could see that the frames were digging into

371

the sides of his face – he pulled them off impatiently and threw them across the room.

They clattered against the radiator loudly before landing on a pile of magazines.

'Oh, come on, Richard,' Rachel said, swishing her long, muscular legs under the covers, her eyes still blurry with sleepiness. 'You've probably broken them now,' she added.

'I don't care.'

She needed a lie-in this morning, what with all the shows, training, promotional duties and posh cocktail parties she had to fit into her schedule. Life had been nothing short of an exhausting blur recently, and she needed a long, deep sleep where not only could her mind repair and rest, but her muscles, too. If only all the torn, overworked fibres in her body could have just a few hours respite . . .

'And no, Rachey, it's not just a moan – things aren't going so well, any more. After the whole drunk-on-stage thing, I thought I could rebuild my career,' Richard grumbled, pulling himself even tighter into a ball and pushing out his bottom lip the way a child does when their mother won't buy them something in the supermarket.

Rachel looked down at her right hand; she was wearing a beautiful ring Lisa had given her. It seemed so extravagant, given how much her mother seemed to struggle with money, but she told her it was a family heirloom and that she wanted to give it to her to celebrate the two of them being in each other's lives again.

It was stunning, and she couldn't stop looking at it.

'I thought the last gig went well? You'd been preparing enough,' Rachel said, sitting up now and giving up on the hope of sleep. She smoothed the covers around herself, looking at the world's best-known superhero in action. Superman's chiselled face was drawn into an expression of determination. A determination that seemed to have slipped from Richard's reach in recent weeks.

'Well, no, it didn't really – ticket sales were down dramatically, and the papers slagged me off again.' Richard sighed. 'And I've had fewer promotional requests, so my agent is worried,' he said, swinging his right leg away from the covers and into fresh air. He moved his toes around a little, watching them. His hair was ruffled and out of place. 'We were hoping I would be selected as the support act at that Hammersmith Apollo thing, remember? I should have had my own show there anyway, before the big incident, but then that came up . . .'

'Yeah, of course.'

'And, well, I found out yesterday I haven't been chosen. I'm so disappointed. It would have been the perfect opportunity to get out there again.'

'Well, why didn't you tell me this last night before bed? Have you been stewing on it the whole night?' Rachel asked, picking up a book from the bedside table and unseeingly turning it over in her hands, as if, maybe, somewhere between the pages of

David Nicholls' *One Day* lay the answers to all their problems.

The whole situation had always been a little awkward, in fact, with Rachel's career flourishing in contrast to Richard's flailing efforts to make a lasting name for himself, particularly after his very public slip-up. Rachel's career had grown into a bright, blooming sunflower while Richard's was now comparable to a thirsty, limp buttercup wilting in its shadow.

But no one actually said that, of course.

'I've been worrying about it but didn't want to say anything,' he said sulkily, closing his eyes tight and making the soft, pale skin of his eyelids crinkle.

Rachel took a deep breath, expelling the air in the form of a loud sigh. 'Have you thought of talking to anyone in the industry who has been around a little longer? Surely all people go through peaks and troughs in the comedy world? People make mistakes, much worse than yours, and they rebuild careers,' she said, looking out of the small window. It was slightly open, and a cool breeze filtered into the room they shared.

'I don't want to.'

'Why?'

'Because it's embarrassing. I've screwed things up, I really have.'

Rachel couldn't understand this: her boyfriend's panic and how it often stood firm and stubborn in the way of actual progress, development and better knowledge.

'So, what are you going to do? Just lie in bed moaning?' she replied, before realising this might not be the softly, softly approach he was looking for.

Richard physically flinched at her words, and turned over so his back was facing her, his ribs moving up and down heavily. She could feel fury boiling away inside him. A bird was singing loudly from a tree by the bedroom window, its feet wrapped around a thick twig, wings extending every now and then for balance. 'Shut up!' Richard suddenly shouted at the small creature, which flitted away in fright.

Rachel was so shocked by his shout and the unfair way he was taking his anger out on a bird that she slapped him hard across the arm.

'Those fucking birds are always there, waking me up with their tweet-twit-twatting bullshit singing,' he said sulkily, pulling a heavy, feather-filled pillow from beneath his head and bringing it down over his ears with force. At that moment, the radio on the bedside table suddenly clicked into life as its alarm went off, in the form of Lady Gaga's 'Bad Romance'. Richard's hand shot out from beneath the covers and smashed down on the stop button. A glass of water juddered but didn't fall.

Rachel looked at Richard and saw a little boy.

The Superman duvet set was an attempt at being a bit retro and cool, much like a lot of the accessories in his home: the strangely shaped designer

375

chairs he had bought with his first six-figure pay cheque; the lamp which defied gravity and was almost impossible for the cleaner to dust; and the bookshelf that had collapsed on the first day it was put up, smashing a 42-inch TV in the process. But now, when she studied him and his handsome frame under those Superman sheets, cowering away from reality, she realised they were indicative of his relationship with the world. He had a lot of growing up to do.

'And, Rachey, I don't mean to be rude, babe, but when are *you* going to sort yourself out?' he asked now in muffled tones, from beneath the pillow.

Rachel's blood started to fizz and thrill inside her veins as she lay in the bed of the man who was supposed to look after her. But she also had to acknowledge that she was angry because she knew, deep down, that she didn't really belong there.

Richard had, slowly but surely, made it clear that he didn't want her around. Didn't want her 'filling the bathroom with bottles of shower gel and mois-turising lotion', and 'littering the wardrobe' with carefully chosen dresses from upmarket City boutiques.

She felt fury now as she looked back on her old home, its large, familiar winding staircases in eggshell white – and how her adoptive parents had not attempted to contact her ever since she had stormed out. She didn't belong there, that was for sure, she reckoned, picturing Rita and Edward eating asparagus tips and drinking wine, perfectly happy without her . . .

In fact, life probably *was* better without her now. Now they didn't have to follow her around the country for rehearsals and shows, hoovering up the dust and rosin from her ballet shoes, and mopping her continual flow of nervous tears.

And she felt fear when she considered the flat where her real mother lived, where leaves blew around in the downstairs corridors, mixed with discarded cigarette packets and regret. She knew that she certainly didn't belong there, either.

Not belonging anywhere, she realised, was a spectacularly empty state of affairs.

Tears started to sting her eyes. Angry tears. 'What do you mean "sort myself out"?' she cried, sitting bolt upright and running a hand through her hair, which had managed to gather together in clumps where she had tossed and turned during the night.

Richard stayed hidden away beneath the safety of the pillow. 'Well, you know . . . You moving in was supposed to be a very temporary thing, Rachey. I'm happy to have you, of course I am, but we weren't ready to move in together before, were we? And now, well, now it seems like this has been, well . . . forced on us,' he finished, the normally steady and strong metre of his well-spoken voice floundering a little under the strain of what he was saying; as though his words were tripping over his tongue on their way out.

Rachel said nothing, pulling the covers back with fury, inviting a blast of air into the warm space they once shared. The cool air obliged and rushed in, making the hairs on Richard's legs stand angrily to attention. She started to pull on the clothes that were crumpled on the floor at the side of the bed, jabbing angry limbs into trouser legs, punching her fists into a faded T-shirt. 'You fuckwit,' she yelled, spitting out the words as she found herself once again stuffing possessions into yet another bag.

'Oh, come on, baby, I didn't mean you have to just leave now, for goodness' sake.' Richard had finally come out of his pillowy shelter and sat up, his face puffy from sleep, eyes small and pig-like.

'Nope, don't you worry, you just stay there bitching and moaning and I'll leave,' Rachel said, almost ripping her phone charger from the plug socket in the wall. 'You're depressing me anyway,' she added, with an angry nod in his direction.

'Where are you going to go?' he asked, running a hand through his hair in confusion, blinking frantically to get a little more clarity on the scene, and the situation.

That was a good question. A question that made her blood run cold. She certainly couldn't go back to her parents and, anyway, her pride would not warrant it. They had done her wrong and the relationship had been severed, in her eyes. She was awaiting a serious apology from them both

378

and, until that day came, she had vowed to never contact them again.

Yet she certainly couldn't stay in this apartment of broken dreams and pretentious furniture.

'A friend's house or something,' she said, realising that she'd been so wrapped up in herself that she had lost sight of her friends and hadn't seen them in months. They would probably now open their doors and greet her with awkward smiles and promises of a sofa. And then they would find something about the way she lived deeply irritating, and eventually sit her on the same lumpy sofa with meek, awkward smiles, and ask her to leave 'at some point soon', because she hadn't really been all that welcome in the first place.

She considered this as she shoved her last few items of clothing into a large Mulberry weekend bag. She had always been under someone's roof, looked after, cared for, and now, in a moment of bright clarity, she understood why her parents had treated her like that: they had been trying to compensate for her abandonment. Rachel had always put it down to the demands of her career, the way her mother took care of everything just because she was tired or stressed . . . She'd realised recently, perhaps a little too late, that all her friends did their own washing and cleaned their own houses. A driver didn't pick them up for events; they didn't have their own stylists for industry parties . . .

But she still needed somewhere for the interim, and there seemed only one option.

Rachel left Richard's apartment with her trademark door-slam.

It took just half an hour for her to make the journey. The bus was packed with the usual crowd: handsome men in suits mixed in with rugged-looking builders and electricians in well-loved overalls; beautifully dressed businesswomen and young girls in torn jeans and Converse trainers.

Rachel looked at her hands, which were wrapped around a bright yellow pole on the 38. Her nails were painted an angry black, she wore a T-shirt with an old 'The Who' album cover printed on the front in faded grey, while her muscular legs were hidden inside a pair of skinny jeans. The only way anyone could tell she was one of the country's most up-and-coming ballerinas was by her swan-like neck and elegant poise. Her thick, blonde hair was pulled back into her trademark ponytail: a neat, clean look.

She wondered where she belonged, in this crazy city where everything seemed so regimented. Where there appeared to be a set social order. But there must be people like her who were just different . . . People who didn't trudge into an office day in, day out; people whose family were mixed up and confused, too.

She knocked on the door three times, lightly.

Lisa answered in her light blue carer uniform.

She seemed to have more wrinkles under her eyes than the last time Rachel had seen her – a few weeks ago in an Asda café. It seemed to Rachel as if Lisa was collecting them like stamps, to show all the places she had been and everything she'd felt along the way.

'Oh, hello, love, you all right?' Lisa asked, looking a little put out but pleased, all at the same time. An unusual skill that only she seemed to be able to master without causing offence.

'Not really,' replied Rachel. 'I need to come and stay for a while. Is that OK?' She blurted it out, clutching the handle of her bag with sweaty palms as her heart rate sped up.

'Well, yeah, of course . . . Look, I have to go to work in a minute, but come in, love.'

Rachel felt a rush inside and knew she was finally welcome. This place, however unconventional or different to her old world, was where she could really be 'home', until she found her feet.

She stepped inside, into the living room, her eyes stinging with the cigarette smoke that gave the room a sepia tone. There were toys and clothes everywhere. She took a deep, sad breath and kicked off her shoes.

CHAPTER 35

'WHAT ON EARTH ARE
YOU DOING?'

Saturday 15 August 2009
Shoreditch, east London
7.30 p.m.

It had been a scorchingly hot day, and the city
was buzzing with the usual excited banter
spilling from bars on every street.

Adam ran his sweaty palms down the side of
his black jeans, and followed Bryony into the bar.
Its walls were covered in painfully cool artwork
and colourful painted lines that resembled the
London tube network. Everyone in The Book
Club, Shoreditch, was desperately trendy. Adam
scanned his eyes over the crowd, noticing thick-
framed glasses, sharp haircuts and mysterious
tattoos, and his familiar feeling of never quite
fitting in returned.

His focus moved back to Bryony, who was now
leaning on the bar. Her long hair was casually tied
into a low side ponytail. She wore a back-to-front
necklace, which glistened in the light as it trickled
down her spine.

A few of the other guys in the place were glancing over at her and it made Adam smile to himself. *She's that kind of girl,* he thought. The kind who made men nudge their mates and point her out, ever so subtly. Adam couldn't blame them at all, and he often found himself quietly amused by the reaction she got when they went out.

Adam bought the first round: a large white wine for Bryony and a Corona for himself. The barmaid wedged a slice of lime into the top of the bottle and it splashed thirstily into the fizzing liquid below.

Bryony sat opposite him at a table that resembled an artist's workbench, with a thick, imperfect wooden surface, stroking the stem of her wineglass with her fingers and gazing at the ice cubes. All of a sudden, Adam found that the bubbling flow of conversation that had always been so easy for them was no longer there. She seemed tired.

Adam felt the condensation on his bottle and started playing with the label.

'Are you OK?' Bryony asked, her straight white teeth glinting in the light as she smiled.

'Yup. Yup. Great, thanks.'

'You look really stressed,' she said, tilting her head to one side and smiling widely, her ponytail brushing across her shoulder. She seemed to come back to life when she was focusing on someone else.

Adam took a deep breath, and for a moment

Bryony wondered if he had grown tired of her. Bored of the moping and the sadness that she could never provide a genuine reason for. Bored of the distance she always kept him at when it came to her life and her thoughts.

'You know, work is pretty full-on at the moment . . .' He trailed off.

Bryony blinked at him a few times, her face as blank as a new canvas. Her eyes had emptied, leaving two huge, limpid pools shining back at him.

Bryony and Adam both knew that his shifts at the café were generally not that 'full-on', that they often comprised him staring out of a window and absent-mindedly wiping down the same table, again and again.

'Is it your masters?' she continued, trying to work out what was suddenly wrong with her friend.

'Yes, that too,' he replied, taking a deep gulp from his drink. 'Listen, Bryony . . . there's something I need to tell you,' Adam said.

'OK, what's that?' she said, smiling playfully but wondering deep down if their friendship was over. Maybe he'd got a girlfriend. Perhaps there was a woman in his life who did not appreciate him hanging around with her . . . She suddenly felt a deep sadness at that even being a possibility, but pushed the thought from her mind. She stared at Adam. He looked strange.

He started to stutter a little but couldn't quite start his sentence, let alone finish it.

She wondered if he was feeling OK. There seemed to be a pallid tone to his skin and his eyes were darting around nervously.

And then, out of nowhere, he leant across the space between them and before Bryony had even realised what was going on, he had run his fingers through her ponytail, and kissed her.

'Adam!' she gasped, pushing him away from her.

Adam jumped back in his seat, to be greeted with the sight of her rigid with fury. He had knocked over her glass of wine in the process, and the sound of shattering glass meant they now had an audience.

'Bryony . . . I'm sorry,' he said, pushing his head into his hands, embarrassed at the swathes of people who had just witnessed his failed attempt at kissing the most beautiful girl in the bar. He looked at her in shame. Her eyes were wide, and she reminded him of a frightened deer. Her response was so extreme. So dramatic. The anger in her eyes was terrifying.

'What on earth are you doing? You're supposed to be my friend! I don't – I don't *need* this, OK? I don't need *you* . . .' she whispered furiously, a nastiness that Adam had not seen before clouding her features.

But, most of all, she just looked scared.

Bryony stared at Adam for a few more moments before standing up, grabbing hold of her bag and storming out of the bar.

Adam sat there for at least five minutes after she had gone, realising that by rushing in like that he had lost the most wonderful thing to walk into his life for a very long time.

CHAPTER 36

THE BEAUTIFUL YOUNG GIRL BEFORE HER.

Saturday 5 September 2009
Covent Garden, central London
3 p.m.

Bryony was nervous.

Jitters had materialised in the pit of her stomach, like a thousand tiny butterflies that had burst into life and were now flapping into her veins. She felt nauseous and short tempered. She had told so many lies about who she was, and now she would have to continue to ensure she was consistent on it all; in some small attempt to understand the monstrous things that had happened to her.

She wasn't even sure if this was a good idea, meeting up with Sharon, a woman who had given so little away. But it was their third meeting now, and she kept coming back. It seemed to be more about Bryony talking, while Sharon just listened, gleaning everything she could from the beautiful young girl before her.

They had arranged to meet in the main square

at Covent Garden this time. As she waited, Bryony half watched a slight, elderly man with wild, matted hair and wellington boots standing on a dented crate, haranguing passers-by with what she considered to be utter nonsense surrounding consumerism, designer labels and the end of the world. Shoppers were startled, scuttling past as they received screams of abuse about the carrier bags in their hands and how they were feeding a society that would soon implode, dramatically and gruesomely – according to him.

Bryony sneezed suddenly and, as she was blowing her nose, accidentally met eyes with him. The man was now throwing his fists into the air, revealing large, gaping holes in the armpits of his green T-shirt.

'You! You over there!' The man pointed at her now, stepping down from his box and shouldering through the crowds. A group of teenagers who had stopped to watch him and giggle behind hands cupped to their mouths started pointing, excited about what was to happen.

Bryony leant back against the brick wall behind her, shuffling her feet so she would be more comfortable as she prepared for an onslaught of criticism. She expected that he'd picked her because she had made an effort today, and looked relatively high maintenance. The kind of girl who spent her Saturdays trawling around Westfield with a credit card and its seemingly limitless limit, not caring about the future or the consequences. But she didn't need his lecture; she wasn't in the mood. And she felt frustrated at how she always attracted attention she didn't want: jeering comedians would always pick her out at comedy clubs so that she would have to quietly escape to the nearest toilet; drunks would always come and sit next to her on the train.

She looked down at her dark blue skinny jeans and her ankle boots, bought for her by her mother in a kind attempt to cheer her up. Her black leather jacket had been a present from Max. He'd found it in an expensive boutique for her twenty-fifth birthday. It was timeless, like his memory, but she would have traded it in, zips, sleeves and all, for just a moment with him.

Everything seemed to go quiet as the man waded through the crowds, like a film in slow motion, a snapped spool of celluloid. He shoved people out of the way as he attempted to get closer to her, abandoning the crate he'd been standing on.

She felt tears well in her eyes as Max had yet again returned to swamp her thoughts, blurring the vision of the strange man, who was now standing in front of her. He was so close that the tip of his dirty nose threatened almost to touch hers, pink and pure, scrubbed just hours before with Clinique.

'Give me a fag,' he demanded.

'No, sorry. Smoking's fucking bad for you,' she said, dully.

'A sandwich?' he asked.

389

'Nope.'

'Chewing gum? Give me some fucking chewing gum!'

'Nope.'

'Crisps?'

'No.'

'A fizzy drink?'

'No!' Bryony cried, raising her arms in the air in frustration, feeling her nerves fray just a little bit further.

'All right, chill out. No need to set your boyfriend on me!' the man said, gesturing at a young man who was walking towards her and staring with interest, but had nothing to do with her.

With that, something snapped inside Bryony, the final, taut thread that had been holding all her emotions deep inside. 'How *dare* you?' she shouted, pushing her fingers into his chest, and drawing gasps of excitement from passers-by who had caught a glimpse of the action.

'How dare I what?' he yelped, his foul breath wafting into her airspace.

'How dare you come to me, giving me all this bullshit about a boyfriend? I don't *have* a fucking boyfriend, OK? And do you want to know what happened to him? Do you?' she screamed, backing him against a tall pillar. Dozens of people were watching now, looks of horror on their faces, silent as the drama played out before them.

'Look, cool it, OK?' the man started to plead now, desperation on his face, his madness ebbing away from him as he backed down. It was all too apparent to Bryony that, away from his soap box, the man was just a shadow of himself, a bully reduced.

'He's *dead*! He's fucking dead, OK? And you have the cheek to come up to me like this, and talk about fags, and chewing gum, and fizzy fucking *drinks*?'

Her breathing was deep and fast, her hands shaking as he slid down the pillar until his bum was just touching the cold cobblestones. He was now cowering beneath her.

'I'm sorry. I'm sorry, OK?' he said, tears starting to fill his eyes, childlike vulnerability all over his face.

Bryony felt a hand on her back, and she shrugged it off, hard, not looking behind her to see who it was. She hoped it would be Max. She hoped she had dreamt the last half a year and that she would find Max behind her now, handsome and beautifully dressed, smelling of the spicy aftershave he always wore, ready to take her away to somewhere safe, where he would kiss her forehead until she stopped crying.

The hand touched her on her shoulder this time, a warm presence.

'Mel?'

She ignored the voice of the woman behind her, still staring blindly down at the man.

'Mel, love. Calm down,' said the woman, her persistence now filtering into Bryony's consciousness

391

and forcing her to turn around. Bryony suddenly remembered who Mel was. It was she, the person she was supposed to be around Sharon, who was now tearfully staring at her, and rubbing her arms with her hands in a bid to calm her down.

Bryony looked down at the ground in shame, as the man got to his feet and darted away back to his box, still shaking from the run-in.

'Love, what was all that about?' Sharon asked, her dark skin, looking purer than it ever had before, set against a baby blue tracksuit top and a silver chain hanging from her neck.

The onlookers had started to disperse, as had the smirks on their faces, which had melted into confusion and laughter.

'God, I'm so sorry,' Bryony said, looking up through tearful eyes and gesturing with her hands for the remainder of the crowd to disperse. To stop looking. And pointing. And staring. And *judging*.

'Come with me,' Sharon said, putting a warm arm around her and leading her into a small pub nearby.

Bryony sank into a large leather chair as Sharon made her way to the bar. She felt all the tension suddenly drain out from her, seeping out of the door and into the crisp autumn air. She couldn't go on like this. She could not continue her existence, pretending that everything was OK and then snapping wildly in public, drawing in audiences who looked on in horror at her breakdowns, which were so naked, raw and painful to experience.

She thought of Adam for a moment, and how he would feel to see her so wild and lost in the fury of tragedy. It was a far cry from the happiness she experienced when she was with him, sharing a huge bowl of crisps and watching DVDs. Would he be disappointed in her? Angry with her, even? Would he eventually get bored and frustrated and walk away from her?

They hadn't seen each other since he had tried to kiss her in the bar. She had told him she needed some time out, but she still couldn't believe he'd put her in that position. She thought she'd made her feelings clear, but then she could hardly blame him for anything; she hadn't exactly been truthful with him herself. There was still so much about her that he didn't know.

After five minutes of queuing, Sharon returned to the table with two glasses of Diet Coke. Bryony stared at her drink as the bubbles rose to the top. A small slice of lemon was bobbing around in its dark depths, brushing against glassy ice cubes.

'What happened there?' Sharon asked, taking a sip of her own drink.

'I'm sorry . . . this stupid guy was just shouting his mouth off in the square, and for some reason he came up to me, and it was fine, until he started talking about a boyfriend or something and I just flipped. Yet again,' Bryony finished lamely, rooting around in her bag and reaching for her sunglasses. She slid them over her face as she felt tears start to drip from her eyes. Her pink lips were pursed, striking against her pale, freckled skin.

Sharon tilted her head to one side and frowned, wondering how she could help this poor girl who had got so lost in grief.

'I keep doing it. I just go mad sometimes. I feel fine when I wake up; well, kind of fine, and then all it takes is for someone to say the wrong thing and that's it . . . I'm gone,' Bryony added, taking a sip of the freezing-cold drink, gritting her teeth to cope with the temperature.

'I understand, Mel. Totally,' she responded, trying to push away the sickening guilt that pulled away at her own heart.

Bryony still felt uncomfortable at being called Mel, but couldn't let it show. She had to be this person; she had to protect her true identity. She didn't even know why she had chosen the name. It didn't suit her. It didn't make sense to her. Melanies were blonde, from the experience of the two Mels she knew. They were healthy looking, and full of hope for a future that wouldn't be blighted by such tragedy.

'Have you given any more thought to making a visit to the prison yet?' Sharon asked, hoping the question would not be met with a tirade of fury.

'I've thought about it – I think about it a lot. But I still can't face knowing who did it.'

'I hate to say this, but do you think it could be the missing piece? That, maybe, in a way, you need to face up to this person to be able to cope with it all?' Sharon asked, realising how hypocritical it all sounded. But the truth was that Sharon had recognised this. She now knew that she would have to face up to her demons in order to move on, in some small way. In order to face all the people who knew what had happened, and had shunned her. Had turned their backs on her and her family. But she was struggling, too.

Bryony took in the words, and rolled them around in her mind. She hated to admit it, but maybe Sharon was right.

They discussed the idea over more soft drinks, which eventually turned into wine as the day melted into night. Candles were lit around them as they sat in the pub window, Bryony still wearing her sunglasses despite the cloak of evening.

A little later, the door to the pub slowly opened, forcing a gust of cool air into the front section, which made Bryony glance up as a shiver ran down her spine. The crate-ranting man from earlier, who now had on fingerless gloves and a gilet with a huge tear in the front, shuffled into the room, his head down, his curly hair bobbing as he moved.

She pulled her sunglasses down slowly as he approached her, her head full of the warm buzz of wine. He suddenly thrust a small piece of off-white paper in front of her and scuttled away, as quickly as he'd arrived.

Bryony crinkled up her forehead in confusion as she watched him run past the pub window and out of view.

'What's that?' Sharon asked, biting her bottom lip in fascination.

Bryony picked up the paper and felt its deep grain, thick and bumpy like soil, at her fingertips. It had clearly been torn from the pages of a posh restaurant menu, or something similar.

She opened it up and read two simple lines penned in the style of an eccentric: sharp jutting strokes in blobby, black ink.

I'm sorry.

Please try to forgive.

CHAPTER 37

CLOUDS WERE GATHERING
IN THE SKY.

Sunday 13 September 2009
Hackney, north east London
10 a.m.

Rachel awoke to the sound of a fight upstairs. On a Sunday morning. On God's day of rest, when the country was supposed to be rising to the smell of bacon and orange juice and, for some, the sound of church organs, the residents of the sixteenth floor of this Hackney tower block were pummelling each other into the ground.

At first she thought she was dreaming the loud bangs that were coming from the floor above, followed by muffled, furious shouts from what sounded like two men. Rachel thought she was in her large double bed in Ealing, and that this noise was coming from outside the sparkling-clean Victorian window of her bedroom, from the world beyond the small frame of the life she lived in. But she quickly realised where she was when she rolled over and fell off the small, inflatable mattress she had slept on, landing on the carpet with a small bump. A smell of stale cigarettes, which clung to the carpet, wafted up her nostrils and made her feel sick.

Now, she realised, her legs and feet ached from her performance the night before. She had rolled in drunkenly at 3 a.m. after post-show drinks with her colleagues. Her head hurt, but a full-blown headache was yet to kick in. Her hangovers always started the same way: with an intense pressure in her skull, which would become a drumming head-ache within the hour, and then be joined by nausea and, finally, guilt.

She sat up and looked at the scene around her. Her head was spinning and she was forced to squint as she struggled to focus on the water glass next to her, gulping down its contents quickly. The living room of Lisa's flat was, as usual, totally chaotic. Her bills seemed to have multiplied over-night in a frenzy of interest rates and missed payments; they were splayed out on the main table next to a calculator.

There was a note on the table from Lisa to say she and Claire were out for the day and would be back at 6 p.m.

Rachel was alone in the flat. Just her, the TV and the opportunity to find out all the information she needed to know. The thumping in her head began: a soft beat in the distance, like a drumstick wrapped in polythene.

She grabbed the glass of water again and tipped

the final few drops down her throat, feeling what seemed like the edges of her brain pushing against the inside of her head as she moved. The sound of the ruckus above suddenly died down; she could now hear dogs barking as a police siren sounded in the car park below. The police came so often to the estate that she didn't even bother looking out at them any more. In her old road in Ealing, the mere flash of a blue light in the corner of a window would prompt curtain twitching and a mass exodus of the nearby houses as people gathered on the pavement, sometimes with tea and biscuits if the incident was interesting enough.

Her hands were shaking a little as a result of her hangover and the ring on her right hand caught her eye. It was overwhelming to look at. Rachel reached into her bag and took two paracetamol, gagging slightly as she swallowed the second. She climbed up onto the sofa, looking out of the window at the concrete jungle she now called home. However short-term this arrangement was going to be, she realised that she was a part of it now.

Rita still had not called or texted her since she had walked out. Not once.

She wondered if her parents hated her now, for walking out of the house and slamming the door behind her. She wondered if they knew how angry she was with them, and how she was just sitting out the days, like a stubborn dog, waiting for them to realise how much pain they'd caused.

Clouds were gathering in the sky, she noticed, and there was a certain degree of heaviness in the atmosphere. Rachel turned away from the window, pulling her knees up beneath her chin and running her hands down the soft skin of her shins, dreaming about her new future. There was a task at hand. It was a difficult thing that she was about to do and she knew it was wrong to pry into other people's business, but she needed some answers.

Rachel was anxious: the last time she had gone rifling through someone else's business she'd accidentally discovered her own in the process, and opened a huge Pandora's box of questions that had changed her life for ever.

Would she go back? Turn back the hands of time, if that meant she stayed ignorant of the whole thing? Rachel wasn't sure.

She turned on the television and found a news channel. Somehow, it made the whole idea she was about to embark on seem more civilised, more educated, more informed . . . A female newsreader wearing a crisp navy suit was gazing into the camera, shuffling a pile of papers. A rolling news banner was running across the top of the screen, but Rachel couldn't make sense of it properly; she had enough turmoil at home. Wherever that was. She couldn't concentrate on anything else.

Rachel slid a cigarette between her lips to calm her nerves, gripping the squashy end between her teeth and lighting it. And, one by one she started going through the letters, photographs and notes scattered on the table in front of her. She assumed Lisa had been going through a box of memories since Rachel arrived back in her life so suddenly, and hadn't been bothered to put it all away. Now they were all mixed up with bills and bank statements.

Lisa's handwriting was slanted, scratchy and angry. The spelling was woefully poor, and Rachel felt a pang of sadness at the pit of her stomach as she realised afresh how different they were; how different her own life could have been.

Rachel ran a finger over the faces in the photographs, trying to match up names, and scribbling in a notebook things she wanted to remember. She also looked at bank statements, adding up the figures in her head.

She tried to find any traces of her father. She came across a snapshot from the early eighties and she became curious. It showed Lisa in a field with some friends, including two men. Lisa looked a lot slimmer, beautiful actually. She was smiling widely. *Could one of those men be my real father?*

When Rachel was finished, she took extra care to ensure that each sheet and photograph was put back in exactly the order they had been in, and that the biscuit crumbs that were sprinkled all over them were back on some of the top pages, just as they had been left.

CHAPTER 38

'THE MOON'S IN A STUPID PLACE IN THE SKY.'

Tuesday 22 September 2009
Finsbury Park, north London
8.30 p.m.

'Do you think Max is sitting on the moon in a rocking chair eating cheese?' The line went quiet. Bryony pulled her legs under her body and pushed herself further out of the window, gripping onto the wooden frame tightly. She could hear Eliza breathing down the line, and the faint sound of cooking in the background. The clattering of utensils. A gentle sizzling from a pan.

'Er, it's possible I guess.'

The line fizzed a little, and Bryony pulled the phone away from her ear and thumped it with her free hand.

'Did you just hit your phone again?'

'No.'

'Yes, you did! I've told you before – it doesn't work. You're like those idiots who sit on the train waving their phones around and trying to get a

402

signal,' Eliza said, flatly. But she was smiling. Bryony could hear it in her voice.

'Can you hear me now?' Bryony asked, staring at the moon.

'Yup. So why would Max be on the moon?'

Bryony smiled widely, a light breeze tickling her face. It was a long, sharp drop down to the pavement below, and she was precariously perched on the window ledge, one leg banging gently on the brickwork. A hum of conversation could be heard from a group of smokers standing outside a pub nearby.

One of the smokers looked up and noticed her. 'Hey, careful, love!' he shouted. The man was surrounded by laughing friends, clouds of cigarette smoke circling. One of them said, 'Nutter,' quietly to their gang, but Bryony heard it.

'Oi, fuck off,' she yelled.

'Bryony! I heard that. You aren't hanging out of the window again, are you?' Eliza sighed, picturing the layout of Bryony's flat and knowing exactly what she was up to and just how dangerous it was.

'It's fine. Chill.'

'So, anyway, *why* would he be on the moon?' Eliza asked again, her voice tinged with sadness. It had been so painful watching Bryony on this rollercoaster journey. She hadn't known Max too well, but she knew him enough to feel his loss, and seeing her best friend in so much torment was sometimes too difficult to bear.

'It's comforting to think as I look up to the moon

that he's there, watching me at night,' Bryony said, still smiling. For the first time in a long time, she was feeling some kind of peace inside. Instead of tears when she thought of Max, she could smile.

Eliza felt a huge lump gather at the base of her throat. But she couldn't be sad. She had to be strong. Bryony could not hear her cry. 'I understand that. I'm going to have a look, too.'

Bryony could hear Eliza unlocking her back door and stepping out into her garden.

Sure enough, there it was. Big, bright and beautiful. 'He's waving at us,' Eliza whispered, cocking her head to the side and feeling her eyes water.

Bryony giggled. 'Do you think he gets to eat whatever he wants up there, and never get fat?' she asked, thinking of all the food he used to love: spaghetti carbonara. Pizza. Hummus. Chocolate cake.

'Yeah, I reckon so. And he gets to have whisky and coke each and every night,' Eliza said, almost able to see him herself now.

There was silence between the pair before a police siren could be heard whizzing furiously past Bryony. It made Eliza wince.

'Do you think he's started smoking again?' Bryony asked, squinting slightly.

'I expect so,' Eliza said, remembering that he used to look like a rock star when he had a cigarette hanging between his lips. He had then developed an awful habit of frantically fiddling with everything around him after he quit.

'Have you spoken to Adam?' Eliza continued.

'No. I haven't heard from him since the kiss disaster . . . I wouldn't be surprised if he never spoke to me again.'

'Why?'

'Because I led him on, Eliza. Not on purpose, but I did. You know, I'd been hanging out with him for months. He thinks I'm single – I haven't told him anything about Max. And then when he kissed me, I stormed out and left him scratching his head . . .'

'Do you think you should apologise to him, Bry?'

'Yes. I really do. I just don't know how.'

'Do you miss him?'

'Unbearably,' Bryony said, feeling a wave of guilt crash over her. And then she said, 'I, I don't know what to do next.'

'Well, first off, Bryony, I really would like it if you would get down from the window.' Eliza tried to hide the emotion from her voice as more tears chased each other down her cheeks.

'I don't want to, though, Eliza. I want to be able to see Max,' Bryony replied quietly, unable to tear her eyes away. 'The moon's in a stupid place in the sky,' she continued.

'Well, put a mirror on the dresser, that one I bought you for your birthday, and angle it just so. Then you can lie in bed and watch the moon all you like,' Eliza said.

'Good idea . . . I've never thought of that.' Eliza could tell from her voice that Bryony was smiling.

Then Bryony continued. 'But I didn't mean that literally, as in what to do next this evening.'

'What did you mean?'

'I mean in life. I feel like there's something I need to do. Maybe I need to move house. It's becoming very difficult now. What do you think?' Bryony felt unable to leave, to shut the door on the home she had made with Max, but she felt uncomfortable staying there. A pile of Max's shirts still surrounded the bed, and if anyone dared move anything they got told in no uncertain terms that it was absolutely not OK. The washing-up regularly teetered out of control, until kind friends decided to roll up their sleeves and help out, while every couple of weeks, Bryony's mother would let herself into the flat and clean it from top to bottom.

Eliza considered this for a moment, pulling her cardigan close to her chest. The flat was messy now, when it never had been before. Max and Bryony used to keep the place in perfect, ship-shape order: there were always beautiful candles burning, new cushions arriving and a collection of cool prints on the walls that they had picked up in markets. It was the kind of home that had made people envious. The kind of love that had made people envious. 'It might be for the best,' she whispered.

'I think I'm ready now. I have stuff I need to do. I feel better, for the first time in ages.'

This was the most positive thing Bryony had said for a long time.

'That's fantastic.' Bryony could hear the smile

in her friend's voice. 'I will help as much as I can. Now will you please get inside now?' Eliza pleaded.

'OK, OK,' Bryony said, swinging her leg round, back into the warmth of her bedroom. 'Night night, darling.'

'Sweet dreams.'

Bryony rang off, sliding down from the window-sill as she did so and landing on the carpet with a soft thud. She got her mirror, placed it on the dresser just as Eliza had suggested, and positioned it so she could see the moon from her bed.

She climbed under the covers and fell asleep almost immediately.

CHAPTER 39

IF SHE WOULD ONLY TRY.

Monday 28 September 2009
Prison cell, High Elms Prison,
south west London
2 p.m.

He had written five letters now. Written in a trembling hand and stuffed into thin envelopes. The address written with care in black Bic medium. A postcode, wobbly, frightened and unsure whether it would really be welcome when it landed on the doormat.

But no replies . . .

The last letter had contained a visit request form so Bryony would be able to visit him in prison should she wish to.

Bryony must hate me, more than it is possible to hate a human being, Keon thought, drumming his fingertips lightly on the table. *Just like my mother hates me and my sister hates me and . . .*

'You all right, lad?' came a familiar voice from his left. Eddie was sitting there, fiddling with a tattered copy of *The Lord of the Rings*. Keon hadn't even noticed him sit down.

Eddie started playing with his bag of marbles, turning them around in his right hand.

I can't take this any more. I can't do this. I'm so sad. I'm so desperately sad I could choke on it. I don't know how to get through it all . . . Eddie thought.

There were a few moments of silence before Eddie emerged from the chasm of his dark thoughts.

'Keon . . . Keon. Hello?' Eddie demanded once more, tearing a small corner from the front cover of the book and rolling it into a ball between his fingers.

'Hey! Don't do that, I want to read it next,' Keon said, slapping Eddie's hand gently and pulling the book towards him. He accidentally dragged it through a puddle of orange juice in the process. He sighed, loudly.

Reading books was the only way he had found to help take his mind off the tortured ticking of the clock, his life silently slipping away into the night as he slowly died inside from the guilt and shame he felt every waking moment. Keon had heard somewhere that it was possible to die from a broken heart. He had broken his own, but he had broken the hearts of others, too. And that was too much to carry on his slim shoulders, day in, day out; following him, haunting him.

His only relief came as soon as he opened a book, when the ghosts that haunted him would slip away to haunt someone else for a while.

Keon had been lost in different worlds; he'd stepped between the pages and smelt the smells and heard the sounds and *seen* it all. All this life and living and existing and breathing that went on beyond the locked doors of his concrete cell. He'd learned new words, too, with the help of a small, tattered dictionary to look them up. Several a day, sometimes. *Assimilation. Unanimous. Hyperbole. Affluence.*

Keon had tried to incorporate them into his sentences, but people didn't understand him, or he used them in the wrong context and got laughed at. He didn't care, though; literature had become his great escape.

'Sorry, mate,' Eddie said, tilting his head forward and looking ashamed of himself.

'It's OK. How are you doing?' Keon asked him, studying his friend's profile.

'Ahh, I'm a bit bored, to be honest. You know, I've been staying in a lot recently, trying to save money and all,' Eddie said, starting to laugh. It sounded slightly hysterical.

Keon laughed, too, a little uncertainly. There was something incredibly funny about Eddie's attitude to all this – it was one of the things Keon liked about him. He had a wry humour, but he wasn't sure whether or not it was meant to be as dark as it was. Keon liked Eddie a lot, depended on him. He really was his only friend in here. In the world, maybe.

'Why don't you read the book?' Keon suggested, sliding it back across the table towards Eddie. Giving him a second chance after he'd begun destroying the cover.

'I've read it. Five times.'

'Oh . . . right.' And there was silence, occasionally broken by the laughter and cries of their fellow inmates. Keon had worked out a good way to tune them out recently, and it didn't annoy him as much these days.

He had started trying to talk to Max at night, which was hard because he wasn't sure if Max could listen. And even if he could listen, why on earth would he listen to him? But Keon had started anyway, by telling him again and again how sorry he was; but it had just ended up sounding stupid. So he had asked Max to give him a sign, to show he could hear. That he was listening. Keon had even once put a piece of paper on the edge of the bed and asked him to move it, or brush it off. But it had just stayed there. All Keon could ever see was Max's crumpled, blood-stained face. It made his stomach clench every time.

Keon wanted Max to tell Bryony to forgive. Somehow. If she would only try. He told him what he planned to do when he was released, even though it was a long way off. All his reading was building up to something: Keon was going to try and make some big changes, start at the roots and

411

hope that new attitudes could grow, saving more lives in the process. He had visions of going around schools to talk to kids one day and talking about his awful mistake, to stop others doing the same, but he didn't know what the best course of action would be just yet.

Keon felt like he knew Max now. He imagined from the kind face that he had seen in the local newspaper that he was well spoken, loved by many people and missed by many more. Keon tried to talk to the man he imagined he had been when he was alive, but then it hurt too much and he had to shut himself away in a book, to read about other people's emotions to get away from his own.

He was going to write one more letter and then he would stop. He would leave Bryony in peace after that, for ever.

'Mate?'

'Yes?'

'Have you got a pen?'

'No. Sorry,' Eddie said, opening the book at page one, yet again.

'So, this is weird . . .' Chantal said, drumming her fingers on the table and staring into Keon's eyes.

Keon felt uncomfortable with this, so looked down at the shiny, grey surface of the table, tracing his finger over some lines that had been carved into the plastic covering.

Chantal's red hair was braided to her head on one side and came tumbling down to her collarbone on the other, before melting into a pile of tempting curls at the bottom. Her green eyes looked so much brighter than when he had last seen her. Her perfume smelt different now. She'd lost some puppy fat. She was growing up and stumbling over some vintage stores along the way.

This was the first visit he had had since he was locked up among society's most hated.

Keon had explained everything in a letter to his friend: the work they had to do in the morning and afternoon; the early lights out; the fatty, high-carb meals that would include a pool of bright orange oil gathered at the edges; the pen battles; and the fact that neither his mum nor his sister had been to see him.

Chantal had lived a few streets away from him at the Fairgrove Estate, but she had moved to south London aged sixteen when her mum got a headship at a school down there. Keon had been gutted at the time, and had always had a bit of a soft spot for her. She was a good girl and she'd always warned him about his friends. She had seemed too good for him and now, looking at her, she was so much more vivid than ever before. He could have sworn her hair wasn't such a shockingly beautiful shade in the real world. He never remembered her having such peach-fresh skin that looked almost impossibly perfect, while her eyes now pierced right through him like daggers, and reminded him of the green seas in holiday magazines. It was hard to take it all in: he almost needed a pair of shades to cope with it all.

'So, how's life?' Keon asked, hoping he wouldn't feel jealous.

'Oh, you know. I'm doing OK at uni and stuff. Got a boyfriend now. Blah blah blah,' she said, chewing gum and glossing over the details. Details Keon desperately wanted to know.

She looked so different. Her style had changed. She'd become a hipster, and Keon could imagine her at student nights, bopping around various clubs and drinking shots with the boys, wearing a Yankees cap and showing off her latest tattoo.

Keon wished he was at university. He could have been.

'So, how about you, babe?' she asked, raising a carefully pencilled eyebrow.

Keon realised suddenly that there was something about her that was quite irritating. The outside world was sitting before him, all draped in leopard print, gold chains and ironic trainers. But he didn't want her to leave.

'Oh, you know, I finished my first novel the other day; marathon training's going well and I just got a first in chemistry,' Keon said, smiling and revealing his perfectly straight white teeth.

There was a long pause. 'I miss you, man,' Chantal suddenly said, leaning back in her chair, her eyes clouding with tears. 'Why did you do it, Key?'

'I told you I didn't want to talk about this,' he said, his features falling. The corners of his mouth dropped and his hands bunched up into fists. He could feel his heart rate climbing.

'OK, OK. I'm sorry.'

'Can you just treat me normally, please, Chants? I just want to pretend we're in a bar, or in a park or something, and I'm not an utter—'

'Stop,' Chantal said, leaning forward and taking both of Keon's hands in her own.

He looked down at her nail varnish, sea-green just like her eyes. She had a gold ring on, with the word 'Pow' emblazoned on it.

'Do you remember how this felt?' she asked, close to him now and smiling.

A few people glanced over at them; they probably assumed she was his girlfriend. A guard started to watch them more carefully.

Her hands felt soft, and Keon suddenly remembered one Sunday afternoon in the park when they were fourteen years old. He had reached out to hold her hand, deciding that he wanted her to be his girl. She had pulled away, and he had never tried again.

'I do, of course. You pulled away, though, Chants,' Keon muttered, his face still showing the sting of it. The heart-fluttering, painful reality of it all.

'I know, I know. I regretted it. You suddenly got really handsome when you were fifteen and I had a massive crush on you, but it was too late because

415

you were hanging with all the cool kids, and the girls were not like me at all,' she said, her eyes like pools again.

'Wow, really? Funny how things change – look at you now,' he said, frightened of how much he desired her. It was impossible, just like everything else. Just like the gun.

She blushed a little and gently pulled her hands away.

'Why did you come and see me?' Keon asked.

'I'm not sure, Key . . . I think first off I know you didn't exactly mean to do what you did. Most of all, I didn't like the thought of you being abandoned, no matter how bad it was. I just kept thinking about you, and I wanted to understand, to make sense of it all.'

'I see,' Keon said, still a little confused.

'Listen, I've got to go in a minute, but I just need to . . .' she said, reaching up under her top and dislodging something from beneath her bra.

Keon watched with interest.

A plastic bag suddenly materialised from the bottom of her T-shirt and she slid it between her knees.

'No, Chants, you can't, you're not allowed, you can't . . .' he whispered in horror, panicked, but it was too late. She'd pushed the packet underneath the table and onto his lap. And they'd been spotted.

'Pens! Fucking pens!'

The prison guard, a tall, thin man with breath

416

that could strip the bark off a tree with one puff, was pacing the floor of the small, dark office, seething with rage. On a wooden desk before him were five different coloured biros, neatly splayed out. Blue. Green. Red. Orange. Yellow.

Keon looked down at his lap, secretly wanting to laugh, but he tried his best to look serious.

'You know the rules, Keon. You've been told all this stuff again and again. You cannot accept or arrange for anything to be given to you during a visit. You nearly caused a fucking security melt-down, you stupid tosser.'

'They are just pens, sir. And, to be fair, I didn't know she was going to give them to me.'

'The rules are the rules,' the guard said, sitting down now and looking at Keon over the table. 'Unfortunately for you, Mr Hendry, there is going to be a price to pay for this.'

Keon envisaged extra toilet cleaning duties, and shuddered inside.

'Any future visits will have to be held with the glass divider.'

Keon rolled his eyes and shrugged.

When Keon came back to the wing, Eddie was playing marbles in the corner of the room. He looked like a kid.

'How'd it go, champ?' Eddie asked, shuffling to the left a little so Keon could sit down next to him.

'Fucking divider,' Keon said, resting his head in his hands.

'Oh, that sucks,' Eddie responded, starting to put the marbles into a small bag.

'Not that I get any visitors, anyway . . .'

Word of the incident had travelled fast. People were whispering and looking at the unusual twosome, crouched down in the corner. The first round of rumour had involved cocaine; the next round had been downgraded to involve weed; and by the time the truth came out, the other inmates seemed pretty disappointed.

Now, the body of a broken pen came sailing through the air and hit Keon in the head. He flinched as it struck his skull and bounced off, hitting the ground with a crisp clatter.

'Ouch! Fuck's sake,' Keon growled.

Eddie started to laugh. Keon glared at him.

'Oh, I'm sorry, mate, it's just a pretty funny story,' Eddie said, between snorts of laughter exploding from his chest.

Keon started to see the funny side, too. He could still remember the look of utter horror on Chantal's face as she was frog-marched from the visiting room. Eventually the laughter trailed off, and Keon suddenly noticed how sad Eddie looked. It was always a bad sign when he was playing with marbles.

'Having a bad day?' Keon asked.

'Ah, no, I'm all right. Just a little tired, that's

all,' Eddie said. 'Hey, they're showing a film tonight – want to watch it?'

'Yeah, sure, man, that would be great,' Keon said, smiling widely and realising that, for the first time, he felt like he belonged.

CHAPTER 40

'THIS AIN'T WORKING.'

Wednesday 30 September 2009
HSBC, Hackney, north east London
10 a.m.

Lisa stood in line at the bank, shaking as she realised that she probably wouldn't have enough money to pay her latest heating bill.

£82.46. FINAL WARNING.

Things had been tight for a long time, but they were slowly getting worse, and she feared what might be uncovered every time she popped into the bank. Lisa looked around her at the people in the queue, and wondered if they were struggling as much as she was. How did other people cope? Was she a bad person somehow, for getting into this mess? How had she got into so much debt in the first place? The figure swirled around her head. £15k . . . £15k . . . Fifteen thousand pounds that she somehow needed to pay back.

She would never be able to pay it back.

She was just trying to get by. There had been no lavish holidays, no expensive clothes; it was just a debt that had built up over the years from a loan she had taken on for Rachel's father before he died, using credit to get by and help with the basic things: food shopping, a new bed when Claire's broke, pots and pans, modest birthday presents for her family. But Lisa had buried her head in the sand, and missed payments. The interest had rocketed and the totals soared, while her wages had stayed the same. Very, very low.

The bill . . . the heating bill, what would she do? What *could* she do? She took a deep breath as she decided she would try and pay, and hope to God it went through. Maybe if it didn't, she could ask for an appointment with an advisor, and beg a gaunt-looking man with acne and dressed in a creased suit for more credit or a deeper overdraft. Anything to help. She imagined herself making more pleading phone calls. 'Just one more week . . . please.'

As she waited in the queue, Lisa stared at a man in the line in front of her. He was tall and well dressed. She studied the back of his head and wondered what it must be like to be financially secure. To be comfortable. To not lie awake at night with a grim emptiness in her stomach as she wondered how she would get through another year.

She looked down at her cream coat, which she'd bought from a charity shop. It was meant to be dry cleaned, but she couldn't even rustle up the money for that. She wanted to get rid of it anyway, as it now always reminded her of that night. Thursday 12 March.

Soon a small screen, which was screwed into the wall, flashed in bright red that a cashier was ready for her. Lisa's stomach cramped as she walked slowly towards the booth. A pretty young blonde girl sat there, wearing a sharp suit, her make-up immaculate. She smiled widely to reveal a set of sparkling white teeth.

Everyone looked so fresh and new. When Lisa looked in the mirror she saw exhaustion; folds of grey skin hanging loosely over her bones. But she had to keep going. Every day, desperately treading water to avoid sinking to the bottom.

'Hello, madam. How can I help you?' the cashier said chirpily, leaning forward slightly in her chair. Her voice was high pitched, and she almost sang like a bird. Her nails were manicured.

'Hi, yeah. I'd like to pay this bill, please,' Lisa said, faking confidence and pushing the paperwork and her card through the slot. *Act surprised,* she told herself, imagining the figures in her mind. She was definitely about to hit her overdraft limit, and was already £1,000 overdrawn as it was. There was no way this payment would go through unless she was due a rebate on something, and it had somehow miraculously landed in her account.

Smoking. Maybe it's been the smoking, she thought, as guilt clawed away at her. The price of a packet of fags had rocketed over the years; maybe financing that habit was what had created this mess, and it was all her fault. Lisa could feel tears stinging her eyes.

The woman looked at the paperwork and started tapping information into the computer. For two minutes, Lisa stood in silence, staring at the computer and trying to mentally programme it into sympathy.

'Right. All done, madam,' the cashier said, smiling brightly with a twinkle in her eyes before pushing the papers back through the slot.

Lisa opened her eyes wide, her heart rate slowing down dramatically. 'Really?' she asked.

'Yes, of course,' the woman responded, looking confused.

'Oh, right, well, thanks very much,' Lisa said, shoving it all in her worn handbag and starting to make her way out of the bank. She kept her head down, feeling as if she'd done something naughty. Cheated the system, somehow.

Well, what a relief, she thought. But, as she walked away from the bank, something stopped her in her tracks. *You should check this,* her instinct told her. Lisa turned around and made her way to the ATM on the outside wall of the bank. Raindrops were falling from the sky, so she pulled the hood up on her coat and gently tied the strings under her chin to protect her hair. She could hear the droplets thumping at the material around her ears, magnifying the sound as if she was inside a tent.

She slipped her card into the slot and typed in her PIN, before selecting the balance option. The machine thought about it for a few seconds; it felt like hours. And then her balance flashed up on the screen. A figure she thought she was imagining.

£3,917.54.

Four digits. Three noughts. *Noughts*. She stared at the numbers on the screen before her, her stomach melting into jelly. Maybe this was all a dream, and she would wake up at any moment to the sound of her daughter, crying out for food and the thud, thud, thud of the usual headache, which hovered over her, day in, day out, like a rain cloud.

Where had this come from? There had to be a mistake . . . She requested a slip to show credits and debits, and pulled her card out of the machine, waiting for the paper, which was eventually spat out of a small slot by the screen.

There it was, £5,000 . . . from MISS R MATTHEW.

Lisa's head felt light, as if it were full of helium. But it was quickly weighed down by another feeling: anger.

'I don't need your charity, Rachel,' Lisa growled, standing over her elder daughter.

Rachel was seated in a rickety chair at the kitchen table. She was still in her ballet tights, her hair sprayed so heavily to her head it felt like a helmet made of straw. She pulled her cardigan around her shoulders as the cold in the flat started to seep into her bones yet again.

Lisa was holding on to her bank receipt, hands

shaking. She was wrapped in a short, green dressing gown and was wearing a pair of moth-eaten slippers that had once had bunny ears at the toes. Two of them had fallen off.

Rachel felt an all-too-familiar sick feeling flooding into her stomach; a feeling of confusion and dread and despair that the world could be such a mixed-up place. She felt like she could never get it right. But instead of anger now, which was her usual knee-jerk reaction, she just felt sad. Her misery was creeping into her soul, and becoming a habitual way of life.

This was the very last reaction she had ever imagined from her mother after transferring some money to help towards the clearing of her debts. She had been so excited about how Lisa would react. That maybe she would have some real respect for her. That this could be home. But she realised now that she couldn't buy that kind of thing, and she felt foolish.

She tried to stay calm and analyse what was going on. Why would a person react like this?

'You basically went riflin' through all my paperwork, right?' Lisa shouted now, starting to pace the kitchen floor.

Rachel looked down at her own feet, encased in a pair of shiny, black Dr Martens boots. 'Well, yes, clearly I did. But I did it to help you, because I know you won't accept help easily . . .'

Lisa came to a standstill, leaning against the metal sink, which was piled high with mugs and baby beakers. 'You know what's worst about this? You come swannin' in here, to my home, expecting me to put you up, and then as soon as my back's turned, there you are, rooting about in my stuff,' Lisa said, between gritted teeth.

Rachel couldn't believe what she was hearing. She started to feel dizzy, only the loud ticking of a white, plastic clock above the doorway keeping her in the room, second by second. *Tick. Tock. Tick. Tock.* 'You didn't have to have me here,' she said, tears pricking at her eyes. Was she being forced away from yet another place?

'But I didn't have any choice, did I?' Lisa cried. 'Because I 'ave already abandoned you, and I couldn't carry the guilt of that again. But you don't belong 'ere, Rachel – you belong in a world of privilege and fucking flashy cars. Not here. It's embarrassing having you here, in this shit-hole,' she finished, bitterly.

Rachel felt sick.

'Why can't you just grow up? By your age I was workin' all the hours God sends to support myself, but you? You just swan around expecting other people to look after you!'

Rachel wiped a tear from beneath her eye, and felt the pain stab deep inside her. She thought she had been safe here. A little bit welcome. But she'd been abandoned. Rejected. Yet again.

'I don't know what to say,' Rachel muttered. She was beginning to feel fury now – her default emotion – at the woman before her.

426

'I mean, come on, you're clearly earnin' a lot of money. Why did you come back to me? Why? Do you not realise how 'ard it was for me to move on from what I 'ad to do?' Lisa said, quietly now, forcing back her own emotions.

'But what about *me*? What about how difficult this has been for *me*?' Rachel replied, her voice wobbling at the end of the sentence. 'I just wanted us to be friends, to put everything behind us. I thought this would help both of us and, as for the money, I can afford it. I don't want you living like this any more – that's the whole point!'

'But what if this is all that people like me deserve?' Lisa turned around so that she was facing the sink. She didn't want Rachel to be able to see her face.

'Oh, come on! You don't have to resign yourself to this!' Rachel replied, deeply frustrated by this woman, this stranger's attitude.

'I need to give the money back, and then you need to leave. This ain't working.'

CHAPTER 41

'I HAVE NO ONE.'

Sunday 4 October 2009
Prison cell, High Elms Prison,
south west London
4.30 a.m.

It was still dark when the ambulance arrived, its blue flashing lights projected onto the brick walls of the prison.

Early-morning raindrops were slipping from the clouds and covering every available surface in a cold blanket of damp. Most of the inmates were asleep, but the sirens jolted them sharply from their beds, prompting them to shuffle towards the bars of their cells and peep into the corridor through sleepy eyes.

There were urgent footsteps as paramedics walked to a cell at the far end of one of the wings, black boots thudding against the concrete floors. A few lights had been turned on so they could find their way quickly. Staff unlocked doors, and whispered to each other in muffled tones.

And soon the sobbing of Keon Hendry could be heard in the distance: 'I have no one.'

A doctor arrived just an hour later, and pronounced Eddie Martin dead.

A prison guard walked quietly into Keon's cell and placed a bag of marbles in his hands.

CHAPTER 42

THE WRITING WAS NOT HIS.

Saturday 10 October 2009
Finsbury Park, north London
2 p.m.

Sara finally felt ready to open the letters that Tom had sent during their crazy break-up. It had been a very difficult thing for them to work out, but it had been put to bed now. She knew he hadn't cheated on her and, in a way, she found it quietly amusing that he had got himself into such a spectacular mess. She was really pleased she'd given him a chance. They could have lost so much.

She'd forgotten the letters were stashed away in a drawer, but had remembered them that morning, after Tom had peeled himself out of bed and headed to his studio.

A smile spread across her face. Should she read them? Was there any point?

She had forgotten that Tom, being the strange creature that he was, had not written her name on the envelope. There was just her address, which he had printed in wobbly capital letters in some

430

attempt to make her think they weren't from him. She knew him that well. He was an artist, after all. Creative. Flamboyant. Brave.

She slid her thumb underneath the thin paper of the first envelope, and tore away the seal until it revealed a slit at the top from which she could pull the letter. She put her glasses on and smoothed it down on the kitchen table. Bright sunshine was filtering through the window and onto the table, casting everything in a luminous glow that made the paper seem so white she had to squint to take it all in at first. *Focus.*

The writing was not his.

Sara's breath caught in her throat. Her brow furrowed sharply as she read the address where the letter had come from, scrawled on the top left-hand side of the page. *High Elms Prison.* Her heart started beating fast.

The writing was young, almost childlike. There was something vulnerable about the crosses on the t's and the dots on the i's, which were formed into small, rough circles. The letter was addressed to someone called Bryony, but the postal details matched her house . . . Sara, totally confused, took a large gulp from her lukewarm cup of tea and started to read.

Bryony,

I understand that the last person in the world you probably want to hear from is me. I also understand if you want to tear this letter up into a thousand pieces, but please. I beg you. Don't. I hope the letters I sent before haven't met with the same fate.

I have some things to say to you, and I hope you at least take the time to read this letter. I have been in prison for what feels like a long time now, although it's been less than a year. Time drags in here like you wouldn't believe. It has given me a lot of time to think, and I have a lot more time ahead of me.

You weren't at the court case. I need you to understand that I'm not a vicious thug, or a young man who did this on purpose in any way. I was young, and blind, and stupid.

I feel like I've grown and aged one hundred years since March, but I'm worried that all my new-found knowledge and wisdom will go to waste . . .

Sara sat upright in her chair, shivers running down her spine. She quickly turned the page over and checked the name at the bottom, because she couldn't wait any longer for an answer.

Keon Hendry. Hendry . . .?

She'd heard about this case – it was all coming back to her. It felt like so long ago now. Such a long time, that she'd totally forgotten about it. She'd read about it when it was all over the news, particularly because it had happened so close by.

432

She remembered being shocked at how close Bryony and Max had lived to her.

She remembered walking past Bryony's flat, on the same road as hers, on the day of the funeral and seeing the cars lined up, and all the flowers. She had fought back a lump in her throat that day, but she had soon become preoccupied with her own problems.

But how had this happened? Sara looked at the envelope. The address was correct. He must have got the wrong house number.

She went back to the next section of the letter. She couldn't help herself but read, consuming the words that seemed to pour so directly from the soul of a troubled being, so desperate to explain himself.

> *I only meant to scare a guy, this young bloke who had been causing me and my friends some grief. But it went horribly wrong.*

Sara felt a lump in her throat now, and looked behind her even though she was alone, frightened in some way that she was being watched.

> *I don't know how I ended up pulling the trigger. I thought the safety was on, which would stop me being able to shoot . . .*

Sara felt bad that she'd held on to these letters for so long, stupidly thinking they were from Tom.

She thought back to a recent drunken night in a curry house when she'd mentioned them to Tom, and how he had looked confused. It was all starting to make sense.

I don't know what you look like. I don't know much about you at all. You never came to any of the hearings, which I was secretly relieved about at the time because I couldn't face you. But now I need to see you, I need your understanding and forgiveness more than anything in the world.

Bryony must have never met Keon, Sara realised. It was possible she didn't even know who he was . . .

But there is a flicker of something within me. I want to do something to make the world better. I want to make a positive difference.

Now Sara started to weep, reading the words scrawled onto the page. She felt unbearable guilt at keeping these letters from the place they belonged. She imagined this man – he was just a boy, really – sitting in prison, wondering why he hadn't heard back from Bryony. She felt pain, deep inside. His pain. Her pain.

Richard Bach, an author I discovered recently, said: 'Some choices we live not only once but a thousand times over, remembering them for the rest of our lives.' That's how I feel. This will never leave me, day and night, in my waking hours and my nightmares.

CHAPTER 43

'. . . BLOW OUT THE FLAME.'

Saturday 10 October 2009
Finsbury Park, north London
8.30 p.m.

A single flame. Gold, white and amber, all at the same time. It was hard to know where the gold finished and the white began.

Bryony lay on the sofa, her body positioned on the worn upholstery, her neck and head hanging down a little so the blood started to rush to her brain. Her long hair swept from her head to tickle the floor, the ends lightly touching the wooden boards.

All the lights were out, the room illuminated only by candlelight. Her phone started to vibrate frantically on the coffee table, rattling away on the glass and flashing MUM. She ignored it.

Bryony had discovered that if she tilted her head this way, and stared at the flame of a candle for long enough, she could see Max's face in the centre of it. She would lie like this for hours sometimes.

436

More hours had been spent doing things like this ever since the bar incident with Adam, which she'd still not managed to patch up yet. She didn't feel ready to see him again. The last thing she had wanted to do was lead him on, and Bryony felt that maybe she'd been a little naïve about the whole thing. What had she expected? Did she really think he wanted to be 'just friends' when he spent hours with her, trying to chase her blues away with bottles of white wine and board games? She found herself smiling gently at the thought of him, and all the lovely things he used to do, but then told herself off for being happy whenever he popped into her mind. So she had just kept pushing the thought of him away, further and further, until she could barely remember what he looked like.

It just wasn't right, she knew. Too early. She would feel bad moving on from a love like Max's in ten years, let alone the minute amount of time that had passed since his death so far.

Her phone started vibrating frantically yet again, MUM lighting up the screen. Bryony reached forward and answered it this time, resentful that she was being dragged away from her quiet world. 'What?'

'Bryony, come on. Be a bit nicer than that, please,' Sylvie chided, gently, down the line.

'Sorry,' Bryony replied, fiddling with the curtain of hair that was dangling towards the floor.

'I really think you need to call Ben.'

'Why?'

'Because he has something to tell you, apparently,' her mother replied, sounding very serious.

'Oh, God, what's that?' Bryony said and sighed, hoping there would be no more drama to contend with.

'Well, I don't know, but he just called again, hoping to get more advice from me.'

'And you have no idea what it's about?' Bryony said, sceptically. She was acutely aware that her mother generally knew everything. She could tell the suitability of a future boyfriend by the mere shake of his hand and could smell cigarette smoke from a mile off. It was terrifying.

'No, I don't,' her mother said.

'OK, I'll call him later,' Bryony replied, with a distinct lack of enthusiasm. She was sure that whatever it was that Ben had to say, as lovely as he was, it couldn't be that earth-shattering. They hadn't spoken for a few weeks; it had all become too difficult to keep discussing the good times when it felt more and more as if they would never resurface in the future.

'Thank you, sweetheart. Look after yourself, please.' Her mother signed off the call with her usual concern.

'I will. You too.' Bryony slid the phone back onto the coffee table and continued staring at the flame. It was flickering slightly on the wick, which was embedded deep in the centre of a small, pink tealight. Mesmerised, Bryony asked Max to just do one thing for her, to prove that he really could hear her. To prove that he could help her find peace. Somehow. 'Max. Please . . . blow out the flame,' she whispered, tears filling her eyes as she realised the lunacy of the moment. She had never imaged that one day she would essentially be a young widow, talking to a candle. But no one was around to laugh at her, so she could do or say anything she wanted.

The flame flickered slightly, and her heart started to race, but then she realised it was caused by a small draught filtering from the window she'd left ajar earlier.

'Please, Max. Please. I need you. You must be bigger than this, than death. You can do anything, you always could . . .' she said in a hoarse voice, giant tears dropping from her eyes and landing on the floorboards with a gentle tap.

She wanted to believe. In films this kind of thing happened – the candle would blow out and then the girl would fall asleep on the sofa with a gentle smile on her face because it was her dead boyfriend's way of saying, 'I'm OK.' And everything, somehow, would be happy ever after.

'I'm going to count down now, Max. This is your last chance. Five . . . four . . . three . . . two . . .'

Beep.

Bryony jumped out of her skin and sat bolt upright on the sofa. She stayed still as stone. The candle continued to burn.

Beep. Beeeep.

She stood up slowly, and shuffled to the intercom. It was now her automatic reaction to dread what could be waiting for her every time it went off. Friends and family always called first, for that very reason. She even ordered parcels to work, and waited downstairs if she had a pizza on the way, just to avoid the sound.

She sometimes wondered whether, if the piercing noise hadn't interrupted her life that horrible night, maybe Max would still be alive.

Beeeeep.

Beeeeeeeep.

'OK, OK, I'm coming,' she growled to herself, pressing the button. 'Who is this?' she said, speaking into the box mounted on the wall. She turned on the hall light because the darkness was scaring her a little.

'Hi. Hi. Look, I know this is a bit strange, but my name is Sara. I live nearby, just a few doors down, actually. I'm looking for a Bryony. Is this Bryony Weaver?'

Bryony took a deep breath and wondered if she should lie, and send this woman, whoever she was, on her way. But something told her otherwise. 'Yes, it is. I don't think I can help you, though,' she said through the crackly line, the only connection between her and this strange woman who was standing on the doorstep outside.

'Will you just hear me out? Please?' the woman said, sounding desperate.

Bryony sighed. 'Sure. What's up?'

'Listen, Bryony. I have some of your mail. Quite a few letters, actually. Our addresses are very similar; they were sent to me repeatedly – the writing makes the 3 look like an 8, and I'm guessing that's how they've always been delivered to my place. They didn't even have a name on them, just the address, so I opened one. I'm ever so sorry . . .'

Bryony swallowed before speaking, and took another deep breath, irritated by this intrusion on her quiet evening. 'It's probably just stuff from a catalogue,' she said, hoping to end the conversation quickly. All her bank statements were online now, as was her phone bill, and her friends certainly didn't put pen to paper any more. And what could be so important it didn't have her name on it? 'Thanks for coming, but don't worry about it. Just throw it away,' she continued.

'No. No, it's not junk mail. I promise you.' The woman sounded so nervous her voice was quavering, as if she was standing in the freezing cold. 'I don't want to say who they're from, well, like this . . .' She trailed off.

Bryony inhaled the candle-scented air deeply through her nostrils and counted to five. 'OK. Do you want to come up?' she asked.

'Yes. I think I should.'

Bryony held the buzzer down and prepared herself for this strange intrusion. She opened the front door to the flat and listened as the woman made her way up the stairs slowly, each step echoing in the hallway. She remembered how this had sounded before, when there were police officers taking the short but steep journey in tight, black boots that had squeaked with each step that they had taken. The journey that had changed her life for ever.

The woman turned the final corner on the stairs and came face to face with Bryony.

Bryony tilted her head and smiled, shocked by how beautiful she was. Her short brown hair was shining in the artificial light and her skin glowed. *She looks just like Audrey Hepburn*, she thought, warming to her almost immediately.

The woman smiled too, but she looked nervous. Overwhelmingly so. She said nothing, but reached out a cold right hand to shake Bryony's, clutching what looked like five or six envelopes in the other. 'I'm so glad I found you in,' she said quietly, before stepping into the flat.

Bryony led her into the living room and put the kettle on. It was something of an icebreaker nowadays, as she no longer knew what to say to strangers. The gentle roil of bubbling water would always get people talking.

Sara sat down on the sofa, but kept her body perched at the edge and her jacket on, as if she wasn't intending to stay for long.

The candle was still burning in the centre of the table.

'How do you take your tea?'

'Oh, milk and one sugar, please,' Sara said, fanning

the envelopes out on the table and placing her hands on her lap.

Within a few minutes, Bryony returned with the drinks, and placed them gently on the coffee table before taking a seat herself. She instantly reached for the letters, unsure as to why this whole rigmarole was necessary when it was probably just what she thought it was. Junk.

'No, wait,' Sara said, leaning forward and looking at her with pleading eyes.

'Why?' Bryony asked, her nose crinkling in confusion.

'Do you know who killed your boyfriend?' the stranger said, now gripping her hands together and biting her bottom lip. The candlelight showed new lines on her face.

'No, no, I don't,' Bryony said sharply, wondering why this woman was asking such intrusive questions. Was she a crank?

'And I don't intend to. Why have you come into my home to ask me about this? I thought you were just dropping off post.'

'Because those letters are from his killer.'

Bryony felt her stomach fold, and the candle suddenly flickered violently in the draught. She moved it gently away, so it wouldn't go out. As she did so, her hands started to tremble, and she shook her head as if she was repeatedly saying no.

'Pardon?'

'I'm sorry, Bryony . . . I said—'

'No way. He doesn't know where I live. He

doesn't *know*,' Bryony interrupted, baffled and confused.

'Your and Max's address would have been read out in court, I assume . . .'

'No. No, no!' Bryony said, starting to tremble all over now.

Sara felt herself panicking, but she had to be strong for this poor girl, whose biggest fears were suddenly sitting on the table in front of her in neat, white envelopes. 'I had to bring these to you. I hope you understand why,' Sara said, suddenly wondering if she'd made a huge mistake. Tom had supported her. He helped her find the courage to go to Bryony's flat, where she had previously seen the funeral cortege all those months ago. He was even waiting outside, just in case. She had left him smoking a cigarette and poking at the shrubbery with the tip of his shoe. 'You don't have to read them, you know. If you want, I can take them away for a while, and leave my number with you, for whenever you are ready. Or even, I can put them . . .' – Sara got up suddenly as she talked, and walked over to the open-plan kitchen – '. . . up here, look. So you can get them down if you ever feel ready,' she continued, pointing at the top of the cupboards.

She'd asked Max for a sign, just a few moments before. Maybe this was it, Bryony wondered, staring at the envelopes and getting double vision.

'No, look, it's OK. Thank you for coming . . .

I'll keep them right here,' Bryony said finally, fighting down the lump in her throat.

'OK, I'm going to go,' Sara said. 'Thank you for the tea, but I really think I should leave you to it.' She wrote her number down on a scrap of paper and left it there, before seeing herself out.

The front door closed quietly, and Bryony was alone yet again, with two steaming cups of tea.

'Thank you,' she whispered.

The tip of the flame flickered and twisted in the air, consuming all the oxygen it could grab in the huge space around it.

Bryony needed to talk to Ben now. This was such a huge thing to deal with and now she needed to speak with him. She picked up her phone, and found Ben's number. She pressed the call button. The phone rang, four times.

'Hello?'

Silence.

'Hello? Bryony, is that you?'

'Yes, yes, sorry. How are you, Ben?'

'Yes, great, thanks. Work's chaos as usual, but—'

'Actually, sorry to cut you off – I don't mean to be rude, but I just need to know something. Mum said you needed to talk to me . . . to tell me something. Is that right?'

'Well, yes. I have wanted to tell you something, for a long while, actually . . .'

'OK, so, go on then. Please,' she said, trying to think what it could be about.

445

'Well, you know the day that Max died?'

'Yes, of course . . .' All the hairs on her arms stood on end, and she felt huge tears well in her eyes.

'He told you he was at work, Bryony. Do you remember?'

'Of course . . .'

'Well, he wasn't.'

'Where was he?'

'He was with me. We were shopping . . .'

Bryony felt herself smarting, irritated by all this. Why was Ben getting so worked up only to tell her that they had been out trying on shoes? She felt a rage rise within her. He'd wasted her time.

'And why would he not tell me about that?' she said, feeling like she was about to snap at him, as she had snapped at so many people.

'Well, that's the thing. We were shopping for a ring.'

She felt the air leave her lungs, and she folded over, in half, like a paper aeroplane. Tears started running from her eyes like wet beads, pouring from her face.

'Bryony, are you there?' Ben could hear a gentle sobbing down the line. 'He was going to propose to you . . . I'm sorry it took me so long to tell you, I just didn't know how it would make you feel, if it would help you or not. But he was my best friend, and I think he would have wanted you to know . . .' he said, breaking down into silent tears himself.

But instead of deep, agonising sadness, Bryony was crying with happiness. Happiness because the man of her dreams, the one she had loved more than anything she'd ever loved in the world, had wanted to spend the rest of his life with her.

'Thank you. Thank you for telling me,' she whispered, squeezing her eyes shut and smiling from ear to ear as her tears continued to fall.

'The thing is, Bryony, things got complicated . . . I hope you'll be ready for me to tell you all this . . .'

There was silence at the other end of the line, so Ben took a deep breath and continued. 'When the police came to talk to me about Max, I asked about the ring but they said there wasn't one at the scene, not on Max, not in his bag, pockets or anything like that . . .'

Bryony suddenly felt a coldness in her stomach.

'But he'd just bought the ring that night so I knew he would have had it with him. I wanted to be sure, though. I took it upon myself to investigate and that was one of the reasons you weren't told right away . . .'

Ben took a long pause before continuing the story. He sounded like he was struggling to catch his breath through his nerves. He could hear Bryony quietly weeping.

'I'd asked a lot of people to keep an eye out, and strangely enough it appeared in a magazine, on the hand of the ballerina Rachel Matthew . . . It's incredible we even found it really . . .'

Bryony sat up suddenly, her hand to her chest. Her heart was thudding and she could feel it beating away at her fingertips. She knew exactly who Rachel Matthew was. The young ballerina from Ealing who had graced the pages of *Company* magazine a while back. She was often in the press. People knew who she was . . .

'So . . . I traced her, and it turns out the ring was given to her by her mother, who found Max when he was lying in the street.'

'What happened, Ben? What the fuck happened!' Bryony started to shout. She felt bad screaming down the phone at him, but this was all too much.

'Calm down, please, be calm, everything's OK . . . Rachel obviously had no idea of the background of the ring. It turns out her mother was heavily in debt, and for some reason decided to keep it, before palming it off on her daughter . . . Rachel's absolutely desperate to return it to you, Bryony, she really is. She's a lovely girl . . .'

Bryony felt like she could take no more twists and turns. She took a deep breath and thanked Ben, apologising for her outburst. Ben gave her Rachel's mobile number and hung up, leaving her alone with her thoughts.

Bryony lay down on the sofa, drifting in and out of sleep. At 2 a.m. she sat up and opened her eyes, to be greeted with pitch-blackness.

The candle had gone out.

CHAPTER 44

IT WAS TIME TO FACE THE MUSIC.

Thursday 15 October 2009
Rosemont Hotel, St Pancras, central London
8 a.m.

Rachel clutched the small, white bag and lay on her back on the bed, digging her fingers into the crinkly paper, which was going soggy beneath her sweaty skin. She'd held it tight all the way back from the chemist to the hotel, working herself into an anxious frenzy every step of the way. She was intensely worried about what was going on in her life at the moment, what the box in the paper bag might say, how her visit to Bryony might go later that day. She was absolutely horrified when she discovered where her mother had got the ring from. She had to face the music. She had to return what was not hers.

She had to finish a love story, she had to ensure its ending was a little less painful . . .

The bed was hard. So hard that she deeply resented the £85 she was paying to sleep in it every night. The cupboards were bare apart from a few dresses draped delicately on wooden hangers, while a pair of boots sat expectantly by the door. She'd shoved all her faded band T-shirts into a drawer with her underwear.

She didn't have much else.

In fact, she resented the whole situation. Living in a hotel, which she only frequented at night. And 'night' was pushing it. She normally got back at two or three in the morning after a show, and woke early for a rehearsal or a mooch around the West End to drink coffee with friends. Sometimes she didn't even go back there, opting instead to stay with a friend or a cast member.

Every day it was the same. A cleaner would scuttle in and tidy her few possessions into a neat pile, and change the bedding, replacing the crinkled sheets with clean ones that had all the softness and comfort of a prawn cracker.

She was still angry at Lisa . . . the sadness had melted away and she was now courting a slow-burning fury about the whole situation. She realised in retrospect that the money transfer might have been a bad idea, but she was shocked at the things Lisa had said in the kitchen that night: the implication that Rachel's return to her life was a huge inconvenience.

The whole thing had worked out in a way she had never expected.

More than anything, she resented feeling like driftwood. While she hadn't been angry before that Lisa had given her up for adoption, she was now.

It's time to do the test, she thought, nerves clawing at her stomach.

She had been feeling distinctly odd recently, and she had vomited in the morning on several occasions. Added to this, she was particularly hungry and sluggish, so much so that it was all pointing towards one thing.

Of course, she knew this would be the worst possible life event that could happen at this stage in her career. There were huge auditions coming up for a role that would mean even more to her than Swanhilda had. They were talking about her dancing abroad now. Maybe even moving to New York.

Everything was just beginning in her career, yet she had no family . . .

In a way, it was perfect. She would be able to just leave the country, quietly, and start again. Find someone new to call family. But if she was pregnant . . . *that will cause all sorts of problems*, she thought.

She hadn't spoken to Richard since the argument in his flat. She had been so hurt by his apathy towards her that she had blocked his phone number from her phone and deleted all the pleading emails he had sent her. In her eyes, their relationship was well and truly over. She'd fallen out of love with him. Nothing could bring her back to him now. Not even a baby.

She closed her eyes and visualised trying to do a *grand jeté* with a huge bump, or squeezing herself into a tutu. It made tears come to her eyes. Would she get fat?

It was time to face the music. And if it wasn't what she thought it might be, she would go to the doctor and undergo health checks. It could be a variety of things. She'd been doing some Googling and had drawn up a shortlist of possible illnesses. From it, she was almost certain she was about to die. Or have a baby.

Rachel swung her legs over the side of the bed and plodded into the bathroom. She did what needed to be done for the pregnancy test and sat on the toilet, pointing her feet towards the ground, twiddling her toes occasionally. Two of the toes on her right foot were covered in plasters from the cuts caused by her new pointe shoes.

Rachel waited. The seconds seemed to go on for ever, but she probably only sat out ten of them.

Nothing . . .

That's good, she thought, now wondering which of the hideous-sounding illnesses she might have. She threw the test in the bin and wandered back into the bedroom, sat cross-legged on the bed and breathed a huge sigh of relief.

Now, she thought. *Time to think about a place of my own to call home . . .*

Rachel arrived at Bryony's flat at midday, her whole body trembling with fear.

One weight was off her shoulders, she now had

to deal with another that had been innocently wrapped around one of her fingers.

The situation was devastating, mortifying, and deeply upsetting for both girls. She had to make this better, even though it wasn't her fault. She had to meet Bryony, and give the ring back.

She rang the bell and waited, her heart pounding in her chest. She felt nauseous. She didn't know how to face someone who had known such agony. While she'd had problems of her own, they paled into insignificance after hearing this story. This was real life.

Bryony eventually buzzed her in and before long she was standing before her in a dark doorway. All the fear melted away. Bryony was stunningly beautiful, and radiated a warmth that put Rachel at ease immediately. This woman had been to hell and back, and now Rachel knew she had the chance to give her something positive. Something beautiful.

No tea was made. There was no small talk. It wasn't the right situation for all that.

The pair sat opposite each other on two sofas, and Rachel reached down into her bag and pulled out a jet-black velvet box she had purchased especially for this meeting.

Bryony started to cry, and dabbed at her eyes with the back of her hand, apologising all the while.

'Don't say sorry . . .'

Three little words – from a famous ballerina to a heartbroken stranger.

'Please . . . Don't say sorry . . .' Rachel reiterated, pressing the box into Bryony's right hand.

And with that Rachel stood up, walked over to the opposite sofa, and gave Bryony a warm cuddle before slipping out of the door and leaving her in peace.

CHAPTER 45

THERE HE WAS.

Friday 16 October 2009
High Elms Prison, south west London
10.30 a.m.

B ryony sat in the visiting room, her heart in
her mouth. This was it. Her biggest fear.
The checks had been stringent when she
had arrived. They had needed to see a passport,
and search her bag.

'He isn't in a good way,' the woman warder had
told her.

'Why?'

'His friend died, fairly recently. I think he needs
to see someone. I think this will mean a lot,' she
said, surprising Bryony with how much she seemed
to care. She had always imagined that prisoners
would be treated with cold contempt; that their
feelings were somehow written off, like the lives
they had destroyed in their wake.

Bryony was frightened of what the sight of him
would do to her. Would she try to attack him?
Shout at him? Would this tip her over the edge?
It felt as though this moment was make or break;

and the prospect of breaking any more than she had done already was impossible to deal with.

The letters had reached into her heart in a way she had never imagined possible. All she could think was that she was meant to go and see him. That all the events in recent days had stacked up and led her to this point for a reason.

She wasn't sure why, or what she was going to say.

A huge glass pane was positioned in front of her: it reflected her face if she stared hard enough at it. There was no sign, smudge or print that gave away it had ever been involved in a previous encounter. Nothing that told the stories of the people who had sat there before her, whose fingerprints might have been left on a surface separating the real world and that of the incarcerated.

Was this right? Was it the right thing to do? Her legs twitched as she sat in the hard plastic chair. She could leave now. Run away. But then a door opened in a far corner of the room, and a wave of calm suddenly washed over her. Her heart started to slow down as *he* was led into the room, by two large security guards.

There he was. Keon Hendry. The man who . . .

He was quite tall, and young. So much younger than she had ever imagined. His skin was a beautiful brown, and he had a certain dignified honesty about his features that made it hard to believe he was capable of such an act.

He was nothing like she'd imagined. He didn't

have the scraggy bone structure she'd visualised, or the scars across his top lip from a nasty fight she'd dreamt up. He didn't have 'E.V.I.L.' tattooed across his forehead. It was a total shock.

Her face was totally expressionless as she watched him walk towards his chair. She didn't know what to say. *He* was alive. His blood rushed through his veins. He could see, even if his eyes could only see the ruins of everything around him.

Keon couldn't look her in the eye. He looked terrified. Exhausted.

He sat down slowly, keeping his eyes on the light blue lino of the floor. His hair was cut short, and was even shorter at the sides. He looked slim, but broad shouldered, too. Like he was growing and growing, and would soon outgrow himself and the prison he was trapped in.

Bryony's heart was still beating slowly. She ran the fingertips of her right hand over the smooth skin of her left palm, a calming technique she had read about years ago and had never used until this moment. She thought for a moment how funny it was that these things were stored somewhere, right in the depths of the brain, for emergencies like these. She was wearing the ring. It made her feel safe.

'Keon,' she whispered, pushing her face towards the glass. To study him. To try and understand. To try and fathom why this young man ever got to this place. Wondering what had led him to that point, from the moment he was born right up to the split second his finger had touched the trigger. His letter had explained some things, but it still didn't really make sense to her.

'Yes,' he said, still glaring down at the ground, desperate to avoid looking into her eyes in case of what he might find.

'Look at me, please,' she said, swallowing the lump in her throat.

He slowly tilted his head up, his eyes meeting hers, red from crying.

And there it was.

The moment she had dreaded and feared in equal measure for so long.

Meeting eyes with him, the kind of man she would normally look at by a bus stop or on a train with interest, because he looked so young, and fresh, and full of the wonderful opportunity that youth brings. But it had all gone to waste. Everything had.

'I'm sorry . . . I'm sorry. I'm so desperately sorry,' he said, starting to cry. His jaw was tight and he looked angry with himself, while the words seemed to tumble from his mouth as if they were water, held back by a dam that had finally burst.

The look on his face frightened Bryony; it made a sick feeling rise in her stomach and she had to start breathing through her nose, slowly. Her legs started to shake but, deep down, she felt calm. It was the strangest state of being she had ever experienced. There was calm there, somewhere within the eye of the storm.

Keon suddenly scraped his chair towards her until he was so close to the glass she could see his breath gathering on the other side. 'Bryony, please. Please talk to me; say anything, I just need to hear you,' he said, as he got himself under control, his tears drying a little. 'You don't know what happened, you don't understand . . . I hate myself for what happened. I wish I could . . . I wish, I wish I could just *die*.'

A security guard made eye contact with her, looking over as if to say he would rescue her if she needed to be saved. She raised her hand and smiled gently, letting him know that everything was OK. She was aware that her action had been involuntary. As if this was all premeditated, scripted, and she was just playing her part.

'The thing is, Bryony, I'm just a boy. A silly little boy. And I need to make this up to you somehow. I need to make this OK, but I don't know how. What can I do? Help me . . . *please*,' he whispered the last part and placed his head down on the surface of the table.

Bryony thought about Max, about how good he was. How good he was inside and out. *What would Max want?* she thought. He would want something good to come of this. Yes, whatever she was about to do, she was doing it for Max. Not for her. This was no longer about her, not really.

'Look at me,' she whispered, feeling tears rise to the surface again.

'Why?' Keon said, looking up again, slightly fearful of what she might do.

'Please. Just come closer,' she said, raising her hand towards the glass and letting it rest there.

Keon put his forehead on the cold, shiny surface of the partition. He was weeping again. As he cried, in his misery he rolled his head around until his left cheek was pressed against the glass, the skin pulling against the surface and making his face look squashed and out of proportion. It was the kind of thing she saw kids do on the bus to make their friends laugh, but it wasn't funny this time.

Not at all.

Bryony let her fingers move to the point where his face was, and felt the warmth of it come through and touch her fingertips. The warmth of a human being who had taken everything away from her, and had made her life so cold.

She stroked the glass as if it were his cheek, as if she was trying to soothe him, and she asked Max quietly in her head if this was OK.

Without looking, Keon raised both of his hands to the surface and pushed his fingertips against it. Bryony lifted her other hand so they were mirroring his on the glass.

And the words just came out. 'Keon,' she said.

There were a few moments of silence.

'Yes?'

'I forgive you . . .'

Three little words.

460

The air rushed from Keon's lungs and he felt as if he crumbled inside, like a falling cliff face.

Bryony felt a huge weight lift from her shoulders; something new was happening, and this was just the beginning, she felt that strongly. It was all she could take for now so, wordlessly, she slowly stood up, her chair scraping loudly against the floor. As she walked towards the back of the room to the door, Keon slid off his chair and collapsed to the floor in tears of relief. A guard walked over to him and rested a hand on his back.

'I'll come back, soon. I just need some time to understand all this,' she said, turning around to face him one more time and seeing him, weak and defenceless like an injured animal.

She turned back and headed out of the door.

Her legs were still weak, but something inside her felt like it was getting stronger. Bryony stood in the dark part of the corridor for a few minutes, her head pressed against a squashy cork pinboard. She smiled and wiped a few tears from her face. Tears of relief.

He was nothing like the monster she had imagined.

There were a few moments of silence. Bryony could hear her own heartbeat, the blood rushing around her body. But the quiet was suddenly broken.

'Mel? Mel, is that you?' came a familiar voice from behind her.

Her back stiffened on hearing it. Bryony moved her head away from the board and turned to face in the direction of the voice.

It was Sharon. She was standing there, dressed in black, as if she was going to church. In her right palm were a few crisp, white tissues. She looked tired, as if she hadn't slept a wink the night before. 'Oh, my gosh. It *is* you,' she said, taking two steps towards Bryony and smiling. She reached out and held on to Bryony's skinny shoulders.

'What . . . what are you doing here?' Bryony asked, feeling an odd sensation in her stomach. The hairs on her arms stood on end again.

'I'm here to visit my son, for the first time. I decided it was time to try . . . He's gone through something quite bad here recently, he lost someone, so I knew I had to come now,' Sharon said breathlessly, trying to smile despite the stress the situation was clearly causing her.

He lost someone . . .

'What's your son's name?' Bryony asked, as everything seemed to go into slow motion. She could hear her quick breaths in her head.

'Keon. Keon Hendry,' Sharon replied, tears welling in her eyes.

Bryony felt a huge wave of shock fill her body. Her legs nearly gave way and she leant back against the wall to steady herself, her body slipping from Sharon's grip. Nausea rushed over her, and she had to take a deep breath. Had Max orchestrated this? Had he made this happen?

Sharon was looking confused.

'Sharon . . . I'm not really called Mel . . . my name is Bryony,' she said, her eyes now overflowing with tears as the realisation truly set in.

Sharon's eyes widened, the colour drained from her cheeks. 'My name is Tynice Hendry . . .' she said.

For ten long seconds they stood in the dark corridor, their eyes glued to one another. Tears started to roll down Tynice's cheeks. Bryony's body was shaking uncontrollably.

Suddenly, Tynice reached across the void and pulled Bryony close to her. Bryony tried to resist, her body stiffening slightly, and she put a hand on Tynice's shoulder.

The walls were caving in. There was a sharp ringing in her ears. She wondered if she was going to faint.

Instead, Tynice held her tightly and kept her upright, whispering in her ear in a desperate tone, over and over again, 'I'm so, so sorry.'

CHAPTER 46

'I THINK I NEED SOME TIME ALONE.'

Saturday 17 October 2009
Rosemont Hotel, St Pancras, central London
3 p.m.

'Congratulations!'

'Oh, good God, you made me jump,' Rachel shrieked as she turned the key in her hotel room door. She had just a few minutes to gather up the things she needed for the evening performance.

'Sorry!' the cleaner cried, jumping up and down in the corridor, which was covered in wallpaper so garish it was positively disorientating. She had a European accent, but Rachel couldn't quite work out where she was from.

'Congratulations for what?' Rachel asked, totally confused.

'For the baby!' the cleaner said, coming to an abrupt standstill but still grinning from ear to ear. Polish. The accent was Polish.

Rachel raised an eyebrow. This was intrusive . . . 'I don't have a baby,' she said flatly, thinking back

464

to the pregnancy test and being able to say it confidently now.

The woman looked startled. 'But I found in the bathroom . . . the test,' she said, going swiftly crimson.

Rachel felt riled now, but clearly this woman had little awareness about how inappropriate this all was. 'Yes, a negative test,' Rachel said, opening the door and stepping into her room, ready to close it behind her again. She would most definitely be complaining about this.

'No . . . no . . . it was positive . . . I, er, I left it in the bin, just in case . . .' the cleaner said, starting to step into the room behind her.

Rachel felt the colour drain from her face. 'Pardon?'

'Yes. It was positive. I'm sorry . . . I couldn't help but notice, oh . . . I shouldn't have said anything,' she continued, flapping her arms and going an even deeper shade of red.

Rachel rushed into the bathroom and pulled the test out of the bin.

There it was. Positive. The line that changes the path of someone's life.

The cleaner was still standing in the doorway, moving the mop between her hands and smiling again. She had tears in her eyes. Rachel wondered if they were tears of joy for her, or humiliation. 'I think I need some time alone,' she said faintly, feeling her head start to spin.

'Yes, yes, of course. If there is anything you need,

let me know, and I will bring it super quickly right away, especially as you are now a pregnant lady,' the woman said, snapping her fingers and spinning on her heel. 'Oh, and you should have plenty of vitamins,' she added, as she left, slamming the door behind her.

A pregnant lady.

Rachel stood there, stunned. Richard's face popped into her mind. He was like a baby himself . . . there was no way he was ready for all this. How would he react?

She kicked her boots off and crawled into bed, pulling the duvet over her head so she was left in cover-induced darkness, her blonde hair splayed out over the sheets.

I was a baby once. She thought about this. She thought about how the start of her life had had such a huge influence on the rest of it. She thought about how frightened she was at that very moment, at how much she had to lose. And yet, beneath all that, there was an undercurrent of excitement . . .

Who could she call? Who would be there for her during her biggest time of need? It dawned on Rachel that she was now in the terrifying position her real mother had experienced: she had to make a massive decision.

CHAPTER 47

'HOW ARE YOU, BRYONY?'

Saturday 24 October 2009
The White Rope restaurant, Crouch End,
north London
Midnight

Bryony had told Adam to meet her at midnight at The White Rope restaurant. Drunk people were staggering around in the street ouside, hanging in small groups outside bars from which erratic disco lights flashed onto the pavement.

He thought she had meant to meet outside and that they would be moving on somewhere else because, generally, people didn't meet for dinner at midnight. *Maybe in places like New York where you can grab your groceries at 2 a.m., get your back waxed at 3 a.m. and then head to a flick at 4 a.m.,* he thought. *But this is London . . . and Crouch End.* So it was something of a shock for Adam when Bryony turned up and invited him into the restaurant.

'But it's closing soon, isn't it?' Adam asked. He felt nervous. This was the first time that they had

seen each other since he had tried to kiss her –
and dramatically missed the mark. It was a long
time ago, too.

He'd almost had second thoughts about meeting
her. The way she had reacted. The fury. It had
shocked him. The memory of that, and the raw
humiliation of the whole thing, didn't make for a
particularly comfortable situation now.

Adam walked over to the front window of the
restaurant, pushed his face against the glass and
looked through. There was just one set of diners
left, while staff wandered around setting tables for
the next day, and polishing glasses. Candles had
flickered away for what must have been hours,
burning right down to their small metal bases, wax
now in liquid form gathered at the bottom of their
glass holders. But, looking further into the room,
he could just make out that near the back of the
restaurant there was a glittering mass of tall, freshly
lit candles. Behind this was a huge sheet of white
fairy lights, dripping down like sparks from a firework. It looked beautiful. He wondered what it
was for.

'Not quite,' Bryony said, a nervous smile on her
face. Her hair was in a plait and she was wearing
a short, black dress with grey ankle boots. She
carried off this Grecian look with her usual elegance.

She looked healthier, too, Adam noticed. There
was a certain glow to her cheeks, as if she'd been
sleeping better or eating more or something.

'OK,' Adam said, suddenly realising he was

about to step into an extremely posh restaurant with a pair of Converse trainers on and a T-shirt that read, 'I like to get down'. He quickly zipped up his hoodie.

Bryony went in ahead of him. It was lovely inside. Straight away, a woman with short, dark hair smiled at Bryony as if she knew her. She looked like Audrey Hepburn. It was a knowing smile, like she was doing a big favour for Byrony because they'd been through something together.

Adam didn't like those 'knowing smiles'. They always meant that something was about to happen – like a stripper or a wedgie. They were rarely good things.

Adam suddenly realised with a sinking heart that this was likely to be the last supper. He imagined Bryony would make some feeble apology about brushing him off all those weeks ago, and say how she liked him but not like that, and that they couldn't see each other again for a while because she needed s p a c e . . .

It was so obvious. Adam breathed a loud and deep sigh, like a tired dog.

'Hello, and welcome to you both,' the woman said, clutching some menus, which were leather-bound and expensive looking.

'Hi,' Adam squeaked, instantly angry that his voice had once again chosen a completely inopportune moment to revisit adolescence.

Bryony started to giggle.

'Please follow me,' the woman said, leading them

to the back of the restaurant and towards the stunning display of lights and tiny flames. In the midst of it all was a specially laid table for two, with a single, fresh candle in the centre.

Adam's stomach squeezed, and he felt his blood suddenly rushing through his veins.

This was for *him*.

Bryony smiled at him, looking at least twice as nervous as she had before. They were ushered towards the table. Adam carefully negotiated the display, trying to avoid setting himself on fire. They sat down, and there was an awkward thirty-second moment where nothing was said at all.

Adam eventually decided to put a stop to it and looked up. 'This is beautiful . . . thank you,' he said. He didn't know what else to say. It was such a statement. So dramatic, but thoughtful, too. 'How are you, Bryony?' he asked now, looking up and seeing her face illuminated by the candlelight.

Adam definitely loved her.

She'd done all this for him.

Even if she didn't love him.

'I'm actually really good,' Bryony said now, smiling, a hint of serenity creeping across her features in the half-light.

'Good. Are you still angry with me?' he asked, smiling his cheeky smile, hoping they could turn the whole thing into one big joke – a ha-ha-isn't-it-hilariously-funny-when-you-make-the-move-on-someone-and-they-don't-like-you-back? sort of thing. *Ha bloody ha*, Adam thought.

470

'God, no. Not at all,' she said.

'Then, if you don't mind me asking, why are we here? You know, in this amazing restaurant, at midnight, surrounded by what looks like eighty per cent of the galaxy?' Adam questioned, raising an eyebrow and smiling.

Bryony looked down and giggled again. 'I hope it's not too over the top,' she said, smiling, looking around at the gloriousness of it all.

Adam grinned, shaking his head.

'So,' Bryony said, taking a deep breath. 'I'm just going to get this out in the open.' She paused, then continued. 'There are things you don't know about me,' she started, running her fingers down her plaited hair. 'Well, only one thing, actually. But it's a big, big thing.'

'OK,' Adam said, waiting for the bombshell to land on the table and blow their worlds apart.

'I met you, all those months ago, at your café. And I guess you will remember that I came into the café on my own rather a lot for a young woman, right?' Bryony said.

'Yeah, you did. And I miss you. I miss making you lattes. You were the best thing to ever happen to that place,' Adam started, realising that he couldn't stop it all coming out. *People are supposed to play it cool, aren't they?* he thought.

Bryony grinned and blushed a little.

A bottle of champagne arrived, putting a halt to their conversation.

When the smartly dressed waiter had left, Adam

noticed Bryony had almost necked her first glass in one. Her usual, straight-talking confidence seemed to have swiftly left the room, leaving her behind. Adam couldn't help but be quietly pleased that he wasn't the only one who had their occasional moments of total social meltdown.

'I came to the café because it was a refuge for me from something awful that happened,' she started again.

Adam topped up her champagne, more and more intrigued by the second.

'I had a boyfriend, Adam. We lived together in the flat I live in now. I'm still there . . . obviously . . .' She halted again. She wasn't making a very good go of this.

'What happened?'

There was silence. Seconds. Ten of them.

'He died.'

Adam slowly moved his glass away from his lips and set it on the table, the last bubbles of champagne dispersing on his tongue. He could almost feel his heart thumping beneath his rib cage. Everything seemed to slow down, all the stars around them seeming to melt into one another. He swallowed hard. So that explained it. The sadness. The distance. The cavernous eyes. The way she held him at arm's length from her at all times.

'I don't . . . I don't know what to—' he started.

'He was murdered. He was shot in the chest by a kid,' Bryony said, matter-of-factly, like a reporter on the TV. Her voice was clipped and almost devoid of emotion.

Adam's stomach turned over. He felt sick. He reached across the table to hold Bryony's hand, but she moved it away. He fiddled with the salt-shaker instead.

'But, anyway. The point is that I have been through a process since he died. I spent a long time feeling totally and completely lost. And, unfortunately, you came into my life right in the middle of it all . . .'

Adam nodded in understanding.

'I didn't want to know who killed Max,' Bryony said. 'I avoided it all. I couldn't love again, I never imagined I would, and I'm sorry you got caught up in it.'

Adam's heart sank. He said nothing.

'But, recently, there's been a change. I ended up going to see the man who did it in prison. His name is Keon Hendry . . .' She trailed off.

Adam's mind scanned back to the case he had read about in the papers – he could recall it now. He could even see Max's face. But he said nothing and let Bryony continue. This was not a time for inexperienced words.

'The thing is, I never thought I would be able to do it. To forgive this guy; this monster who took away the love of my life. But I did, I have,' Bryony said, smiling now.

Adam realised now what it was that had changed about her. A certain stress had ebbed away from her body, while the glow to her cheeks that he could see came from within. He cleared his throat, unsure of what a person should say in a situation like this. For something to do, he unzipped his hoodie, not caring any more about the slogan on his T-shirt. It was a moment that put everything into perspective, because nothing really mattered that much . . .

Adam realised that the overall feeling for him was that of relief. Relief that it all now made sense. 'I'm glad of that, Bryony. I'm so glad you did it. I can only imagine how much you miss Max, and how you will for the rest of your life,' he said, shifting a little in his seat. But he knew, deep down, that what had happened to Bryony was too momentous for him to ever really grasp.

She started to speak again.

'I think the time has come when I've realised that I have a really good thing in my life. Well, a person. Oh, sod it – *you*,' she said, glancing up at him. 'You actually have no idea how much you helped me, Ad. I think you saved me by just being my friend. You were more than a good thing in my life . . . I'm not sure I could have done it without you. And when that really good thing tries to kiss you, but you aren't in the right place and you push it away, you might possibly regret it later . . .' she said, looking down at the tablecloth, which was a brilliant, sparkling white.

Adam was a little confused. He didn't know how

he could have made such a difference. He felt like he'd never made a difference to anything.

'I hope you understand that after Max died I never imagined having feelings for someone else. It felt wrong. Criminal, in fact. You just arrived in my life and I tried to fight it by pushing you away.'

'I totally understand,' Adam said suddenly, wanting to reach out to her.

Bryony continued – had to continue – as if he hadn't spoken. 'And so you have a little time to think about things, and big events happen in your life and you realise that you did the wrong thing . . .'

Adam gulped. Was he hearing this right?

'So I want to ask you if I am forgiven . . . I was so cruel to you . . . But I need those words . . .' she said, looking down at the table again.

'Well, of course, Bryony. I forgive you,' Adam replied, almost in disbelief. 'But I don't think this is something that requires forgiveness. It was what it was; I timed it all wrong, it was just wrong. I won't do it again, I promise,' he said, pursing his lips.

Bryony took another sip of champagne, seemingly lost in thought.

Their waiter had tried to return to get their food orders, but the intensity of the conversation had kept him away. Now, seeing a pause, he darted forward, only to wheel away again as Bryony started talking. He walked off, shaking his head.

'But, what if I want you to do it again?' she said bluntly, her eyes wide.

'Pardon?'

'Well, I guess what I'm saying is that if you tried to kiss me again, I would almost definitely kiss you back.' She paused. 'I, I can't make you any promises. I learned that we can't promise we will always be there for anyone in this life . . . but I want you to know how I feel about you.'

'What, here?' Adam said, pulling his head back and looking around the room in an exaggerated fashion, making her laugh. 'But there are so many people. And they're all looking at us,' Adam said with irony, a nod to the last time he'd tried it.

Bryony surveyed the now totally empty restaurant, collapsing into laughter again.

'Now?' he asked again, more quietly this time.

Bryony just looked at him and nodded.

'OK, you asked for it,' he said, pulling away his serviette, which he had stuffed down the front of his T-shirt, and placing it next to his empty starter plate.

Bryony watched him walk around the table. The candles flickered.

Adam knelt down next to her chair, feeling something wonderful wash over him. He put an arm around her slim waist, and held her hand.

And he did it. He kissed her. And she kissed him back.

When he slowly pulled away and looked into her eyes, they were filled with happy tears.

'Bryony,' he said. 'Whatever happens with us, I understand – whether we are friends, or more than that. But I need you to know that I have another three little words for you . . .'

Bryony started to smile a little, and wiped a tear from her eye.

'I love you.'

CHAPTER 48

THE PHONE RANG.

Thursday 17 June 2010
Ealing, west London
2.50 p.m.

Rita held Margot in her arms, and stared at her face. She was fast asleep, her mouth and forehead moving every now and then as she dreamt of the world she was yet to experience.

Everything was tiny. Her eyelids were minute, her lips were small, her nose a mere button in the middle of her face. Her skin was so soft that she could barely feel it when she touched it. She was the most beautiful thing she'd ever seen.

Rachel was upstairs in her bedroom, pacing the floor and waiting for a phone call. It was nearly 3 p.m. That was when they had said they'd call. She had a dreadful feeling she might not get the role. Things were so different now. She'd just had a baby; she hadn't been able to train for months. If she did get the part, she would have just three months to perfect it. And she would have to juggle her career with the demands of motherhood.

478

She was terrified.

The only thing they had to go on was her reputation. Her previous performances. The reviews and photographs. The name she'd made for herself before her life had changed for ever. She wanted this role so badly, not just because it was a bigger, better role, but because she wanted to prove that it wasn't all over now that she was a mother. Rachel felt she owed this to the thousands of women in similar positions. Not just ballerinas and celebrities, but mothers-to-be who worked in offices and hospitals and shops, and found themselves juggling a career and a brand new life. Often alone.

When she had found out she was pregnant, it had taken just a few hours for her to make her decision. She had swallowed her pride and gone straight to Ealing to speak to her mother, for the first time in a long time.

Her parents had been the most supportive they had ever been, welcoming her back with open arms. And she had realised that this life of hers, however unconventional it was, *could* work. OK, things would be hard, but the way her mother's face had melted into an unspoken forgiveness from the moment she arrived on the doorstep had proved everything to her.

I forgive you – three little words – unspoken, but dancing across the features of her mother's face. It showed that Rita and Edward loved her more than anything in the world. And, really, she now knew that was all she needed.

Richard knew about his daughter. He had tried to persuade Rachel to consider other options, including adoption, but the decision had been clear to her. Life had not followed the path she had expected, but she had a new responsibility now and it felt right. In his own way, he had tried to show as much support as he could, but he simply dilly-dallied in the background, unsure of what to say or do. He would see Margot as much or as little as he wanted, and he showed his support financially. But Rachel didn't *need* anything from him any more.

The phone rang. 'Hi. Is this Rachel Matthew?'

She sat down heavily on the bed and bit her lip, looking up to the ceiling and hoping. Wishing. Praying.

'Yes, this is she.'

'Hi, Rachel. It's Marc.'

Rachel felt her stomach fold over with nerves. This was it, a huge, pivotal moment.

'We've thought about this very carefully. It has been a difficult decision. So, after much discussion here, I wanted to let you know that you have been successful . . .'

Fireworks went off in Rachel's imagination, and she felt breathless. 'Successful,' she repeated, just as her father materialised in the doorway.

As soon as Edward saw her face, he quietly jumped for joy, somewhat bashfully, whacking his elbow on a shelf in the process.

'Yes. Congratulations, Rachel. You will be Princess

Odette in our next production of *Swan Lake*. How do you feel?'

Silence.

'Rachel?'

'Sorry, yes, I feel wonderful! Thank you so much. This is a dream come true,' she replied. She wasn't good at taking compliments, because she had always felt deep down like she was a bad person or as if she didn't deserve it. Impostor syndrome, that's what it was. But she was going to take this one, because she'd earned every moment of it. 'Thank you.'

She smiled at Edward, who was now wiping a tear from his cheek. She'd never seen him cry before.

'We'll be in touch soon with details of the training but, please, go and celebrate,' Marc said, before ending the call.

Rachel felt as if she was floating down the stairs in her old Ealing home. The one she had grown up in. The home where she had said her first words, learned how to walk, and danced for the very first time in a tutu small enough to fit a teddy bear.

'*To forgive is to set a prisoner free and discover the prisoner was you.*'

Lewis B. Smedes